Shattered Faith:

The Cost of Eternity

By
A. L. Beck

Table of Contents

Dedication

For Garry,

who never fails to make me laugh, supports me in my lunacy, and has always been there in the darkest of days.

I love you. X

Chapter One

"The right information at the right time is deadlier than any weapon." – Westworld

Quinn was a terrible Scientologist—always had been. He'd never managed to get the proverbial hang of it. Even with all the classes, the auditing, the Sec Checks, the purification rundowns, he could never quite fall into step with everyone else. That was likely why he couldn't pull away from Elijah's firm grasp. Elijah's hand clamped just above his wrist, where a black reusable shopping bag full of Scientology promotional flyers hung.

"Quinn, please, listen," Elijah pleaded.

"No! Why should I? You abandoned the Church! You've already been declared! Why should I listen to anything you have to say?"

Despite his standard protests, Quinn couldn't pull his arm free. He couldn't look past Elijah or ignore him with that thousand-yard stare Scientologists were infamous for. Instead, he was caught by Elijah's blue eyes, so like his own.

"Quinn," Elijah repeated, shaking his head slightly. The curly hair that had once been a perfect jet-black was now heavily streaked with silver, with wide patches sprouting from each temple. Quinn glared at him from under his own chocolate curls that seemed determined to fall into his eyes.

People still hunting for post-Christmas bargains whirled around them, moving in every direction but avoiding the two men as if they were encased in a bubble.

Quinn heard voices echoing off the beige walls and perfectly white ceramic tile floors of the huge mall. Despite the constant glut of people, everyone seemed far away. It felt as if he and Elijah were alone in the crowded place.

"I spent nearly twenty years in the Church. I was in good standing and upstat a lot during that time. Why would I want to destroy something I devoted my life to for all those years?"

"How should I know?" Quinn snapped. "Maybe the psychotherapists got to you, or Big Pharma, or something! They probably paid you a lot. How much was that jacket, eh?"

"And maybe, just maybe, I want to have a conversation with the son I haven't seen in years."

Years? Yeah, I guess it has been years, Quinn thought.

Since Elijah had been posted at the Guelph Org and forced to leave Calgary, Quinn hadn't seen him, and there had obviously been no contact since Elijah had left the Church. He couldn't even remember the last time he'd seen his father. Quinn wanted to say something, to snark back at him, but there was a sadness in Elijah's eyes that wouldn't let him. He couldn't stop looking at Elijah, memorizing his face, his expressions, his clothes, the way his hair lay on his head, the fruity smell of his cologne that reached him despite everything around them.

He hadn't noticed Elijah in the crowd, hadn't realized he was there until he felt the grip on his wrist. He had turned to find himself looking into familiar blue eyes, a square face, a perfectly straight Roman nose. Elijah was clean-shaven. The last time Quinn had seen him, he'd had a scruffy, unkempt beard much like Quinn's own. It had taken a few seconds for Quinn to realize who he was looking at.

Elijah wore a heavy, mottled caramel-brown faux-suede coat with a zippered front, which opened to reveal a plain light-blue T-shirt. His beige khaki pants didn't have a single crease, as if they'd just been pressed. He had gained weight and was more filled out than he had been. He was almost unrecognizable compared to the thin, scruffy man he'd once been.

Quinn had never seen his father looking so well or so well-dressed. "We don't have anything to talk about anymore," Quinn heard himself say. He hadn't realized he was going to speak, but as soon as the words left his mouth, he knew them to be true. What was there to talk about with a Suppressive Person, after all? Church doctrine dictated that just talking to Elijah for a few moments would be enough to harm Quinn, both physically and mentally.

"I know it's not easy to talk about something other than the Church, but I'd like to try if you'll give me a chance." Elijah smiled sadly, white teeth beneath that perfectly straight nose Quinn had always been slightly jealous of.

Quinn looked away.

"I don't think that's a—"

"Elijah! *Mon cher ami,* the Scientologists are here. Did you see them?" came a heavily accented, unfamiliar voice over the crowd.

Quinn looked up while Elijah glanced over his left shoulder.

The owner of the voice walking toward them wasn't like anyone Quinn had ever seen. He stood about Quinn's height—around six feet tall—thin, with squarish shoulders and long, lanky limbs. Legs like twigs in blue jeans stuck out from beneath the threadbare hem of his T-shirt. His thin arms were covered in tattoos, brightly coloured flowers and leaves that ran all the way down, even over the backs of his hands to the first knuckles.

At first glance, he seemed all arms and legs, or would have, if his complexion hadn't been so startling. His white skin made him look like a ghost despite his ombré green T-shirt. His hair was long, falling just past his elbows, parted far to the right and swept left, hanging over much of that side of his face and almost completely covering his left eye. A black hair elastic tied it off just below his chin.

White. Perfectly straight, perfectly white hair that didn't come from age; the half of his face Quinn could see showed a young man about Quinn's own age. Ghostly skin.

The man was an albino.

Quinn had heard that there were albinos, but he'd never actually seen one. He blatantly gawked as the man turned on his heel to glance behind himself for a second, then turned back to Elijah.

"Did you want to leave?" the man asked Elijah. His Québécois accent was clearer now, that distinct sing-song way of speaking unmistakable. A few steps closer and he was at Elijah's shoulder. Now Quinn could see his face more clearly: the hair pulled over, a nicely shaped straight nose, lips not too full, a heart-shaped face with a pointed chin.

Quinn met the strange man's right eye and caught his breath. The light from the mall's sunroof hit the eye just as he stepped to Elijah's side and lit the light amber, almost yellow colour. Quinn had never seen anything like it and found himself staring, agape.

"Larkin." Elijah let go of Quinn's wrist only to slide his hand higher, closer to the elbow. "I'd like you to meet Quinn. Quinn, this is my best friend, Larkin Childs."

The albino looked at Quinn, meeting his gaze without hesitation. "Quinn? Your son, Quinn? *Tabarnak,* how wonderful to run into you!" He extended his right hand for Quinn to shake. "Your father speaks of you all the time!"

Quinn extended his left hand cautiously, as if afraid the strange man might bite. He glanced down to see what looked like a bright yellow chrysanthemum tattooed on the back of the man's hand. He half expected the white hand to be cold, as if he were grasping dead flesh, but it was warm.

Larkin's grip was firm.

Quinn desperately wanted to hide under his hair as the odd man squeezed his hand.

"It's so nice to meet you, finally." Larkin smiled with neat, white teeth.

"Hum… nice to… meet you too," Quinn mumbled at last.

"Larkin and I have been friends for years," Elijah explained, his hand still on Quinn's arm. "He's helped me more times than I can count."

Larkin snorted. "That's what friends do, no? They help each other."

"Did you help him blow, too?" Quinn found himself saying. "Did you help him abandon his eternity? His family?" He surprised himself with how bitter he sounded.

"Actually, no," Larkin replied without missing a beat. "He had already made that decision before we met." He glanced around again and leaned toward Elijah. "I don't think we should keep standing in the middle of the hall, though. They're sure to spot us if we stay here; I do stand out in a crowd." The more he spoke, the more obvious his distinctly sing-song Montreal accent became.

"You're right. Quinn, please, just sit and talk with me for a little bit. Just a few minutes…"

He hesitated, ready to say no, knowing the Org members would be furious and would never allow such a thing. Being in the company of a Potential Trouble Source (PTS) would mean a long interview with Barbara in Ethics, endless sec check (Security Check) sessions with Patricia, and possibly even being labelled a PTS himself. A slippery slope that could lead to Quinn being declared a Suppressive Person and thrown out of the Church, a thought that made his insides tense and sent a chill down his spine.

Never mind that simply hanging around with a PTS could make Quinn physically ill, or cause him to commit overtly hostile acts against the Church. He knew all this and what the punishment would be if he were caught, and yet…

…and yet he found himself looking into Elijah's eyes. They were pleading, accompanied by a warm smile he hadn't realized how much he'd missed. His focus shifted from his father to the strange pale man.

"All right," he sighed at last.

Chapter Two

It was Larkin who found them a table in the food court, settling in a sunken area right behind the Dairy Queen and sushi stand.

"We're out of sight here. Even if they go to the toilet, we're still out of sight. We should be good here."

"Thank you, Lark." Elijah sat with his back to the wall on the large, padded bench.

Quinn took the plain, stackable plastic chair on the opposite side. "Are you worried they'll catch you doing something wrong?" he grumbled as he sat.

"Kesse? 'Wrong' is a matter of perspective, *tsé.* But I'd rather not get into a scene in the middle of Chinook Mall. It may be the biggest mall in Calgary, but a messy scene'll still attract a lot of attention."

Quinn looked up to see a faint smile on Larkin's face, as if this were all the most natural thing in the world.

"Mon ami," Larkin said to Elijah, "I'll get us some sushi, *hein?* Conversation goes so much easier with food."

"Thanks, Larkin. I appreciate it."

Quinn watched as Larkin walked away. Despite his lankiness, the pale man moved through the crowd like a dancer.

"I'm sure you have questions." Elijah folded his hands neatly on the table.

"Why?" Quinn demanded. It was the only question that mattered. "Why did you do it? Why did you leave?"

Elijah looked down at his folded hands for a long moment. "It... wasn't an easy decision, or one I made on a whim. I knew what it would mean... for us. For you."

"Then why?"

"There's no one reason. I wasn't happy. I never saw you or your mother; I never spent any time with either of you. I didn't like the way you were being treated, and it didn't seem the techniques were working for you. Every time I saw you, your anxiety seemed worse. You looked miserable. I didn't look good, either. I looked in the mirror and didn't recognize myself. I was a zombie. Then there was the money."

"What money?"

"All the money they talked me into donating. All the church courses they had me put on credit cards. The inheritance from my parents, the car, my mother's jewellery—everything went to the church. There was no money left. Nothing.

"I started getting calls from collection agencies, asking me to pay off the credit cards. I told them what I made at the Org, and they pointed out that I'd lied on the applications. You know as well as I do, they tell you to lie to make sure you get the cards. The collection agencies were threatening to send me to jail. It's considered fraud to lie on a credit card application.

"I went to the Org begging for help. I went to my commander in tears, begging him to tell me a way out of it, begging to know what to do. He told me to just ignore them and join the Sea Org; then they wouldn't be able to touch me. That was his solution: 'Join the Sea Org.' I'm pretty sure that's why your mother joined—to avoid the collection agencies."

"But it's all for the greater good! Once we Clear the planet..."

"And if that doesn't happen? Or if it takes a hundred years? I can't hide in the Sea Org forever. Besides, that would mean leaving you and your mother, leaving Canada, and going to Clearwater or Los Angeles. I looked at all my books, all the awards, all the certificates, and suddenly didn't know why I was doing it. I wasn't happy, I still wasn't Clear, and then there was you."

"Me? You're going to blame this on me?" Quinn's eyes narrowed. "You're going to blame me for your decision?"

"I don't blame you. I just saw how unhappy you were. I saw my own misery reflected in your face, in your eyes. I started to question everything—everything Hubbard wrote. And then there was the e-metre." He paused.

Quinn held his breath.

"I deliberately lied during an auditing session. I lied, and the metre didn't react. Nothing. It wasn't a small lie, either. I made sure it was a whopper. I wanted to test it. I knew then I couldn't do it anymore. I was miserable every second of every day, and for what?"

"For your eternity," Quinn said, the standard response, though his conviction felt weak. "You'll never break the cycle, you'll never clear your bank unless you go on with it. You'll never get to Clear."

"That's just it. I've done a lot of reading since I left. Quinn, there is no bank, no reactive mind, not really. Others who were in the church and went Clear, who went on to do their OT's, their Operating Thetan Levels—they got all that way and then left because they realized there was nothing to believe in."

Quinn shook his head at the words no reactive mind. "No. No, that's not true. You're lying to me. You just have a lot of MU's."

Quinn had been taught his entire life that MU's—misunderstood words—were the only reason someone couldn't learn something or question something Hubbard wrote. He had never questioned that, not once. But no bank? The idea that there was no reactive part of the human mind, where engrams and negative emotions were "banked" or stored, was ridiculous. And why would anyone who went past Clear and reached the highest Operating Thetan levels leave? Quinn dismissed it without hesitation.

"Oh, I understood." Elijah began to pick at the skin on the edges of his fingernails. "There were no words I didn't understand. I just didn't believe it anymore. The e-metre didn't react. The credit card companies were threatening to put me in jail. I never saw you or your mother, and when I saw your mother, all we did was fight.

"I was miserable. I just wanted to die and get it over with. I kept thinking it would be okay if I just died right then. I was okay with death. I didn't want to go on like I was. Nothing mattered, not even my life. When I realized my life had no value even to me, when I felt nothing, that scared me. I was empty, drained, and death just seemed preferable."

He stared at his fingers as he picked and yanked skin away, his face shadowed.

Quinn could see that, despite how well-dressed he was, Elijah looked older, worn. The lines on his face seemed deeper, the shadows darker than Quinn remembered. His eyes looked watery, from the cold outside or from emotion.

"But," Quinn's voice hushed, "there's another life. Your next life…"

"When I'm supposed to go back to the church and pick up right where I left off. Remember, that's what the contract we signed says— that we'll go back in our next life. A new life where I'd be just as miserable as I was, or worse."

Shaking his head, Elijah looked up abruptly and met Quinn's gaze, blue eyes meeting blue eyes. "Just the thought made me sick. The thought that I wouldn't be able to escape, that even death wouldn't be a release, drove me crazy. I couldn't stand it. I couldn't handle the thought of that. I thought I'd lose my mind. I couldn't see any way out."

Quinn watched in silence as Elijah sighed. He didn't know what to say, what to think. His brain whirled, trying to understand everything, and yet he felt blank at the same time.

"Getting rid of my reactive mind, getting rid of engrams—none of it seemed to matter. No engram, no horrible moment of pain or heartbreak in my past seemed worth the pain I was in every second of every day. I couldn't remember the last time I'd been allowed to sleep through the night, or the last time I had a decent meal, when I laughed or even smiled. All I could remember was exhaustion, hunger, and anger."

"Anger? I don't unders—"

"The more I thought about how horrible I felt, the angrier I became. I started lashing out. At first I was just snappy and argumentative, but then…" He looked down at his hands again.

Following his gaze, Quinn saw he'd pulled the skin from the edge of his left ring finger until it bled.

"I lost it," Elijah said. His eyes stayed fixed on the fingers he was torturing. "I just snapped. I lost it on someone at the Org—someone of a lower rank. I can't even remember now what he did, just that it was something stupid and unimportant that pissed me off. I don't remember grabbing him; I don't remember throwing the first punch, but I must have.

"I was told I punched him square in the face, hard enough to knock him down. The next thing I remember, I was sitting on his back, slamming his face into the floor with both hands as hard as I could, over and over and over."

Elijah stopped picking at his fingers and covered his face with both hands. "I broke most of the bones in his face. They had to take him to the hospital; he had a seizure right there on the Org floor."

Moments passed before Quinn spoke. Elijah sat with his face covered, a picture of guilt and pain, a large drop of blood on the edge of one finger.

"W-what did Ethics do?" Quinn leaned forward, listening closely.

"Ethics? Nothing." Elijah let his hands fall, revealing a pained expression.

"Nothing?"

"Nothing. They said it wasn't unethical, that I hadn't done anything wrong, and that he'd deserved it."

Quinn pushed back from his father until his spine met the chair. "I don't believe you. They didn't do anything?"

"Not a thing. Quinn, I could have killed that man. As it was, I hurt him so badly he's probably never going to be the same. There was so much rage in me that I could have done it and not even known until it was too late. That's when I knew I had to get out. At any cost, at all costs, I had to get out. For my sanity… maybe even for my soul, I had to leave. I didn't know who I was anymore.

"And I'll tell you something—I'm not the only one. There are others who left for much the same reasons. They didn't believe in it; they didn't believe we were doing the planet any good. They were afraid of losing themselves to anger, to fury, just like I was. A lot of people have left."

Quinn frowned. How could Ethics do nothing? Not out-ethics? People leaving? Abandoning the fastest-growing religion in the world? No.

"No," he said firmly. "I don't believe you. Even if you're right, even if you had to get out, I don't believe that there are a lot of people who want to leave, want to abandon their eternity. I just can't believe that."

Shaking his head, Elijah answered, "Quinn, Ron Miscavige left."

"What?!? No!"

"Yes, he blew as well. He was OT 8, the highest Operating Thetan level there is, and says now he doesn't believe in any of it. Do you really think he had MU's as well? Do you really believe he just didn't understand some of the words? If the father of the church leader leaves—"

"No!" Quinn slammed his hand on the table. "It's a lie!"

"Quinn." Elijah's quiet voice carried over the tumult of the crowd. His face darkened into a frown. "I know you haven't attested to Clear yet—you're not that far up the Bridge—but after I left the church, I learned that all that's required to have the Clear Cognition is to say to your auditor, 'I've just realized that I've been mocking up my own Reactive Mind all this time, my whole life. But I'm not doing that any longer.' That's really all you need to do to go Clear. None of them will tell you, so I know you're going to doubt what I'm saying, but it's true. I would never lie to you about that."

"That's another lie," Quinn hissed through his teeth. "That's just stupid. That's a lie some SP or shrink told you to say."

"But you don't know for sure, do you? Before I left, I was further up the Bridge than you must be now. You don't know for certain what I was taught because they won't tell you."

"You're an SP, a Suppressive Person. You want to destroy the Church. Why the fuck should I believe you?"

"Quinn—"

"Here we go!" Larkin interrupted in a sing-song tone.

Quinn looked up and saw the albino holding a beige plastic tray.

"Elijah, I got you green tea."

"Thank you." Elijah sat back.

Larkin set the tray on the table to their left and began to hand out food. He passed Elijah a small paper cup of green tea, then a rectangular, covered plastic tray. Sitting, Larkin placed his own tray and bottled water in front of him and served Quinn.

"Quinn, I wasn't sure if you liked sushi, so I got you an extra couple of things you can try. If there's anything you don't like, just leave it and we'll eat it."

Once again, Quinn felt pinned by Larkin's whiskey eye, as if he were a butterfly in a display case under that gaze. The face around it stayed blank and emotionless.

"Why did you tell me all that?" Quinn demanded of his father as he finally looked away from Larkin. It was harder to ignore the food than the albino; just the sight of the unfamiliar dishes made his mouth water and his stomach growl.

"Because you wanted to know. You asked why I left. I didn't tell you because I'm trying to get you to leave, but because I think you have a right to know. I'm not proud of what I did, Quinn, of anything I did. I have to live every day with the shame and guilt of what I did in the church. That was one incident. There were many… many more.

I have nightmares. I've cried more times than I can count. I left Guelph and came back here because I wanted to be close to you, to be here if you needed me.

I met Larkin, and he's become my dearest friend, my confidant. I've cried on Larkin's shoulder and vented to him over and over. He's helped me more than I can ever repay him for."

Larkin reached over and put his hand on Elijah's shoulder. Elijah covered his mouth with his right hand, as if he were going to be sick. He didn't speak, didn't even look at his friend, but Quinn saw Larkin's fingers curl as he squeezed Elijah's shoulder in what had to be a comforting gesture.

"Tabarnak," Larkin snorted, giving his shoulder a small shake. "This is too dark a conversation for lunch. *Mon cher ami,* we shouldn't keep the boy from eating, *hein?"*

"No, you're right." Elijah sighed and pulled his hand away from his mouth. "He should eat. He needs to eat."

Quinn looked down at the trays in front of him. Several rolls of things he couldn't name sat beside pieces of pinkish fish roughly the length of his thumb, each on a small pillow of rice. In another plastic tray, only a few centimetres square, sat bright yellow rectangles with a dark band around the middle, about a centimetre wide.

"What are these?" He picked up the smaller tray.

"Those are called tamagoyaki," Larkin answered. "They're a kind of Japanese omelette, so it's cooked."

"Cooked? You mean the rest of it isn't?" Quinn gave him a skeptical look.

"No." Elijah smiled. "The fish is raw. Raw fish is a Japanese delicacy. You'll like it."

"A lot of people get nervous about raw fish, so you might want to try the omelette first," Larkin suggested.

Quinn looked at the albino's face. It seemed expressionless, perfectly blank, as if nothing around him touched him at all. Even as he held Quinn's gaze, his lack of expression didn't change. Quinn looked down at his hands, then at the two trays.

"I don't know where to start."

"Here." Elijah leaned forward to open the small tray with the omelette strips. "There are little packets of soy sauce if you want it, and the green stuff is wasabi. It's horseradish, so it's hot."

"I personally don't put much of anything on it." Larkin opened his tray. "I like how delicate it is, *là."*

Quinn studied the perfectly rectangular, bright yellow strips. A faint smell of egg reached his nose. His mouth watered; his empty stomach growled in anticipation.

"How do I eat these?"

"You're supposed to use chopsticks," Elijah said gently, "but they can be hard to learn. You can just pick them up with your fingers."

Cautiously, Quinn picked up one of the yellow rectangles and saw the neatly formed rice oval beneath. He took a careful bite. The slightly sweet egg and mild rice tasted surprisingly good. He was keenly aware that both Elijah and Larkin were watching him as he set the bitten piece down and tried to open a packet of soy sauce. His hands were shaking and sweaty. He could feel sweat starting to build on the back of his neck.

Desperate to get them to stop staring at him, Quinn blurted the first thing that came to mind. "Isn't there too much of an age difference for you two to be best friends?"

Larkin's right eyebrow, the only one Quinn could see, lifted, though his face didn't change.

Elijah chuckled. "I don't think so. Besides, I thought having a friend about your age would help me understand you better. But Larkin's… unique. I'm not sure Larkin's interests and experiences apply to other people."

"I would hope not," Larkin retorted with a snort, munching on a roll of something Quinn couldn't identify. Quinn noticed that while his face still looked blank, his right eye seemed faintly amused. *That's weird, his eyes don't match his face.*

He found himself drawn to the odd man, watching how the tattoos on his hands shifted as he picked up his food and ate, and wondered why he wore his hair in such a strange way.

After wrestling with the packet, Quinn finally managed to get the soy sauce on the egg and rice. The tang of the sauce surprised him, but he liked it. The omelettes were gone in a moment. He opened the other tray without further hesitation and began to eat one roll after another as quickly as he could. He had no idea what each roll was, but he didn't care.

"Everything is delicious."

"I'm so happy to see you, Quinn, to be able to sit and have lunch with you." Elijah spread a bit of the green wasabi paste onto one of his own rolls. "Don't eat too quickly and make yourself sick."

Have lunch with? Oh, no, how long have I been here?

Quinn sputtered around his food and jumped to his feet. "I've got to go. I've got all these flyers I haven't handed out—"

"Quinn…" Elijah started, then trailed off.

"Wait." Larkin pulled a small white plastic bag out from under the tray. "Take your food with you." He leaned across the table, gathered the tray that still held a couple of sushi rolls along with the unopened water bottle, and put them in the bag.

"I understand." Elijah sighed. "I really wish you could stay longer, but I understand."

Quinn took the plastic bag from Larkin's hand, their fingers touching for a brief moment. Again, he found himself caught by the light-yellow eye, wondering how it had come to be that colour.

"Quinn, give me the flyers you have." Elijah stood.

Quinn pulled them out of the black shopping bag and handed them over. Elijah turned and passed them to Larkin, who tossed them into the recycling bin.

"There, you've handed them all out," the albino said, with the slightest hint of a smile. "Now you can't get in trouble for it."

Quinn shoved the plastic bag with the sushi into the other one and turned to leave.

"Quinn, wait," Elijah called.

Turning back, Quinn watched his father step toward him with his arms outstretched. "Please," Elijah said, "let me hug you in case I don't see you again for a long time."

Quinn wanted to refuse. He wanted to tell him he was being banksy, letting his emotions get the better of him, but the words caught in his throat at the sight of Elijah's pleading eyes. Sighing, Quinn let Elijah hug him. A moment or two passed before he released the stiffness in his shoulders and put his arms, just slightly, around his father's waist in response.

They stood there for a few moments, neither saying anything, while Quinn just wanted to get away before someone saw them.

Finally, Elijah stepped back, holding Quinn by the biceps, and stared at him until Quinn grew uncomfortable and looked away.

"My son," he said with a smile.

Quinn tried to find something interesting on the floor to look at.

Elijah went on, "Please remember that I love you and I'm proud of you, no matter what. And I'm always here for you."

"Here. Meaning, if I want to blow?" Quinn shot back with a frown.

"Meaning, for anything. Anything at all. Even if you just want to talk, I'm here."

"Quinn, take this," said Larkin, who had gotten up and moved to Quinn's side without him noticing. Quinn looked down and saw a simple white business card between the tips of his long fingers.

"What's this?" Quinn took it and read:

Versailles Vintage & Friperie

Owner: Larkin Childs

432, 16 Avenue NE., Calgary, AB.

Beneath that were two phone numbers, one apparently for the store and the second, Quinn guessed, a cell phone number. He quickly shoved the card into his back pocket.

"In case you can't get in touch with Elijah, you can always call or text me. That's my cell phone, *là,* " Larkin said.

"Yes," Elijah added, "Larkin can always get hold of me. So if you can't, for some reason, you can text or call Larkin. He'll be able to help you if I can't."

"Any time, day or night," added the albino, his visible eye smiling again. Although his face still looked oddly blank, his gaze held Quinn's. "You can always reach me."

Quinn mumbled a "thanks" as he turned, forcing himself to look away from the albino's eyes. He cast one last glance at Elijah and hurried back up the ramp from the lower level and into the mall.

Chapter Three

The promotional stand was set up deeper into the mall, at one of the intersections where the different hallways met. Warren, the executive director of the Calgary Org, had picked the spot deliberately to try to contact as many non-Scientologists, known as "wogs," as possible.

With hands going cold, Quinn felt sweat forming on the back of his neck and noticed how shallow and rapid his breathing had become. Worst of all, the rash under his arms was starting to flare up. *It itches. I know if I scratch it, it's going to hurt more.*

The rash flared every time he became anxious or stressed, so Quinn was used to it. That didn't stop the maddening itch or the overwhelming urge to scratch it raw. The more people crowded around him, the worse the itch got and the shallower his breathing became. He pushed his way through the crowd until he reached the Scientology information stand.

He spotted Perry standing by the plastic folding table laden with books and pamphlets, all neatly arranged. Near the corners of the table stood two wooden A-frame folding signs with "Free Personality Test" and "Free Stress Test" written on them in bright, cheery red letters. Taped to the front of the table was another sign that read "Hubbard Life Improvement Centre" in neon green letters against a bright orange background.

Standing above most of the crowd, Perry looked like a flagpole in a three-piece brown suit. Very tall and thin, with straight black hair buzzed very short on the sides, he wore a light mauve dress shirt and a mud-brown tie to complete the look. He shot Quinn an annoyed glance as Quinn finally managed to approach the table.

"Where have you been?" Perry demanded, licking his lips and twitching his shoulders.

"...I... ...was handing out pamphlets as ordered, Sir."

"Where? I sent Jeremy and Blaise to look for you, and they couldn't find you." His tongue moved in his mouth like a worm, wiggling. He shifted from foot to foot and shook out his right hand for no apparent reason.

"I was down at the food court." That's not a lie, at least.

Perry frowned. "I'm sure they went that way." He glanced toward the food court, then back. "How did you do?" he demanded. His tongue sat in the left corner of his mouth before darting back to the right. He had a habit of moving his lips and tongue in ways that had nothing to do with what he was saying. It never failed to give Quinn the creeps.

"I... gave away... all of them."

Perry leaned over, snatched the bag from Quinn's arm, and looked inside. "What the hell is this?" His hands twitched as he shifted his feet again.

"I... picked up something to eat."

Perry fixed Quinn with a skeptical look over the top of his round, white plastic-framed glasses. His dark brown eyes hopped about like chickadees, rarely settling in one place unless he was trying to intimidate. "Was that before or after you handed out the flyers?" he asked, pursing his lips. "And what made you think you had the time to eat, eh? None of us has had anything."

"After." Quinn looked down and away. "I'm sorry, Sir. I ate as quickly as I could." The rash was both itchy and aching now.

"Hmm." Perry took a couple of steps back and licked his lips. Biting his lower lip, he shifted his weight onto his right leg before handing the bag back to Quinn.

"I worked really hard, Sir. I did my very best to talk to people."

"Well, that's something. We'll stop you from becoming a more degraded being! We'll get you Up Stat yet!" He smiled and punched Quinn's left shoulder in a playful manner.

Quinn smiled, then rubbed his now-sore shoulder once Perry turned away to scan the crowd.

"Where's everyone?" Quinn asked, desperate to change the subject. Perry hadn't reached Clear yet, but he was Barbara's right hand, and she had gone Clear years ago. Who knew what she'd taught him?

"Everyone's handing out flyers. Here, sit down and sell some books. The Church needs you to. We have to get our enrolment numbers up. You need to try harder!" Perry leaned in, palms flat on the table, pinning Quinn with his gaze. His voice took on an almost desperate edge. "We all have to do better! We all have to do our best to Clear the planet, and you're not pulling your weight, Quinn. You did well today, but you need to do better all the time. You need to get your stats up, way up."

Quinn stared at the piles of books—*The Way to Happiness: A Common Sense Guide to Better Living* and *Dianetics: The Modern Science of Mental Health*. The flyers sat in neat, obsessively straight stacks at each corner of the table to make it easier for people to grab one as they walked by.

"Yes, Sir. I'm sorry, Sir. I'll do better."

Perry huffed, picked up a handful of flyers, and walked off into the crowd. Even with his height, Quinn lost sight of him in a moment. He leaned forward to straighten the pile of flyers Perry had knocked askew before sitting down.

Stop a stranger and just start talking to them... The thought made him feel sick, but he tried his best to postulate the outcome he wanted: to sell a book. He focused on it, telling himself over and over, *I will sell a book, this will happen. I will sell a book, I will.*

He sat and watched as people passed him by until a heavy-set man with thick red hair and a beard stopped to look at the books. The man looked about forty and wore a Calgary Flames jersey.

"Hum...," Quinn mumbled, "do you have any questions, sir?"

"Yeah." The man picked up a copy of *The Way to Happiness* and flipped it over to look at the back. "Is this any good? I mean, does it help?"

"Oh... y-yes, it does. It's very p-practical and s-sound advice for l-l-living a b-better and happier life."

"But wasn't Hubbard just a writer or something?"

"Well, yes." Quinn's mind raced. He remembered something he'd read somewhere and decided to go with it, reciting it verbatim as best he could. "But his life was too... varied and... um... He had a really broad influence. Like... there's a tribe in... Africa who know and revere L. Ron Hubbard as an educator. There are... factory workers in Albania, I think it is, who know him only for his administrative discoveries. There are children in... China...who know him as the author of their moral code, and readers in dozens of languages who know him for his novels."

He was proud of himself for managing to say that much. He smiled at the man, but in truth, he was smiling at himself. He felt lightheaded, as if he'd been holding his breath for too long.

The man looked at Quinn somewhat skeptically. "What do you mean by 'their moral code'? And how would a tribe in Africa know Hubbard?"

"Through this book. It's a guide, a code to use throughout your life to have a better life."

The man started flipping through the book at random.

"It's not a hard book to read," Quinn added, hoping to make the sale. "Each principle is explained, and how it relates to happiness, and each explanation is thorough but simple enough for anyone to understand."

"Yeah, I think I'll pass, but thanks anyway."

"Oh. Oh... I'm sorry to hear that. Would you like to take a f-f-flyer instead?"

"No, thanks," he said as he walked away.

Quinn hung his head. He'd tried; he really had, but it hadn't worked. *How do the others do it?*

He put his elbows on the table and covered his face with clammy hands, the failure tightening the knot of anxiety in his chest all over again.

I don't get it. I don't know what I'm doing wrong. Was I too efforty? Patricia keeps saying that it can happen, that if you put too much effort into something, it blows back on you. Maybe that's what I did, put too much effort into it, so it didn't work? Why can't I sell books and talk to people like the others? They make it look so easy...

Still, I did manage to talk to someone, that's a win, right? Even if it's a small one, it's still a win.

The rash under both his arms had started to throb. He pulled his hands away from his face and looked around again. No one was even pausing to look or giving him the chance to try again. For a few minutes, he just sat there looking around until he remembered, "The food."

He popped one of the big oblong pieces in his mouth. He kept chewing each piece longer than he needed to, since he was enjoying the taste so much. His mind wandered even as he reveled in the experience. *Elijah. What are the odds that I would run into Elijah here?* There were literally thousands of people swarming the place, and somehow his father had spotted Quinn amongst the crowd.

What does he really want? Is he trying to get me to blow? Well, of course he is, isn't he? That's what people like him do, isn't it? He didn't make a big deal of it, though.

"And maybe, just maybe, I want to have a conversation with the son that I haven't seen in years," was what he'd said.

Is that true? Did he really just want to talk? No, he's an SP. He can't be trusted. I'm sure he's trying to manipulate me somehow. Maybe some psychiatrist gave him tricks to try and manipulate me. I bet that's it. I wonder how much they paid him?

Mom would lose her shit if she knew I'd seen him. She's hated him since he left. He made himself our...my enemy. I have to remember that. That was his choice, his action. He made himself an enemy of the Church, our enemy. He made that choice; he chose to leave us behind. Leave me behind. He frowned at that. He left me behind. He didn't care enough to stay in the Church. Warren would probably say that Elijah hates me, that the fact that he left proves that.

Quinn felt his face frown, his eyes narrowing as he thought. He remembered Elijah's eyes, how they'd had a pleading look. How kind they'd looked. He remembered Elijah's smile, the way that he'd hugged him. He remembered the feeling of his arms around him, the warmth of his embrace.

Elijah's voice played out in his mind again. "My son, please remember that I love you and I'm proud of you, no matter what. And I'm always here for you."

No, I can't trust him even if I wanted to. He just said that to get me to lower my guard. He's out to destroy the Church, Mom, and me. He's out to destroy everything we've worked for. He doesn't want us to Clear the planet. He doesn't want us to succeed. He doesn't want me to succeed. He doesn't want me to go up the Bridge because then I'll be way more evolved than him. Because I'll leave him behind, show him just what he could have been if he hadn't given up. Yeah, he'll probably be pissed when I go Clear. When I'm Clear, and I've learned everything, and I can do all the fantastic things that Clears can do, he'll be jealous then! And no anxiety! I'll be able to talk to anyone about anything and on any subject! All the knowledge of the world will just be there in my head for me to use.

Yes, I'll be far, far evolved beyond Elijah once I go Clear. He's just jealous.

Seeing his path clearly before him, Quinn smiled. Up the Bridge to Total Freedom was the only path worth taking. If only he could get the hang of talking to people and stop freaking out about it.

Quinn's thoughts ran along the same lines for some time until he looked up and saw Brittany and Mark striding through the crowd toward him.

Mark was an older man of Asian descent; his straight grey hair had receded far back from his oval face to the crown of his head. His worn, threadbare, tight blue jeans highlighted the fact that he was bow-legged.

Brittany, by contrast, was in her mid-twenties, like Quinn. Her wavy, long blond hair fell to her waist, accentuating her long, reed-like frame, although the shapeless, ill-fitting black sweater hid her natural curves. Quinn watched as she stopped to speak to a man, touched his elbow, and tried to give him one of the flyers she held. She flashed a broad smile, her long, angular face lit up with her obnoxiously cheerful, fake Theetie-Weetie personality. Quinn saw the man refuse the flyer and forcefully pull his arm away from her grip; the anger on her face was plain.

That's weird; she couldn't get him to take it. Huh.

Quinn smiled as they came up to him. "How'd it go?" he asked.

"Awesome!" Brittany said brightly. Her face shifted from anger to cheerful in a fraction of a second as a big smile spread across her face. "We talked to a ton of people, gave away lots of flyers." She placed the remainder of her flyers back onto the pile on the table. It looked much like the stack she'd originally taken.

"Oh, definitely," agreed Mark as he set down his own thick stack. "Pretty much everyone I talked to was really interested. I'm sure we're going to see some new members soon."

"How'd you do?" Brittany pointedly asked Quinn.

"I did really well, too. I gave away all my flyers, and I actually managed to talk to people. I was a mess, but…"

"You make too big a deal out of that so-called anxiety," Brittany snapped, her face suddenly dark with frustration and anger. "It's all in your head, you know. Stop using it as an excuse and just get over it already!"

"I try…" Quinn said quietly.

"Talking to people isn't hard," said Mark, his soft voice clipped. "You just open your mouth. Any idiot can do it."

"Except Quinn," Brittany smirked.

Quinn looked away so she couldn't see how much she was upsetting him, how banksy he was starting to become. *Why doesn't she see how hard it is for me? I thought she knew me better than that.*

"How'd you do, bitches?" came a voice over the din of the crowd.

Quinn looked up and saw Perry coming back through the crowd with Blaise, Rochelle, Dickson, and Jeremy trailing behind him. It was Blaise who'd called out, an alligator smile spread across his face, but it faded when he saw Quinn.

"Did you have another panic attack, Quinn?" he asked, sounding annoyed.

Quinn tried to square his shoulders. "No, I actually gave all my flyers away," he said with a smile. "And a guy came by the table, and I was really able to talk to him."

"You mean you actually sold a book?" Rochelle looked down her pointed nose at Quinn. She tucked her shoulder-length chocolate hair behind her ear and peered over the plastic red frames of her cat's-eye glasses at him.

"Yes," Quinn quickly lied, then looked away. He'd never gotten along with Rochelle. There was something about the way her glasses sat on her very round face that bothered him. He looked up at Perry instead. "Did I do all right, Sir?"

"Not too bad," came the smiling reply, "but you have to keep it up."

Quinn couldn't keep the smile off his face. The simple comment made him feel warm and happy, as if his path really was the right one.

"All of you need to remember what we're doing here," Perry went on. "The more we push, the more groups like the Canadian Security Intelligence Service are going to push back. Don't forget that CSIS works closely with the CIA and the pharmaceutical companies to pump more drugs into the population of North America than any other organization. Don't forget for a minute that L. Ron discovered that a select group of people are running a secret government that controls every aspect of modern life, finance, the media, and pharmaceuticals. It's all controlled by this secret, shadow government; they run everything. We're not just fighting ignorance; we're fighting evil, Suppressive People out to destroy the planet! The more gains we make, the more they're going to fight against us! They're using every weapon at their disposal to stop us!"

Perry's voice rose in pitch as he wound himself up. His tone grew louder with every word, his tongue wiggling wildly. No one from the small group dared to interrupt. Instead, they made small sounds of agreement and nodded.

"L. Ron found out and exposed what these people were doing, but because these SPs control the media, this atrocity has been allowed to continue! That was back in 1966, and they're still in control! We aren't just up against individual SPs; this is an enemy that's out to destroy the entire planet! The more ground we gain, the more they try to shut us down!

"There is a war coming, a huge battle for the fate of humanity, and we are the foot soldiers on the front line! If we have to die for our ethics, then we'll die knowing we're not bound to this world anymore and that our next life will be even better!"

There were more murmurs of agreement. Rochelle even went so far as to clap, a gesture quickly mirrored by Brittany, who was not to be outdone.

"We've done well today," Perry went on, "but we can't rest on our laurels; we need to keep it up. We need to get our enrolment numbers up. We can't let down our guard, not even for a minute! The fate of the entire world is up to us!"

He paused to absorb the light clapping coming from every member, Quinn included. His lips pursed and then opened so everyone could see his tongue wiggling from one side to the other, as if it were independent of his will.

"Come on," Perry ordered, his voice still strong and loud, cutting through the general background noise, "break down this stall and let's get back. We still have classes."

"Yes, Sir!" was the unanimous reply.

There was a sudden flurry of activity from the group. Quinn folded the two chairs and leaned them against the wall before turning to help Blaise carefully fold up the signs, while Mark and Dickson worked on folding up the black metal legs of the table. Despite his slight frame, Quinn picked both signs up easily and tucked them under his right arm, the chain rattling against the wood. He hung back with the signs while Mark and Dickson each picked up one end of the table and walked off with it, Brittany and Rochelle following with the boxes of books. Blaise and Perry each took two chairs. The troop marched along the echoing halls, calling out polite "excuse us" to shoppers in their way.

Quinn followed at the end of the line. *I wonder if Elijah and that guy, Larkin, left yet? What if Perry sees them? He'll lose it! He'll never believe that I didn't see them or talk to them!*

Please don't still be there. No, I have to postulate the result that I want! I have to have the will and make it happen! Neither of you will be there! Elijah! Larkin! You'll be gone! You will not be there in the food court! Disappear!

His stomach jumped with a sudden rush of panic, making him feel nauseated from the food he'd eaten. His eyes scanned the crowded mall as they walked, desperately searching for white hair, but all he saw was a sea of brown and black, with the occasional dyed pink or purple thrown in.

He tried not to let out an audible sigh of relief as they finally walked down the ramp from the food court and out into the sharp, frigid air of the parking lot.

It was a win; he'd actualized that they wouldn't be there, and they weren't. He was deeply proud of himself, using his abilities as a Scientologist to affect the behaviour of both an apostate and a never-in like that. He smiled.

"Oh, my God." Blaise looked down at his phone as he walked through the automatic door. "It's -22 Celsius but feels like -28! That's nuts! Guess you won't be cleaning the van early tomorrow morning, eh, Mark?"

The intensity of the cold slapped Quinn's face and seemed to suck the air from his lungs, making his chest tighten and his face burn. He felt the hair in his nose start to freeze as he breathed. It was far too cold to snow, and the tiny breeze that had picked up seemed to slice through his thin coat and shear the flesh down to the bone.

Quinn gritted his teeth as they walked toward the van. He heard the snow squeaking under his running shoes, heard the sharp crack as he stepped on a patch of ice. His left leg shot out from under him, sending him lurching sideways and stumbling. The weight of the signs under his arm pulled him forward at the same time. He managed to keep his balance but lost his grip on the signs, which clattered loudly to the hard ground.

Jeremy was a few steps ahead and turned at the sound. "You ok, bud?"

"Yeah, I think so. These damn shoes don't have great traction." He bent down to gather the signs, puffs of fog from his mouth swirling like dragon-breath, his hands aching in the cold.

"I hear ya. That's the thing I hate about winter. If you dress for the cold outside, you sweat to death inside, and if you dress for the inside, you freeze your ass off outside!"

"You should still wear boots, Quinn." Brittany had stopped walking as well. "You're going to keep slipping with those runners."

"But then my feet would sweat all the time we're inside, and then my boots will be sweating, and my feet'll freeze anyway."

Brittany wrinkled her nose, an expression that made her resemble a mouse. "Your feet sweat?"

"They do when I'm wearing boots, and the furnace is cranked up inside."

"I'm the same," chimed Rochelle.

"Really?" Perry asked her. "You both should really work on that. I don't think that's normal. You should really get that under control."

Quinn felt his face break into a smile. The intense cold hitting his teeth made the moisture on them freeze. He ran his tongue over them to warm them again. He enjoyed banter like this, when they could all just chat and joke, like any group of friends who had known each other for years.

The bluish-grey van stood out like a beacon of warmth and comfort, its spotless beige interior beckoning them. It was an old Dodge Caravan that, to use Blaise's phrase, was "old enough to vote."

"I just got a text from Barbara," Perry was telling Blaise. "Apparently, it's going to be really cold next week as well, so everyone had better bundle up when we go to the farm!" Quinn smiled at the thought, even as those around him complained about the cold.

The cattle farm was owned by the Clark family, one of the biggest donors to the Calgary Church and probably their most vehement supporters. In exchange for their generous support, the Org parishioners would work on the farm, mostly cleaning out the barn, feeding and watering the livestock, and sometimes doing general repairs. The parishioners had been told repeatedly to constantly be on alert, since it was easy for such a massive animal to cause harm if they weren't careful.

Quinn didn't mind working to clean the huge barn, shovelling out the waste. He found working with his hands relaxing. While the others hated it, Quinn was always the first to volunteer to work there. He loved the animals, loved being outside. Much easier than studying the coursework. *I feel so stupid when trying to learn that stuff.* He didn't feel stupid when he was working with the cows. There was nothing to ponder; everything just was what it was, and the cows just seemed so present; they lived in just that moment, nothing else.

Studying and coursework weren't as enjoyable as working with the cows. Quinn always had trouble with LRH's writings; he always felt he was too stupid to comprehend, that he didn't quite get what LRH was saying. Quinn knew he was expected to understand, but always felt like he was trying to decode some secret message that eluded him.

He was still smiling, thinking of the farm, as he clambered into the far back bench seat of the van, sitting on the driver's side.

Jeremy climbed in beside Quinn, followed by Blaise, while Brittany and Rochelle sat in the front, with Dickson squishing himself in beside them.

As the highest-ranking officer, Perry took the front passenger seat, while Mark hopped into the driver's seat; the older man wouldn't allow anyone else to drive it.

"Turn on the heat, Mark, for God's sake!" Dickson said. "I'm freezing my nuts off!"

"Don't be impatient," came the reply. "It's going to take a while for the van to heat up anyway." He pulled the van out of the parking stall and turned left, heading toward 58th Avenue.

"Why can't we get a van with heated seats?" Dickson continued.

"We don't really need that, do we?" Perry responded. "Do you have that much havingness?"

"I do when I'm freezing my ass off! Then I have a lot of havingness for heated seats!"

"I thought you were freezing your nuts off?" mused Blaise with a smirk. "Just how big are your balls that you can sit on them and confuse them with your ass?"

Jeremy barked with laughter. "I don't think you're supposed to sit on your balls, Dick! Doesn't it hurt? I bet you can hit that high note in *Closer to the Heart*, eh?"

"Well, Geddy Lee can't hit it anymore, so someone has to," Perry chimed in, causing everyone to laugh.

"Oh," countered Blaise, "he can hit that note. You just have to grab his nuts and squeeze! Then he'll definitely hit it, but only once!"

All of the men groaned and laughed while the two women snickered.

Once at 58th, Mark turned right, heading toward Macleod Trail. As he made the turn, the van suddenly fishtailed to the left.

The conversations stopped.

Brittany let out a loud squeal.

Mark's arms became a blur as he fought to regain control.

Quinn gritted his teeth. Bracing his feet against the floor, he felt the wheels slide on a patch of black ice.

Quinn threw all his mental strength into postulating the outcome he wanted, using every mental resource he had to keep the van from crashing. It was the most powerful thing he knew to do, and the only thing he could do at that moment.

Don't hit the median, he ordered the van silently. *The van won't hit the median. Mark will get it under control. We will not crash.*

The back end of the van fishtailed, almost going onto the median and putting the van sideways across the road. He braced for impact while at the same time willing the van not to crash.

Abruptly, the wheels caught the pavement, and the van lurched forward, awkwardly settling back onto the road.

"Everyone ok?" Mark called back to the passengers. "Sorry, I didn't see the ice."

"Black ice?" Jeremy asked.

"Yeah. They need to get the sanders out here again. Why the hell don't they plow the roads properly in this city?" Mark fussed.

There was a relieved laugh from Perry. "Haven't you lived here for twenty years or something? You should be used to it by now."

"Yeah, but I still remember back in Ontario, they at least knew how to plow!" Mark shot back with a nervous laugh. "Out here, they wait for a Chinook to do the work for them!"

Quinn stopped listening to Mark complain about Calgary roads in winter; he complained about the roads in summer as well. Instead, Quinn smiled to himself as he looked left and out the window. *I did that,* he told himself. *I postulated what I wanted to happen, and it happened. I really did that. I can't believe it. I actually made us not crash.*

In a week where Quinn hadn't had a single win, this was his second one. He was thrilled and had to bite his lip to keep from mentioning it. He was sure everyone in the van had done the same thing—used their minds to postulate the van not crashing—but he was equally certain that he alone had prevented a wreck. The feeling that his training worked, that he really was on the right path, made him so happy he didn't want anyone to dull it, even a little. The thrill made him feel so warm that when the heater finally came on, he didn't feel it.

But then the guilt hit him like a fist. *Maybe I pulled it in. Maybe meeting Elijah and that guy made Mark hit the black ice in the first place. Yeah, that must be it. I managed to stop the crash, but I caused it in the first place. Shit.*

The guilt swept the joy away as if it had never existed, and Quinn felt the cold again.

They were still discussing the near-accident by the time they got back to the Org.

"Just remember," said Blaise in a voice that made him sound like a TV announcer, "black ice can happen to anyone! Be sure to talk to your children about the dangers of black ice!"

"You make it sound like they're smoking it!" Perry laughed.

"Maybe they are! Is that what happened, Mark? You smoked some black ice there, bud?"

Quinn wore a false grin as everyone began gathering the promo materials out of the back before heading inside.

Chapter Four

Books. He remembered the books.

One wall was lined with shelves, too full for bookends. He loved books and had wanted to look through them.

But he couldn't do what he wanted because he was sitting in a straight-backed wooden chair, feet dangling helplessly below him, facing a seated adult who looked like a mountain. The man leaned toward the six-year-old, brown eyes fastening on him with a hard, cold look that chilled his heart. Quinn squeezed the edges of the wooden seat, the sharp corners digging into his palms.

"Bull baiting is a very important lesson to learn," the moderator, a young teenager herself, explained. "With so many people and organizations trying to bring down the Church, it's very important to learn how to tune them out, so that absolutely nothing they say or do can affect you. Everything will just roll off your back.

"Quinn, you sit there, and you will not react to anything that is said to you, understood? Don't even look at him—look past or through him. If you must react, laugh, but you can't let them think they're getting to you. No matter what's said or done, you can't react. Understand? Don't dramatize or overreact."

Quinn understood the instructions; he wasn't stupid. But the adult in front of him was terrifying. If the cold eyes didn't make him shiver, the nasty smirk on the man's face, lips pulled tight in skin stippled with dark late-day stubble, certainly did.

At first, Quinn managed to keep his serenity, but the yelling and insults went on and on until his composure crumbled like cheese.

"You're disgusting." The man leaned within inches of the child's face, the smell of stale coffee overpowering. "You smell. Did you know that? The other kids have been calling you 'Horse' behind your back because you smell like one."

Quinn bit his lower lip, trying desperately to melt into the back of the hard wooden chair. His eyes pricked with tears.

Don't cry. Don't dramatize. Don't cry. Don't react. Don't flinch. Don't cry.

He bit down harder, hoping to focus on the pain instead of the tears threatening to spill.

"You're a fuckin' suppressive," the man snarled. "Why don't you change your clothes and take a shower? Or are you too stupid to do that yourself, eh? You're pathetic!"

"Good," came the moderator's voice from behind Quinn. "Keep going," she encouraged the man. "Push. Push him harder."

Quinn squeezed his eyes shut so tightly that the muscles in his face started to hurt. He felt hot tears leaking out from between his lashes.

"OPEN YOUR DAMN EYES, YOU MOTHER FUCKING LOSER!" the man abruptly bellowed. He must have leaned closer still, because Quinn felt his breath on his face, felt spit strike his skin.

Quinn shook with fear. The smell of coffee on the man's breath was sickening.

"Laugh at him, Quinn," said the moderator, her voice high and thin as if it might crack. "Laugh at him like it's the funniest thing you've ever heard."

Quinn lowered his face, too terrified to laugh. He could taste blood from biting his lip so hard.

"Look at you! You can't even open your eyes because you'll start to cry like a little baby! That's it, isn't it? Are you gonna cry, baby?" the man berated. "If you're not a baby, then you must be a little faggot, eh? You queer, boy? You're a little fag that can't control themselves? Eh? That's it, isn't it? You get off on guys, don't you? You jerk off to men! You gettin' hard, little boy?"

Mind blank with fear, Quinn couldn't guess the meaning of the words.

"Yes! That's the way, keep pushing! Keep trying to make him react! Quinn! You need to face him! Open your eyes and face him!"

Quinn squeezed his eyes tighter. He knew he couldn't; he'd never be able to keep from crying. Suddenly, the chair grew warmer, almost hot, spreading down his thigh.

"Oh, my God! You disgusting little brat!" the man yelled. "You peed all over yourself!"

The moderator was yelling at Quinn to get a mop and a bucket to clean up after himself. "Don't worry," she told the man. "You did a great job! He just has to learn to control himself better."

He trudged along a dim hallway to the janitor's room, struggling with the heavy, wheeled mop bucket already half filled with brownish-grey water and the wooden-handled yacht mop that was longer than he was.

He watched his feet as he walked back, dragging the dingy yellow bucket behind him to the class. Quinn had to use both hands to haul the mop into the air and plop it down with an audible wet smack onto the tiled floor.

The moderator yelled, her voice like a high-pitched squeal. "You need to clean up after yourself, keep in your exchange, and take responsibility for your actions. Remember that. Everything has to be in ship-shape!"

"Yes, Sir," Quinn replied automatically, already having learned that superiors were always addressed as Sir, regardless of gender or age. He pushed the chair out of the way and began moving the mop back and forth as best he could. The handle balanced on his left shoulder, most of it sticking up behind him like a flagpole announcing his shame. He watched the dark ropes of mop strands move and bend as he pushed them around the floor, watching the patterns they made with unseeing eyes.

"Quinn!" The moderator's yell snapped him out of his daze. "What's wrong with you? Don't you know you have to clean the chair first, or it'll just keep messing up the floor? It's dripping! Come on, you already know how to do this, remember? You've done it before in your past lives, so you shouldn't need to be reminded! How many times have we gone over this stuff?"

"Yes, Sir," Quinn replied. "Of course, Sir, my apologies."

He hauled the heavy mop back into the bucket and trudged off down the hallway to find something to clean the chair. He was keenly aware of the huge wet spot on the front of his jeans, the warmth long gone, leaving him cold and miserable. He silently prayed to whatever deity might hear him that no one would walk down the hall and see him, see his shame. The friction of the wet denim rubbing his thigh started to chafe painfully, making him walk with his legs apart like a movie cowboy.

He was dismayed to find that the spray bottle of cleaner and the roll of paper towels sat on a shelf far above his reach. He finally noticed a broom leaning in the back corner. Grabbing the handle near the head, he coaxed the roll of paper towels toward the edge of the shelf and knocked it to the floor.

Bolstered by this small success, Quinn slowly manoeuvred the bottle toward the edge, only to watch in horror as the plastic hit the floor and broke, cleaning liquid splattering everywhere.

Already distraught over his loss of control, this was too much for him. His face twisted, his chest tightened. He crouched down, covered his face with his tiny hands, and began to sob. He had no idea how to fix this.

He cried in frustration, knowing he was supposed to already know how to do these things, told again and again that he'd done them in past lives. But he had no idea how he was supposed to recall something he couldn't remember experiencing. He knew he'd be screamed at, told to "Knock off the bank" for his emotions, since emotions were negative. He was angry with himself—for failing the bull baiting, for being stupid, for always being at fault—and with nowhere else to put it, the tears came.

Quinn's eyes snapped open, just as they normally did at this point in his dream. He sat up slowly and pressed the heels of his hands against his closed eyelids until he saw stars. *That damn dream again. I hate that dream. And on one of the few nights I'm allowed to get a whole four hours' sleep, too. Damn it.*

The bull-baiting dream was a regular visitor. The memory of the emotional pain and humiliation felt just as strong in his sleep as it had on the day it happened, and it reminded him exactly how early he'd been taught that his feelings were wrong.

Quinn swung his legs over the edge of his cot. The cold ceramic tile felt like ice under his bare feet. He hung his head and shoved his fingers into his tangled hair. With a sigh, he got to his feet and padded quietly across the room to the door. He paused, fingers already on the handle. Mark shifted and muttered something in his sleep.

Quinn's eyes drifted to the poster hanging at the head of the bed, something from a TV show Mark used to watch faithfully. Even in the dark, he could make out the white background and the dark shadows of trees, and above them another shadow, a supposed UFO. He could make out the caption in white block print:

I WANT TO BELIEVE

Quinn didn't believe in UFOs, or ghosts for that matter; the present was challenging enough without adding to it.

He turned the knob and pulled the door open as quietly as possible. Squeezing through the smallest gap, he slipped into the hallway and padded along the dead blue-grey carpet that muffled his footsteps.

He barely glanced at the notice board beside the bathrooms, and didn't bother to read the "Golden Rod" notice hanging there. This one was against Brittany, who had been found guilty of restimulating Tom. Brittany had pulled it in herself, had done something that made him sexually desire her; the details of everything she had done to cause this were clearly laid out in neat bullet points. Tom's transgressions were noticeably absent, as he was clearly the victim. The notice would hang there for weeks, even months, for every Church member to read.

Quinn had glanced at it when it was first posted but had ignored it since. He remembered all too clearly when his own Golden Rod notice had been hung; he remembered the embarrassment, the guilt, the pain of being glared at and mocked. He shoved the memory aside, refusing to relive it again.

He opened the bathroom door. It moved easily, giving only the barest squeak from the hinges. Four bright, crisply white urinals lined the wall opposite the door.

Quinn stepped into the room and went straight for the stall. He wanted to be alone, to de-stress from the nightmare. Sitting down, elbows propped on his knees and face in his hands, he relieved himself.

As he pushed his way out of the stall to wash his hands, he thought of the wonderful, happy future his teachers had promised him as a child, a future that still seemed as far away now as it had when he was six. He looked at himself in the mirror: curly hair sticking up at odd angles, dark circles under his eyes, and even his beard crooked.

I guess they didn't count on how much I'd fuck up, he thought as he headed back down the hallway to his room. *I mean, it's obvious I'm messing up and sabotaging myself and my progress up the Bridge. What other explanation is there? It's obviously my fault.*

Not for the first time, Quinn promised himself he'd work even harder starting tomorrow, that he'd commit himself even more to his studies and work. He'd double down, make everyone proud of him, finally start to live up to the potential his teachers and his mother, Joni, had seen in him all those years ago.

Elijah never saw my potential, he decided. *That's why he was always trying to sabotage me. He still is, him and that weird friend… what was his name…?*

As he crept back into his room and slipped into bed, Quinn's mind wandered back to the meeting with his father and the strange albino man.

Oh… yeah, Larkin. That was it. Larkin. I've never heard that name before. Odd name for an odd guy, I guess.

He settled back into the mattress, pulling the sheet up around the back of his head. He bent his knees until the soles of his feet were pressed flat against the wall behind him.

Oh, well, I guess it doesn't matter, it's not like I'm going to see them again, is it?

He felt himself starting to drift into sleep again, smiling to himself as he looked forward to his life's work with renewed vigour. As he drifted, the image of the albino's face appeared in his mind's eye.

I wonder why the hell he wears his hair that stupid way? You can only see his one eye…

He drifted deeper. His last thought, before sleep pulled him under, was to wonder what the strange man might look like if that hidden eye weren't covered by a white curtain of hair.

Chapter Five

Patricia was down from Edmonton for auditing sessions with the Calgary parishioners, and it was Quinn's turn. Patricia was the only auditor in the province, so she spent most of her time at the larger Edmonton Org. Quinn was thrilled to have an auditing session; auditing was the foundation of their faith, after all. That was how he ended up telling her his great withhold, the encounter with Elijah and the strange man.

He sat ramrod straight in the small auditing room. A large blue-grey piece of equipment sat on the desk. It had a large oval base supporting another oval section, which was attached to a smaller rectangular section that stuck out to the side. Two long braided cords were attached to the machine, the other end of each cord connected to a bright silver cylinder, known as a "can." The back of the machine faced Quinn, but turned the other way, he would have seen the white face with its dreaded black needle, along with three buttons, a dial, and three small rectangular digital displays. Two video cameras were mounted in the room, one in each corner, their lenses pointed at the desk, red lights glowing like eyes in the dark.

"Now, go back to the beginning and go over it, pick up any additional data you can contact," Patricia instructed.

"Elijah saw me in the mall, he grabbed my arm and said he wanted to talk to me," Quinn repeated. He'd lost track of how many times he'd gone over the story, each time adding a bit more detail he'd forgotten.

"I hear you," Patricia interrupted, "but help me understand why you would willingly talk to an apostate. A known Suppressive Person."

"I was curious. I wanted to know why he left. I guess I thought maybe I could talk him into coming back, going back on the Bridge."

"You guess?"

"No, I'm sure that's what I wanted. I thought if he told me why he left, I could address whatever it was he was thinking and get him back."

"You're not on the Blow Team, Quinn. You don't have the training for that. You should have contacted Barbara, Perry, or Blaise. They can handle those situations. You can't."

"I know, but there really wasn't time; it happened so fast. One second I was going through the crowd, and the next he had my arm."

"All right, go on."

"I figured he was going to try and talk me into leaving, but he said he just wanted to see me. Then his friend came along, this weird guy called Larkin. It was Larkin who suggested we go to the food court. He said he was worried that the Church members would see him, because he 'stands out in a crowd.' That's what he said: 'I stand out in a crowd.'"

"There's something," Patricia whispered to herself. "Go on."

Quinn continued, "I wanted to know why Elijah left. He told me he just wasn't happy. He said that he thought I didn't look happy and that he didn't think the tech was working. That he spent all his money on the Church, and that creditors were coming after him. He wasn't happy that he never saw Joni or me, and he didn't want to join the Sea Org. He said he'd rather die than stay in the Church. That's what he said: 'I just wanted to die and get it over with,' and he didn't want to come back to the Church in his next life.

"He gave me this bullshit story about how he lied during an auditing session, and the metre didn't react. He even tried to tell me that he beat the shit out of someone at the Org and that Ethics didn't do anything. He said he was scared of what he did.

"Then he said there were all these people who got all the way through their OT levels and then just… left. He tried to tell me that Ron Miscavige left! I mean, of all the stupid lies to tell. Like the father of the Chairman of the Board would leave, the whole thing was pathetic. And then he tried to tell me that all you need to do to have the Clear Cognition is to say to your auditor, 'I've just realized that I've been mocking up my own Reactive Mind all this time, my whole life. But I'm not doing that any longer.' That's really all you need to do to go Clear."

"You're kidding." Patricia stared at Quinn while keeping one eye on the needle.

"I know, right?" Quinn laughed. "It's the stupidest thing. Like I could trust anything he said."

"So, you didn't believe him."

"No. It was all just bullshit." Quinn laughed again and shook his head, pleased with his certainty.

"Well, it's a relief to know that you didn't believe him. Your needle is definitely going wild, but it must be reacting to the dangerous and negative things that were said by the SP. Tell me about this SP's friend, Tarquin, was it?"

"Larkin."

"Right, Larkin. Tell me your impressions of him."

Quinn had to give her question some consideration. Not because he didn't want to tell Patricia about the man—that was unthinkable—but because he didn't know where to begin. "He's... odd," he finally started. "He's an albino, covered in tattoos. I mean covered, all up both arms and legs. Long straight hair that he wears on the left covers his left eye. He has yellow eyes. I've never ever seen that before. I didn't know anyone had yellow eyes. Tall, thin, from Quebec. He has a thick accent."

"So, his appearance was odd."

"Yeah, but it was really strange, his face... there's no expression, or hardly any. It just always seems blank. And even when he did smile, his eyes were hard and they didn't match the smile."

"What do you mean, his eyes didn't match the smile?"

"Just that. His face would smile, just a bit, but his eyes didn't smile. They looked… cold. It was really weird."

"Go on. There's something there." The needle was still moving.

"I… I didn't talk to him much, but he seemed nice. Elijah said that Larkin was his best friend. Elijah said that he thought having Larkin as a friend might help him to understand me better, since we're closer in age."

"So, he's using this so-called best friend for his own purposes. Interesting."

"I didn't think of it that way."

"That's what SPs do, though, isn't it? They use people for their own gain and then throw them away until they need to use them again."

"I guess. I really don't like to think about how an SP thinks."

"Even though the SP in question is your biological father?"

"No. I can't guess what he thinks. I can't understand why he does anything."

"Let's go back to this friend, Larkin. Tell me something positive about him."

"I don't know, like I said, I didn't talk to him all that much."

"You must have some positive impression about him. Your needle is clearly telling me that you do."

"Really?"

"Yes. You know the body has a whole electromagnetic flow, and the metre is simply measuring changes in the resistance of that flow. A change in resistance indicates a thought, an engram that's causing resistance to the electromagnetic flow. As we go through our auditing, there should be fewer and fewer distractions to the electromagnetic flow as you work through each engram. Your needle is showing that you're clearly not done with Larkin. So, tell me something positive about him."

Quinn considered. "Well, I guess being so odd-looking, it kind of makes me want to know why he's like that. He's... interesting, I guess."

"Right. Let's go back, start at the beginning, and run through everything you remember. Try to pick up more details as you go along."

Quinn started to repeat the story again, just as he had before, and as he would do many more times over the coming hours. It was part of the process: working through the memory of the event over and over until the e-metre needle stopped reacting to it. Only when it stayed floating upright and almost motionless would the engram be declared dealt with. Only then would his emotionally charged reactive mind stop grappling with the engram, leaving his logical mind in control.

Quinn believed that once all his engrams had been dealt with, both in this life and his past lives, he would finally become Clear—finally become the version of himself he was supposed to be.

It was nearly 4 a.m. by the time the auditing session was finished, but Quinn was too exhilarated to sleep. He felt fantastic, like there was nothing in the world that could bother him or touch him. He was so happy he felt like he could dance. This feeling was the best thing about being a Scientologist: the feeling of taking control of your life, of your fate. There was no uncertainty, no doubt, just relief and joy, and for now it made his loyalty to the Bridge feel utterly right.

Chapter Six

It was just a short walk from the Org to the dorms where Quinn lived. Once an L-shaped, two-floor strip mall, the building had been purchased by the Church after a fire gutted the place. Instead of tearing it down, the entire congregation had been recruited to restore it. None of them had any construction experience—not in this life, anyway. They were assured that everyone had done all this before in a previous life they weren't able to consciously remember, and that the physical work would act as a trigger to help them recall those hidden memories.

He had vivid memories of using a sledgehammer to knock down walls burned black, pulling out handfuls of black wire like stiff witch hair. He still had the indented scar on his left foot from when the sledgehammer slipped from his hands and smashed into it, breaking two bones.

Quinn was convinced that his construction memories must have been buried very deeply.

It was all normal to him: raising money for the Church and the new Ideal Org in Calgary, recruiting new members, working to Clear the planet, and studying the Founder's writings. While Quinn didn't think he ever really mastered a lot of the basics, eventually, slowly— ever so slowly—he began his work up the Bridge to Total Freedom, where the state of Clear awaited him.

Going Clear was the goal for every Scientologist, the ultimate state of spiritual superiority. Clears were said to never get sick, to be perfectly logical, to never let their emotions get the better of them. Their emotional "Reactive Mind" permanently bowed to the logical "Analytical Mind." They could recall every instant of their life in perfect eidetic detail. Clears could move objects with telekinesis, could read minds, had removed all their engrams and dealt with any pain or emotional issues that lay within them. Clears were more creative, more fulfilled, and able to achieve any goal, no matter how lofty, with ease.

Past Clear were the Operating Thetan Levels (OT's), where students learned how to operate outside of their own body by "exteriorization," to control other people at will, and even create their own personal universes. Clears and those who had passed the OT Levels were superior beings who could make the world a better place. Everyone was told that they worked tirelessly to eliminate war, crime, hunger, and poverty. Clears and those who had gone on to the OT's were real-life superheroes.

Who wouldn't want to be a part of that? Who wouldn't want to create a utopia? Quinn wanted it as much as anyone. This was his purpose, his lifelong ambition: to help Clear the planet, thereby saving the world and the human race with it. It was the purpose of the Church, the goal of every Scientologist. To work diligently throughout your lifetime toward that goal wasn't really a hardship; it was the right thing to do. The only thing to do.

Quinn was delighted to work as a server at the party celebrating the Founder's birthday three weeks later. Everyone would be able to watch their Chairman of the Board in his annual birthday speech. It was exciting, and the preparations took up so much effort that he forgot about Elijah and his strange friend.

"Don't forget," Perry told everyone, "Our biggest donors are coming to hear the Chairman of the Board speak, so we have to get everything right! Everything must be exceptional! White Glove isn't good enough! This will help to get everyone's stats up, so get busy!"

Everyone scurried around like mice until everything looked perfect. The food, drinks, decorations, the large TVs—everything had to be spotless and perfectly arranged, nothing even slightly out of place.

The servers were dressed in shiny, dark grey suits and white shirts. The women wore short black pencil skirts and heels, with white shirts and black ties.

Quinn was surprised that only twenty people actually came, but it didn't matter once the live feed started. His eyes widened as he saw the packed auditorium of the Fort Harrison hotel, the elegant gold and white decorations, everyone dripping with glitter and jewels.

"Oh, I wish I could be there," Quinn sighed as the lights dimmed and the concert that opened the show began. "Just once, just one year."

"Me too," whispered Brittany, standing close to him. "Can you imagine being with Scientologists from all over the world? It would be amazing!"

"I heard that this year's party is breaking all previous attendance records," added Rochelle. "There are more Church members every day. It's amazing to think of millions of people, all working together to Clear the planet. And we're a part of that."

"Incredible," sighed Quinn, and he clapped enthusiastically when David Miscavige, the ecclesiastical leader of Scientology and the Chairman of the Board, dressed in a smart black tuxedo, entered.

"Tonight's the night we celebrate L. Ron Hubbard's birthday," began the COB as the deafening ovation ended. "It's a night we traditionally shower him with the gift he most wished for on his birthday in return for his legacy—the legacy of tech."

Their leader continued, "So, you want to know why tonight is going to be an epic celebration? It's because tonight the clouds of heaven itself are going to part with a deafening thunderclap, and the gifts of expansion are going to rain down like a torrential hundred-year storm!" There was a huge roar and applause from both the crowd in the Florida auditorium and in the Calgary Org's meeting room.

The Chairman went on to list all the posthumous awards and accolades that had been presented to the Church founder. There were 800 new recognitions from various city governments, law enforcement agencies, ambassadors, legislators, and global leaders. No other religion in the world had received more accolades; no other religious founder was more adored worldwide than LRH. The number of awards would have been completely unbelievable were it any religion other than Scientology.

The presentation continued with audiovisual segments by their late founder, L. Ron Hubbard, including a welcome speech that had been recorded fifty years earlier.

Everyone hung on the Commodore's every word as he spoke of executives studying all Scientology organizational policies until they were able to apply those policies not by rote, but by instinct. This was the vital point: that Scientology's principles were innate and that you should be able to apply them by instinct.

If you couldn't, you had clearly done something wrong.

Quinn couldn't help but hang his head, knowing he must be doing something wrong. But his gloom vanished like smoke as the Chairman continued to discuss the ever-expanding Church. He talked about the plans to open another Ideal Org in Puerto Rico. The Ideal Org program had been something that the Chairman of the Board had been overseeing for several years. Just as Christian churches were elaborately decorated to honour their fictional God, Ideal Orgs were highly decorated with marble and gold to honour the founder. The impact of the Ideal Orgs couldn't be underestimated; they were bringing more people into the fold each day. Calgary was destined to have an Ideal Org of its own once enough funds had been raised.

And Quinn was a tiny part of the glorious whole, part of the fastest-growing religion on the planet. He thought his chest would burst; he was so proud to be part of the only organization that was making a real difference in the world.

Once the party was over, everyone was chatting about how amazing the celebration was. It was thrilling, inspiring, and motivating. Quinn promised himself he would work harder, study harder, and better his stats until he was on the same par as everyone else in the Org. He would devote himself completely to the Church and its goals, with no room for anything else. This is what matters. The Church and going up the Bridge, Clearing the planet, and making the world a utopia—that was all that mattered. Nothing else. He was not an individual; he was part of a much larger whole that would change the world. What in Quinn's small life could be more important than that?

He was still riding the emotional high the next day when he was called into Barbara's dark office. Quinn's shoes didn't make a sound on the deep, blood-red carpet as he stepped into the ethics officer's room. The back wall was covered in dark floral wallpaper on which hung countless awards, certificates, and diplomas that Barbara had earned during her Scientology career, each in identical plain white frames. The only light came from the small, cheap black plastic gooseneck lamp on her desk, as she didn't have a window. He was convinced that the Org's ethics officer purposely made her office look like a dungeon.

"Sit down, Quinn," she said without looking up from her laptop screen.

He pulled one of the red plastic chairs away from her desk and sat.

Barbara picked up a piece of paper and tossed it across the desk. "Sign it."

Quinn picked it up and gave it a cursory glance.

"Elijah dropped his meat body," Barbara said before Quinn could make sense of what he was reading. "You're not to go near the memorial or have any contact with anyone connected to it. Sign the order, confirming you understand."

He was stunned. "Dead? How? When?"

"Doesn't matter, does it? Just sign it."

With shaking hands, Quinn signed the paper, the ink fixing his obedience even as his mind reeled, the high of the night before colliding with the sudden, ordered absence of his father.

Chapter Seven

Walking back to his room, his knees threatened to give out. With clammy hands, he rummaged through his drawers until he found the business card he'd hidden. It was as if he was watching himself from a distance, as if it wasn't him who was moving, who was secreting the card into his jeans pocket. It was someone else who tried to hurry to the bathroom without looking like he was hurrying.

Only when he sat in the bathroom stall did he feel he could breathe again. He hurriedly wrenched his flip-phone and the secret card from his pocket:

Versailles Vintage & Friperie

Owner: Larkin Childs

432, 16 Avenue NE., Calgary, AB.

He stared down at the card for a few moments, hardly believing what he was going to do.

Slowly, he pecked out the number into a text message, and then even more slowly pecked out the message. Quinn didn't text often, partly because his ancient phone made texting difficult, and partly because he didn't have anyone to text.

He wrote the message four times, repeatedly deleting it and starting over. Finally, he typed it again and quickly hit send, only to wish he hadn't. The message was simple:

"Is it true?"

He stared at it in disbelief that he'd actually sent it. He was grateful that the volume was turned off when he got a reply,

"Who is this?"

He hesitated before texting back, "Quinn."

The response was immediate. "Yes, I am truly sorry. Elijah passed away yesterday afternoon."

"How? Was he sick?"

"*No*, the doctors said it was a brain hemorrhage. It was very sudden. No pain."

Elijah, dead? Dead. Gone. He kept staring at the phone, not knowing what to think. The memories of their last meeting at the food court rushed back. Quinn tried to remember every word, the feeling of his father's arms holding him, every detail that had been so easy to forget; he now desperately struggled to remember. There were no feelings, nothing he could identify. He felt a stillness inside as if he was waiting for something.

He looked down as he received another text.

"There will be a small memorial in two days, if you would like to come. You can catch a cab and then text me, and I'll send you the address."

Smart not to send the address, Quinn thought. *Otherwise, Tom and a few others would be there to watch it, to keep me from attending.* He stuck the phone back into his pocket without replying and hurried out of the bathroom. He kept his head down and did everything exactly as he was supposed to do for the next two days. Only when he was in the bathroom stall did he dare take out his phone. He looked at it for a moment before going into his text messages and rereading the text from Larkin about the memorial.

Today, he thought, *that's today. I can't go, I don't have the clearance to go. But I feel like I should. Like I should say goodbye. I never got to when he blew, maybe I should go and say goodbye now. But I can't get permission to go. I guess that Larkin guy will be there.*

The image of Larkin's whiskey-yellow eye popped into his head. The image was as clear as if the man were sitting across the table. He remembered the way the flowers tattooed on the back of his hands moved, the bright colours rippling with the skin. He recalled his sing-song accent with perfect clarity, the intriguing speech pattern running through his mind.

He looked down at his phone again. A reminder popped up on the calendar:

Purif @ noon

Damn, I really don't want to do the Purification Rundown; the funeral would be a breeze. I want to go; I think I need to go. I want to say goodbye. I want to go. Am I really going to disobey direct orders? But I really want to go. I want to see... The thought drifted away as he suddenly wasn't sure how to finish it. The memory of yellow eyes wouldn't let him.

Chapter Eight

The Purification Rundown was a detoxification program meant to rid an individual of the harmful effects of chemicals lodged in the body's fat stores, which created a biochemical barrier to spiritual well-being. Drugs taken years before could suddenly reactivate and affect the mind and body if they weren't cleansed. In practice, it mostly meant hours in a sauna and massive handfuls of vitamins to help clear the toxins. Quinn hated it only because he hated the sauna—having to sit there for hours, sweating out the impurities.

He kept looking down at his routing form, which told him he had to go to the Purif after class. The routing form, akin to a schedule, told Org staff members where to go and what to do when they got there. The superior officer would check off that something had been done before sending the person on to the next thing. Skipping one step to do another, or doing tasks out of order, was strictly forbidden. Your entire day was planned for you. No decision-making required. Everything was structured, orderly, and followed the Founder's writings to the letter.

So Quinn was surprised when Blaise and Brittany rushed in, both looking flustered.

"Quinn!" Blaise called. "I know we're supposed to be doing the Purif, but Rochelle broke a shelf in the filing room. There's shit everywhere, and she's being super emotional, so Brittany is going with you instead. Barbara already okayed it."

"Of course, that's fine," Quinn replied.

"She cut her hand when it broke," Brittany added helpfully. "There's blood all over the place."

"Really?"

"Yeah," Blaise muttered, "I might have to go with her to the hospital to get stitches. It's pretty deep."

"How the hell'd she break it?"

"I'm not sure," Blaise responded. "She said she sort of leaned on it when she was filing, and the shelf snapped. She should know better than that. I bet she was Dev-Ting and trying to sneak in a nap. That's why she leaned on it."

"Rochelle doesn't normally do that," said Brittany in her defence. "I've never seen her Dev-Ting, pretending to be busy when she's not. She works hard."

"Well, she wouldn't be doing it right if you noticed, would she?" Blaise snarked back.

"It's ok," Quinn interrupted. "I can go with Brittany instead."

"Hyson will go with you," Blaise added. "He's going to escort you both and then take you back to the dorm for clean-up duty."

"Yes, Sir," both Brittany and Quinn replied.

Hyson was one of the many security guards employed by the Org, mostly to protect against break-ins. Clean-cut, with jet black hair and ochre skin, Hyson loved to regale them with stories of his days as an MMA fighter and the training he'd done around the world. Brittany always seemed fascinated and would ask Hyson question after question, anything to keep him talking. Quinn was convinced she liked him, but hadn't seen anything to really write a KR about.

The spring air was crisp, and dirty snow still clung to the sidewalks as they headed out along McLeod Trail back to the dormitory and the sauna. Quinn turned up the collar on his old denim jacket as he followed Brittany and Hyson, who began to chat. He looked up at the overcast sky and noticed a perfect chinook arch. The grey clouds hung low, and the arch—a crisp, bright slice of blue beneath the grey— looked particularly picturesque.

Quinn trudged along while Hyson chatted and Brittany hung on every word. He noticed how she laughed lightly, how she tucked her hair behind her ear, how much she grinned. *Oh, yeah, she's into him.* But his mind kept drifting away from the pair in front of him, sliding back to his lost parent and the strange man with whisky eyes. *I wonder who will be there. No one from the Church, obviously. That Larkin guy will be there for sure...*

A sudden blaring of car horns from behind jolted him out of his thoughts. Looking over his shoulder, he saw a man on a bike riding against the crush of traffic. He was yelling and swinging a dirty yacht mop at the cars, challenging the speeding vehicles like some knight in a fairy tale. Quinn could hear him yelling over the din of traffic and the roaring horns as cars swerved to miss him and each other. A black Beamer nearly took out a Tesla as it swerved around the mop-wielding knight in a panic. He heard Hyson yell, heard Brittany let out a pained, "Oh," as they watched helplessly, waiting for the inevitable.

When it came, it was a dark grey minivan hemmed in by cars on both sides.

Quinn held his breath as the man on the bike forged ahead and the hulking machine bore down on him.

Brittany screamed at the sickening sound when the man and vehicle collided, at the horrifying sight of the man flying over the hood, his head snapping back, then landing with a gut-wrenching bang against the windshield. The mop went flying and struck another car, causing its windshield to shatter, while the bike vanished beneath the body of the van.

Quinn was still holding his breath when Hyson ordered him and Brittany not to move while he called 911. Two lanes were blocked, bringing traffic to a sudden halt, and those going in the opposite direction slowed to a crawl as people tried to see what had happened.

"God, I hate rubber-neckers!" Hyson said to no one in particular as he rushed toward the mangled man. "Goddamnit, move! We need an ambulance right now," he yelled into his cell. "Possible fatality!"

Brittany still had her hands over her face. "Is he dead? Is he dead?" she asked through her fingers.

Quinn wasn't sure she was talking to him, but replied anyway, "It didn't look good; he might be."

Brittany groaned.

Several cars stopped, and their drivers got out, phones at the ready to film the accident. Other people came out of the businesses behind them to see what was going on. People behind the minivan did the same, getting out of their cars and rushing to help the injured man, while the woman who had struck him exited her vehicle, wailing and screaming in panic. After a moment's hesitation, Brittany went to help.

Quinn was rooted to the spot, watching the chaos, listening to the screaming and shouting, when the thought struck him. *No one's paying attention. I can't help anyway. No one's paying attention.* He looked at the accident again, then glanced over his shoulder at the sidewalk.

He took a step backward, eyes picking out Hyson and Brittany in the crowd. Hyson was still on the phone with 911, yelling while trying to keep people away from the injured man. Brittany was trying to comfort the wailing woman.

Quinn took another step back. No one paid any attention. Another step, and then he turned and began to walk away, walking not toward the Org.

He hunched his shoulders as he kept going, walking quickly toward the only place he could think to go: Chinook Mall.

He pulled his phone from his pocket and quickly sent a text: "Where's the memorial? Send me the address."

To his surprise, the response was quick, as if Larkin already had the phone in hand. The address in the city's northwest was followed by: "Take a cab. I'll pay for it. Don't worry, just come if you can."

Reading the message, the thoughtfulness touched him. He hadn't considered how to pay for a cab, hadn't considered how he'd get to the memorial at all. He had just started to move, as if pushed by instinct. Now that instinct had a direction.

He tucked the phone back into his pocket and kept walking past the strip malls, the restaurants, the smells that tried to drag him inside. He kept his eyes on his feet, ignoring everything as his worn sneakers carried him along. It was only a few blocks before he saw the mall looming on his right.

He fidgeted as he waited for the light to change so he could cross the street, glancing around to see if anyone was coming for him. He bolted across as soon as the signal changed. Cutting across the mall's parking lot, he all but ran, heading toward the theatre where he was sure he'd find a cab. Instead, he noticed a bright yellow cab parked near the main entrance. Quinn rushed over and went to the driver's window.

"Can you take me here?" He shoved his phone with Larkin's text on the screen toward the older man's face.

"Yeah, sure, hop in."

He hurried around and climbed into the back seat, right behind the driver. It wasn't until the driver started making his way through the parking lot, heading towards McLeod Trail, that the thought came to Quinn, *What have I done?*

Chapter Nine

We're here, I think, he texted.

Whatever he'd been expecting, this wasn't it. There was a music studio and store in the front. The memorial space was at the back, and the stairs led down into the basement.

"Um… a friend will be out to pay my fare," he mumbled when the driver looked at him for payment. The man gave Quinn the stink eye just as Larkin's white hair appeared. Larkin headed straight for the driver's door.

Once Quinn was out of the car, Larkin turned and grasped him by the arms. "It's good to see you, *mon ami,* I just wish it were under better circumstances." His only visible eye looked swollen, as if he'd been crying. He was dressed in dark pants, dark dress shoes, and a navy polo shirt. His white hair was tightly braided and tied off at the end with a black satin ribbon in a bow. A brightly coloured enamel locket stood out against the dark fabric, orange and yellow tulips framed in bright green leaves against a white background, tiny sky-blue forget-me-nots dotted here and there.

"Um… thanks, I guess."

"Come, we haven't started yet. Your father would be thrilled to know you made it."

He led Quinn down the narrow cement steps, carpeted in threadbare green, the walls painted stark white, and into the basement. There were a couple of dozen strangers milling around, many of whom turned to look at Larkin as he brought Quinn inside.

The walls were covered in fake wood panelling that failed to make it look less like a basement. Padded, stackable chairs were arranged in neat rows facing a wooden lectern. A large framed photo of Elijah stood on an easel beside it. Enormous white wicker vases overloaded with white and yellow flowers stood on either side, with more filling the area behind the lectern.

Larkin was saying something, but Quinn didn't hear him. Instead, he walked directly to the lectern and to the photo; the fresh, sweet scent of the flowers reached his nostrils.

Quinn barely recognized him. The photo looked like it might have been taken at a Stampede event. Elijah wore a bright blue and orange plaid shirt and a white cowboy hat, a massive grin across his face. He held up a can of beer, toasting the photographer. He looked happier than Quinn could ever remember seeing him.

"I love that picture," said Larkin from behind.

Quinn jumped, having forgotten he was there.

"That was a year ago," Larkin continued. "He was at a work Stampede BBQ, and he texted me that picture. I don't even know who took it."

Quinn didn't answer. He was too busy looking at the shiny brass urn that sat on a white pillar next to the photo. "He was cremated?" he asked at last.

"Oui, that was his wish. Come, sit here in the front," Larkin said, gesturing to a chair with a sweep of his arm.

Quinn sat down stiffly in the second chair from the end while Larkin took the outside seat beside him. A moment later, a man in a dark grey suit with a round face and receding reddish-blond hair approached them.

"Did you want to start now?" the man asked.

Larkin nodded and whispered, *"Oui,* thank you, Mike."

"Everyone," called Mike as he reached the lectern and took his place behind it, "please be seated." There was a rustle of movement as the guests began finding their seats. "We're here to celebrate the life of our good friend, Elijah Ryan. As his boss, I can say without hesitation that Elijah was a model employee, someone who could always be relied upon. Any time there was a party or something we did at work for charity, Elijah could always be counted on to be the first to volunteer. When we set up that family fun fair to raise money for cancer research, he agreed to be in the dunk tank. Clients absolutely loved him because he always took extra time with them and explained things in a way they understood.

"Elijah had a good heart, wanting nothing more than to help other people, and that was especially true of his friends. He was the kind of guy who would give you the shirt off his back. And while Elijah was an excellent worker, it was his kindness, warmth, and understanding that I think we'll remember him for most. He was probably the least judgmental person I've ever met, and I often wondered if all the time he spent in an organization where love, empathy, and understanding weren't always the norm gave him such compassion and insight."

Quinn bristled, knowing exactly which organization Mike was referring to. He stiffened, jaw set, wanting nothing more than to jump up and defend his Church—or to walk out. His feet, however, seemed rooted to the carpet. *I should've known this would happen, that they'd start attacking the Church! They just can't resist the need to try and destroy everything LRH built! Why the fuck did I even come here?*

"Whatever the reasons behind it," Mike went on, "there can be no doubt that he was a wonderful friend to everyone here, and his sudden and unexpected loss has left deep holes in our hearts. I would like to invite anyone who would like to come up here and say a few words. We'll start with his best friend, Larkin."

Quinn looked at the side of Larkin's face. While he still wore that strangely blank expression, his eye was downcast, his teeth were clenched, and his hands were balled into fists on his knees. He was unsteady as he slowly got to his feet. *Is he shaking?*

Larkin made his way to the lectern, said a quiet "thank you" to Mike, and turned to face the crowd.

"Mes amis," he started. "I am not someone who makes friends easily, but I considered Elijah to be my best friend. He was, in fact, the first friend I made when I moved here to Calgary, and he never wavered in that friendship. Some of my fondest memories are of the time he spent helping me set up my shop. *Le bon Dieu* knows he didn't have to do any of that, but once he found out I had just moved here, he immediately volunteered. I have wonderful memories of the two of us covered in dust, working to get everything set up. He was interested in everything, the stories behind every piece. Elijah knew that store and the stock almost as well as I did.

"As Mike said, Elijah didn't judge anyone for anything; he was unique in that he just accepted people for who they are, regardless of their past transgressions. I could open up to him in a way that I couldn't with anyone else, tell him things I hadn't ever told anyone else. I never once had to worry about his reaction or him repeating anything. Telling Elijah secrets was like telling a priest; they went no further. Elijah was someone you could count on—if you needed a shoulder to cry on at three in the morning, he was there, and *le bon Dieu* knows how many times I cried on his shoulders. He had what they call broad shoulders to bear all of us and our problems, while not talking about his own. I think he preferred dealing with other people's problems instead of dwelling on his own.

"En effet, he wasn't one to dwell on anything negative for long. He loved to laugh and could start giggling over some trivial thing until he couldn't breathe. I can't tell you how many comedy movies he and I roared through, how many stand-up comedians we watched or saw live. I remember him just howling at a Gabriel 'Fluffy' Iglesias show, to the point that I thought they'd kick us out."

He liked stand-up? I wonder if I get that from him? I wonder who his favourites were? I guess I'll never know now.

"Elijah could light up a room; he was everyone's friend, loved everyone he met, and didn't deserve to pass so soon. He…"

Larkin stopped and dropped his head, covering his mouth with his hand. Quinn stared as the man's shoulders began to shake. Abruptly, he ripped his hand away and slammed his clenched fist on the lectern with enough force that the sound rang around the room and bounced off the walls.

"Oh, *mon cher ami,* how will I ever get through the New Year's without you? Eh? *Qui me soutiendra et me gardera du noir, maintenant que tu es parti, Elijah?*"

Cupping his face with both hands, he sobbed loudly.

Mike went up and put a hand on Larkin's shoulder, gently leading him away and back to his seat next to Quinn. Larkin sat and folded himself in half, bending at the waist until his face, still in his hands, was almost touching his knees. Quinn couldn't hear if Larkin was still sobbing, but his back and shoulders shook, and Quinn felt something twist in his own chest—anger at the Church, loyalty, and a grief he didn't know what to do with, all colliding in the dim, floral-scented room.

A tall, thin, dark-skinned man with glasses and a shaved head stood and read a poem, but Quinn wasn't paying attention. *This isn't what I thought a wog funeral would look like. I thought it would be… bigger. Grander. They don't believe that they'll meet them in another life, so I thought it would be a bigger thing than this. It just seems…shabby. Maybe that's me with too much havingness, but I really thought it would be a bigger thing than this.* He remembered the glamorous, massive event the Church had held for the Commodore's birthday, with its rich white-and-gold decorations. This memorial for a dead man isn't even in the same league, Quinn found himself getting more and more annoyed at how shabby and poor it seemed by comparison.

He looked over at Larkin, who had regained his composure, his face resuming its blank expression. His eye looked red, which made the unusual amber colour seem deeper and stand out all the more. *Why the hell did he break down like that? Wogs clearly aren't in control of their emotions, that's for sure. Are they all going to be that griefy? Are you supposed to cry at these things? It's just his meat body that he's dropped, that's all.*

Quinn had never actually been to a Scientology funeral, but he felt sure that the knowledge that you would meet again in your next life meant that there would be no tears, no deep emotions taking over and overstimulating the reactive mind. *We leave our meat body behind and embrace our thetan, the being of pure thought, spirit, and light that we really are. Your body and mind are just things that you have and get dropped when you don't need them anymore.*

He only half listened to the other stories, although everyone said much the same thing: how good a person Elijah was, how he'd helped them, how he'd been there for them. *I'm surprised they didn't try to nominate him to be a saint,* he sneered to himself. But Elijah wasn't in heaven. Heaven was a made-up thing that didn't, and had never, existed. Quinn was on his feet the second the last speech ended. The anxiety had eaten away at him during the service, and he couldn't sit still any longer. He stood and looked behind him at the gathered people, several of whom were watching as if they expected something of him.

"Quinn," Larkin whispered from his seat, "did you want to say anything?"

The thought made his hands so cold they started to ache. The idea of getting up to speak to a bunch of strangers about a father he barely knew made him angry. He looked away, back to the photo of the smiling Elijah, and shook his head no. *I don't know him,* he thought. *That version of Elijah. I can't say anything even if I wanted to. What could I say? He walked away from his Church, he abandoned his family, that he left his immortality behind to live in the MEST? That* *he left...left **me** behind?* He shook his head again, more firmly this time. No, there was nothing to say.

"All right." Larkin stood, turned to the crowd, and thanked everyone for coming, signalling that the service was over. Pleasant, soft music came on from overhead. As the audience stood and shuffled, conversations broke out throughout the room. People began coming up to Larkin, telling him it was a wonderful service and shaking his hand. Several of them tried to speak to Quinn, offering condolences, which only annoyed him more.

Larkin turned to Quinn, creating a space for him, and Quinn unleashed his thoughts, loud enough that others nearby turned toward the commotion. "You keep saying you and Elijah were best friends," he blurted out. "But I don't see that you had anything in common with him. How the hell were you his best friend?"

"Eh bien, peut-être he was more my best friend than I was his," Larkin replied. "I can't say for certain."

"So he was your best friend, not the other way around."

"Perhaps."

"And you, his so-called best friend, couldn't do better than this to send him off? This is bullshit!" He shoved past everyone and headed for the stairs that led to the door.

"Quinn!" Larkin called as Quinn shoved through the group, shouldering people out of the way as he put his head down and almost ran.

Once at the top of the stairs, in the weak spring sun, he inhaled deeply. He felt like he'd been holding his breath and only now, in the sun and the fresh air, could he breathe. Shoving his hands into the pockets of his jeans, he headed toward the street, wondering how to get back to the Org.

"Quinn! Wait!" Larkin called after him.

He turned to glance behind, not noticing the patch of ice masquerading as a puddle in the middle of the parking lot. The turn put him off balance, so when his foot slipped and shot out from under him, he ended up sprawled on the asphalt, wondering how he'd gotten there. He was still trying to process what had happened when he looked up and found Larkin there, holding out his hand to help.

"Are you hurt? That was quite a spill."

"I'm fine!" he snapped, shoving Larkin's hand away as he clambered to his feet. "I'm fine! You're a helluva best friend, you know that? This was the best you could do? He never finished going up the Bridge! He never got to Clear! That means he got sucked back into this nightmare of death and rebirth! He's not going to be a pure thetan, a spirit being! And this was how you said goodbye? This cheap, pathetic shit show? 'Oh, Elijah was great! Oh, Elijah was a wonderful friend! Oh, Elijah was the person you called when you needed help, and he was always there!' He's so amazing, and this was the best you could do? A service in a basement? I don't think you gave a shit about him!"

"Quinn…"

"No! This was just sad! It seemed like everyone just wanted to talk about themselves! 'This is what Elijah did for me! This is how he helped me!' It was hardly even about him! I want to know why! Why do you think this was good enough, if he was so fucking wonderful?"

"Quinn, Elijah made all the arrangements himself. These were his wishes."

"Oh, yeah, sure! I thought you said he died suddenly!"

"He did; it was a brain aneurysm. We were having dinner at his place. We were talking, and all of a sudden his face just went slack and he slumped to the ground. Mid-sentence, he just looked startled and then dropped."

"Oh, really? Then how did he make all the arrangements?"

"He'd done that some time ago. He always said he wanted something small, something without a lot of fuss. He used to joke that he didn't want his memorial to cost two arms and a leg."

"Oh, then I guess this was all he could afford, huh?" he shot back with a bitter laugh. "The Church would have paid for everything if he'd stayed! We could have a proper goodbye, but nooooo! He had to throw it all away, all his security, his friends, his family! And for what? This pathetic excuse of a MEST life?"

"Non."

"No? What do you mean, 'no'? Am I wrong?"

"I mean, *'non'*, there wasn't very much money in Elijah's estate, so I paid for everything. I just paid for it; the decisions about where and how it was done were your father's, not mine. This is what he wanted, Quinn."

"What?"

"The location, the way the service was, the fact that it wasn't religious, these were all Elijah's decisions. He had it all planned in advance. I don't know why he wanted to plan it down to the last detail when it seemed he had a long life ahead of him, but he did. Me? Throw me in a cardboard box and toss me out with the garbage, I don't care, but Elijah did care. This was all him, Quinn. The only decisions I made were about the flowers. I would have paid for it no matter how elaborate or expensive, but this was what he wanted. Everything was your father, everything."

"Why did he want something like this? Why did he die just like that? It must have been a mass of repressed trauma that surfaced, to suddenly just kill him like that! No sickness, no nothing! I want to know why! Why did he leave? Why didn't he deal with whatever engrams ended up killing him? I wanna know why!"

"Quinn," Larkin reached out to put his hand on Quinn's shoulder, but Quinn slapped it away and took a few steps back.

"Why?" he demanded again, yelling. "Why did you get to spend so much time with him? Why did he leave the greatest religion on the planet? Why did he abandon everything?" Tears spilled from his eyes.

"Je ne sais pas, Quinn." Larkin sighed. "I don't know why he was taken as he was. He should have died an old, happy man. They say the good die young, and in your father's case, that's the truth. He should have been a light in the world for much longer; it's very unfair."

"I want to know why he left! Why did he abandon us! And why..." he became quieter, "and why all of you know him in a way I never will. Why is he a stranger to me, and all of you know him so well?"

Larkin sighed. *"Je ne sais pas,"* he repeated. "But I might be able to suggest a way you could get to know your father a little better, even now."

"How?"

"You can talk to us. Everyone here—listen to their stories and get to know him through us."

Quinn shook his head. "No, I'm not going back in."

"Eh bien, then talk to me. I can tell you everything I know about your father. Listen, Quinn, why don't you come back and stay at my place for a while? We'll talk about your father, or whatever you want."

"This is just a trick to get me to leave the Church, you wog!"

"No, it isn't. And I'm not asking you to leave, at least, not forever. In three days, I have to deliver a chaise lounge to Canmore. Why don't you come with me? Stay at my place for a few days, we'll go to Canmore, and then I'll drive you back to the Org myself."

"I still say this is a trick."

"Non, I swear it isn't. In fact, I'd be grateful for the company." He looked down. "Your father was supposed to come with me; we were going to drop off the chaise in Canmore and then go on to Banff for a

couple of days. Your father loved Banff; he went as often as he could. He was looking forward to it, and… ever since he passed, I've been dreading it. I don't want to make that trip alone, knowing it wasn't supposed to be that way. *S'il vous plaît,* Quinn, you'd be doing me a great favour."

"You promise we can talk about Elijah? Do you swear not to keep me from leaving? Swear to take me back to the Org any time I ask, even if we haven't gone to Canmore?"

"But of course."

"How do I know I can trust you?"

"You don't, not until you try to, *mon ami.* But your father did trust me, if that means anything."

Quinn looked at Larkin—at the one amber eye, the colour all the more intense for its redness from crying; at the oddly blank face; at the bright white hair covering half of it. He looked down and noticed the tattoos on the backs of Larkin's hands, peeking out from under the long sleeves of the navy polo shirt. *This might be my only chance.*

"Ok, I'll go." He raised his arm to flex his shoulder and winced.

"Are you sure you're not hurt*, mon ami?* "

"I think I landed on my arm near the elbow."

"Come, let's get you something for the pain, eh?" Larkin's hand lightly touched Quinn's shoulder blade as he escorted him toward the old, beat-up white pickup he drove, and Quinn—still furious, still loyal to the Church, anything else was unthinkable—nonetheless stepped into the first choice that might let him know his father at last.

Chapter Ten

He clung to the handle above the window, legs aching from pressing the imaginary brake on the passenger side. His entire body was ridged with fear. *This is it, this is how I drop my body. They're right when they say your life flashes before your eyes. This is how I die, in this truck with this weird guy.*

By contrast, Larkin seemed perfectly calm and in control as he wove through the afternoon traffic, speeding past the other cars as if they were parked. He slammed the gear shift around as if punching it, and the engine roared. "Quinn, may I ask you a question?"

"S-sure." *I'm going to have whole track engrams from this for sure!*

"You used a word I don't understand. My English is good, but I don't think I've ever heard the word 'mest' before. What does it mean?"

"Oh! MEST stands for 'matter, energy, space, and time'. That's what the physical universe is, just matter, energy, space, and time."

"Ah! It's from Scientology then, eh?"

"Yeah, the physical universe isn't as important as our spiritual being, our thetan. It's just stuff that all gets left behind when you drop your body."

"When you pass away?"

"Yeah."

"Ah. I see."

"MEST isn't important, that's what LRH's technology helps you do: stop worrying about the MEST and focus on the spiritual universe."

"So, the beauty in the world isn't important? It doesn't matter?"

"Oh, it's not that the world isn't beautiful, it's just that our spiritual being is more important. Our thetan is free of mental pain. It's happier, peaceful, and more joyful than we can ever be when we're in the MEST."

I wonder why I can talk to him like this, but I can't do it when I'm trying to sell a book? He gritted his teeth as Larkin whipped the truck around a corner fast enough that it threatened to tip over.

"So, you look forward to the afterlife, like Catholics do."

"But, it's not an afterlife like that, there's no heaven. If you don't go up the Bridge of Total Freedom, if you don't follow the teachings of LRH, you get sucked back into the MEST and are born again."

"Scientologists believe in reincarnation?"

"For those that haven't gone up the Bridge, yeah. Didn't Elijah tell you any of this?"

"He talked about his experiences there, not the dogma."

"He never told you anything?"

"Very little, as it happens." His hands darted along the steering wheel as he weaved between cars, triggering a swarm of angry honking. "I knew another member of your church long before I met your father. She talked about what the goal was, the dogma. Mais, it was many years ago, so I've forgotten most of it."

"Really? Did you ever study any of it? Take any classes?"

"*No,* I read Dianetics once, but I admit I found it very confusing. My English isn't always the best."

"Oh. Is English not your first language?"

"*Non*, I grew up *à Montréal,* so French was what I cut my teeth on. I learned English in school and from television and movies."

"Really? I just figured everyone in Quebec knew English, too."

"It depends on what your parents want," he said as he screeched to a stop at a red light, causing Quinn to pitch forward despite his seatbelt. *"Ma mère était une fière francophone,* so she didn't want us to learn English until we knew French completely."

"Us?"

"My brother and I."

"Oh. Is your brother like you? I mean, is he…well…"

"An albino?"

"Yeah."

The corner of Larkin's mouth twitched a hair upwards. "Two albinos in the same family? *Je pense qu'il y a* better chance of winning the lottery."

I only understand half of what he says. "Oh. I never learned French."

"Non? I thought it was mandatory in school."

"I went to a Church-run school, so it wasn't necessary."

"C'est de valeur! But I'm sure you'll pick up a few words, even in a few days."

Assuming I live that long….

The hair-raising drive ended as Larkin drove past Peter's Drive-In and turned into a small strip mall parking lot with a detached two-story building at the front left corner. Only after Larkin shut the engine off did Quinn dare to breathe.

"I thought we were going to your place?" he asked after peeling his hand off the window handle.

"We are. I live above my store."

Quinn slowly got out of the truck, his legs and arms aching. He looked up at the unassuming square brick two-story building. The front entrance with its big windows faced the parking lot, while a grassy patch with bushes and a couple of small trees faced the street. In the centre of the grass was a large pole that held up a big square backlit sign that read, *"**Versailles Vintage & Friperie**"* in fancy gold letters against a deep blue background.

Quinn turned to see Larkin standing on the bottom of the truck, door still open. His head was above the roof, and he had turned his face into a strong gust of wind that had picked up, eyes closed. The wind blew his hair away from his face. Quinn took him in clearly for the first time and could see the perfect symmetry of his eyes. The sun caught the white hair, making it shimmer and giving him an angelic look.

A pronounced scar ran from his left ear down the side of his face, tracing the jawline until it ticked upward near his chin. The scar had a brownish tint compared to the rest of his skin. The left ear was dark and misshapen. He was still staring as Larkin opened his eyes and hopped down.

"I love the wind here," he said, noticing Quinn's gaze. "The summer wind here is different from anywhere else."

"Oh." He didn't know what to say. *I wonder what Larkin would look like if he smiled, just a big ear-to-ear grin. Probably never happens.*

Following Larkin to the glass shop door, eyes glanced at the large pieces of stained glass that hung in the window. Beside the front door with its white protective grid was a porchlight, featuring a bright red dragon holding a white globe light in its talons.

"Bienvenue dans ma boutique, mon ami," said Larkin as he held open the door.

Quinn had been in thrift stores before; indeed, all of his clothes were second-hand, but he'd never seen anything like this. Thick, dark green carpet slightly gave way beneath his sneakers. Glass cabinets and carved wooden china hutches overflowed with porcelain figurines. Sparkling crystals; porcelain dishes with perfectly painted floral borders; fancy purses hanging from cabinet corners; dolls and teddy bears stared blankly forward. There was a wooden rocking horse with glass eyes peeking out from under a thick mane; mirrors and dark landscape paintings hung on the walls near the ceiling, jostling each other for space. Black-and-white photos of long-dead people stared gloomily at him. Hanging lights cluttered the ceiling so closely that hardly any space remained between them.

He was so busy looking around at everything that he didn't notice the woman standing near the back until she spoke, "Hey. How'd it go?" Her deep voice startled him. He looked up to see a tall, broad-shouldered woman with rich, sepia skin, long grizzled dreadlocks, and warm dark eyes.

"As well as you could expect," Larkin sighed. "Quinn, meet Sandra, my best employee. Sandra, *mon ami,* meet Elijah's son, Quinn."

She nodded at Quinn. "Hey. I'm sorry about your Dad."

"Thank you." She had a small eyebrow ring above her right eye.

"Where's the spaghetti lamp?" Larkin looked up at the ceiling, where there seemed to be the smallest of gaps.

Sandra's face lit up in a big grin, a kind smile. "Sold it," she replied.

"*Non!*" came the incredulous reply.

"Yep. About an hour after you left, this guy came in and lost his mind over it. Said he'd been looking for one for ages. Didn't haggle, just paid the full amount."

"*Pour de vrai!* See, that's why you're my best employee! *Bon travil,* Sandra!"

Her grin got bigger. "What can I say? I'm good!" she laughed.

How the hell did he notice something was even missing in all this mess? Quinn wondered, but asked instead, "What's a spaghetti lamp?"

"They're lamps whose shades are made of strings of spun lucite, a type of plastic," Larkin replied.

"They're very 1970s," Sandra added. "But, all that vintage shit is cool now."

"'Vintage shit'," Larkin repeated with an amused click of his tongue. "Maybe I should change the sign to 'Get vintage shit here', eh?"

"How about 'Vintage Shit Shop'?" Sandra suggested.

"That does sound better," Quinn agreed, feeling the need to join in the amusement.

Larkin snorted and muttered something in French under his breath while Sandra laughed.

"You have a lot of havingness, don't you, Larkin?" Quinn said as his eyes kept hopping around and around.

"Havingness?" Sandra asked, her eyebrow ring jumping upwards.

"The need for physical stuff."

"Is that another Scientology word?" Larkin asked.

"Yeah."

"Ah! But none of this is mine, it's stock to be sold."

"There's so much of it."

"Of course, there is. You never know what someone is looking for, so it's good to have a bit of everything, *tsé*."

"How do you remember all of it? Or find anything?"

"You should see the basement," Sandra quipped. "Larkin'll sell anything that isn't nailed down, right?"

"Well…" he replied thoughtfully, "nails can be removed, so…" Sandra let out a bark of laughter.

"Come, Quinn," he said, "before I have to defend my business any further, let me show you upstairs to my apartment."

Chapter Eleven

The bright red door to Larkin's apartment was located near the back of the store, close to the dumpster. A narrow staircase led upwards to a second door, which opened into the apartment itself.

"Bienvenue," Larkin said as he ushered Quinn inside.

A large studio space greeted them, floor-to-ceiling windows letting in the afternoon sun, which gleamed on the spotless wood floor. Builders' beige walls were almost invisible behind old paintings in elaborate gold frames right up to the ceiling. Like the store, there was stuff everywhere: paintings of anthropomorphic animals, china cabinets of porcelain figures and Blue Mountain–style animals, decorative plates, crystal, vases, and even some very old-looking stuffed toys.

Quinn's eyes hopped about like chickadees. "Wow," was all he could say.

"I like to think of all of this as extra stock." Larkin's gaze followed what Quinn was taking in. "I'm happy to sell any of it if someone's looking. There's a half bathroom by the front door, *icitte.*"

Half bathroom? How do you have half a bathroom?

"There's the TV over here." Larkin pointed to the large flat screen facing a sickly mustard-coloured couch with unsightly orange, yellow, and brown flowers, and another that featured more oversized orange flowers against a cream background with broad wooden arms. An overstuffed chair in plain orange velvet completed the scene.

"The bedrooms are upstairs, *là,"* he continued, indicating a black iron and glass staircase that ran up to the second floor. "There's a full bath upstairs as well. And there's the kitchen and the laundry; please feel free to help yourself to whatever's there, and you can use the washer if you like."

"Thanks."

"Would you like to see the guest room now? Or would you like something to drink first?"

"Sure, coffee would be great."

"Chu désolé, mais je n'ai pas de café, I rarely drink it. I do have tea, *t'en veux-tu?"*

"That's fine."

"Help yourself to any of the books as well," Larkin added. "You may read whatever you like."

Quinn hadn't noticed the books among the clutter, but further to the left of the couches was an oak desk, complete with a computer, almost buried in books and bookshelves. The shelves bowed under the weight, and more tomes lay on their sides atop the others. Quinn wandered over to look at the titles, finding books on art and antiques, as well as mythology, religion, history, art, vegetarian cooking, and books about the Palace of Versailles, most in French.

"You have your own library."

"Hm? *Oui,* I've always liked to read."

Quinn made his way towards the kitchen and sat down on one of the wicker barstools with forest green cushions at the counter, while Larkin set out a pair of large, mismatched porcelain mugs.

"We can have tea and talk on the roof." Larkin tossed a tea bag into each mug. "I go up there to smoke."

"You don't smoke inside? Even in the winter?"

"I try to avoid it as much as possible. I've seen what decades of smoke can do to antiques, *là.* It's never pretty. Smoke and tar build up on the piece and can destroy it in some cases."

"Oh, I didn't know that. I guess you have to be pretty smart to do this antique thing?"

Larkin chortled quietly, although his blank expression didn't change. "I wouldn't say I'm particularly smart, but I have learned some things along the way. Someone told me that you have to understand the time that a piece was made to understand the piece itself. And to weed out the fakes."

"Fakes?"

"Mon Dieu! There are always people trying to fake antiques of one type or another for money. Some pieces can be worth thousands, tens of thousands."

"Really?"

"There's more money to be made in fakes than in the real pieces. You can sell a fake painting as many times as you want; the real one you sell only once."

"Yeah, but that's stuff like jewellery, right?"

"Non, paintings, furniture, even toys. Fake jewellery is easier to spot and harder to replicate."

"Really? And that stuff is worth a lot of money?"

"To the right buyer, yes." He turned away to pick up the now whistling green kettle from the stove. "There's a huge black market for antiques, so I have to be careful," he went on as he poured the water into each mug. "For antique dealers, their reputation is everything, so I have to be very… Ah… what's that word *en anglais? Ciboire!* Vigilant! That's it! I must be vigilant and make sure that no fakes are sold in my store, unless they're reproductions, of course."

"Isn't reproduction a fake, though?"

"Non et oui, properly reproduced pieces are clearly marked, you don't even need to have a trained eye to see it. What would you like in your tea, Quinn?"

"Oh. Just black is fine."

"Bien, here you are, *là,"* he handed Quinn his mug, taking the other for himself and adding milk to it.

"Thank you."

"Bienvenue. Enweye."

He headed towards another door, almost hidden beneath the staircase, on which hung a framed poster of *Doctor Who.* It was minimalist, with most of the poster taken up by the words: *"Courage is not just a matter of not being frightened, you know. It's being afraid and doing what you have to do anyway."*

The walls along the narrow staircase were lined with similar posters and framed photos, all from the same show. Quinn followed cautiously, afraid to bump into anything. He blinked as Larkin flung open the blue door at the top of the stairs and stepped into the light.

A wrought iron bistro set in bright white sat in the middle of the nearly empty roof, under an off-centre patio umbrella with a mint green shade. Cedar trees in large whiskey barrel pots sat one in each corner, their scale-like leaves waving peacefully in the wind. Larkin strode over to the table, set his mug on the glass top with a clack, and pulled out one of the chairs.

"Asteure." He sat and turned around to face his guest. *"Hâle-toi une bûche.* Where would you like to start?"

"At the beginning, I guess." Quinn took the other chair and set his mug down in front of him. "How did you meet Elijah?"

"I had just decided to move here." Larkin pulled a pack of cigarettes and a plastic lighter out of his back pocket. He pulled one from the pack using his mouth, then cupped his long fingers around it to light it. The cool breeze picked up and whisked the grey smoke around his head before dragging it away. Long, spider-like fingers dragged the brown glass ashtray, already bursting with ash and butts, towards him.

"I'd been living in the US for years, and I'd had enough. I needed a new start, so I decided to come back to Canada. I'd briefly lived in Calgary years ago, so I decided to come back here." He sipped his tea.

"Why didn't you go back to Quebec? To Montreal?"

"Too many old ghosts, I wanted to have a fresh start in a new place. Reinvent myself, as they say. I had bought the shop and the reno work was being done, so I decided to check out my competition. There used to be an antique store on McLeod, you probably don't remember it."

"Actually, I do. It's a crystal shop now, isn't it?" Quinn took a sip of his own tea and sputtered. It was still too hot to drink.

"Oui. En tu cas, I decided to go in to see what they had, what their pricing was like, that sort of thing. There's only one other customer in the place, *j'ne sais pas* where the owner was. As I'm looking around, I walk behind the other customer and see he's looking at a Kit-Kat clock. You know those clocks that look like a black and white cat, and the eyes move back and forth, and the tail moves as it ticks, *là?*

"He had one in his hands, and I couldn't help but peek over his shoulder at the price. *Mon Dieu*, I saw the price and started to laugh! He turned around and looked at me, and I said, 'I wouldn't pay that, it's only worth half.' The man was Elijah, and he was looking at it as a gift for his roommate. I told him that I had a Kit-Kat clock, and that I'd happily sell it to him for half that, if he could stand to wait a few months until I got the store opened. We started to chat, had lunch, and became friends all in the same day."

Larkin huffed, amused at the memory. He drank more tea after tapping the ash off the end of the cigarette.

"And he offered to help you set up your shop? You mentioned that at the funeral."

A cloud of smoke wrapped itself around Larkin. *"Oui,* but that was a bit later. I had to go back to Florida to tie up some things first, and by the time I got back, the bulk of the construction was done. Your father helped me set things up. He unboxed all the stock I'd brought with me."

"But what did you talk about? I mean, it doesn't seem to me like you and Elijah had anything in common."

"Everything. Elijah was interested in everything. That meant that we could talk on a wide variety of things he'd learned along the way. *Mais,* it was really our… *Comment je peux dire?* Life experiences, our pains that bind us. Elijah talked about leaving the church, having to start over again, and creating a new life for himself. I'd done the same, so we understood each other."

"So, he told you he blew? That he abandoned eternity and his family?"

"Well," he began with another puff of smoke, "he didn't put it like that, but yes."

"And you didn't tell him to go back?"

Larkin snorted. "Who am I to tell him that? That's not my place to pass moral judgments."

"But, didn't you know it was wrong? Scientology does so much good for the world, for the people! He would have improved so much as a person if he'd stayed! Scientology–"

"Is not for everyone."

"Yes, it is! It works for everyone. All they have to do is accept it, work at it!"

"And perhaps your father wasn't ready to do that." Another puff of smoke obscured his face for a moment. "I left the religion I grew up in as well, so I understand. It's not an easy thing to do, I can tell you that. It's a decision that comes with guilt and fear, all the things that were instilled in us since we were children. Having no contact with either you or your mother was one of the things he felt the most guilty about."

"Oh, sure. He didn't show it."

"You weren't here to see it, Quinn. I can tell you with complete honesty, it killed him inside. It was something that haunted him, daily, *là.*" The smoke curled about him as the breeze died. The smell was intense, causing Quinn to clear his throat. Larkin sipped his tea.

"Just last year," Larkin went on, "Elijah gave me a porcelain cat figure, black and white with a pink bow tie, to commemorate how we met, a reference to the clock. He remembered things, thought about things that you wouldn't expect. I know he worried for both you and your mother. He worried that you weren't happy, that you weren't thriving."

"He shouldn't have. What could happen if I were with my Church family, my real family?"

"It would have eased his mind if he knew you were happy, Quinn." Another puff of smoke. "That's all he wanted, *là.*"

Quinn frowned.

"Your father worked for an investment company in the accounting department, that's where he met Mike, his boss. They became friends and used to go hiking in Banff and K country together."

"Maybe I should be talking to Mike then."

"*Oui,* you should. Absolutely."

"Instead of you, I mean."

"If you'd prefer, I'm sure Mike wouldn't mind. He might not have the room for you to stay, though. He has a little one under five. Not the quietest place to stay, I'm sure."

Quinn tried another sip of the cooled tea, not feeling the need to respond.

Larkin sat unmoving but for the smoke that trickled up and away from the cigarette, now in the ashtray. His white hand reached out to pick up the red mug again.

"He did well at his job. Elijah was careful; he took his work seriously and had an eye for detail. His boss loved him."

"That's Scientology. It teaches you to spot the details, to make sure everything is perfect. Everything accounted for. If you work for the Church, you have to have an eye for detail."

"That served him well then. We spent a lot of time talking about the stock I had," Larkin went on. "At first, *de toute façon*. It was like making small talk, *là*. A way to get to know each other better. He loved the stories of the pieces, the same as I did. Old pieces have their own history, their own stories. If you have a good eye and good memory, you can learn much from antiques. The stories people tell you about how and where it came from, that their *arrière grande-tante* was given it by her lover, who was killed in a far-off war somewhere, are like legends. There may be a bit of truth, but the true story has been so distorted over time that there's not much truth left. They make for great stories, while the truth can often be... less exciting, but interesting all the same."

"It's just stuff, though, the physical stuff doesn't matter. That's why I said you have too much havingness, putting too much importance on physical stuff instead of your spiritual well-being. That's why people get themselves into trouble, that's where a lot of pain comes from."

"That's true," came the voice through the smoke, "but physical things can be triggers for some people."

"That's what I mean. They're just triggers for pain when the stuff isn't important at all."

"Not triggers for pain, *là*. Antiques can be triggers for memories of loved ones lost and of past times. That's what people talk about; it's not the thing they see, it's the past. Their past. There are tears as often as there are smiles, sometimes both at the same time. Sometimes there are painful memories, but I've found that for most people the painful memories are overshadowed by the joyful ones."

"Yeah, but the need to get and have stuff is what causes so much pain."

"Greed is a vice, *oui*. But your father didn't have a greedy hair on his head, *là*. He was generous to a fault."

"Mike said that, too."

"Oui. Your father actually learned how to make vegetarian meals just for me. He knew I didn't always cook for myself, so sometimes he'd bring over all the food and cook here. Other times, I would cook, so we ate together a lot."

"You don't like to cook?"

"Actually, I do, I just can't always be bothered to cook for myself alone. I like cooking for other people, so I always made sure to make a great meal. Your father loved my mac and cheese, for example. I used to make double and let him take home the leftovers. In the summer, we would drive around to all the yard sales, we'd look for things that people were selling cheaply but were actually worth a great deal."

As Larkin talked, Quinn listened in spite of himself, realizing that every story was a piece of a life he'd never been allowed to see—and that, for now at least, he was choosing to sit here and hear it.

"You don't find stuff like that all the time, do you?"

Another puff of smoke and a long drink of tea. "More than you'd think. What's the saying *en anglais?* One man's trash is another man's treasure? People can't always be bothered to look things up, so they sell them for cheap. Anything can be worth money to the right collector."

Quinn frowned. "So you don't tell them that they could get more for whatever it is? That's pretty shitty, you know."

"*Non,* it depends on what it is. If someone was selling a real *Fabergé* egg for twenty dollars, I'd tell them. But even if you do, sometimes they can't be bothered to go to the effort of selling it themselves. If they're clearing out *l'appartement de grand-mère,* they may not have the energy to go about selling everything separately. I can do that for people. I sell their things on commission, so either they get rid of it by selling it for cheap, or they can let me help them get more for it. Antique dealers live or die by their reputation, so it does me no good to cheat anyone.

"*En tout cas,* we spent many a summer day doing that, driving around to the garage sales, laughing at nothing and everything. Your father loved to laugh; he'd laugh at the silliest things, enough that he'd cry. I remember one time, we were at an estate sale and the people were selling a car. They mentioned the car had a moonroof. Your father asked me, 'What's the difference between a sunroof and a moonroof?' I couldn't resist it, *mon Dieu,* so I said 'About twelve hours,' and it just set him off! He roared!"

A smile spread across the normally blank face. It started as a half-smirk that gradually broadened into a full smile, showing Larkin's beautiful white teeth.

Quinn was surprised at how much that smile changed his appearance, how human it made Larkin look.

"As many days as we spent driving around and laughing, there were as many nights we spent crying into each other's beers, *pour ainsi dire.* That's how I know how much he worried for you and your mother—he told me. He even told me that he would take the train up to that laundromat in the northeast where you go to work sometimes. He'd hang around outside just to try and get a glimpse of you, just to see if you were ok."

"How did he know when we were going there?"

"*J'ai aucune idée.* Most of the time he came back saying he hadn't seen you, or anyone from the church. There were a few times, however, when he did see you, and he would come back and tell me how well you looked. He was proud of you, Quinn."

"So… he spied on me? Yeah, that's not creepy at all."

"It was all he felt he could do. He said that if he tried to speak to you, it would make more trouble for you, and he didn't want that."

Quinn had to admit that was true. Elijah coming into Church-run anything would certainly get Quinn in trouble with Ethics. Any interaction with a known SP would have to be reported, and every second of that interaction would be gone over multiple times during auditing. As the son of a Suppressive Person, Quinn was already under extra scrutiny and had been ever since Elijah blew.

Larkin gulped down the last of his tea. "Would you like another cup of tea, Quinn?"

"No, I'm ok, thanks."

"*Bien,* I'm just going to get another one. I'll be right back."

Quinn sat and stewed. *So, Elijah's a saint, a wonderful guy, really a best friend to everybody. Everybody but me, that is. Proud of me? How in hell could he be proud of me when he dumped his faith, dumped Mom, and me? He wouldn't have known how I was doing in my work or the classes, or how far up the Bridge I was. How proud* *was he of me? If he'd have come back, gone through Ethics, and gotten back into the fold, then **I** could have been proud of **him!** But no! Did he know how bad that would look for Joni and me? Being the son of an SP is bad enough; I can't imagine how bad it was for Joni being the wife of one! No wonder they divorced.* He was still thinking by the time Larkin got back.

"*Eh bien.*" Larkin returned to his seat. "Is there anything you would like to ask me about your father, Quinn?"

"I don't know…it's just a lot, you know?"

"*Oui, je comprends.*" He lit another cigarette and inhaled deeply. Quinn looked at the strange man, at his cobweb hair, his long white fingers, at the amber eye that felt like it saw into his soul. The smoke from Larkin's cigarette curled about until it seemed to circle his eye, highlighting it and making Larkin's stare more penetrating. Suddenly feeling uncomfortable, he looked away.

"Where did you live in the States, Larkin?"

"Oh, all over. I was in Florida before coming here."

"Oh! Where? The Church has its headquarters in Clearwater, the FLAG base."

"I know, I lived in Sarasota, but I've been to Clearwater and saw the building."

"Really? You're lucky. I really want to go to the FLAG base!" Quinn spent the next while grilling Larkin for every detail about the base, the people he'd seen there, about Clearwater itself, everything he could think of. Eventually, Larkin suggested ordering pizza for dinner. Quinn found himself staring at a medium Canadian pizza, unsure how to proceed. "Is this really all for me? You're not having any?"

"I wouldn't eat all that bacon and pepperoni, *mon ami*. If it were just the mushrooms, *c'est bon*. I'm happy with my vegetarian one."

They ate in the living room, with Larkin putting on a documentary about China's terracotta warriors. "Your father loved programs like this," he said. Quinn was intrigued; he'd never heard of the terracotta warriors. Riveted, simply absorbing the new information, he ate without thinking, until he abruptly realized he'd eaten more than half the pizza and was desperately overfull. "Oh, my God, I can't **move**!" Quinn laughed. "I can't remember the last time I was this stuffed!"

Larkin let out an amused snort. "That's a good thing, *là*. I would be a terrible host if you left here hungry."

After the end of the program, Larkin showed Quinn to the guest room upstairs, which was next to Larkin's own, with the bathroom across the hall from both on the right. It was a comfortable room, and the beige walls were again invisible behind numerous vintage paintings and photographs. Although the print above the head of the bed of a fox-headed person, posed standing with crossed ankles like in a magazine ad, with the words "Fashion Animals," made Quinn smile in amusement.

Quinn opened the window before crawling into the clean navy-blue sheets and pulled the fluffy blanket with the wolf print up to his chin. The bed was so much softer than he was used to, and he quickly started to drift off.

I don't know what else to ask him about Elijah, Quinn thought as he started to slip away. *I can't ask him about every conversation they've ever had, can I? I should try to find out what awful things he said about the Church, just to get proof that he really was an SP. Larkin's not exactly an open book. I should try to find something I can use to convince him to join the Church. Maybe then I won't have to spend so much time in Ethics for taking off. If I get Larkin to join, that'd be a huge win for me and the best thing for him. Yeah, I just need to find something I can use. I have to get him to talk more, then I'm sure I'll find something. Yeah, that's it, I just need to get him to talk about himself, I need to get to know him better.*

His thoughts became jumbled as he drifted further and further into the comforting darkness until it wasn't possible to distinguish thoughts from dreams.

The bright early summer sun was streaming in through the window by the time Quinn cracked open his eyes. *I guess I don't have to get up,* he thought as he stretched. *I don't have anywhere I have to be. I can't remember the last time I got to sleep in.* He rolled over onto his stomach, but eventually the need to pee forced him to get up. He tiptoed towards the upstairs bathroom, since the apartment was as silent as the Rocky Mountains. He glanced at the time on his old flip phone as he got back to the room. *Holy shit, it's noon?*

He dressed quickly and headed downstairs, only to find the apartment empty but for a note on the kitchen counter:

Mon ami Quinn, I've gone downstairs to the shop, but please help yourself to anything in the kitchen. I'm sure I have some snacks in the cabinet. Please also watch whatever you like on the TV, or come downstairs if you like.

This was followed by instructions on how to get into the various streaming services Larkin subscribed to. The idea of just sitting around watching TV was enticing; it was something that Quinn never had the chance to do. There was always too much Org work that had to take priority over everything else. He was tempted, but he just couldn't do that; he felt guilty. He needed to be doing something, anything, so instead he headed downstairs and into the store.

He walked in to find Sandra on a step ladder, trying to dust all the hanging lights, and Larkin sitting in the back on his computer. They both looked up when the shop door opened.

"Quinn! *Bon après-midi!* Did you sleep well?"

"Yeah, I'm sorry I slept so late, that's so down stat!"

"Down what?" Sandra asked.

"Down stat. Unacceptable."

"It's a Scientology term, *là?*"

"Yeah, it means you did something really wrong."

"Well, don't worry about it. Larkin was sleeping on the couch until a few minutes ago!" Sandra snorted.

"Cibole," said Larkin by way of a reply. There was another floral sofa in the back room, featuring large purple and blue roses against a cream background.

"You were asleep?"

"I don't always sleep well at night, so sometimes I have a nap, *là.*"

"Hey, can I help you with anything, Sandra?" She didn't need to be asked twice and quickly put Quinn to work dusting the lighting fixtures, an easy task for him. He quickly impressed her by working both quickly and efficiently. Larkin spent his time on the computer, checking online auctions for valuable items that he could sell in the store. He began regaling Quinn with stories about the pieces he was looking for online, as well as items in the shop. It seemed everything had a story of its own, and Quinn quickly became intrigued, drawn in by every detail.

"Hey, Larkin?" he asked while dusting the Royal Doulton figurines, "you said you lived in Calgary before? When was that?"

"Hein? Oh, years ago. I was only here a few months, maybe a year."

"Why? Didn't you like it?"

"Non, I liked it, but it was time to move on, explore new places, *là."*

"Where did you go?"

"Hm, I think I went to Edmonton for a while, but I got bored there, so I went to BC after that."

"I was born in BC, but I haven't been there since I was a little kid."

"*Oui,* I remember your father telling me that. The church wanted you to come to Calgary to go to school here, but your parents wouldn't allow you to go alone."

"I could have come alone. The Church would have taken care of me. Kids are just adults in smaller packages."

"Your parents couldn't tolerate being apart from you. Joni refused to allow you to leave without her. Your father said they had a terrible time, that the church elders wouldn't allow them to go with you. Eventually, they had to allow the church to take you, and then they hopped in a car, drove to Calgary, and just turned up at the Scientology building here."

"Really? I didn't know that."

"*Oui.*"

The evening passed much as it had the previous night, only this time Larkin ordered Chinese food. Quinn suggested watching a horror movie, eventually settling on *Silent Hill*, as neither of them had seen it. "I never get a chance to watch TV at the Org," he told Larkin.

"Well, you can watch whatever you want here, *là.*"

They eventually got to bed after midnight, which was pretty early for Quinn, who immediately slipped into a deep, dreamless sleep.

The next day, Larkin asked Quinn to go with him to a lady's house who wanted to sell a Georgian dresser. "If I buy it, I'll need help moving it," he explained.

"You might have to get money from the safe," Sandra said, "if it's what she says it is."

"Safe?" Quinn asked.

"Larkin's got a safe downstairs that really oughta be in a bank," Sandra replied. "It would take dynamite to break into it. It's in the basement because it's so freakin' heavy, it would bust through the floor."

Once in the truck, Quinn again found himself clinging to the handle above the window, Larkin's driving just as wild as they headed towards the northeast quadrant of the city. Desperate to rid his mind of the thoughts of imminent death, Quinn asked:

"What's Montreal like? I've never been there."

"Ah! Montréal is beautiful! There's a reason that Québec is called *La Belle Province*! I didn't really appreciate it when I was living there, but I look at photos and I see it now. And the food! *Je pense que cuisine Québécoise* is just as good as anywhere in the world."

"Have you been back? Like, for a visit?"

"Non."

"Why not?"

"Too many old ghosts."

"Do you have family there?"

"Oui, ma tante, mon oncle et mon frère y vivent tous."

"And you don't want to visit them?"

"Non." The tone of that one single word made it clear that Larkin didn't want to discuss it further.

"Oh. What about your parents?"

"Both dead."

"Did they just die recently?"

"Non, many years ago now."

"Oh."

There was silence for a time before Quinn became uncomfortable enough to break it:

"I'm…guessing you had all those tattoos when you met Elijah?"

"Oui, I've had them for years. I got them when I was still in the States."

"Why? I mean, why all of them?"

Larkin let out an amused huff. "They say tattoos are like potato chips, you can't have just one."

"So, you got them on a whim?"

"No."

O-kay, strange. "Didn't they hurt?"

"Everyone always asks that. Of course they hurt, *esti,* but I always found they hurt more when healing than when you're having them done, *là."*

They eventually came to the community of Castleridge, each duplex looking much like the others, with the same square outlines, neutral siding in beige, grey, or white, and small square front lawns. Quinn would never have known one house from the next but for the house numbers. A small lady in a blue hijab that complemented her green eyes opened the door and led them upstairs.

"The man said it's Georgian," she told Larkin as he began to inspect the beautiful wooden dresser. "I'd like to sell it."

"Oui, madame. Icitte, Quinn, help me move it away from the wall, I need to see the back, *là."* Quinn watched him get onto the floor and begin examining the back, even taking out a small flashlight from his pocket to examine the markings. He opened drawers and looked at the sides, and took out a couple completely to look at the back. He reminded Quinn of a doctor examining a patient, methodical and intent. Eventually, Larkin straightened.

"I'm so sorry, madame, this dresser isn't Georgian, it's a reproduction."

"A…what?"

"A reproduction. It's a very good one, it's beautifully done, but I'd say it's no more than 50 years old. It's not original, but an original in such beautiful condition would easily be worth five or six thousand to the right collector. This is probably worth less than half.... *Madame?"*

The two men stared at the woman as she put her head into her hands and began to sob. They stood helplessly while she cried.

"My…husband," she eventually stammered through her tears, "he's not a good man. He gets…angry…especially with our children. I threw him out and we're getting a divorce, but I thought he was paying the mortgage, and it turns out we're so far behind. I thought I could sell some things to pay for it, but..."

"Se démener comme un diable dans l'eau bénite," Larkin muttered to himself.

"I'm sorry?" the lady sniffed.

"Pas important," he replied. He reached into his back pocket and took out his wallet, and while both the woman and Quinn stared at him, he took out a massive wad of brown $100 bills and handed it to the woman.

"Oh, no!" the woman exclaimed, putting up her hands. "I can't!"

"Yes, ma'am, you can," Larkin's voice was firm; clearly, he was not going to take no for an answer. "You will take this, you will save your home, and then you will take your children to have a day where they can be children and forget the pain, for a time. Take them wherever they want to go." He tried to press the bills into her hands, and when she didn't take them, he turned and placed the entire thing on the dresser.

"But, but why?" she stammered.

Larkin stepped closer to her and placed a white spider-hand on her shoulder. "Because," he said softly, "I grew up in an abusive home, and I know how the pain lingers. Let your children be children for a day, yes? And let me take this one burden from your shoulders. *Enweye*, Quinn." He turned and headed back down the stairs, with Quinn hot on his heels. As soon as Quinn got in the truck, Larkin threw it in gear and took off down the street.

"Larkin," Quinn panted as he struggled to put on his seatbelt, "how much did you give her?"

"Enough that she won't have to worry about the mortgage for a few months."

"But, why? Why would you just give her money like that? It's better to help people work out their problems and their issues instead of just bailing them out."

"Is it? Sometimes, *mon ami,* the best thing you can do is to bail someone out. That helps to get them back on their feet, and then they can help themselves."

"But, you don't even know her. Why would you do that?"

"It doesn't matter, she's a person in pain who needs help, and I'm able to provide that help. So I did."

"But, I don't understand…"

"You don't have to, my friend. I could do it, and I did."

Quinn fell silent, not knowing what else to say. *He grew up in an abusive home…maybe that's his ruin. He must have all kinds of engrams. Yeah, I think that's what I can use.*

Chapter Twelve

Early afternoon found them loading the carefully wrapped chaise lounge into the back of Larkin's truck. The gleaming, deep red cherry wood went surprisingly well with the tiger-print fabric of orange and black.

"I keep wondering if they're going to film *un porno* on this, *ciboire*."

Quinn couldn't help but giggle. "I've never actually watched a porno," he noted. "It's considered down stat. You get in trouble for indulging in it."

"You're not missing anything much," Larkin replied.

Larkin easily wove between cars and transport trucks along the highway to Canmore as it wound its way through the foothills, past the wide green fields and the occasional river. As they went further north, the farms were replaced with spruce and fir trees that crowded the space along the highway. Massive limestone boulders bulged out of the ground, the pale grey in stark contrast to the green trees. Wildflowers of yellow, blue, and purple danced among the stones, tossed by the perpetual wind created by the traffic.

Then came the bend, the curve in the highway that Quinn had been waiting for. He watched delightedly as the very first mountain came into view, the highway running just a few kilometres from its base. It wasn't remotely the biggest mountain, but it was the first that marked the end of the foothills and the true beginning of the Rocky Mountains.

The early afternoon sun made the grey rock glow, as if lit by divine light, perfect for the tourists who stopped along the highway to marvel at it. They drove past the enormous Mount Lougheed that loomed darkly over the highway, casting its shadow across the speeding vehicles.

"*Regarde ça*," said Larkin, indicating the car beside them with a nod of his head. "All that camping gear on the roof, they must be planning on staying in Banff for weeks."

"I went camping once. We went to Kananaskis."

"Oh? Did you enjoy it?"

"Yeah, I liked it, but I don't think the girls did. I was in one tent with the guys, and the girls were all in the other tent. All of a sudden, Brittany started screaming, and they all ran out of the tent. Turns out, Brittany said she 'heard something sniffing' the tent and it scared her!"

"What was it?"

"A deer. It took off as soon as the screaming started. I don't think Rochelle has ever let Brittany forget it," he laughed.

Once they took the right-hand exit to Canmore, the peaks of the famous Three Sisters could be seen guarding the town. Most of the buildings were styled like traditional chalets, with orange Douglas fir wood used on every fence, every bench, and on almost every building.

Larkin began taking turns that Quinn couldn't follow, somehow managing to avoid hitting the tourists that crawled every which way, oblivious to the heavy traffic around them.

Eventually, they came to a large house at the end of a cul-de-sac that was surrounded by bushes. Lots of polished wood and huge windows that spanned its two floors made it seem to emerge from the trees like part of the forest itself.

A tall, thin, bald man with dark skin came out to greet them as they pulled into the gravel driveway. Larkin called to the man in French as he got out, while Quinn smiled and gave a polite nod to the stranger.

Larkin chatted with the man as they untied the chaise, the pair speaking French that Quinn couldn't hope to follow. *"T'as une superbe maison, Edouard,"* Larkin said at one point. "It's a beautiful home, isn't it, Quinn?"

"Oh, yeah, it's amazing!"

"Merci, merci," the man replied. "Let me show you where to put it."

The house was no less impressive inside. Orange Douglas fir wood made up the walls, ceilings, and exposed roof beams, set off by dark slate floors, with the forest visible from every window. They carried the chair towards the back of the house and set it up in the media room, which looked out over the massive deck and the backyard. There was no fence between the yard and the wilderness.

Quinn looked around while Larkin and Edouard chatted, and he noticed something move on the edge of the brush. He watched as a doe carefully stepped into the open yard, her ears perked forward, one delicate foreleg raised as she hesitated before gracefully stepping onto the lawn.

"Look!" Quinn breathed, interrupting the conversation.

"Oh!" Edouard said, "That's Beatrice."

"Beatrice?"

"Oui, she comes to visit often. She probably has this year's fawn hidden somewhere." Then, seeing the enraptured look on Quinn's face, he added: "Here, let me get the bag of carrots."

Quinn followed the man as he led the way to the enormous kitchen and out the sliding glass door onto the deck. He watched in amazement as Edouard called to the mule deer, who elegantly stepped towards him. Edouard held out a baby carrot to her, and she stretched out her neck to snatch it quickly. She kept looking about as she ate, the crunching of the carrot loud in the quiet.

"Here, Quinn," Edouard called quietly, "would you like to feed her?"

"Really? Can I?" He glanced at Larkin, who looked like he might smile.

"But of course!" He handed Quinn a few of the baby carrots while Larkin took out his phone and filmed. "Just hold it out for her with an open, flat hand, just in case she nibbles you a bit."

Quinn held his breath as the creature daintily came to him, only to realize just how big a deer actually was. He felt dwarfed by the animal, but her deep brown eyes made him think of a puppy. She took the offered carrot but didn't snatch it, appearing more comfortable, licking her nose after she finished her treat. She stood close enough that Quinn could have reached out and stroked her neck. He held out another carrot. He felt her nose brush against his skin as she took it and felt her warm breath on his hand. He looked up at Larkin, face beaming.

Larkin's one eye seemed to be smiling. He managed to feed the deer five or six carrots before something startled her, making her leap away from Quinn, only to pause, looking around, ears erect and one forefoot raised, poised for flight, before stepping back into the brush. Quinn could not have been more delighted.

"Larkin! Did you see that?" he asked like a child.

"*Oui*, I saw it. I filmed everything."

"Beatrice normally comes in the early morning; it's a surprise for her to come so late in the day," Edouard commented.

"Oh, I can't wait to tell them about this back at the Org! Larkin, will you send me the video?"

"Of course."

"That was amazing! I've never been so close to a deer! Oh, my God, thank you," he said to Edouard. "Thank you so much for letting me do that!" He was just about dancing as they went back to the truck. "I can't believe a wild animal just came and ate out of my hand like that! That was amazing! I can't believe I pulled something so wonderful in!" he kept repeating as they headed back down the gravel driveway.

At the end of the street, Larkin stopped for much longer than he needed to make sure the way was clear. Quinn looked over only to find Larkin staring at him with an intense expression, his whisky-coloured eye boring into him.

"Why are you looking at me like that?" he asked uncomfortably.

"Let's go to Banff," came the reply.

"What?"

"Banff. We're almost there anyway; it's maybe half an hour away. Your father loved Banff, and I'd like to show you one of his favourite places, Moraine Lake."

"Moraine Lake? I've never heard of it. I've heard of Lake Louise."

"It's a man-made lake. They flooded a valley that had an abandoned mining village in it to make a place for divers. But your father thought it was one of the most beautiful places in the world. I… would love to show it to you, Quinn."

"And you'll take me back to the Org after that?"

"*Oui.*"

Quinn hesitated, knowing he should get back and that the longer he was away from his duties, the more trouble he'd be in. But he found himself not really wanting the trip to end; he had come to like the odd man. Larkin was calm and collected like a good Scientologist, but at the same time, he was so different from anyone Quinn knew, and he was the only friend he had outside of the Church.

"Do you think we'll see any more animals in Banff?"

"I think it's almost certain," Larkin told him as an impish smirk spread across his face.

"Ok then, let's go to Banff and Lake Moraine."

"C'est beau!"

Chapter Thirteen

The road to Moraine Lake was winding, snaking through the trees, its course like a river. At one point, Larkin stopped the truck at the sight of a huge bull elk by the roadside, happily feeding on the grass and wildflowers.

The small parking lot and building that appeared around a tight corner startled with its sudden contrast to the greenery. A wide footpath wound along the lake to the left and into a campsite.

Quinn watched as Larkin donned a wide-brimmed grey hat, vintage sunglasses with round gold-tone frames, cigarette at his lips. "Why the hat and the glasses?" he asked. "We're not going to be here all day, are we?"

"*Non*, but the sun is not kind to *aux albinos*, so I 'ave to take care. I burn almost immediately."

"No sun tanning then, eh?"

There was an amused huff. "*Non*, and sunscreen with SPF 1,000 is essential." Quinn grinned.

They followed the path, walking past the docks with boat rentals and guided tours. The path dipped to an open area of rocks and sand that led down to the blue water. Mountains loomed around the shore, enclosing the lake like a fence.

"This," he told Quinn, "was Elijah's favourite place in the world. He asked to have his ashes scattered here."

"He did? Are you going to do that now?" The thought wasn't horrifying; it just provoked curiosity.

"*Non*, I will, but I'm… not ready yet. In time, *tsé*, in time." Larkin picked one of the two picnic tables and sat, making sure he remained in the shade.

Quinn walked towards the edge of the shore, carefully picking his way across the rocks. He went out onto a thin spit of land, clambering over the boulders to the water's edge. The crisp breeze was cool as it tugged at his curly hair and beard. The lake ran off and vanished to his left, and he found himself admiring the mountains that rose directly in front of him. The pine and fir trees bristled thickly along its steep flanks like porcupine quills, becoming sparser until they stopped completely, leaving the bare grey rock to scrape the sky. Snow still clung to it, highlighting the ragged peaks and running down the steep sides like whitewater. Clouds drifted, casting shadows that deepened the grey stone, the dark trees, and the blue water. The sounds of the tourists faded as he watched the slow waltz of mountains, clouds, and water; an unending dance moving to a melody unheard by the clattering crowds.

Time didn't exist; the only indication he had of how long he'd stood there came when he went to move stiff muscles that balked. He rubbed his chilled arms as he headed back, catching a whiff of Larkin's cigarette as he approached. But the cigarette was burning unnoticed, held by loose fingers as Larkin roughly rubbed his eyes, then pinched the bridge of his nose. Half a dozen cigarette butts, each carefully pinched out, sat on the table in front of him next to his sunglasses. He covered his left ear with a cupped hand.

"You ok?" Quinn asked as he sat down opposite.

"Ah, I'm fine, it's just…" His stiff posture caused Quinn to realize that he'd been crying. "I feel as if he's here, your father. I feel like he's here with us; his ghost is standing at my shoulder."

"You really miss him, huh?"

Larkin sniffed and nodded.

He watched Larkin regain his composure. *I want to touch him,* Quinn thought. *I want to… I don't know, pat his arm or something. I really want to touch him, his hand, maybe? Why the hell do I want to touch him so much? Just to make him stop, to stop rollercoastering…*

yeah, that's it. Just to stop him from this banksy shit. He didn't move; instead, he deliberately folded his hands on the table to stop them from moving. He watched while something inside kept telling him to reach out, until Larkin finally straightened, snuffed out the cigarette between his thumb and forefinger, and rubbed his eyes.

"*Pardonne-moi, mon cher ami.*" He sat back, only for his eyes to go wide. "*Chu désolé*, Quinn. I shouldn't have said that. Habit."

"Why?"

"It means, 'Forgive me, my dear friend.' That's what I used to call your father. *Mon cher ami*, or just *cher* for short."

"Oh."

"*Écoute*, it's getting late, why don't we stay here in Banff for a night, eh?"

"What do you mean?"

"I mean, we just stay here and go back to Calgary tomorrow."

"You said you'd take me back whenever I wanted," Quinn bristled. "That was the deal."

"Yes, that's why I'm asking if you'd like to stay. If not, we'll go back right now. I just thought you might want to 'ave dinner and go back tomorrow, that's all."

"So, if I say no, you'll take me back?"

"But, of course."

The trees rustled in the breeze. The buzzing of a boat suddenly seemed very loud. A fat chipmunk dashed across the ground near them, looking at the pair inquisitively to see if they'd spilled anything.

"I think I'd like to stay. There's great food in Banff, isn't there?"

"Of course, there's many wonderful restaurants in town."

"Yeah, no, yeah," he said finally. "Let's stay."

Larkin sat back with an unexpected smile that flashed briefly across his pale features. "Excellent! Maybe we should splurge and get Beaver Tails, *là*?" He carefully gathered up the cigarette butts and tucked them into the pocket of his denim shorts. He began describing the deep-fried delights known as Beaver Tails as they walked back, making Quinn's mouth water.

Two men going in the opposite direction looked at Larkin; one elbowed the other and started to laugh. They seemed drunk, one slurred something Quinn couldn't catch, but Larkin clearly did. He turned and stared both men down, his face hard and jaw set. The one who'd spoken turned back to face Larkin, spreading his arms wide as if he was going to embrace him.

"What?" he drunkenly demanded. "You got something to say?"

"No, but clearly you did, *monsieur*. Perhaps you'd care to say it to my face, *ostie*?" The tone clearly marked his words as an insult.

"Fine!" The man spat as he walked up close to Larkin. "You look like a freak."

Larkin said nothing but continued to glare at the man.

Getting no verbal reaction, the man continued, "What kind of faggot are you? You one of those He/She's? That's it, isn't it? You tranny! You fuckin'..."

He never got to finish the sentence. A blur of movement so fast, Quinn wondered how it had happened.

One second, Larkin was facing the man, and the next there was a thump and a crack, and the man was lying flat on his back, looking up at the sky.

"*Sacréficie*! You should be more careful, *monsieur*," Larkin said. "The footing isn't sure here; it's so easy to slip, *ostie*." With that, he turned on his heel and started to walk towards Quinn, leaving the man to gather himself up. The man got to his feet and immediately charged.

Quinn let out a yell of warning.

Larkin's face didn't change. He rounded on the man, and his leg slammed into the man's knee from the side. The stranger hit the ground hard, this time falling to the side, grabbing his leg, and howling in pain.

Larkin leaned down, his face close to the stranger's. "I would suggest that you stay down," he said as he turned and walked away. "Come, *cher*," he said to Quinn as he walked past, "let's go." The stranger's friend was pulling the man to his feet and helping him limp away towards the campground.

"Larkin," he gasped as they reached the truck, "why did you do that?"

"Hm?" He seemed unconcerned as he climbed into the driver's seat.

"I mean, he just called you a name; was it worth that violence?"

"Ah! Drunken idiots like that are dangerous. Better to knock some sense into them before they come after you again and make a total nuisance of themselves."

"How do you know you didn't really hurt him? I think he hit his head."

"I doubt it. Drunkards often fall or get hit and just walk it off. They're so drunk they're loose. They don't brace for the fall, so they just… bounce."

"You sound like you fight a lot," Quinn said as he climbed in beside Larkin.

"Looking the way I do, I have. The fights come to me." His tone was indifferent, as if this was something that happened daily.

"So, that happens a lot?"

"Not all the time, no, but often enough." He put the truck in reverse and began to back out of the parking spot. Just as he got back and shifted it into drive, Quinn put his hand on Larkin's arm. Larkin looked at him.

"I'm sorry," Quinn said. "I'm sorry that happened to you, and I'm sorry you lost your friend. And you can call me your dear friend, if you want to."

Larkin spoke in a quiet voice. "*Merci*, Quinn. I'm… touched." He cleared his throat. "*Eh bien*, we won't let it ruin our day, *tabarnak*. Let's get those Beaver Tails, eh?"

Chapter Fourteen

The Calgary Org wasn't much to look at; it was hard to be impressive on the second floor of a tiny strip mall. The Org had been renamed the "Hubbard Life Improvement Ministry of Calgary Inc." to bring in more people.

"I'll show you around." Quinn opened the mall's glass door, revealing the grey stairs that led to the second floor. He headed up with Larkin following. When Quinn saw Larkin looking unimpressed, he was quick to add, "We're only here until we have enough money to buy a building for an Ideal Org. Then we'll be in a much, much bigger, nicer place."

"*Vraiment*? That will be nice," Larkin said flatly.

The Org was divided into two sections, separated by the tiled stairs. A brightly lit reception desk and bookstore were on the left. The reception desk was made of light maple so that it would appear as welcoming as possible.

Quinn noticed Angela carefully watching Larkin from reception. To him, she always looked ill, and the fluorescent lights deepened the shadows of her face and did her no favours. The dark circles under her eyes were a testament to her struggles to remain on-line. The Org was small enough that most members had to take on double or triple duties, which kept most of them off-line, just as Quinn was.

Maybe I should do a KR on Angela, Quinn thought as he looked at the woman. *She's always sick, so she must be connected to an SP somehow. Perry's been after me to do one, so maybe I should do one on Angela.*

The store was probably Quinn's favourite part of the Org, with the light maple bookshelves and neatly arranged rows of all of L. Ron Hubbard's books, essays, and audio tapes of lectures, all lined up in orderly rows.

Large windows ran from halfway up the wall to the ceiling along the left side of the room. Light blue-grey paint showed between the bookshelves. The store was carpeted in rich navy blue with a tone-on-tone herringbone pattern. It was neat, clean, and orderly, with the different coloured spines of the books giving the room a cheerful air.

Larkin looked right, to the door nearest him. A gold-toned sign with the words "Staff Only" embossed in black was stuck to the glass door, and the world beyond looked very different from the brightly lit store. A dark maroon carpet ran down the straight hallway, past doorframes of dark, almost black oak on the left and the same large windows on the right. Small pot lights set in the suspended tiled ceiling couldn't chase away the gloom entirely, leaving shadows in the corners like piles of dust.

Only the first office door was open. A massive mahogany desk filled the room, the front covered in ornate carved scrolls. Quinn didn't know the number of times he'd polished that desk, using cotton-tipped swabs to get into every single crevice.

A banker-style brass lamp with a dark green glass shade sat on the desk, beside a dark green desk blotter. Next to the blotter, six fine black-bodied fountain pens with silver clips were lined up, while an office-style black phone sat on the right. One wall was covered in bookshelves, the books all neatly bound in navy faux leather with embossed gold lettering. Every book written by L. Ron Hubbard was there, ready for use. A prominent black-and-white portrait of LRH hung on the wall opposite the door.

Larkin stood for some time, looking into the open office, betraying nothing; he might as well have been a mannequin.

"That office," a voice called from behind them, causing Quinn to jump, "is for the Commodore, our founder, L. Ron Hubbard."

Quinn looked back and saw an older man halfway up the stairs. He was largely bald, with a ring of white hair that ran behind his head to each ear. Aviator-style silver-framed bifocals sat perched on a downward-turned fleshy nose, in front of bulging grey-blue eyes. He was wearing a beige sweater with thin horizontal black stripes over a white dress shirt. A black tie at the collar only accented his thin, ropey neck. Baggy black dress pants and dress shoes completed the look. "We keep it for him as a token of our respect," he concluded as a tight smile appeared on his thin, colourless lips.

"And for his inevitable reincarnation and return to the fold," Larkin replied in a matter-of-fact tone. He'd barely glanced at the man before turning back to the office.

The older man's eyebrows went up in surprise as he came up the last few steps to the landing. "Indeed," he said. His eyes darted from expressionless Larkin, who appeared to be ignoring him, to Quinn, whose hanging head betrayed his desire to sink into the tiled floor.

"Quinn, welcome back." His face broke into a big, welcoming smile. "We've really felt your absence, and I'm so pleased that you've come back. Everyone will be thrilled to hear that you're home. We've missed you deeply. Please introduce me to your friend." His voice had a clipped, proper tone despite its cheerful cadence. He folded his hands behind his back like an army sergeant.

"W-W-Warren, s-s-s-sir," stammered Quinn nervously, "this is L-Larkin Childs. L-L-Larkin, meet W-Warren Tresaster."

Larkin didn't extend his hand, didn't even glance at Warren. "Pleasure," he said curtly.

"Warren... is the... executive director here." Quinn didn't know what else to say.

"Ah. You're the one in charge, *là*."

"The board of directors is in charge." Warren smiled and spread his arms as if giving the pair a blessing from on high. "I'm merely the captain of the ship, guiding it along."

"Ah."

"I take it you are... familiar with the tenets of our Church, Mr. Childs?" Warren asked again as he clasped his hands behind his back.

"I am." Larkin's voice betrayed nothing.

His eyes were dark, and he still wasn't looking at Warren, a fact that turned Quinn's insides to ice. No one ignored Warren. No one.

"Yes," said Warren with a smirk, "I seem to remember that you were friends with an apostate of ours, Elijah Ryan. He must have told you a great number of... exaggerated stories about our faith, I'm sure."

"Elijah is... was... my friend, *oui*, but he didn't have to tell me about Scientology. I was already familiar with it."

For a brief second, shock and annoyance flashed across Warren's face. His eyes narrowed, and his hard mouth turned down sharply at the corners, only for him to regain his composure and reclaim his toothy smile. The changes happened so quickly that Quinn doubted whether he'd seen them at all. Larkin, however, continued to ignore the man.

"Really? You've had occasion to take a couple of courses, perhaps?"

Larkin didn't respond; he kept looking at the open office. "Beautiful desk," he finally said, his back still towards Warren. "Mahogany. Looks roughly nineteenth century, with Chippendale Rococo-style carvings. The *rocaille* scroll work on the front is very typical of the period. No way to tell for certain if it's an authentic Victorian piece or high-quality reproduction without examining it more closely, *n'est-ce pas*, Quinn?"

Warren answered, "Very good. It's an authentic piece, I can assure you. I arranged the purchase myself."

"A great many things in this life are passed off as things they are not. Many things... such as pieces like that, are made to look authentic, but are not," Larkin replied without looking around.

"Very true, very true. We have a term for it in Scientology, it's 'apparency'. It takes a keen eye and an even keener mind to know the difference."

"*C'est vrai*, but even with the best of intentions, we can be deceived. Especially if we want to believe something is real when it isn't."

"Only if one isn't careful."

Larkin finally turned around and fastened Warren in his gaze. "As they say, 'the road to hell is paved with good intentions'. That is the English phrase, *n'est pas*?"

Warren smiled more, a toothy, crocodile grin. "They do say that, don't they? Please, Mr. Childs, allow me to show you around."

"Quinn has kindly offered to give me the grand tour, *merci, Monsieur*."

"Well, perhaps you'll allow me to join you?" His left hand appeared from behind his waist as he motioned for them to go into the store.

Larkin didn't move, but Quinn quickly stepped over and opened the door.

"Oh, that's just offices and a file room," Warren explained as Larkin still didn't move, indicating the dark red hallway. "Nothing of any great interest, I assure you. The bookstore and classrooms are much more interesting." He gestured again for Larkin to go into the store, but the albino didn't twitch. For a moment, Warren and Larkin stared at each other, blank expression facing exaggerated grin.

It couldn't have been more than a few seconds, but it seemed a ridiculous amount of time to Quinn before the albino finally walked in without a backward glance, Warren following right behind.

Quinn trailed after them and closed the door, frowning; he couldn't shake the feeling that he was somehow missing something important between the two men.

"Where did you learn about Scientology, Mr. Childs?" Warren asked as he walked past Angela, whom he ignored.

Quinn's eyes met Angela's. He gave her an almost imperceptible shrug.

"I've met other people involved with Scientology. They saw fit to explain it to me," came Larkin's reply.

"Really? That was good of them. Which Org were they involved with?" Warren was full of questions.

"The specific name escapes me, *malheureusement*." Larkin glanced around at the displays.

"Oh, that is a shame. Perhaps you remember the city? We encourage our members to spread our philosophy, so I'd be happy to send a note of thanks to whomever shared the good word with you."

"That won't be necessary, *merci*." Larkin stopped at a table that displayed a dozen or so copies of *Dianetics* that were neatly stacked, but for one that had been set on a clear plastic display stand. He looked down at the books with a blank face.

"Here," said Warren as he moved closer to the albino.

Quinn saw Larkin pull away from Warren, although his feet didn't move.

Warren picked the book from the stand and went to hand it to Larkin. "Please, Mr. Childs, take it on the house, so to speak. I'm sure you'll find it most enlightening and informative."

Larkin didn't move to take it; his eyes seemed to have found something more interesting on one of the other shelves. "As it happens, I've read it already, *Monsieur*." His feet remained firmly planted.

"Really?" Warren couldn't keep the surprise out of his voice as he set the book back down, careful to make sure it was perfectly aligned and the entire stack was straight. "I'm delighted to hear that. And, please, call me Warren. May I ask, what did you take away from your reading?"

Larkin didn't look back at the older man. "It was some time ago, but it seems to have not made much of an impression, I'm sorry to say."

He doesn't really sound all that sorry, Quinn thought.

"Some great works are like that. They don't make as much of an impression when we are younger, but we find them so much more informative and inspiring when we reread them as an adult, wouldn't you agree, Mr. Childs?"

"*Oui,* I would, I would indeed." Larkin turned his back on Warren again and wandered deeper into the store. "However, some books are only worth reading once, as you've absorbed everything they offer in the first reading, so a second would only be redundant."

Quinn was still standing near the reception desk, feet riveted to the floor. His gaze bounced from one man to the other as if watching a tennis match, feeling caught between pride in his Church and a growing unease he couldn't name.

"Some books only seem simplistic," Warren went on, alligator grin glued to his face, "but, upon further examination, are far more complicated and interesting than a cursory reading would lead one to believe. Perhaps only a more advanced, more highly evolved mind is able to see past the simplistic façade to the true depth of the work."

"Which you have, *non*? A more evolved mind?"

"Which all Scientologists have, including our young Quinn here. It is, however, a skill that can be learned, Mr. Childs, by someone who is willing to absorb the lessons."

"I've found that lessons can be like smells." Larkin picked up a biography of L. Ron Hubbard and began absently flipping through it, apparently looking at the pictures. "Pleasant at first, but then they become increasingly overbearing once they get absorbed into the furniture. Quinn tells me that you've already gone Clear, *Monsieur*. Congratulations."

"Warren, please, Mr Childs, and thank you."

"A shame that the benefits of improved eyesight and hair regrowth have... eluded you, despite your achievement." Larkin finally met Warren's eyes again and smiled. "*C'est de valeur.*"

Quinn could see that Larkin's smile was fake. *Is he smirking?*

Like a shadow, a frown flashed across Warren's face, only to vanish a second later. "A temporary situation, I assure you."

"Ah!" Larkin was still smiling as he set the book down and turned away.

He is smirking!

"I'm a little surprised that you know about some of the benefits of going Clear, Mr. Childs."

"You are the first Clear that I've met in person. I must say that I find the results a bit... underwhelming." Continuing his tour of the office, he looked at the books on the shelves, picked the odd book up to look at the spine, and flipped through a few pages before setting it back on the shelf.

Quinn finally managed to pry his feet from the floor. He wanted to tell Larkin to be careful. As a Clear, Warren was considered one of the most intelligent and powerful people in the Org. Clears were able to read minds, which alone made him a thing to be feared, and Warren's word was law, despite his protests to the contrary. And yet...

Larkin seemed comfortable and was holding his own. He was nonchalant in his conversation, as if they were discussing the weather.

Warren exhaled a scoffing sound. "Are you suggesting I should demonstrate my abilities like a circus sideshow? Isn't that what the

Devil asked of Jesus, to prove himself? As I recall, the response was something along the lines of, 'I have no need.'"

Even then, Larkin didn't glance back at the older man. "Comparing oneself to Jesus is a cardinal sin."

"Only to Catholics. To Scientologists, there is no such prohibition."

"So it would appear. *Mais*, it seems you have misread your audience, *Monsieur*."

"Are you a Catholic, Mr. Childs? Unless I am mistaken, a Catholic who doesn't regularly practise is referred to as a 'lapsed Catholic', a person deeply despised by the Church."

"An extreme position that is no longer adhered to, *Monsieur*. *La Révolution Tranquille* saw to that; more than one extreme position was addressed and corrected."

"Catholics were once referred to as 'Papeists', weren't they? We don't feel the need to pay homage to a myth created by people to shield themselves from the truth."

"*Non*? Better to pay homage to a fallible person, then?"

"All people are fallible, Mr. Childs. Isn't the Pope fallible? Truly great men are able to rise above their weaknesses and create something incredible that lasts well beyond one lifetime. It takes a person of advanced intellect to recognize their failures, thoroughly address them, and then rise above them. Only then can a man create a legacy that lasts beyond one mere lifetime."

"As the Bard said, 'Some men are born great, some achieve greatness, while others have greatness thrust upon them', *n'est pas*?" Having walked around the majority of the bookstore, Larkin walked back towards Warren and stood just a few metres in front of him as he spoke. His hands tucked into his pockets, looking entirely relaxed and unconcerned. He met Warren's gaze and held it, examining the man like he was a mildly interesting microbe on a slide.

"An interesting statement, Mr. Childs."

"Indeed, Shakespeare is full of 'interesting statements', in particular on the nature and effect of tyrants."

"What are you insinuating?" Snapping back, Warren frowned dangerously. Witnessing the hostility on Warren's face, Quinn's hands became clammy. He knew that frown; he'd seen it. He knew Larkin was on thin ice, that Warren was livid and would explode any second.

Larkin, for his part, simply smiled another fake smile and held up both his hands in supplication.

"Ah! I insinuate nothing! Forgive me, I'm *Québécois*, so sometimes my English isn't as...subtle or as clear as I might like. I was simply discussing Shakespeare. I assume you've read the works of the Bard? An intelligent man such as yourself?"

"Sadly, my ongoing work for the greater good, for the benefit of the entire planet, prevents me from engaging in such...trivial, off-purpose pursuits." Warren was still frowning, but the tension had eased slightly.

"Ah! That is a shame, for it is often in such trivial pursuits we learn the most about both ourselves and humanity."

Warren's smile got bigger, something Quinn didn't think possible. Warren was straining to smile, the effort causing him to grit his teeth. "Nevertheless, such pastimes must be set aside in favour of far more important work. Speaking of which, I must get back to my own. Quinn." He was still smiling as he turned his gaze to the sweating man. "Please come to my office after you've finished showing Mr. Childs around, won't you? I'm sure you remember that I told you before you left that I'd like to discuss your trip with you upon your return."

Quinn replied without hesitation: "Y-y-yes, s-sir." *I told you that I'd like to discuss your trip... I don't remember that. When the hell did he say that?*

Warren nodded to both of them, but his eyes seemed glued to Larkin. "If you'll both excuse me."

Larkin inclined his head as Warren turned and walked away, hands swinging purposefully by his side. Angela was again completely ignored.

'Discuss your trip'... I'm dead. That's it, I'm dead. I'm in so much shit. Quinn sighed.

Larkin, however, had caught the sigh. "*Ça va bien,* Quinn?"

"Huh? Yeah, I'm fine. I'm just thinking about the 'talk' Warren and I are going to have."

Larkin looked concerned, his eyes dark as he moved to his side. "Quinn..."

"No, it's ok," Quinn said as he held up his hand. "I knew I was going to get in trouble; it's not like it's the first time." He tried to laugh it off, but Larkin's visible eye still looked displeased. "I've been through Sec Checks... Security Checks, before."

"Nevertheless," Larkin leaned closer to Quinn and whispered: "If you'd rather delay it by extending your vacation, say the word."

He was close enough that Quinn could feel the exhalation of breath on his ear, a feeling which distracted him and tickled, causing him to break out in goosebumps.

"No, it's fine, Lark, really. Let me show you the classrooms."

He led Larkin through the double glass doors on the far-left side of the store. There were two classrooms, each with a long, conference-style table with chairs arranged on each side. Copies of L. Ron's work lined the shelves along with binders full of transcripts of lectures. Dictionaries sat in the middle of the tables, ready for word clearing. Another large photo of Hubbard graced the far wall opposite the door, of him sitting at a desk wearing a dark suit, white shirt, and tie. The classrooms were empty; there appeared to be no one about the Org at all.

"This doesn't look like classrooms as I remember them." Larkin looked inside.

"No, it wouldn't. They're mostly for individual study instead of someone leading a group."

"*Hein*? What's the point, then? You could just as easily study at home."

"Too many distractions somewhere else. It's much easier to study in a place for it, and there's always someone to answer questions and to help you as well, which you wouldn't get at home. Besides, when you get to the higher levels, the OT levels, there's a huge risk. What if you accidentally leave a book open somewhere? If someone reads that material and they haven't been prepared for it, it can be dangerous."

"Dangerous? How?"

"It can make people very sick, or even kill them."

Larkin raised an eyebrow, his eyes hopping back and forth, searching Quinn's face. "Has that ever happened?"

"Well, it's never happened here, but I guess it has. I mean, how else would they know?"

Further down, near the far end of the hallway, was the small auditing room. It contained a plain, simple wooden office desk and chair, with a blue upholstered straight-backed chair in front of it.

Another photo of Hubbard adorned the wall; it was a close-up, portrait-style photograph where Hubbard was looking directly at the camera. The deep lines from his nose to his mouth were softened by his wry amusement.

The most prominent feature of the room was the large, blue-grey piece of equipment on the desk, the famous E-metre. The back of the machine was facing the glass window in the door, but had it been turned the other way, they would have seen the white face with its dreaded black needle, along with three buttons, a dial, and three small, rectangular digital displays. There were two video cameras in the room, one in each corner, with their lenses pointed at the desk.

"This is the auditing room," Quinn explained. "It's so small because it's totally soundproofed, even the door. That's an e metre on the desk, it measures and weighs your thoughts and reads your emotional responses to questions. Patricia's the auditor, so she sits in the big office chair, facing the needle so she can watch it and monitor it."

"Auditing sessions are filmed?" Larkin asked, indicating the two video cameras with an uplifting of his chin. "I didn't know that."

"Oh, yeah, they're all filmed. It's just for record-keeping. One camera films you when you're being audited, the other one films the e-metre and the needle. I guess when you get to the upper levels, you could look back at them and see how far you've come. See yourself talking about all the things that used to be a problem and aren't any more. That would be pretty cool."

"Indeed."

He led Larkin down to the very end of the hall, which led into the meeting room. Painted a light beige with a light grey carpet, it featured a raised stage area whose wooden sides, along with a podium, were all stained cherry wood colour. There were a couple of long meeting tables, with brown folding assembly chairs arranged along one side, all facing the stage.

Mounted on the wall, just to the left of the stage, was another black and white framed photo of a more casual, older Hubbard whose long, scraggly grey hair hung about his ears and stuck out at odd Einstein-like angles from his head.

"This is the meeting room," Quinn spelled out. "Whenever Warren has to talk to all of us, or if we have a group class or informal fundraiser, we use this room."

"Do you have fundraisers often?"

"Yeah, but normally we try to put on bigger shows and raffles and things for the public members to try and get them to donate. We use this room if we're planning a show or something as well. That's pretty much it, Lark. What do you think?" Quinn turned and began to walk slowly back towards the store.

"I must admit, it doesn't look like I thought it would," said Larkin as he fell into step beside Quinn. "It's very...clean. Organised. It almost looks like you could eat off the floor."

"Oh, it all has to be spotless. Clean as a whip and ship-shape!" Quinn smiled, almost laughing.

Larkin smiled back, the briefest flash of a smile that showed his white teeth.

Quinn felt his heart lift at that, felt the room brightening from it. "Like I said, it's only until we have enough money for an Ideal Org. Apparently, the COB is anxious to have more Ideal Orgs in Canada. Sorry, COB stands for...."

"Chairman of the Board, *Monsieur* Miscavige, your leader."

Quinn was startled. "You really do know more about the Church than you let on, eh?"

"Hmm. I know many things, my job requires it, but I don't always have the opportunity to use all that I know."

"You should come and take a course, Larkin. The communication course might be really useful. You said your English isn't what you'd like; I'm sure it would help. To be honest, though, I've never had an issue with your English."

Larkin smiled again. No teeth this time. He exhaled in amusement. "*Merci*, Quinn, *mon ami*. I fear my English is as good as it will ever be."

"You don't know that; there's always room for improvement."

"True. But a lesson once well learned is difficult to unlearn."

"What do you mean?"

"Never mind." Larkin shook his head. "*Ce n'est pas grave.*"

"What does that mean, *'ce nest'*...?"

"*Ce n'est pas grave*, means 'it doesn't matter'. Perhaps I should teach you French, Quinn. What do you think?"

Quinn let out a bark of laughter despite himself. "That'll be the day! I don't think I have a head for languages! I have enough trouble with English!"

"The way they used to teach languages, I'm not surprised. *Mais*, lessons with me would be different."

"How?"

"Well, the first thing I'd teach you is how to swear like a proper *Québécois*! There's an art to it, *tsé*."

"There's an art to swearing?" Quinn chuckled and beamed at Larkin.

"But of course! We *Québécois* don't do things by halves, *là*! I read somewhere that you can tell what a particular people and culture are most afraid of by how they swear."

"Really?"

"*Oui*, for us *Québécois*, it's religion and God. So, all our swear words are religious terms. We're most afraid of *le bon Dieu* and his angelic warriors."

"What about English?"

"Largely bodily functions, which means you Anglophones are scared of yourselves, a concept which I've never understood."

Quinn began to laugh as they walked down the hallway and through the store. Angela had left the reception empty. He opened the door for Larkin, and the two of them walked out into the stairwell. Quinn hesitated, suddenly not wanting Larkin to leave.

"Will you walk me to the truck, Quinn?" he asked, perhaps sensing the other's reluctance.

"Sure."

Larkin led the way. His long limbs easily took him down the stairs.

Quinn trudged behind, feeling clumsy by comparison. The toes of his running shoes were scuffing the steps. He almost tripped over his own feet, only catching himself by the handrail.

Larkin looked up as the sound of Quinn's stumble echoed in the stairwell.

"Are you all right?" he called up.

"Oh, I'm fine. Just clumsy."

Once he reached the bottom, Larkin stood waiting for Quinn. He even held the door open.

Quinn mumbled, "Thanks," as he went through it. He walked to Larkin's beat-up pick-up; the white vehicle somehow looked even more rusted and worn sitting in front of the Org than it normally did.

"I guess this is it," he said without looking at Larkin, gazing downward towards his feet. "I...don't know when I'll be able to see you again, Lark, so I wanted to thank you. Thank you for letting me come to Elijah's memorial, thank you for letting me stay with you, and for the trip to Banff."

"I take it you enjoyed the trip then?"

Quinn looked up to find that Larkin was standing close to him, his thumbs hooked into the belt loops on his denim shorts.

"Oh, yeah, absolutely! I really did! I can't believe I got to feed a wild deer! It was great! I really liked...hanging out with you."

"As did I."

Quinn looked up to meet Larkin's whisky eyes. He found the other meeting his gaze, but his eyes were hopping back and forth like yellow canaries.

"Quinn, I meant what I said, that I consider you a friend. And I'd very much like to see you again. I enjoy your company a great deal."

"I...like hanging out with you, too. I just... I'm in trouble for taking off, so I just don't know when I'll be able to see you again. You're...well, you're the only person I know outside the Church."

"*Vraiment*? I'm honoured."

Quinn looked at Larkin for any trace of sarcasm or condescension. He saw none, just those amber eyes darting back and forth.

"No, really," Larkin continued, as if reading Quinn's mind. "I know it can be difficult to make friends outside of church, so I appreciate that I am your friend." Quinn opened his mouth to reply, but Larkin continued, "Quinn, I want you to know that if there is ever a time when you need that friendship, when you need somewhere to go, you can come to me."

"What are you saying?" Quinn frowned. He felt something shift inside him, something angry.

"Just that. That I'm your friend, and if you want to come and talk, or have dinner, or if you need a bed for a night, my door is open."

"Why would I need a bed? I live in the dorms."

"I know, but that building burned down once, *n'est pas*? What if it catches fire again? Or you get locked out by accident? You'll need somewhere to stay."

"Or if I want to leave the Church? That's what you're really saying, isn't it?"

"*Non*, I'm not."

"Yes, you are! God, I should've known!" Quinn felt himself snap to anger, the switch flipped completely. He started to pace, throwing his hands in the air in frustration. "This is why none of us have wogs as friends, it always comes back to that! 'Leave the Church!'" He felt his anger rise, felt it catch in his throat like he was going to vomit.

"Quinn..."

"No! I'm not listening! Even if Elijah left, that doesn't mean that I will!" He tried to look past Larkin, to stare through him the way all good Scientologists were taught to look through someone who was an SP. But Larkin's whisky eyes kept catching and holding him. Quinn found himself unable to look past the albino, unable to keep from meeting his eyes.

"And if you choose to stay, that doesn't mean we're not friends. I would've been Elijah's friend whether he was still a Scientologist or not."

"That's easy to say now! You already got him to leave, so I'm next, is that it?"

"You know that's not true, *mon ami*. Elijah had already left when I met him."

"But you made it easy for him to stay out, didn't you?"

"I don't know that I'd call it 'easy'. He had many sleepless nights about it, shed many tears. But if you're asking if I would throw my friend out just to force him to go somewhere he didn't want to be, then you're right, I made it easy by letting him stay somewhere safe and warm, by not kicking him out into the street."

Quinn had stopped pacing and was looking at Larkin, watching him, trying to read him, but his face showed nothing. His body language seemed just as blank. His posture was relaxed, leaning back against the front passenger fender, his ankles crossed, the bright floral tattoos that ran down his limbs gleaming. There was no hint of deception or vitriol, only his eyes moving, following Quinn.

"Elijah...cried...about leaving?" he asked at last.

"But of course. He'd been in the church for a long time. It wasn't a simple thing for him to walk away from."

"And...me? Was it easy for him to walk away from me?" Quinn looked away, down. He couldn't believe he'd asked that; he was ashamed to have asked such a question. But now that he had, he was frightened to hear the answer.

"He shed more tears over you than anything, I think."

Quinn met Larkin's eyes again. "Really?"

"*Oui*. He didn't like to speak of it too much, I think he worried that I'd think him a complainer, but I know he loved you, no matter your differences in views."

Quinn suddenly felt sad and looked away again. *He loved me. He really... did he really?*

"Quinn, two people can disagree on certain subjects and still be friends, remember that. You and I are friends, no matter what. Friends watch out for each other; they help each other in times of crisis, no matter the cause. That's what I want you to remember, *mon ami*, if you remember nothing else. Friends help and support each other. That's just what they do, that's friendship."

Larkin stood, staring at Quinn as if he were considering something. His eyes moved as if looking for something in his face.

Quinn started to open his mouth to speak when Larkin reached out and put his hand on the younger man's right shoulder. He abruptly pulled Quinn towards him, firmly enough that Quinn didn't think of resisting. He found himself in Larkin's arms, in a fiercely tight hug as Larkin's arm wrapped around his shoulders. He stiffened as he felt Larkin slapping his back affectionately with his hand, only to then be let go and find himself at arm's length. Larkin was holding him by the biceps with a slight smile on his face.

Quinn was straight as a board. *What is happening? Why does this feel... good?*

"Come anytime for a visit, *mon cher ami*. I'd love to get together for lunch or dinner. I'll even cook. My door will always be open to you." With that, Larkin went around the front of the truck to hop into the driver's seat.

Quinn stood there, watching the pickup vanish into the afternoon traffic. He felt strangely empty now that Larkin was gone. For a moment, he imagined himself running after the truck, calling to Larkin to come back. *Yeah, run down the middle of MacLeod, that's a great idea. I'll get run over before I get a block.*

Elijah cried. He cried about leaving the Church. Does that mean he regretted it? He could have come back. He'd have been in major shit, but he could've come back. Elijah cried. He cried about leaving....me. He never saw me much anyway, so why? Why would he cry about me? It's not like the Church doesn't take care of me. So why? I don't understand.

Quinn turned to look up at the second floor. There, standing in the window of the stairwell, was Warren, watching, his hands folded behind his back.

Quinn cast one last look in Larkin's direction before turning to walk back through the door of the Org and trudging up the stairs towards Warren.

Chapter Fifteen

"Again, tell me again."

"He said, 'I won't push, encourage or even force you one way or the other, whether to leave or to stay.'"

"What else?"

"That's all. We...never really talked about the Church."

"Your needle says differently."

"No, we really didn't. If anything..."

Quinn was convinced it was the shaking of his hands that was making the needle dance. He gritted his teeth and shifted his grip on the right can, trying to hold it as loosely as he could without making it obvious. He slid his left hand down, gripping that can nearer the bottom.

Stop it, he willed the uncooperative needle, *stop moving, damn it.*

"Yes?" the interviewer prodded.

"If anything, I think he avoided talking about the Church. The conversation he had with you was the most I've ever heard him say about it."

His palms were sweating and his breathing had gone shallow, all of which made the auditing session worse. He looked up to see Warren frowning down at the *e*-metre; Quinn could see the reflection of the moving needle in his glasses. He'd never been audited by Warren before.

"I'd like to change topics," Warren said without looking up. "Tell me about Larkin Childs."

"A-a-about L-L-Larkin?" Quinn swallowed hard. *Get a grip.*

"Yes. What did he tell you about himself?"

"Hum...well, he was born in Montreal."

"Good. What else?"

"Um…he left when he was...I don't remember."

"Yes, you do. I'll ask the question again. How old was he when he left Montreal?"

"Ummm... mmm... eighteen, I think."

"You think?"

"He was eighteen."

"What about his family?"

"He didn't really talk about them. His parents died when he was a kid."

"How old?"

"I'm sorry, I don't—"

"How old was Larkin when they died?" Warren's tone made it clear that *I don't know* or *I don't remember* were not acceptable. An answer was expected, demanded.

"I...um... twelve...he was twelve. I'm sure that's right. His aunt and uncle raised him after that."

"Names. Did he give you their names?"

"No."

"And he's, what, thirty now?"

"Yeah, I think so."

"What are his feelings in regards to the Church?"

"I don't know."

"He was friends with a known apostate, so surely he must have said something negative about the Church."

"Actually, he didn't."

"Your needle says differently."

"N-no, he didn't. Really."

"What negative things did he say about the COB?"

"Nothing. I didn't know he knew who the Chairman of the Board was."

"You're telling me he knows that? Who the COB is?"

"Yes."

"What negative things did he say about LRH?"

"Nothing. All I've heard him say about LRH is what he said to you tonight."

Warren looked up at Quinn over the top of the silver frames, fixing him with pale, watery blue eyes and a warning tone. "Quinn..."

"No, really. Nothing. He didn't say anything. I swear."

Warren sighed audibly. "Is there something that happened that made a particular impression on you? Patricia will go over everything when she sees you, but I want to know why your needle is reacting like this."

Because you scare the living shit out of me? "Mm, I don't think—"

"Quinn." The cold snap of his voice made Quinn shake even more. *What can I tell him? I have to tell him something. Anything. Think, damn it.*

Wait, I know... "Well..."

"What?"

"There was this lady, she asked Larkin to come out and appraise a dresser she had."

"Yes?" Warren stopped watching the needle and looked at Quinn over his glasses.

"Well, it wasn't worth what she thought it was. I can't remember, Victorian? No, that's not it, it was... Georgian... I think that was it. It was supposed to be Georgian, but Larkin said it was a reproduction."

"So, not worth what he was anticipating?"

"No, not even close. This lady...she burst into tears. She said she'd sent her husband to jail because he'd been abusive, and she needed the money to pay the mortgage or she would lose her house. She told Larkin she'd sold everything she could, but nothing was worth much, so she didn't have enough."

"And? Go on."

"Well, Larkin gave her the money. He'd taken money out of this big safe he's got and he just...gave it to her." Quinn paused, remembering the look of joy on the woman's face, the way she'd hugged Larkin while weeping. "He told her to use it to save her house and told her to do something nice for her children."

I know what it's like to be a child and live with an abuser. Quinn was sure that's what Larkin had whispered to the woman, but he didn't want to tell Warren that. *What the hell's wrong with me? I should tell him everything; why can't I?*

Quinn didn't understand his own reluctance. Everything he'd been taught said he should tell Warren without question, without hesitation. But he couldn't. He hung his head slightly in shame, aware of the tight knot in his stomach.

"How much money did Larkin end up giving her?" Warren asked, snapping Quinn back to the present.

"I don't know exactly, it had to be enough to cover her mortgage payment. It looked like a lot. And she was so happy! It showed me how much good there's still left to do in the world, how one thing can help a whole family, and how much it meant to them."

"Mmm," was the only sound Warren made. For a long moment, he just sat there, not really looking at the needle, staring at nothing.

"I assume that your friend paid for this little...excursion?" he asked at last, without looking at Quinn.

"Yes."

"And you said he has a large safe?"

"Yes."

"Where?"

"In the basement of the shop."

"Have you seen what's in this safe?"

"No."

Now Warren looked straight at him, meeting his gaze without blinking. "Then how do you know that he took money from the safe?"

"Sandra mentioned it."

"Sandra?"

"She works in the shop for Larkin."

"I see."

Looking away, Warren opened a drawer. Quinn's heart sank. He knew what that drawer contained, the only thing it contained.

Warren pulled out what looked like a notepad, approximately 5.5 x 8.5", and set it down to the right of the e-metre.

Even upside down, Quinn could see the bright red crest and the big *Golden Age of Tech* title in fancy red lettering. Below that, in large, simple black letters, were the words *Ethics Chit*. A block of italic text sat beneath. Quinn sighed as Warren began writing. *Well, you knew you were going to get one of those, didn't you?*

Warren wrote for a moment, then tore off the top page and handed it across without looking up. Quinn set down the can in his right hand, took the paper, and stuffed it into the front pocket of his jeans.

"Quinn, you know this is for your own good, right?"

Quinn looked up, barely able to see Warren's eyes for the reflection of the dials, but he could tell they were looking over the top of the bifocals at him, pinning him to the chair.

"I know being audited by me is...unusual, but I felt I had to have this *comm* with you. Quinn, I do understand, believe it or not."

Quinn swallowed hard but said nothing.

"I was very close to my mother," Warren went on. "It was a devastating blow after she left the Sea Org. Right after she finished OT VIII, she blew. No one saw it coming. She'd been one of the most devoted members, working with LRH himself, at his right elbow, and she threw it all away."

Quinn hesitated before whispering, "She did?" He was shocked; he didn't think he could breathe.

"I was horrified," Warren continued, eyes still fixed on him. "To have worked for the Church for so long and then just...throw away everything she'd ever believed in, like it was so much trash. To spit in LRH's face like that, I couldn't understand." He closed his eyes briefly before locking Quinn in his sights again. "Obviously, I had to disconnect from her. She became our enemy overnight, but I wasn't sure I could do it. I admired her so much. She always seemed to work harder than anyone else and devoted herself more than anyone. From my first days in the Church, I thought of her as the pinnacle of virtue, the most devout officer. I wanted to speak to her, to demand to know how she could do that to LRH. That wasn't an option, obviously..."

"Obviously," echoed Quinn.

"I walked around in a daze. I didn't think I'd get through it. I was rollercoastering badly, but I was able to get past it with the help of my family. My real family, that is. That's what the Church is, Quinn, we're a family. My fellow Sea Org members kept telling me to let her go, to get over it. My superiors wouldn't let me dwell on it; they kept me in line, kept me busy, kept me focused on what was really important, so that I was able to keep the whole thing from becoming an engram. By the time I heard about her dying, it didn't faze me at all."

Quinn didn't know what to say. He just sat there, looking at the older man's almost neutral face.

"We've let you down, Quinn. I personally let you down. I'm sorry."

The words jolted Quinn out of his silence. "What? No, no, you didn't, Sir!"

Warren placed his palms on the desk and pushed his chair back. He rose slowly and walked around the desk to sit on its corner, one leg dangling. He looked down at Quinn with a smile that managed to look kind and sad at the same time.

"Oh, yes, we did. I did. I'd forgotten how much the support of my real family meant to me when my biological family betrayed me. I forgot how much I leaned on them. You're younger than I was and...I suppose I thought you were stronger, more resilient than I was. We should have been there for you, so that you wouldn't have to turn to a...wog."

"Sir...."

"No, it should have been us that you turned to. I should have been there for you, and I wasn't. That was terribly out-ethics on my part, for which I hope you will forgive me. I'm sure your friend means well. I'm happy he was able to help you when we didn't, that he picked up that slack for us. But, Quinn, my dear boy, no one really understands what we're doing here. Please remember that. No never-in will be able to understand what it means to work for the greater good like we do. Wogs will drag you down, even if they don't mean to. Your Larkin may be a good friend, but he'll never understand you or be able to help you as well as we can. Please don't forget that. It won't take long for the enemies of our Church to get hold of him, just like they do everyone else, and use him to try and turn you against all of us. It would be an unbearable loss to the Org if you were to leave. There's simply no one who can replace you, you know. I know Brittany and the others would be just devastated. For your own sake, keep in mind who your real family is. You are much too trusting. You always have been, and I don't want you to be hurt when the psychotherapists and Big Pharma inevitably turn him against you. All right?"

Quinn stared up into eyes he'd never seen look so kind, at an expression he didn't recognise on Warren's face. *My real family...* "I'll remember, Sir. Thank you."

"Good." He started to slide off the desk, then paused as Quinn spoke again.

"Sir?"

"Yes?"

"Thanks...for telling me all of that. I...had no idea."

There was a flash of teeth as he smiled. "You're welcome. I'm sure I don't need to remind you that this was a private conversation. I'd rather news of my own personal failings not be spread around the entire Org."

"Of course! I won't tell anyone, I promise."

"Excellent. I knew I could count on you, Quinn." He got up and walked back around the desk, pulling his chair in and casting his eyes back down to the e-metre. "Tom!" Warren called out without looking up.

Quinn flinched involuntarily. He heard the door open behind him.

"Yes, Sir?" Tom's deep, booming voice rang off the walls.

"Please escort Quinn to the hole...gently."

"Gently?" Tom sounded surprised.

"That's what I said," Warren snapped, looking up and frowning at Tom. "Do I need to repeat my orders?"

"No, Sir," Tom answered quickly.

Warren, apparently satisfied, smiled slightly before looking at Quinn. "Quinn, you will hand that chit to Patricia when you see her, as she will be discussing your...absence with you further. In the meantime, you are to remain in the hole and think about what you've done and everything we have discussed. Understood? And Tom, when you come back, you can join everyone else at the farm."

"Ye-es, Sir," Quinn stammered.

"Yes, Sir," said Tom briskly.

"Good. Both of you may go."

Quinn pushed the chair back, got to his feet, and left without a word or a backward glance. *Gently.* Quinn had never heard Warren say that before, but it apparently meant Tom was simply to walk him back to the dorms without laying a hand on him. Tom never spoke, and Quinn didn't dare break the silence. He did, however, steal a quick glance at Tom and found the older man looking furious beneath his massively bushy eyebrows, his mouth carved into a deep frown.

Chapter Sixteen

The Hole.

Every Org has one or access to one, so Warren said. The place of punishment for any parishioner who went against the tenets of the Church or the will of the director.

The concept had started with David Miscavige, the Chairman of the Board. The Hole had been used to punish senior management members of the Sea Org who had gone against Miscavige and the Church.

Warren had boasted about how genius the concept was, and once he had assumed the leadership of the Calgary Org, creating a Hole became a top priority.

The Hole for the Calgary Org was located in the dorms. While the rest of the dorms had been rebuilt from the fire that had destroyed the former strip mall, the Hole had been more or less left alone. It was a stifling, tiny, windowless room that might have been a closet or storage room at some point. It was barely big enough for a twin mattress, a sink, and a bucket for a toilet.

The mattress sat directly on the tiled floor and had a flat pillow and a ratty, itchy wool blanket that was a dingy blue-grey from too much use without being washed.

Soot still blackened the once grey-green walls from the fire; it smelled like urine, ash, and despair. A single light bulb hung from a bare wire from the ceiling, but there was no switch in the room for it to be turned off. The switch was outside the door, so the light was under the guard's control. Almost every member of the Org had been in the Hole at least once, with the exceptions of Warren and the members of the Board of Directors.

It wasn't Quinn's first time in the Hole. Once he heard the door lock behind him, he sat down on the lumpy mattress, propped his back against the wall, and looked down at the paper he'd been given. On each side of the "Golden Age of Tech" crest were blanks that had been filled in:

To: <u>Ethics Calgary Org</u>   Date:

Via: <u>Sharon H.</u>   CC<u>: Patricia M.</u>

From: <u>Warren T.</u>

He hadn't bothered to fill in the date, which was more than a little unusual since it was against procedures. Quinn didn't bother to read the italicised text beneath the words **"ETHICS CHIT"**; he'd read it so many times he could recite the quote from the Commodore himself by heart:

"It means that they must chit students who bring a body and ask for unusual solutions; they must chit all discourteous conduct; they must chit all roller-coaster cases; they must chit all suppressive action observed; they must chit snide comments; they must chit alter-is and entheta; they must chit derogatory remarks; they must chit all dev-t. Anything in violation of ethics or dev-t PLs must be reported." - L. Ron Hubbard.

Ref: HCO PL ETHICS CHITS 1 July 1965, Issue I

Beneath all of that was another fill-in-the-blank:

Qn: <u>Quinn Ryan</u>

Finally, beneath that were Warren's tersely written notes:

Last week's schedule:

Sun 6 am - 1 am   On time

Monday   No show

Tuesday   No show

Wednesday   No show

Thursday   No show

Attended an event with a known PTS after requested permission was denied.

Direct violation of orders; punishment to be determined.

W/O CSW should be considered blown (4 No Shows); time needs to be made up.

Warren's signature, a knot of right-leaning slanted lines that looked like a squiggle, appeared beneath the notes.

Quinn did a double-take at the words "punishment to be determined". *I've never seen that before. 'To be determined?' What the hell does that mean?*

Quinn kept staring at the Ethics Chit, kept reading and rereading "punishment to be determined". The unknown terrified him and was very much out of his realm of experience.

He felt a sinking feeling in the pit of his stomach. Biting the fingernail on his right middle finger, he stared at the chit in his left hand. *I think I'm in real, real trouble.*

He sat there, bare lightbulb overhead, staring at the paper. He ran over Warren's auditing session in his mind, trying to decide why he hadn't wanted to talk about Larkin's life with his commanding officer. It somehow felt wrong, like Larkin had entrusted him with secrets that weren't Quinn's to reveal. And yet Warren had shared secrets with Quinn as well, hadn't he? He couldn't believe that a superior officer, a **Sea Org member**, would open up in such a way. It was unheard of, but Quinn saw it as an honour. He was now responsible for Warren's secret, just as he was for Larkin's, and he knew that his promise not to reveal those discretions to anyone wasn't an idle one.

We've let you down, Quinn. I personally let you down. I'm sorry. For your own sake, keep in mind who your real family, your real friends are.

My real family ...my real friends.

The Church is my family, too. I don't really have anyone else, just Joni. And my friends, I really don't know anyone outside the Church.

Wogs, they'll drag you down, even if they don't mean to. I don't want to be dragged down, I don't want to lose the progress I've made. I don't want to go back down the Bridge again!

Quinn, two people can disagree on certain subjects and still be friends, remember that. You and I are friends, no matter what.

I don't think Larkin would drag me down on purpose, but just hanging around with a Wog can make you sick. I don't want to get sick all the time from hanging around with Larkin. I don't want him to affect my progress.

Your Larkin may be a good friend, but he'll never understand you or be able to help you as well as we can. Please don't forget that.

No, he wouldn't really understand; he can't without any training.

Friends watch out for each other; they help each other in times of crisis, no matter the cause of that crisis. That's what I want you to remember, mon ami, if you remember nothing else. Friends help and support each other. That's just what they do, that's friendship.

It's nice to have a friend who's not in the Church, though. We talk about other stuff, nothing deep or anything, just ...stuff. Larkin makes me laugh, and he knows so much! So much that I had no idea about!

It would be an unbearable loss to the Org if you were to leave. There's just simply no one who can replace you, you know.

Even though I'm down stat all the time? Even though I mess up all the time?

I know Brittany and the others would be just devastated by your loss.

I'm not so sure about that, but I guess Warren would know better, wouldn't he?

He kept staring at the chit in his hands, the words seemed to have a weight that they hadn't before, as if they were imbued with more meaning than before.

My real family.... Maybe they really do care after all? I mean, if Warren says they don't want to lose me, that must be the truth. He wouldn't lie to me, after all! Sea Org members don't lie! Not to other Scientologists, anyway! To Wogs or SP's, sure, but not to us!

There was a click as the light outside was suddenly turned off. He shifted over, pulled the flat pillow close to him, and lay down on his left side, his right arm folded beneath the pillow. He stared into the blackness.

Maybe...maybe Warren's right. Maybe it's not worth having a friend who's a Wog, a never-in. If I hang around with him too much, I might lose everything. Lose my progress up the Bridge. Lose my eternity.

Lose my home.

Lose my real friends.

Lose my real family.

I like hanging out with Larkin; I enjoy it. I really enjoyed those three days....But I don't think it's worth losing everything for a Wog friend, is it? I could lose everything in my life for one single friend.

Is hanging out with Larkin worth all that? No, it's not. It really isn't. Warren's right, it's not worth it.

I knew I could count on you, Quinn.

He kept staring into the black, ruminating over everything, until the day's stress and tension eased and he started nodding off. Bending his knees, he pulled his feet up until he could rest the soles against the wall behind him.

The last thing he thought of as sleep pulled him under was the scar on Larkin's face and ear, wondering how he'd received them and wondering what the scars would feel like if he were to touch them.

Chapter Seventeen

Warren stayed in the auditing room long after Tom and the pre-clear had left. Quinn's description of large amounts of money simply given away ran through his mind.

Thirty years old. Born in Montreal. Warren rested his elbows on the desk and interlaced his fingers, resting his chin on them.

Warren was a careful man by nature. He had risen in the Sea Org ranks because he never left a job undone and was thorough to the point of nitpicky. He'd served on the Blow Team with distinction, recovering more potential apostates than anyone. He did this by going through everything, every scrap in their auditing and ethics files, before he made a move. That was the best way to find someone's ruin, the leverage he could use to get them back in line, back with the program. He'd used the same method to get money when he'd served as a registrar, turning what he knew about fellow parishioners into pressuring to give more than they could afford.

He was keen enough to see an opportunity where others missed it. One of his proudest upstat moments was browbeating a man into giving all the money intended for his wife's tattoo shop rent to the Church instead. That had been back in Clearwater, and he'd won an award for it. He'd been given a team of young FSMs to lead and had pushed them hard, working the phones and visiting parishioners at all hours, often more than twenty hours a day.

As much as he demanded of others, it was no more than he expected of himself. His team had brought in more money than anyone, a rate of success he had driven and maintained.

And now another opportunity was presenting itself; he could see it. He needed more information if he was going to use that opportunity to its full potential. However, there were no ethics files to read, no auditing notes to mine.

That left two sources of information which, while helpful, wouldn't necessarily provide a ruin he could use. One would most likely be biased, self-serving, and incomplete. *In such a case, there was only one course of action. Use both.* As LRH had written:

The foremost law, if one's ambition is to win, is of course to win.

Having confirmed a course of action in his mind, Warren got to his feet and headed out the door. His stride was purposeful, focused. He strode past the bookstore reception desk without so much as a glance at Angela. He'd call her into his office later; she was excellent stress relief. Placid, easily manipulated, and ready to respond to the slightest command—just the way he liked it. She'd been down on him several times, but she'd baulked at full penetration, citing her marriage as an excuse. It was a situation he planned on correcting, and tonight was as good a time as any to do just that. There was no doubt in his mind; she just needed the right push.

The thought of her should have been distracting, but it wasn't. He simply compartmentalized it for later.

Warren went into the private half of the Org. His office was at the far end of the hall, just beside the file room at the very end.

He opened the door into the peaceful sanctuary that was his office. The back wall was covered in countless awards, certificates, and diplomas he had earned during his Scientology career, each one in an identical gold-toned frame. They were a testament to his power within the Church, his unquestioned authority.

A black pleather couch sat just inside the door. Warren's desk was plain, with a black desktop computer and an old black office phone in the middle, a simple white gooseneck lamp beside them.

Warren went to the chair and toggled the lamp on. He reached underneath the desk and felt around until his fingertips found the small plastic box glued to the underside. He opened the lid with a click and removed the key inside to unlock the top drawer. He pulled out a brown pleather-covered address book and began to flip through the entries. It didn't take him long to find the one he was looking for:

Frere, Murray, followed by a phone number.

He laid the book on the desk and held the pages open, tucking the receiver under his right ear as he dialled. The phone rang only twice before a deep, husky voice came on the line.

"Yeah?"

"That's a charming greeting."

"I'm busy. Whataya want, Warren?"

"That's not the way to speak to your biggest client," Warren said with a frown.

There was a snort of amusement on the other end of the line. "What makes you think you're my biggest client?"

"Please, let's not play with each other. I could have that hefty retainer from the Church revoked in a moment, and you know it."

"Fine," Murray sighed. "What is it you need?"

"I want you to look into someone for me."

"Somebody else blow from the Church?" the man asked.

"No. This person could either be a source of trouble or a great whale."

"You don't know which?"

"Not at this point, no."

"And you want to know which they are."

"Yes. More than that, I want you to dig up everything you can find on them," Warren said as he leaned back in his chair and kicked off his shoes, leaving them haphazardly under the desk.

"So, fact-finding."

"Isn't that what private eyes do best?"

"Mm, 'kay, I'll do it. Email me whatever you know. Have you gotten approval from your management yet?"

"Don't worry about that, that's not going to be an issue."

"If you say so."

"They're not going to say no to me, Murray. Haven't you learned that by now?"

"Yeah, whatever you say, Warren. Just email me what you have." Murray didn't say goodbye; he just hung up.

Warren should have been offended, but he didn't care about the man enough to bother. Murray was just a useful wog whose obedience could easily be purchased. There were dozens, hundreds, just like him—people who would never be smart enough to join the Church, but who were useful when needed.

He hit the power button on the computer tower and turned on the monitor as it began to power up. He loosened his tie as he logged in and quickly went to his email.

He hammered out the email to Murray with everything he knew about Larkin Childs, using his preferred typing method of two fingers pounding the keyboard into submission. Once it was sent, he opened up a new email and began to compose the one that really mattered:

Subject: Request permission for fact-finding mission

Sir,

I request approval to employ the PI on retainer at the Calgary Org to begin a fact-finding mission. A person who may be a PTS has recently come to my attention. While under normal circumstances a PTS would need to be addressed and handled, I have information that leads me to believe that this PTS could be a potential whale; he has access to invaluable resources if he can be turned. The benefits would be two-fold: Firstly, a PTS would be handled and neutralised, and secondly, a new whale, who is a large source of funding, would be available to our registrars here at the Calgary Org.

There is a definite possibility of turning this PTS into a pre-clear; however, I need more information about the PTS to make this happen.

I do not foresee this as being a difficult assignment, as this PTS already has a connection to one of our pre-clears on staff, and the potential benefits far outweigh the minor costs in gathering the required information.

I await your positive response.

Yours,

Warren Tresaster

He reread the email three times before sending it. Since any email of this type had to go through multiple levels of approval, it might be several days before he received an answer. That didn't concern him; he was confident the request wouldn't be refused. And if it was, it would simply become a pink-legs mission he could run anyway.

Pink-legs missions weren't uncommon in the Church, and every member of the Sea Org had been instructed to read and word-clear the essay many times. It was the COB's favourite, an essay about personal power—the highest of all Ethics Conditions. Warren could have recited it from memory.

The Founder had read a biography of Simón Bolívar, the South American revolutionary leader, and his mistress, Manuela Sáenz. While staging a successful liberation, the pair had failed to consolidate their power and use it to make a fortune for themselves and their supporters, which, in LRH's view, made them complete failures.

As LRH had written, the people at the top didn't need to know everything:

…and if he's in power really, he won't ask all the time, "What are all those dead bodies doing at the door?" And if you are clever, you never let it be thought HE killed them — that weakens you and also hurts the power source. "Well, boss, about all those dead bodies, nobody at all will suppose you did it. She over there, those pink legs sticking out, didn't like me."

Pink legs had become a meme in the Sea Org; you got the stats up any way you could, and any questions about how those stats were raised were answered with *pink legs*—meaning you really didn't want to know. The end justified the means.

He sat back and stretched, arms over his head, deeply pleased with himself. One compartment of his mind closed on Larkin and money; another clicked open, and he smiled.

He picked up the receiver again and punched in the extension for reception. The phone was answered on the second ring by a soft female voice.

"Yes, Sir?"

"Angela, come to my office, please."

"Yes, Sir."

While he waited, he removed his sweater and folded it neatly on the desk. When he was finished, it was as perfectly square as if he'd just bought it. He bent down to pick up his shoes and aligned them precisely under the desk. He was loosening his tie further when there was a faint tap on the door.

"Come," he called.

Angela cracked the door open just wide enough to slip in sideways and then closed it behind her. She stood with her back pressed against the door, eyes downcast.

He smiled, noting that under her plain black cardigan she wore a pink-and-black snakeskin-patterned top and a long black skirt, her feet in plain black thong sandals. Her hazel eyes looked huge beneath her heavy brows.

"You wanted to see me, Sir?"

"Angela, come here, my dear." He put on his warmest, most fatherly smile. He turned his chair slightly and patted his lap. "Come, sit."

She crossed the room cautiously and perched on his knee. Warren took her knees in his hands and drew them up fully onto his lap so that her feet were off the floor and one arm rested around his shoulders. Her tiny frame felt almost childlike. He looked up and saw her biting her lower lip.

"Angela, my dear, let me just say you've been working very hard. I've seen how many duties you've taken on, and I'm extremely proud of you."

She startled. "Thank you, Sir," she whispered.

"I know how hard you've been working to stay online, and while it's commendable, I can see it's taking its toll on you."

"I'll do anything," she murmured, barely above a whisper, "to go all the way up the Bridge."

"I know you will." His hand rested on her knee, his fingers beginning to gently squeeze through the skirt.

"It's just…"

"What is it?"

"It's taking me so long to get up to the next level. And my husband, too. It's taking so long and it's so expensive…"

"Oh, I know, my dear, I know." His tone was soothing. "Don't you remember LRH himself said he wanted to make the courses free? But you know how desperately we need the money to stand up against those who would destroy the Church and stop our humanitarian work.

All the Narconon programs would have to close, and we desperately need them—especially now, with the downturn in oil and gas. You've seen what a ghost town downtown Calgary is becoming. Empty offices, crime rates going up, more people than ever in this very city who need our help."

"Oh, yeah, I know, it's just that…"

"You'd like to move up the Bridge more quickly."

"Yes!" Her sudden enthusiasm would have caught a lesser man off guard. Warren simply smiled.

"You're still on the Method One Co-Audit, correct?"

"Yes. Even though you've been helping me make case gains…"

"You're still on Method One."

She looked away and nodded. "We're running out of money, and we can't get any more credit cards. Perry filled out more applications for us, but they were turned down. Warren…I'd…like…." Her right hand slid down to rest against his crotch. He was already hard; the pressure of her palm only sharpened the sensation as she began to rub. Leaning closer, she whispered in his left ear, like a naughty child afraid of being overheard. "I'll suck it for you. I'll even swallow, if it will get me off Method One."

Warren smiled as sweetly as he could manage. "While I would deeply enjoy having you make another case gain, there is a way for you to reach the next level tonight. Not tomorrow, not next week—tonight."

Her hand stilled. Her eyes widened. "Really? How?"

Instead of answering, he slid his hand down from her knee, along her shin to the hem of her skirt. His fingers slipped beneath the fabric and began the slow journey back up, tracing the line of her shin to her knee again. He cupped the joint, feeling the bone and soft tissue under his palm, then let his hand wander higher to her thigh.

She started to squirm. "Warren…"

"Everything we do is in the service of the Church, isn't it?" His voice stayed low and patient. "We only go up the Bridge so we can help others do the same, so we can Clear the planet. The greatest good for the greatest number of beings, correct? And you've said more than once you want to go up the Bridge so you can keep doing good for the world, haven't you?" His hand slid further between her legs, resting halfway up her thighs, rubbing and caressing the warm skin. "Did you know, my dear, that sexuality has been part of human religion for thousands of years? Oh yes. Humans used sexuality as a way of connecting to the divine, of touching what they couldn't see. Such acts were considered sacred, an act of communion, done in service of their god. LRH studied such ceremonies extensively."

"I know what you're thinking, but this is not cheating, my dear. This is a religious act, an act of devotion. Once you reach the next level, I can post you to Division 2. You'll be a registrar. Oh, you'll exude so much theta you'll have donations flooding in."

"Registrar?" She pulled back slightly to look at him, but the glare from the lamp obscured his eyes. "You think I could do that?"

"Oh, yes." Warren slipped his arm around her shoulders. "I know you can. I used to manage an entire team of FSMs—I can help you. I've always believed in you, more than anyone on staff. Remember me telling you that? No? Shame. You really do need to learn to listen more carefully, my dear. You'll be more upstat than you've ever been; you'll do more to keep Scientology working, for the entire world, than you ever dreamed. I can help you, my dear, if you let me."

He drew her closer so he could lean in and kiss the left side of her throat.

"But my husband…" she whispered.

"You're worrying too much. You'll be able to help him with his auditing," Warren breathed between kisses, using his teeth to nip lightly at her skin. "And I may be able to see my way to allowing your auditing to give him more case gains than normal, simply because of your new position and that raw theta I can't resist."

His hand slid all the way up; he could feel the cotton of her panties under his fingers, the heat beneath.

"Really? You'll help him?"

"Please try to pay attention, Angela, my dear. Yes, we will both help him—you and I. It might work very well to have you both as FSMs, working as a team. I know it's not normally done, to have a couple posted to the same position, but exceptions can always be made…"

He pulled back to meet her gaze. "If you're willing to put in the effort, that is."

She moaned quietly; her breathing was growing heavier, her teeth worrying her bottom lip as she shivered.

"We talked about this before, remember?" he continued. "But I'll ask again: are you willing, Angela, to make the sacrifices necessary for the greater good—for the planet? For the Church? For LRH himself? To make his vision come true?"

She hesitated for a fraction of a second and then breathed, "Yes."

Warren smiled. "You've made the right choice, my dear."

His hand slid back down her leg and out from under her skirt. "Would you be so kind as to go over to the couch and undress for me, please?"

She nodded and slipped off his knees, crossing the room with a hesitant gait. She took off her cardigan and automatically began to fold it.

"No," Warren said from the chair. "Just drop it on the floor. And turn this way—I'd like to see you."

She obeyed, letting the cardigan fall in a heap. The snakeskin-print top was a cami; her bare arms looked thin and pale as she pulled the fabric up over her breasts, then over her head, dropping it onto the cardigan.

Warren pulled his tie free, folded it, and set it neatly on top of his sweater.

Angela slid her skirt down and let it fall to the floor, kicking it aside with her sandals so that everything lay in a dark tangle on the carpet. Warren began unbuttoning his white shirt as he watched her stand there in black lace bra and black cotton panties, her arms hanging limply at her sides.

"Black," Warren chuckled. "Were you hoping I'd ask you to kneel for another case gain, my dear? You know how it affects me when you wear black."

Angela didn't answer. She looked down as she reached behind to unhook the bra. Warren hardened further as she eased the straps down her arms and pulled the bra away. It was the first time he'd seen her bare, and his mouth began to water at the sight of her breasts, fuller than they'd appeared under clothes, drooping slightly with their own soft weight.

She didn't look at him as she slid her panties down. She wasn't shaved; he could see the mousy brown curls that spread slightly down the sides of her thighs. He licked his lips as he stood up from the chair and shrugged out of his shirt.

"Now, my dear, please sit on the couch, right in the centre."

She did, knees together, facing him.

"Good. Now open your legs. Wider, yes, as wide as you can. Put your heels on the cushions, one on each side. Yes, that's it. Now use your hands to spread yourself open, please. Yes, that's right."

He let the shirt drop; he was too aroused to bother folding it. Reaching for the lamp, he twisted the neck so the light became a spotlight, forcing her to squint. Now he could see everything: every hair, the rise and fall of her chest, the sheen of moisture between her legs that betrayed her own arousal.

"Yes, that's perfect. Now I'd like you to pleasure yourself with your fingers." His voice stayed soft, coaxing. "There's no need to hesitate. Nothing we do in this sacred space is wrong, remember? Nothing is done that isn't in service to the greater good. You are free here, free to explore your body in a way you've never done before but always wanted to. Yes, that's the way. Yes, I want to hear you moan."

He kept his eyes on her as he undid his pants and stepped out of them and his socks. Warren never wore underwear; tonight, he was grateful for the habit.

"You're...sure...this...ah...isn't cheating?" she asked, fingers moving quickly over herself.

"Are you questioning me?" His voice dropped, low and dangerous.

"No, Sir! Ah!" She looked away, eyes fixed on the pile of clothes on the floor.

"Then I'll have to repeat myself." His gaze never left her. "If you were paying attention, you'd know this is a religious sacrifice. The concept of cheating doesn't exist here."

He moved towards the couch, licking his lips. Kneeling in front of her, eye level with her, he watched every movement.

"No, no, don't stop. Climax so you're as ready as possible. Here, let me help you."

He reached up and slid his index and middle fingers inside her. She was already wet; he could hear the soft sound around his fingers, and she cried out anyway.

"Yes, yes, this is a prequel," he murmured. "I can feel how ready you are. I knew you wanted this. I knew you wanted me to take you."

"To…ah!…get…ah!…higher…"

"Don't speak unless I tell you!" he snapped. "Yes, to get higher on the Bridge. Moan as I'm penetrating you with my fingers. Yes, that's it. You're getting the couch dirty. I knew you wanted this. I know everything about you, my dear. I know you better than you know yourself. Remember that. Yes, cry out as you climax. Be as loud as you like."

She groaned heavily and shivered, a spasm running through her whole body. She fell back as her hand slipped away.

Without a word, Warren pulled his hand back and looked at his fingers, slick from being inside her. He smiled as he put them in his mouth and licked them clean.

She watched him blankly, eyes dark, breasts heaving as she panted.

He took her shoulders and pushed her down into the couch so she was half sitting, half reclining. She was limp and didn't resist as he lifted her right leg and set her heel on the back of the couch, then pushed her left leg out until her foot found the floor.

"Women can climax many times in a row, did you know that?" He positioned himself between her legs and over her. She stared up at him, eyes wide and glassy. "You've just climaxed, but you're going to cum again and again as I take you. Pleasure is part of the sacred act, an integral part of sacred sexuality—just as pain is. It's not forbidden here the way it is in Judeo-Christian culture. You will enjoy this. I know what you want. I know how to give you pleasure you've never known before."

With one swift movement, he was inside her.

"Moan," he told her. "Moan as I'm taking you."

The only sounds were the wet, rhythmic noise of his thrusts and her moans, punctuated by his grunts. He bent his head and took her right nipple into his mouth, sucking on it as hard as he could while he moved inside her.

She cried out, a sound that blended pleasure, pain, and fear.

He felt it stretch, the nipple lengthening the harder he pulled. He bit down hard, and she cried out again, clearly in pain. He pulled out of her and shifted to her other breast; he didn't want to climax too quickly. Harder and harder he pulled as she writhed beneath him. Another sharp cry tore out of her as he bit down again.

"You like the pain," he muttered as he straightened up. "I know you. I know your darkest desires. I know how to fulfil them."

A moment later, he was inside her again, grunting as she cried out. Holding her hips, he dragged her towards him with each thrust so he could drive as deep as possible. He felt her spasm and shiver again in another climax and smiled.

"Moan," he ordered, and she did. "Keep moaning. Moan as if you were a slut who begs for it."

She obeyed, her moans matching the rhythm of his thrusts.

He was sweating now as his pace grew harder and faster, the sounds louder, the slapping of skin on skin quicker, the moments between thrusts shorter. He threw his head back. "Tell me," he ordered. "Say you want it."

"Yes," she whispered, eyes blank, staring at nothing. "Yes, do it."

"Beg me to do it. Use that dirty word."

"Please, fuck me." Her voice was flat.

"Again."

"Fuck me."

"Louder. Scream it. Tone 40."

"FUCK ME! PLEASE FUCK ME! SIR! PLEASE!"

He climaxed. He thrust into her a few more times and then pulled out, some of his semen dripping onto the couch.

She lay there, unmoving, staring up at the ceiling.

"That was excellent, my dear," he panted, looking down at her. "Excellent. Round two will be even better."

She didn't speak.

"In a little while," he assured her. "I'll take you on the desk. Yes, you'll like that, I promise. I'll be able to be rougher now that you've had it once. I'm going to eat you, devour you. You'll climax again and again tonight."

She stayed silent as he reached out and began to fondle her left breast.

"Yes, you'll learn to like it rough, won't you? Speak. Say you want it rough."

"Yes, Sir. Please, Sir, I want it rough. I want you to fuck me again, Sir. When you fuck me, please be rough with me, Sir."

"Tell me to rape you."

"Please…please rape me, Sir. I won't fight—"

"Now, there's no fun in that, is there?" He kept stroking her breast, smiling. "When we get to that point, I'll want you to fight back. I want you to resist, because the pleasure you'll feel when I overpower you will be the most intense thing you've ever experienced. The pleasure, the pain, the need for more. You'll love it."

"Yes, Sir."

"Good girl. Keep this up, and you'll be Clear in no time, with my assistance. Just remember, this is what you wanted, this is what you needed, no matter what happens. This is for your own good and for the greater good as well."

"Yes, Sir. Use me, Sir, for the greater good."

"Say it. Say it's what you wanted—to be used for the good of the Org."

"I want this. Use me for the Church."

"Good girl," he said softly. "I knew you did."

Chapter Eighteen

He must have been asleep, because he didn't hear the click of the light switch—only the sudden blaze of the bare bulb, so intense after the blackness of hours or days that it hurt. He shielded his eyes with his hand and squinted as the door opened. Tom brought in a plastic straight-backed chair and set it down facing Quinn. No sooner was the chair in place than Warren walked in and sat, posture fastidiously straight. Quinn immediately leapt to his feet and saluted his superior officer, only to be waved off.

"Quinn," he said, "there's no need for such formality."

"Yes, sir," Quinn replied, relaxing his stance but remaining on his feet.

"Quinn, I've been thinking about your unauthorized excursion, and I think I know a way we can… oh, shall we say *salvage* your position within the Church."

"I'll do anything, sir," Quinn said at once. "I know I was wrong. I know I should never have gone. It's one hundred percent my fault."

Warren nodded. "Yes, that is not in dispute. But I think I may have a way to turn your mistake into a benefit, for both yourself and the Church as a whole."

"Really? How?"

"I had the impression during our auditing session that you're rather fond of this Larkin, aren't you? You consider him a friend?"

"Um… yeah, I guess I do."

"And of course you want what's best for your friend, don't you?" He pressed on without waiting for an answer. "I myself found your friend quite interesting, and it seems that he's more aware of the teachings of the Founder than I would have expected. That not only makes this Larkin interesting, it makes me concerned for him."

"Concerned?"

"Yes. As you know, some of LRH's writings are only allowed to be accessed by people who have reached a certain level on the Bridge. However, it appears that your friend has been given access to some of our teachings, and he may not have been ready for them. I don't believe he's been given the proper training, and having that knowledge without the training puts him at risk of illness or physical harm. Do you see what I'm saying, Quinn?"

"I... I'm not sure."

Warren sighed audibly. "It's simple. He needs proper training to absorb LRH's teachings, which he hasn't received. If he was given this information by some squirrel—someone who's using the tech without being trained in it—then Larkin is highly at risk. So, I've decided on a course of action that will allow you to redeem yourself and help your friend at the same time. You, Quinn, will convince him to join."

"I will?"

"Yes, you will. Both for your good and his. Clearly, the man is highly intelligent, and it would be a great shame to allow someone of such intelligence to fall victim to all the negative forces in the world, wouldn't it? The government, Big Pharma, the RCMP. I think you need to rescue your friend from all of it. Now, now, I know you're going to say you've never been very good when you've been posted on Division 6, and that's true. However, this doesn't involve you talking to strangers, which I understand is difficult for you. This is helping your friend, sharing the most important aspect of your life with him and helping him to better himself in the process."

"But how can I do that?"

"The simplest way I can think of: by spending more time with him. So, I want you to go to your friend and convince him to hire you at his store."

"A wog job?" Quinn asked, disbelieving.

"Yes, I think a wog job will do the trick nicely. It will allow you to spend a great deal of time with him, as well as bring money into the Church, since your wages can be used to pay for your classes and additional training. Remember, every single new member we gain helps us to Clear the planet, helps us achieve our ultimate goals of world peace and the end of poverty, hunger, war, disease, and drug use. Every single person we bring in brings us one step closer to those goals. Your friend could be instrumental in helping us, and by bringing him into the fold, he'll help *you* as well.

"Now, how about we get you cleaned up and you can go visit your friend, yeah?"

"But how am I supposed to get him to give me a job? What if he doesn't want to hire me?" Quinn protested.

"You must convince him, Quinn. Don't accept 'no' for an answer. Remember your training, and remember this is for the greater good. If you do this, your transgression will be forgiven and you'll be back online again. If you have to pay him multiple visits to convince him, then so be it. Tug on his heartstrings if you need to, but you *must* get a job with this Larkin. That will allow you to spend as much time as required to convince him that he needs to join.

"Get him to take one class, and we can do the rest. Now, that doesn't sound so hard, does it? Unless you're not serious about going Clear, of course. Get a job and convince him to take one single, solitary class."

"Of course I'm serious about going up the Bridge and going Clear! One class, that's all?"

"That's all. You can do that, can't you, Quinn? I have total confidence in you. I know you can do this. The end phenomenon is to get your friend to join us. I know you won't disappoint me, will you?"

"No, sir! I won't fail you!" Quinn saluted again, desperate for Warren's approval.

"Excellent. Now, go back to the dorm, get cleaned up, and start to plan how to get that wog job, hm?"

"Yes, sir."

Warren was smiling to himself as he walked out of the hole.

Chapter Nineteen

He stood across the street at the bus stop, staring at the store. The smell of burgers from Peter's Drive-In drifted on the breeze, and his stomach growled. He lingered there, hoping Larkin would come outside so he wouldn't have to walk up and actually open the door—while dreading that exact possibility at the same time. Two buses stopped; he waved them away. Eventually, he walked to the corner and waited for the light to change.

How in hell do I do this? 'Hey, Larkin! How about giving me a job? The Org Director says you have to...' Oh, yeah, that'll totally work. Come on, Quinn, you fuckin' idiot, you bonehead, you have to do this, you can't fuck this up. You have to do this.

He held his breath as he stepped off the sidewalk and into the street. He was so focused on Larkin's shop that he missed the car whipping around the corner until it screeched to a halt, the bumper centimetres from his knees. For a moment, he couldn't even understand what the driver was yelling, or why he was yelling at all.

"Why don't you look where you're going?" shouted the driver.

All the tension and fear that had been building in Quinn rose to the surface like some dark sea monster breaking through. "Why don't you look where you're driving? I have the light! You almost hit me! Open your fuckin' eyes and get off your fuckin' phone or whatever the hell you were doing instead of paying attention, bud!"

"Me?" the man screamed back. "You walked in front of my car!"

"Bullshit!" Quinn snapped. "I have the light, you idiot! You ran the stop sign!"

The yelling went back and forth until the driver got out of his car and walked up to Quinn. Quinn's nerves failed him; he was sure he was about to get beaten up. He froze, bracing for the punch, until he heard a familiar voice.

"Kessé qui se passe? Pourquoi tous ces cris? Quinn? Is that you?"*

Quinn looked over to see Larkin stepping off the sidewalk and heading toward him. "This moron went through the sign and nearly hit me!" Quinn spat, exasperated.

"This fuckin' douche canoe walked in front of my car!" the driver screamed at Larkin.

"I had the light!" Quinn protested again.

"Ostie de colon, tabarnak! Ostie de câlice de tabarnak, c'est pas possible comment que t'es cave!" Larkin snapped at the driver, speaking so quickly the words all seemed to blend into one. "I've seen you run that sign before! I know you and your fuckin' souped-up car! *T'es donc ben niaiseux, t'es une ostie de vidange!* Get in your car and drive!"

The driver kept yelling as Larkin put his arm loosely around Quinn's shoulders. *"Est-ce que tu vas bien,* Quinn? You aren't hurt?"

"I'm fine," Quinn muttered, shooting another death glare at the driver.

"I swear to *le bon Dieu,*" Larkin said as he began leading Quinn toward the sidewalk. "I've never seen so many people run stop signs or red lights as I do here! Not since I left Montreal, anyway."

"Do people drive crazy like that in Montreal?"

"Ah! *Tabarnak,* they're the craziest of the crazy! You either learn to drive the same way or you get run over! Are you sure you're alright?"

"Yeah, I'm ok. Thanks."

"Pas de problème! I heard the yelling and thought I recognized your voice. Come, I'll get you some tea, calm the nerves, eh?"

Minutes later, Quinn found himself sitting on the floral couch in the back of Larkin's shop, a steaming mug of tea cupped in his still-shaking hands.

"You sure you're ok?" Sandra asked. "You look pretty shaken up."

"I'm fine, he didn't actually hit me."

"Man drives like an idiot, *ostie!* Even for here!" Larkin looked at Quinn as he sat down on the computer chair. The desk was just to the left side of the couch, with a tiny kitchenette beyond it, where Larkin had boiled the kettle on the hot plate. "I must admit, I wasn't expecting to see you so soon, *mon ami.* I'm delighted you're here, *tsé.*"

"Yeah, I got permission to come."

"Oh? I thought you were in trouble for leaving without permission."

"Yeah, it's just…"

"*Oui?*"

Abruptly, he had a flash of inspiration. "Yeah, Warren has been asking everyone to get jobs outside of the Church," Quinn lied. "That way, we can bring more money to put towards the Ideal Org. But, I don't really know anyone outside the Church but you, so…"

"You thought you'd come here and ask for a job?"

"Yeah."

For a moment, Larkin simply looked at Quinn before sitting back in his chair. "No," he finally replied.

"No?"

"No. Sandra, would you be so kind as to take an early and long lunch? I'd like to talk with Quinn."

"Yeah, no, absolutely," Sandra replied, and quickly headed for the door.

Quinn watched her leave before looking back at Larkin. "Why won't you give me a job?"

"Because, if I were to hire you properly, there would be taxes to pay, paperwork to fill out, and many records. I don't think your Warren would like that. Besides, I would prefer not to give money to any church, *ostie.*"

"Why?"

"I don't have much use for churches since I gave up being Catholic."

"Please, Larkin! Warren wants everyone to do this, and the only reason he's willing to let me off the hook for taking off to Banff is because he wants me to get a job. I don't know anyone outside the Church!" His anxiety suddenly took over, and he began to hyperventilate. "I don't even know how to apply for a job, or what I should apply for. I don't know how to do this, and I don't want to fuck up again..." He let the sentence drift, unable to finish.

"*Vas-y doucement, Quinn.* Take it easy, just breathe. Focus on your breathing and try to slow it down."

"I'll... get... in... in so much... tr-trouble if I... f-fail again."

"*C'est naze ici,*" Larkin sighed. He pinched the bridge of his nose and squeezed his eyes tightly closed.

"What do I do?" When he didn't answer, Quinn prodded: "Larkin?"

"*Tabarnak,* there's only one thing to do."

"What?"

"*Tu devras travailler au noir.*"

"Huh?"

"You'll have to work under the table," Larkin repeated. "Then there's no taxes, no paperwork, you'll be paid in cash, and I don't need to know what you do with it."

"You can do that?"

"No, it's not legal, strictly speaking. But many people do it." He sighed again. "I will be in trouble with the CRA if anyone finds out, though, so you mustn't tell anyone. Even Warren. The whole point of working for cash is that it's not traceable, there's no record of anything."

"I don't want you to get in trouble with Canada Revenue."

"Ah, don't worry. Just don't tell everyone that you're being paid in cash, and it should be fine. Like I said, people do it all the time."

Quinn's face brightened. "Really? You'll give me a job?"

"Yes. I can always use another pair of hands to move heavy things around. Even though Sandra is very strong, I don't like always having to ask her for help. Minimum wage here in Alberta *est ridicule,* so I won't insult you by giving you that."

"I'm ok with minimum wage! Really!"

"Are you sure?"

"Yeah! I'm fine with that!"

"*Eh bien,* if you're really sure."

"I won't tell anyone, and minimum wage is perfect! I won't get you into trouble, Larkin."

"*Oui, oui,*" Larkin held out his hand to Quinn. "We have a deal, then?"

Quinn seized his hand, squeezing it fiercely. "Yes! Oh, definitely!" His breathing had steadied, and now he couldn't stop grinning. "Can I start now?"

"*Hein?* If you like. We'll see how enthusiastic you are after a couple of weeks."

I'm in, Quinn thought. *I'm in. I actually did it! Now, I get to spend time with Larkin and try to convince him to take a class. One class, that's all Warren wanted. Just one class… I can do this! I'm not gonna fuck up for once.* He couldn't stop grinning.

Chapter Twenty

"This is for me?" He stared down at the money on the countertop in disbelief.

"*Bien sûr.* Fifteen dollars per hour, and you worked 20 hours, that's $300. Of course, there are no taxes taken out." Larkin had dark circles under his eyes.

Quinn kept looking down at the three brown coloured bills. "I've never seen a hundred-dollar bill before," he said at last.

"Would you prefer smaller bills, *là?*"

"No! No, this is fine." He quickly scooped them up and tucked them into his wallet, as if afraid that Larkin would take them back.

"Don't spend it all in one place!" Sandra called as she came up from the basement, a large, fat porcelain vase in her hands.

"Huh?"

"Sandra's being funny, *mon ami.*"

"Oh. Hey, you want a hand?" His mind was racing as he helped Sandra set the huge piece up in the front window. *Three hundred dollars? For twenty hours' worth of work? I've never even **seen** that much money at once! In the Church, everyone works fifteen to twenty hours **a day,** and I think the most I've ever been paid was twenty dollars! Does everyone get paid like this? Is everyone rich? No wonder they're always asking people for money, they must have it to spare! Three hundred dollars for twenty hours, I can't believe it! Larkin said they'd take taxes normally, but geez! And he even drives me back to the Org, so I don't have to spend money on the bus! This'll help to pay for so many classes! Classes… Right, I can't forget I have to talk Larkin into taking just one class….*

He'd tried over the last few weeks to bring up Scientology to Larkin over and over again, who seemed astoundingly uninterested.

Floundering in his mission, Quinn had gone to Warren seeking assistance, suggestions not only on what to say but on how to say it. He'd been given a script, which he'd dutifully memorized, but was having trouble figuring out an appropriate time to bring it up. He waited until Sandra went for her lunch before trying again:

"Hey, Larkin?"

"Hein?"

"You don't sleep well at night, do you?"

"No, not always."

"Why?"

"I'm a, what does Sandra call it? A night-owl."

"Do you have nightmares?"

"Doesn't everyone, *ostie?*"

Knowing the next line in his script, Quinn wondered if Larkin would follow it as he and Warren had practiced. He took a deep breath. "Are the nightmares because of the abuse?"

"_______________"

Quinn looked up from the Royal Doulton figurines he was rearranging to find Larkin staring at him, his whisky-coloured eye fixed on him like a yellow laser.

"Kessé?" he said in a quiet tone.

"You know, the abuse. You told that woman that you remembered what it was like to grow up in an abusive home. Is that where your nightmares come from?" Larkin said nothing, but kept staring at Quinn until he felt uncomfortable enough to plow forward with his script. "What if you could get rid of all that pain and start sleeping at night? You'd be so much happier and freer. You could be filled with joy and light, and you'd see the world as the wonderful, amazing, beautiful place it is."

"*'N'importe quoi'* would be what I'd say," Larkin snorted and looked down at the art book he'd been reading.

"What does that mean?"

"It translates to, 'That's bullshit'."

Quinn went on with his script. "And you'd be right to think that. It sounds too good to be true, but I know it's true because I've lived it. I've experienced it myself, but that doesn't matter. You'll never know if it works for you, if it's true for you, until you experience it, until you try it for yourself. You…"

"Arrête ça. Toute suite."

"What? I don't unders–"

"Stop it. Now." Larkin repeated. "Right now."

"But–"

"Toute suite! Stop it."

"I was just–"

"I know what you were *just* doing. I won't have it."

"But–"

"No. Not another word." Larkin took off his rectangular-framed reading glasses, dropped them onto the open book, and pinched the bridge of his nose. "Quinn, you are my friend; the son of my dearest friend, and I enjoy having you here, but I will *not* allow you to keep trying to convert me. Understand this, it will not happen. *Le bon Dieu* himself could come down from on high and order me to join, and I'd still refuse. **It will not happen**, understand?"

"But it could help you. Remember, you told Warren your English isn't what you'd like it to be? They can help with that. LRH's tech is amazing, and it can help you improve every aspect of your life if you just give it a chance."

"No. Never."

"You don't know if it's true for you until you try it, though! Why not take just one class and see what it's all about? One single class can't hurt, right? It wouldn't even cost much, an introductory class is only twenty…"

"**NO!**" He shot up from the chair and slammed both his palms onto the counter, kinking the pages of the book. "***T'a fermes-tu, ta gueule?*** You will never get me to join! Do you understand that? Never! I lived near Clearwater, remember? I've seen what your church does to people! I know how it destroys people, families! I've known for decades what your beloved LRH was about, and I would spit on his grave if I could! It-Will-Never-Happen. Do you hear me, Quinn? Never! And if you insist on this *stupid* song and dance, I won't allow you to work here any longer! I will demand you leave and not return, *tu comprendes?* Now, kindly shut the fuck up and drop it." Sitting, he returned his glasses to his nose and scowled.

Quinn's script had warned him to expect resistance; counterarguments were likely to follow, but nothing could have prepared him for the ferocity of Larkin's rage. He stood there, looking at Larkin, who now appeared as detached as ever. He was at a loss. "Larkin, I–"

"Get out."

"But I–"

"Get out. Now. I don't want to see you."

Quinn froze. "But what about–"

"Get out! Now! Right fuckin' now! **OUT.**" His final word echoed, seemingly ricocheting off the light fixtures like a punch.

Quinn ran out the door, not even realizing he was doing it until he was outside. Pacing around and around, a knot in his stomach tightening. He was sweating profusely; the sweat ran into his eyes and stung. *Oh my God! Oh my God! What am I gonna do? He kicked me out! He said he'll never do it! Never! And he'll toss me out if I keep trying! He'll never take a class, he'll never convert! I'm gonna lose the only chance I have of making it up, of getting back on track! I'll have to go back and admit that I messed up again! I've lost...*

His pacing quickened, and as fear took over, he began hyperventilating. His stinging eyes began to water, leading to tears that rolled down his face.

I've lost my only friend. That's it. It's over. My only friend outside of the Org, and he's gone. He'll never let me come back! I'll never see him again! He's my only friend and he's gone! I'm such an idiot! I'm so stupid! No wonder I have no friends! No wonder I'm always fucking up! No wonder I'm such a loser! I'll never see him again, never again. I'm... Alone. I'm alone again. All alone...

He slumped against the shop wall and sank to the ground, pulling his knees up to his chest. Folding his arms across his knees, he buried his face in his elbows and wept. Yet another failure in a lifetime of failures, and the weight of all the losses was too much. Quinn gave in to anxiety and sobbed until he felt the vibrations in his spine; the muscles in his face hurt from grimacing. He had no idea how long he'd been sitting there when he heard a familiar voice.

"Quinn?"

He looked up to find Larkin standing over him. He started to crawl to his feet, but Larkin's hand settled on his shoulder, stopping him. Larkin sat down beside him, a pack of cigarettes in hand. Pulling one from the pack, he popped it into his mouth, cupped the end in his long fingers as he lit it, and inhaled deeply. The resulting puff of smoke lingered in the air. "*Je suis vraiment désolé,* Quinn. I am very sorry."

Quinn sniffed but said nothing.

Another puff of smoke hung like acid. "*J'ai la langue à terre,*" he continued. "I am too tired. I haven't slept in…ah, a week maybe? I don't know. I'm overtired, and that made me snap at you, and I shouldn't have done that." Larkin looked at Quinn and sighed. "Let me tell you a story. When I lived in Sarasota, and I was looking for an artist to do my tattoos, the woman I found lived in Clearwater. She and her husband were both Scientologists."

"They were?"

"Mm. I didn't care, *tsé,* people can believe whatever they want, who am I to judge? But just after we started working together, her husband committed suicide. He shot himself in the head, and it turned out that all the money that was supposed to be used for the rent on the tattoo shop and their house had all gone to the church. All of it. Thousands upon thousands over the years. My artist was distraught. Not only did she lose her husband, but she was going to lose her home and her shop, and it was all because of Scientology."

But Quinn had stopped listening; he stopped because all his life, his Church training had told him exactly how to deal with someone disrespecting the Church. He simply looked through them and tuned them out, so even though he was looking at Larkin, he didn't actually see him.

Larkin went on, "So, we made an arrangement. I would pay the rent on the shop and the house to pay for the tattoos. She agreed and worked harder than anyone should to get them done to earn the rent. If I gave her money, I was afraid it would go to the church, so I just paid the rent myself. She eventually decided to try to sue the church, saying that they were responsible for her husband's death, but no lawyer would take it. When the church found out, they decided to sue her for defamation or some such nonsense. They had lawyers, but she didn't."

Quinn was still giving Larkin the infamous Scientology thousand-yard stare. He wasn't listening, but he let Larkin talk. That was the correct standard response. *Don't argue, don't try to reason with them, just let them talk. Let it all pass through. Don't take any of it in.*

"After the work was done," Larkin continued, "I went to her home to give her the rent for that month and found her sister there. Hmph. I hadn't known she had a sister, but it turned out the church considered her sister a Suppressive Person, so my tattoo artist hadn't seen her in years. My artist hung herself in the garage because she was going to lose everything to the church. She'd done it a few days before, and her sister had gathered everything from the house that was related to Scientology. Every book, every award, every medal, everything, and she was burning them out on the front lawn. I can't bear to see any book burnt, so I saved one or two. There's a copy of <u>Dianetics</u> on my bookshelf that was hers; there are notes in the margins and highlights on every page."

Just let him talk in one ear and out the other like it's nothing. Just be still and be in the moment, and don't let anything he says sink in or bother you.

Larkin looked at Quinn, his one eye intense, forcing Quinn to meet his gaze. "Quinn, my tattoos are the last pieces of artwork she ever created. She was an amazing artist, and when I die, her work will rot away forever. It will be as if she and her husband never existed. I saw the pain that Scientology caused her and her sister. And I saw the pain it caused your father to be away from you and your mother. I watched his heart splinter if he caught a glimpse of either of you, saw how it killed him to not know if either of you was safe or happy. I've seen that pain firsthand, and I cannot, will not, ever be a part of it. Do you know what I mean?"

Quinn nodded. "Yeah, I get it," he lied, and added, "Warren wanted me to get you to take a class, but I really want to help you. Honestly! I think it would help you a lot, and that's what I wanted." His eyes went wide; he looked away. "I wasn't supposed to say that."

Larkin snorted. "You may not have had that in your script, but it was honest. I know you wish to help, *mon cher ami,* but you can't, believe me. No one can."

They sat side by side quietly for some time. The only sound was Larkin's breathing as he smoked.

"Larkin?"

"Hm?"

"Are you still mad at me?"

"I was never mad at you. I'm just cranky."

"So, we're still friends?"

"Yes, if you want us to be."

"Of course, I do! You're the only friend I have outside the Church, you know that. I don't want us to stop being friends."

"I'm glad to hear that."

"Hey, can I try your cigarette?"

Larkin cocked an eyebrow. "*Pardone?*"

"Let me try your cigarette, please?"

"Why?"

"It's supposed to relax you, isn't it?"

"They say that, but I don't know that it does." He handed Quinn the cigarette, and Quinn took it awkwardly with his left hand. "Don't inhale too deeply," Larkin suggested.

The sudden jolt of pain and coughing that followed was more intense than Quinn would have believed. His throat hurt, his lungs burned, he coughed and coughed until his head was pounding and his nose was running. He blinked at Larkin through watering eyes.

"Not so relaxing the first time, is it?" Larkin was almost grinning.

"How do you do that?" Quinn sputtered around his choking; the coughing fit ended with him gagging. Horrible as it was, it was better than the panic attack that had now subsided.

"Been doing it forever. Come, let's go back in, and you can wash your face before Sandra comes back. Otherwise, she'll want to know why you're all red and puffy."

"My face is red and puffy?"

"If it wasn't before, it's more so now that you've tried to smoke." There was a slight smile on Larkin's face; even his one eye looked happy, and the sight made Quinn's heart soar.

Chapter Twenty-One

It was drizzling in the southwest where the Org was, but in the northeast, the rain hadn't started yet, although the dark grey, low-hanging clouds threatened.

It was cold, especially for early June, so Quinn had chosen to wear his favourite sweater over a blue T-shirt. Known around the Org as "*that* sweater," the solid, unbroken colour had been described as "bile green," "snot green," and "cow shit green" by various church members. It was Quinn's only possession that he genuinely loved. Not only was it soft and cozy, but he knew that no other staff member would bother to try and take it because of the revolting colour; no matter what, it was his and safe.

He yawned heavily as he forced limbs that seemed to weigh a thousand pounds to move. Getting off the bus at Edmonton Trail, he yawned again and waited for the streetlight to change. He was delighted to have managed to get to Larkin's shop just past 10:30 a.m.

He'd spent all night preparing flyers for the Org's upcoming promotion and membership drive at the Calgary Stampede in a month, basic Division 2 work. Division 2 was easier than Division 6A. While Division 2 would prepare flyers and other promotional materials, Division 6A would be responsible for actually handing out the flyers at Stampede, talking to the general public, and trying to talk them into signing up for a minor course.

Being posted to Div 6A was a nightmare for Quinn; promoting the Church in the face of overtly hostile rejections made his anxiety so much worse. He was certain his post would be changed to Division 6A to work the booth at the upcoming Stampede. He preferred working on the flyers, even if he didn't finish until 3 a.m.

He'd still been up at 5 a.m. sharp for his shift on the reception desk, a position he didn't like either, but at least he could divert most questions to other staff members. He'd only eaten part of his breakfast.

The discoloured eggs and grey oatmeal served at the dorm were even more bland than normal, something Quinn had not believed possible, so he'd only taken a few bites. That meant he'd arrived early for his morning shift.

The reception phone hadn't rung once that morning, so Quinn spent the time opening and sorting mail. Anything addressed to a particular staff member was opened and then set aside for the *HCO* (*Hubbard Communications Office*) to review, which meant Warren and Sharon.

The *HCO* was part of Division 1, responsible for security and ethics, and as such, it was their job to review all letters to staff to make sure they contained nothing negative towards the Church. Once the letters had been reviewed and censored, they would be passed out to the staff members to whom they'd been intended. If the letter was overtly hostile, it would be placed into the staff member's individual file as evidence of their possible connection to any *PTS* (*Potential Trouble Source*) or *SP* (*Suppressive Person*), and then filed. Most members would only see those letters as part of a Sec Check due to an ethics issue, at which point they'd be confronted with the never-before-seen evidence against them. Sharon especially seemed to take great pleasure in bringing out such letters and confronting staff with them. It didn't happen often, but when it did, she made sure everyone in the Org knew all about it, privacy be damned.

Quinn never bothered to read them. In fact, he had been encouraged by Barbara to do just that, as it would give him the ability to write a KR (*Knowledge Report*) about anything he found in them; even the most minor violation of Church policies was out of ethics and needed to be reported. If Quinn did it, it prevented Sharon from doing it, which was most likely what Barbara wanted. But Quinn never felt he was good enough to pass judgment on anyone else, as he probably had far more KRs written about him than by him. This was out of ethics as well, since writing KRs on other members was a requirement, but he had trouble doing it. So he just opened the envelope, logged it in the Excel tracker, and set it aside.

Then he'd made sure the flyers were all out on display and neatly organized, dusted bookshelves, cleaned the desk, sorted supplies, and generally kept busy, even though there really wasn't that much that needed doing. Known as *Dev-Ting* or *Developed Trafficing*, it entailed making himself look busy without anyone catching on that he really wasn't doing much. He just puddled around, looking like he was doing something important, until Barbara finally told him he could leave for his "special mission" at his "wog job" around 10 a.m.

"We expect to see more progress very soon, Quinn," Barbara had told him before he left. "We talked about this, remember? We need this. The Church needs this, don't forget the end phenomenon. Don't fail us."

Quinn had replied with the expected standard response: "Yes, sir. I won't fail, sir."

It had been a long morning, which he hadn't helped by nodding off a few times on the bus and almost missing the City Hall stop where he changed buses. Now, standing on the corner of Edmonton Trail and 16th Avenue, he stretched as he waited for the light to change and started to feel more awake. The thought of spending the afternoon in the shop with Larkin brightened his mood considerably and quickened his step as the light finally changed. He crossed 16th Avenue and then turned right towards Larkin's store.

The butterflies in his stomach appeared again as he got closer to the shop. His anxiety began nagging at him. *What if he's not there? What if Larkin had an accident? What if he tells you to leave?* He reminded himself that Larkin was his friend—his best friend, really— and if anything had happened, Sandra would have told him. At least, that's what he was trying to convince himself. As he got closer to the shop, his happiness finally outweighed his anxiety.

The bells on the door jingled merrily as Quinn opened it, and a broad smile spread across his face. He saw Sandra first; the tall woman had her back to him, a dark river of dreadlocks running down to her waist. Stretching up, she was rearranging a couple of the lamps on a high shelf. She glanced around at the sound of the bells.

"Hey, Sandra! How are you?"

"Hey! Fine, how're you doing?" Her voice, warm, deep, and rich, seemed to fill the shop. Quinn liked Sandra; she had a warmth about her that made him smile. He'd liked her from the moment he'd met her. She was upbeat and cheerful, but not in an overwhelming, *Theetie-Weetie* kind of way.

"Can't complain," he answered. "Where's Larkin?"

"In the back and in a mood." Sandra rolled her dark brown eyes. "Maybe you can cheer him up. I'm tired."

"*Chu pas de mauvaise humeur!*" A familiar voice came from behind the wall in the back room behind the counter. Quinn didn't have to know French to guess the meaning.

Sandra rolled her eyes again. "Sure, you're in a great mood," she muttered.

He felt his face breaking into a bigger smile as he headed back to find Larkin frowning at his computer. His rectangular gold wire-framed reading glasses perched precariously on the end of his straight nose.

Quinn noticed that he'd pulled his white hair more to the side than normal, so that both his eyes were visible for a change.

"No, you're not in a bad mood at all!" Quinn said with a grin. "What's up, Larkin? What's the matter?"

"*Bon matin, mon cher ami. Ça va?*"

The grin on Quinn's face grew wider. "Ok, I actually understood that one!"

"Bon!" Larkin said without looking up; Quinn thought he saw him smiling slightly behind his fingers. "And what's the reply?"

"Wait…I know this… *Pas mal?*"

"Très bien!" said Larkin. *"Très bien!* I may teach you Québécois yet! I'm just going to scan and save all these receipts…" Larkin turned in his chair and, for the first time, looked up at him. "Quinn, *mon ami,* exactly what are you wearing?"

"What? Oh, you mean this?" Quinn said in mock confusion as he pulled at the front of his sweater to look down at it. He felt the grin growing to the point that his cheeks were starting to hurt.

"Oui. Where on earth did you find a sweater in…that…colour?"

Quinn laughed. He was happy to have a break from the Org, and Larkin's attention pleased him even more; he felt completely relaxed. "Isn't it awful?" he asked brightly. "It was just so ugly I had to buy it! It was only two dollars and it's really warm, actually."

"It'd have to have some positive quality," Larkin replied with a snort. "It looks like you dipped it in pea soup…after you ate it and then threw it back up again!"

Quinn laughed harder and nodded in agreement. "So, what are you doing again?" He leaned against the door frame and casually crossed his ankles. He felt relaxed, far more than he had just a few minutes ago.

"I'm just scanning all these receipts and saving them to the clients' files," Larkin replied. "It's tedious. I avoid doing it, but I have too many, so I need to scan them to get rid of the hard copies."

"You keep files on all your clients? Everyone who comes in and buys something, do you have a file on them?"

"Non, mon ami, not to that extent. These are special clients, ones with black credit cards. They only come in when they want to pick up something I've found for them. They make requests, ask me to find a

particular piece, provide me with a budget, and I get paid a commission once I find it for them. Some of them have a running tab, so I have to keep every scrap of communication, every email. I make notes about every phone call, every receipt, everything. I have to keep track of it so there are no questions, no misunderstandings."

"I can help, if you want." Quinn leaned over Larkin's shoulder. "What do you want me to do?" His face was close to the top of Larkin's head, and he caught a whiff of his shampoo, a warm citrus scent. He inhaled, savouring it. The smell reminded him of the three days they had spent together after Elijah's funeral. He had a sudden urge to bury his face in Larkin's hair and wrap his arms around the albino's neck and shoulders in a hug, a flight of fancy he dismissed immediately.

"The scanning is the simple part, I can do that, but it's the renaming and filing that takes time. *Assieds-toi ici* and I'll show you." Larkin got up, and Quinn took his place in front of the computer; the chair was still warm. Quinn enjoyed the heat from Larkin's body that lingered against his back, buttocks, and the backs of his thighs. It felt good, almost cozy. He settled comfortably into the chair.

"Here," Larkin leaned over Quinn's right shoulder to take the mouse in his right hand. He moved the cursor across the computer screen while Quinn watched. "The scanned pages are here, in the G drive, but I scan a big pile at a time, so you'll have to look at each page in the PDF."

Quinn found himself distracted by the sound of Larkin's long hair brushing his shoulder. He was certain he could hear it, the whispering of white hair against the weave of the sweater. He could feel Larkin's left hand on the back of the chair, could feel the weight of it as Larkin used it to brace himself as he leaned over. He abruptly became aware of how shallowly he was breathing, the sound of his heart pounding in his ears, almost drowning out Larkin's voice.

"Now, the client files are here," continued Larkin. "They're all alphabetical by last name." He must have leaned in closer; his voice was almost a whisper in Quinn's right ear. He was so close that Quinn could hear the exhalation as he spoke, could feel his breath, the warmth of it against his cheek, his ear. He caught the scent of peppermint and wondered if Larkin was wearing some kind of cologne.

"When you pull the page out of the PDF and put it here in their *receipts* folder," Larkin went on, "you just rename it like this: 'Receipt,' then the date on the receipt—year, month, day—then a dash, then just a word or two about what it was. It doesn't need to be detailed, just 'chair' or 'table' or 'vase' will do. Then another dash, then their name, last name, comma, first name. *Comprends?*"

Quinn was holding his breath as Larkin leaned over him. He nodded, unable to speak.

"*Icitte,*" Larkin said, moving the mouse to open a file. "*Là, là,* you can see how I do it. Just follow the same pattern when you save the page."

Quinn's hands had suddenly become so cold they ached, while at the same moment, he felt a trickle of sweat crawling down his back. He desperately wanted to take the sweater off; it felt like it was constricting him, preventing him from drawing a full breath. Larkin's face was just centimetres from his own; if he turned his head, he could easily kiss his cheek.

He had a sudden picture in his head of doing just that—turning to Larkin and pressing his lips against the man's cheek—only to imagine Larkin turning his head and responding in kind, kissing Quinn's lips.

Wait...what?

"It's simple..." Larkin said, quietly, almost purring in Quinn's ear; Quinn's stomach jumped in response, butterflies appearing from nowhere.

Yes, turning around and kissing you would be simple, but....

"...but, it's repetitive. You can pull up YouTube or whatever to listen to music if you like," Larkin said, breathily. He reached over, leaning even closer to Quinn, and he pulled his black earbuds out from where they'd been tucked in beside the tower and handed them to the stunned man. *"Tiens, prends ça."* The smell of peppermint was even stronger and seemed to have been paired with old dust, but Quinn couldn't tell where it was coming from.

Quinn might have mumbled a "thank you" as he took the earbuds, but his mouth had gone so dry he wasn't sure if he'd spoken. There was a shock as the tips of Larkin's fingers brushed against his palm. Quinn stared at his hand, hyper-aware of where Larkin had touched him. "I'll scan more in for you, *mon ami. Merci beaucoup* for doing this for me," Larkin said as he straightened.

Quinn swallowed hard. "N...no...problem," he managed to spit out. He felt Larkin's hand on his shoulder, his long fingers gently squeezing his flesh. Even through the layers of clothes, Quinn's mind was focused entirely on the feeling of Larkin's hand on him.

"Would you like some tea, *mon ami?*"

"Hum...yeah, sure." As Larkin moved away, Quinn began to breathe heavily, panting after holding his breath so long. *What the hell was that?* The butterflies seemed determined to make his stomach jump into his throat. The image of Quinn turning his head and kissing Larkin's cheek sprang into his head again, as clearly as if he'd seen it himself, a third party watching from a distance.

Why the hell would I think of doing that? Why would I want to? Why did I freak out like that? Was it an anxiety attack? Panic attack? But this felt different than a panic attack; there hadn't been the urge to get away, to get out into the cool open air that Quinn normally felt. And yet, his heart had been pounding, his hands had gotten cold, and he hadn't been able to breathe. Quinn pulled the sweater off over his head. Trying to catch his breath, he tossed it roughly onto the floor near his feet.

So, what was it?

Chapter Twenty-Two

The image of Larkin responding to Quinn's kiss sprang into his head again, clear as water. *What am I thinking? It's wrong, perverted, disgusting for two men to be together! I'm disgusting to be thinking like that! What the hell is wrong with me? I must be sick, that's the only thing it can be. I'm sick. It's making me crazy. I can't be... I can't be.... I'll be stuck at the 1.1, one-one on the tone scale forever!*

This is so unethical! It's wrong, LRH said...it's perverted... Anyone who's gay is 1.1, "one-one", an overt...overtly hostile, out to destroy the church and everyone in it. Anyone who's one-faced is two-faced. They smile in your face and then stab you in the back. Sneaky, treacherous, liars, and manipulators.

But ...that's not me, is it? Obviously, I'm not out to destroy my own church! I'm not trying to destroy everyone! My friends, my mother! I don't say one thing to someone's face and then do the opposite when they're not there! That's not me at all. At least, I don't think it is.

As for being a pervert... Quinn found he couldn't finish the thought, having no idea how to. He certainly never thought of himself as perverted or an overt, even when he'd kissed…

Malcolm.

Quinn tried his best not to think about Malcolm. He had long since forcibly pushed the memories out of his mind, but now found them all coming back to him in a rush.

Malcolm.

He suppressed the pang of guilt, the feeling that filled his stomach and made him sick. Emotions bubbled up from nothing and seemed to strangle him, making it hard to swallow, hard to breathe.

It was happening again, those strong emotions he couldn't control, let alone stop, but this time it wasn't Malcolm, it was Larkin. And it was worse. He could feel it, feel the intensity starting to choke him. The butterflies, the shallow breathing, the sweating, the aching, itchy rash.

But why? What did I do to make this happen? I have overts that I've committed and haven't admitted to, is that it? I can't think of anyone who could be suppressing me. Is it Larkin? Am I being suppressed by him? No, there has to be something I've done, some wrong I've done.

This was part of church doctrine. If something bad happened to you, it was because of an "overt", a bad or incorrect action that hadn't been resolved. An overt act draws negative energy to you, causing bad things to happen to you. You pulled the bad thing in yourself. Alternatively, if someone in your life was against the church, they were a PTS, and being around them also drew negative energy to you. Either way, whether you did something wrong or were allowing someone else to be negative around you, it was your fault, and that meant you had to fix it.

No, that's not right, that can't be it. There was that one time when he talked about the lady who did his tattoos, but nothing since. Think! What have I done to pull this in? Even if it was true, even if I wanted to…wanted Larkin…what would he say? How do I know he wouldn't reject me? I don't even know if he likes guys! What am I saying? I mean, look at him, he's fantastic, and those eyes! Women must just throw themselves at him all the time!

"Is something wrong, *mon ami*?"

Quinn was jolted out of his thoughts. He looked up to find Larkin standing there, a full mug of tea in each hand, his white eyebrows furrowed in concern. His whiskey eyes were shadowed.

"No!" Quinn said, too quickly and too loudly. "No, it's fine! I just…I'm…I'm just tired, that's all."

"Ah! Didn't you sleep well last night?" Larkin asked as he set a plain dark blue mug near Quinn's hand.

"I slept fine, but I was up late working."

"Oh? What were you working on?" Larkin took a step back to lean against the counter, crossing his ankles as he brought the mug to his blush-pink lips.

His lips... Quinn looked away. "Preparing flyers to hand out. I was just writing out the text that Warren wants and dragging and dropping pictures into Word. Nothing too hard, but it's hard to get it to look nice. I'm kind of picky about it, so it takes time."

Feeling he was on familiar ground, he could talk about his work with the Church while he fought to calm himself and settle his stomach.

"Warren writes the text?" Larkin tilted his head, studying Quinn as he took a cautious sip of tea. He glanced down at his own mug, watching the steam curl up from the dark liquid.

Quinn ran the question through his mind to see if there was anything overtly hostile in either the comment or the tone before responding, but found nothing. Perhaps Larkin was just curious.

"Sharon actually does the first draft, but Warren, Barbara, and Tom all have to go over it as well; it's a regulation. Warren gets the final say, so all I really have to do is copy and paste it, check for spelling mistakes, add pictures, and figure out the layout. Sometimes there are bulletins from senior management or international management that have to be added without changing anything, not even a comma."

He felt better, more relaxed, as whatever had gripped him began to subside.

"*Verbatim*," said Larkin around another sip of tea, seemingly in response to nothing.

"Pardon?"

"There's a word for that, when you can't change anything. It's '*verbatim*', *en français* it's '*mot pour mot*'. When you're copying or relaying something exactly as written, without any change or deviation, you're copying or relaying it *'verbatim'.*"

"Oh! Yeah, I did clear that word, I guess I just forgot," said Quinn as he turned back to the computer.

Yes, he was feeling calmer now. His breathing felt normal again, and the butterflies were finally settling.

But what if I really did want Larkin, and if he felt the same way? What would I do? What would I do if I knew for sure…

"I'll scan a pile of receipts in for you, *mon ami,*" said Larkin. "Take your time with them; there's really no need to rush. I keep them for my own records and for taxes. This doesn't need to be done right away, and there are a lot of receipts, so feel free to take your time and take breaks. *Comme je te l'ai dit,* it's tedious, so feel free to take lots of breaks."

"Yeah, no, for sure." Quinn watched as Larkin turned his back to him to start gathering up a large pile of papers. *What would I do if Larkin wanted me? What am I saying? That's stupid! Why the hell would he want me? I'm not special, or even good-looking. There's no way. But, what if…*

'Mon ami'….that's what he calls me. 'Mon ami' means 'my friend', nothing more. 'Mon cher ami' is my dear friend, but still…my friend. Not my boyfriend, my friend. But, sometimes he just calls me 'cher' …' dear'.

Quinn watched as Larkin began piling the pages into the top feeder of the large scanner that stood on the far side of the room. He was standing with his weight on his left leg, while the right leg was bent slightly at the knee in a relaxed position, tilting his butt to the side. Quinn had a clear view of the right side of Larkin's face and noted that his expression was now brighter as his mood had improved.

He tried to recall how often Larkin's phone had gone off during their time together, but couldn't remember. It seemed that every time it had gone off, it was related to work, to the shop.

Does that mean no girlfriend is texting him? I've never heard him mention anyone, ever...so maybe there isn't anyone? And what if there isn't? What does that matter? We're both men! Even kissing him would be out of ethics, an overt act...perverted. It would just make bad things happen to me...and maybe to Larkin. LRH said so, didn't he?

I can't ...I just can't go through that again. Not again. I don't want anything bad to happen to Larkin. So why do I keep thinking about it? The imagined image of Larkin kissing him popped back into his head again. *What would that be like? What would Larkin's lips feel like? What the hell am I thinking?* He shook his head, trying to loosen the thoughts from his brain. *What would he taste like? Would he taste like Malcolm, or would he be more like Brittany? Something completely different? NO. How would it feel to have his tongue in my mouth?*

The thought of Larkin's tongue in his mouth caused a familiar but unwelcome feeling starting in his pants.

STOP THAT.

He thought he heard Larkin's voice, but he seemed far away and Quinn couldn't be sure what he was saying, or even if he was really hearing Larkin's voice at all. Was he asking a question?

What would it feel like if he started touching me...down there? JUST STOP THAT, RIGHT NOW. STOP IT! The feeling in his pants grew stronger. Quinn was grateful he was sitting, as it had already gone beyond his ability to hide it. He started biting his lower lip, hoping to use the pain to regain control of himself. *What do two men even do together? Malcolm said he knew... QUIT IT.* He shook his head again, but the thoughts refused to become unstuck.

"Quinn?"

What would two men do together? Besides oral and jerking each other off, that is.

"Quinn?"

What would it be like to be with Larkin? To sleep with Larkin? Not just any guy, but with Larkin.

He couldn't think of any other man at that moment; even Malcolm's face seemed to have vanished from his mind. There was only Larkin and his eyes.

"Quinn!"

Startled, Quinn jumped and looked up at Larkin standing right in front of him. The papers were gone from his hands; he was leaning on the desk, palms braced on the edge, looking straight into Quinn's face. His hard amber eyes were frowning but softer somehow.

"*Mon cher ami,* are you sure you're alright?" he asked.

"I'm fine!" Quinn said quickly, and again much too loudly. "Why?"

"Because you were just staring at nothing and didn't answer me when I spoke to you. You had an…odd…expression on your face as well."

"S-sorry! I…I didn't hear you, I guess. Sorry."

"*Cher,* why are you apologizing? Hm? What have you had to eat today?"

"Eggs and oatmeal," Quinn replied, careful to leave out the amount he'd actually eaten.

"An odd combination, *là.* Perhaps you haven't had enough? If you don't eat properly, it can affect your blood sugar and make you ill." He turned on his heel and headed to the fridge, despite Quinn's protests.

Quinn pulled his chair closer to the desk, trying to hide himself.

Please don't let me have to get up. Please don't let me have to get up. Please don't…

Going into the bathroom and jerking off would have been the quickest and easiest way to deal with it, but that was an overt act he'd have to confess as well. He didn't feel like incurring a fine for it, either. He'd been fined $15,000 when he'd been caught with Malcolm, a debt he was still decades away from paying off with his $20-per-week Org paycheque. Masturbation would tack on another $3,000-plus fine that Quinn also wouldn't be able to pay. All he could do was sit there and hope his distress would go unnoticed.

"Here."

He looked up to find Larkin holding out a bright green apple, a soft smile on his face. "Eat this, and drink your tea before it gets cold. And you're staying for dinner."

"I shouldn't—"

He hesitated before reaching out, but finally put his hand out after a moment. There was a flicker of anticipation, expecting Larkin's fingers to touch him again, but when Larkin placed the apple in his palm, the size of the fruit kept their hands from brushing.

Quinn was both relieved and disappointed as he set the apple on the desk.

"You're staying. No discussion. You're staying. What would you like?"

"Oh, anything's fine, whatever you want, Lark." Quinn knew it was better not to argue. Once Larkin's mind was set on something, there was no changing it.

"Do you like Vietnamese food? I know a good place we can order from."

"Vietnamese? I've never had it. Is it like Chinese?"

"A bit," said Larkin, still watching Quinn closely. "I find it lighter than Chinese. Chinese can sometimes be greasy, and Vietnamese isn't, *là*."

"Sure, that sounds great! I'll eat whatever you feel like, Larkin." He smiled, and the albino finally turned away, picked up his tablet and his tea, and headed over to the ugly couch to check his online auctions. He set the steaming mug on the arm of the couch, where it wobbled precariously before settling. He slipped off his sandals and pulled his feet up, bending his knees so that he was curled with the soles of his feet against the back of the couch.

Carefully sipping his own tea, Quinn turned his attention back to the computer and the pages Larkin had scanned. *Maybe if I concentrate on this stuff, it'll go away and I'll feel better.*

He put his earbuds in, found YouTube on the computer, and was surprised to see that Larkin was still logged in.

Curious about what Larkin watched online, he started poking through the history while sipping his tea. There were a lot of videos in French with titles Quinn couldn't decipher, but they looked like historical documentaries. There were also a lot of music videos, mostly by artists Quinn had never heard of.

Geez.

He became so interested in Larkin's history that his unwanted erection finally began to fade. *Finally.*

Eventually, Quinn picked a playlist at random and started working on the files. The list contained wildly different styles; it was jarring to be listening to folk music one moment and heavy metal the next, but he kept listening as he worked.

Quinn had his head down, concentrating on the files, when he felt Larkin's hand on his shoulder again. He jumped and pulled out the left earbud.

"*Chu désolé,*" Larkin said with a small smile. "I didn't mean to startle you, Quinn. I just wanted to check and see how you were doing."

"Fine!" Quinn replied hastily, the butterflies rising in his throat again. "It's going fine! You listen to a lot of different kinds of music, don't you, Larkin?"

"*Hein?* What do you mean?"

"Well, I was looking at your YouTube playlists. I think you've got everything on here!"

"My playlists?"

"Yeah, when I go into YouTube, it's your page and it has your playlists on it."

Larkin set his mug down and put his hand on the back of Quinn's chair, leaning over him again to look at the screen.

Quinn held his breath. *Not again, oh God. Please, not again.*

"Ah! I didn't think of that! I forgot that I was still logged in when you pulled up YouTube!" Larkin chuckled as he straightened up. "Not that it matters, *mon cher!*"

"Ummmm… I did sort of go through your history, Lark."

"*Peu importe, cher.* Go through whatever you like. My secrets keep themselves."

That sentence struck Quinn as odd, unusual enough that he turned and looked up at Larkin. The other man was meeting his gaze, an amused look in his eyes and a slight smile on his face. He must be joking. Quinn tried to laugh in response.

Larkin was still smiling as he glanced at the computer screen again. "Alannah Myles? I haven't listened to her in a while!"

"Who's Alannah Myles?"

"She's a Canadian singer I used to listen to all the time. *Mon Dieu,* I had such a huge crush on her when I was about nine or ten!" His chuckle threatened to become an actual laugh. "She's actually very good, has a good, strong voice. Oh, *tabarnak!* She had this long, dark curly hair and the most gorgeous legs! Killer smile! *Oui!* I had a real thing for her!"

"So…you really liked her, huh?"

Of course, he did. Why wouldn't he have a crush on a female singer when he was a kid? That's normal, isn't it?

"*Oui,* her, and Julie Masse, Luc De Larochellière, and the lead singer of Les BB!" Larkin outright laughed, remembering.

Quinn stared at him. It wasn't a loud or boisterous laugh, but it was filled with warmth and genuine happiness. It was so rare to hear Larkin laugh that Quinn couldn't help but stare.

"The fantasies of youth, *non?*"

"Julie who?"

"*Ici, je vais vous montrer,*" Larkin said, leaning over again to pick up a scrap of paper and write the names down. "If you put their names in the search bar on YouTube, I'm sure they'll all come up."

Larkin looked up as the bells jingled when the front door opened. He moved away from Quinn to go greet the customer.

Curious, Quinn started typing the names into Google instead; he wanted to see pictures.

Julie Masse… She's cute, I guess. Blond hair… I wouldn't have thought she was Larkin's type, though… bleached blonde! Geez! Les BB… odd name for a band… wait, the singer is a man! And this last one, Luc De Larochellière, another man…

That's two women…and two men.

So, wait, he's had crushes on both men and women? Does that mean he likes both? Is that possible?

His Org-taught knowledge of human sexuality had focused on homosexuality as perversion, while heterosexuality was "normal." He didn't even know the word for someone who liked both.

He glanced over at Larkin, who was showing the customer—an Asian man in his mid-forties—a large, oval-shaped, coloured Murano glass vase with a spiderweb pattern in dark chocolate. Quinn listened for a moment as Larkin explained why there was no serial number on the vase the customer could Google to check its value.

Google, of course! Why didn't I think of that?

After checking again to make sure Larkin wasn't looking, Quinn quickly went back to the Google homepage and typed: *"What do you call someone who is attracted to both men and women,"* and hit search.

The first response appeared in a neat little text box. Quinn read:

A literal dictionary definition of bisexuality, due to the prefix bi, is sexual or romantic attraction to two sexes (males and females), or to two genders (men and women). Pansexuality, however, composed with the prefix pan-, is the sexual attraction to a person of any sex or gender.

Beneath that, there was a link to a Wikipedia article, which Quinn didn't bother to follow. *Bisexuality…bisexual.* Now that he'd seen the word, he felt certain he'd heard it before, but couldn't remember where. The other word, pansexual, was unfamiliar to him.

Maybe it was from when I was clearing words, maybe it was in the dictionary. Bisexual. Is that what Larkin is? And if he is, then maybe… Maybe he wouldn't reject me if I told him…

Told him what, exactly? That I…like him? Do I want to be more than his friend? What am I thinking? He put both hands to his temples and squeezed, trying to force the thought from his head. He squeezed his eyes tightly closed in a childlike effort to regain control. *It can't be. This can't be happening again! They'll find out, Warren and Sharon, they'll find out. And Patricia! She'll definitely know! This is it, they'll expel me! Kick me out! They'll declare me! I'll be on the street! I'll never see Joni again!! And Larkin…*

What would they do to Larkin? Oh, God, not again! Please, I can't do it again, please not…

"Quinn?"

Quinn looked up and found Larkin watching him from the doorway. He moved closer and put his hand on Quinn's shoulder. "Quinn, *mon ami,* you've been acting very strangely since you got here. *Dis-moi ce qui ne va pas,* Quinn."

"Sorry," said Quinn with a sheepish smile.

"Tell me what's wrong."

"N...nothing's wrong, Larkin! Honestly!"

Larkin frowned, clearly not believing him. "All right." He turned away, nevertheless.

Oh, shit. I have to get it together. I have to snap out of this, I have to get past it, or he's going to start asking more questions. I have to… "Did the guy buy the vase?" *Maybe, if I talk about something else..*

"*Non,* he didn't, *c'est de valeur.* Quinn." Larkin had turned to go back into the front of the store.

Quinn found himself staring at Larkin's back. "Yeah?" he cautiously replied. His eyes began to wander without him realising it, until he was staring at Larkin's ass, nicely shaped and firm. Quinn kept trying to look away, but found he couldn't.

"Why don't you take a break for a bit? Go out the back and get some fresh air. Take a walk around the parking lot; it might make you feel better. And take your apple, maybe eating will help."

"Oh …sure. Thanks, Larkin." He wrenched his eyes away from Larkin's ass and slowly, shakily, got to his feet and looked down to see that his unwelcome erection had mercifully gone down enough that he could get up and walk. Grabbing the apple, he went outside the back door so that no one would see. He leaned on it as he closed it behind himself and exhaled in relief.

Chapter Twenty-Three

I don't know what that was, but it can't happen again. It can't. I can't let it happen again. I don't wanna lose…. Lose? Lose what? He couldn't finish the sentence; he didn't know how. He moved away from the back door to walk to the right of the bright green dumpster, past Larkin's ratty-looking white pickup truck.

He looked down at the apple Larkin had given him, bright, solid green with a hint of yellow near the base. The sky had brightened; the dark grey clouds were breaking up. A warm wind picked up and began to swirl between the buildings, catching Quinn's hair and pulling at his shirt. He took a bite of the apple as he leaned against the building.

Every apple Quinn had ever had in his life had always seemed the same: deeply red, mushy but dry, with a bland, vaguely sweet taste that was tolerable but not especially enjoyable. This was hard, crisp, and deliciously tangy. It was so juicy that Quinn found himself wiping the juice out of his beard.

My God! How is this so different? Where does Larkin even get this stuff? It's like I've never had an apple before in my whole life.

He stared at it, at the bite he'd taken out, admiring the perfectly gleaming white flesh. *Wow.* He took another bite, and his mind wandered again, slipped back into what felt like a lifetime ago.

Malcolm.

He had noticed the tall, dark boy at Church events immediately, as both he and Brittany were the only ones there close to Quinn's own age. Malcolm had a deep, husky, warm voice that Quinn enjoyed listening to. Dark skin tone, closely cut hair through which his scalp sometimes shone, and a warm smile. Quinn had made a point of working with both Malcolm and Brittany at every event, something Warren and Sharon were happy to agree to, deciding that three good-looking young people, happily chatting and laughing as they worked, were exactly the right look for the Church. They were exactly what was needed to draw in new blood.

Their parents were public Scientologists, so they weren't on staff and didn't live on Church-owned property. Malcolm and Brittany even went to high school, coming to the Org at night to work into the small hours and on weekends.

High school.

Quinn had never attended anything but Church-run classes, so he would pester his new friends with questions about school. What did they learn about? What food was served in the cafeteria? What were the teachers like? Was it true that schools had security guards with guns? And that both teachers and guards were beaten by the principals?

Malcolm had actually laughed at that, while Brittany snickered, and Quinn had looked at them both, horrified. On and on, Quinn's questions seemed to never end, much to his friends' amusement, and their patience seemed limitless.

Quinn adored them both, but every time he thought of Malcolm, he would get excited—excited to see him, to talk to him, excited just to be around him—his stomach quivering with butterflies. He adored Brittany, too, loved talking to her and being around her, but Malcolm was different. He considered Malcolm to be his very best friend, his confidant. With Malcolm, Quinn felt he could say anything without fear of a KR. It was only when he was around Malcolm that he felt confident, capable, and happy, like he could do anything as long as Malcolm stood by his side.

Perhaps inevitably, Sharon decided that the three should be posted to Division 6A.

"The three of you radiate so much raw theta," Sharon told them, "that the best possible thing for the raw general public is to see the three of you. Real, active Scientologists working to Clear the planet. The three of you together are so powerful, they'll line up for courses!"

Malcolm and Brittany were beaming; it was a huge compliment. Quinn just wanted to crawl into a hole. He hung his head, trying to hide behind his unkempt curly hair.

It was the first day of handing out flyers and selling copies of *The Way to Happiness* after the massive 2013 flood that had destroyed much of the downtown core. They were posted near Inglewood, their targets the city workers and members of the Calgary Highlanders who were assisting with flood relief and clean-up of the seemingly endless mud and debris left behind by the overflowing Bow River.

Quinn found himself stammering and stuttering whenever he tried to speak, his hands shaking so badly the flyers ruffled in his grip. More than one wog had asked if he was okay, if he needed medical help, to which Quinn could only stammer, "I…I...I'm...fine."

When Malcolm saw how badly Quinn was sweating and how his hands shook, he made it a point to stand right beside him and take the lead.

It wasn't until they got back to the dorm and Quinn stood watching himself vomit that Malcolm began to pester him about what was wrong. It was Malcolm who finally got Quinn to admit to suffering from anxiety and terrible panic attacks, something he didn't talk to anyone about but Patricia, the auditor.

"Don't worry about it," Malcolm had told him. "If you get somebody really snarky, I'll handle them. Just fake it, smile, and nod. I'll be there with you, so don't worry."

And he had. Malcolm had stayed near Quinn the entire time, leaving Brittany to flirt with the male city workers and the Highlanders to get them to take flyers, while Malcolm and Quinn handled everyone else.

"Sorry, not into cults," or "Yeah, no," were the more polite responses, while the word *"CULT"* was yelled or screamed at them more than once. Every time that particular word was thrown at them,

Quinn would visibly flinch, as if it had physically struck him across the face. The rash under his arms was weeping constantly and was both itchy and painful.

In dealing with the raw public, Malcolm was Quinn's complete opposite. His warm smile, his ease at speaking to strangers—even in the face of overtly hostile rejection—were a constant source of amazement for Quinn. Malcolm's ease relaxed him and made it a little easier, but it still didn't stop Quinn from throwing up every night for the entire time they were working the flood line.

They were in the bookstore alone together, metres from where Mark was manning the reception desk, when they were finally able to speak about it. Their voices were hushed as they took all the books off the shelves to dust and restock.

"I don't know what to do," Quinn whispered to Malcolm, glancing over his left shoulder to see if anyone was listening. "I can't seem to get over it, and even though I've never missed an auditing session, they can't seem to find the engram that started the damn thing. I haven't had a real case gain in, I don't know how long."

The rash began to itch, and Quinn had to scratch his right armpit. It hurt to scratch and made it weep sticky, clear liquid, but the itch was too painful to ignore.

"Can't you just tell them you don't want to do Div 6?"

Quinn snorted. "That would probably guarantee that I'll be there forever. I think they figure if they keep forcing me into it, I'll get over it, but..." He glanced over his left shoulder again to make sure Mark wasn't listening. Malcolm did the same, both of them needing reassurance that their hushed conversation wasn't being overheard.

"Nothing makes it better," Quinn continued. "I think the more they put me in Div 6, the worse I get. It's because of an overt or an SP in my past or in a past life or something. Maybe there's a bunch of locks I haven't gotten through yet..."

This was the standard response, but Quinn couldn't keep the sadness out of his voice. He resisted the urge to scratch again; now his left armpit was itching badly enough that it hurt.

"Yeah, that's what they say. I don't think it works that way, though. I know someone at school who has anxiety. It's nothing she can control; she even takes medication for it."

"But she's a wog, right?" Quinn whispered back. "She wouldn't know. Don't they make kids take psych drugs and stuff at a wog school, anyway? She'd get better if she were on the Bridge, getting audited."

"No one forces you to take drugs in high school! Besides, auditing hasn't worked for you, has it?"

Quinn hesitated before answering. Auditing not working? The thought alone was ridiculous, outrageous. Blasphemy!

"I haven't done enough, I guess, or I'm not going deep enough, but I can't seem to find the time to schedule more. I just don't understand why it's getting worse. I have to be doing something wrong. It's me, I mean, it has to be, right? I'm fucking up somehow."

"Maybe auditing alone doesn't work for everything. Maybe you need something else as well, touch assists or something?"

"Touch assists are for an injury or an illness."

"What do you think anxiety is? It's a kind of illness. Maybe you need to get reconnected to your nerves or something, then maybe you'll start to feel less nervous. You should tell Barbara about it, maybe a locational assist…that might work."

Barbara had decided it was a fantastic idea and suggested that Malcolm himself perform the locational assists on Quinn. Since the Calgary Org was so small, it wasn't uncommon for people on the Bridge to help each other this way.

It required Malcolm to write a Completed Staff Work report (CSW) that Barbara first reviewed and approved, then submitted to Warren for final approval. The detailed report had to clearly state what the problem was, why Malcolm's suggested course of action was the best solution, and what the inevitable positive outcome or case gain would be. Failure was not allowed.

Malcolm was slightly higher on the Bridge than Quinn, so the idea of him performing the procedure wasn't unusual. At first, he performed the touch assists on Quinn in the Org's study rooms before having the idea that getting out into the fresh air might help even more. Another CSW was written, and this plan was, surprisingly, approved by both Barbara and Warren immediately.

They'd spent days together, walking around the still recovering city, marvelling at the mass destruction, Malcolm guiding Quinn by having him look at different objects and focus on them, concentrating on each object until he could block out everything else. Malcolm then used touch assists on Quinn's arms, trying to get the rash to calm down.

It worked at first, perhaps because Quinn felt relaxed around Malcolm anyway. Malcolm varied it by performing other touch assists as well, touching Quinn's head, arms, and legs with the tip of his index finger while Quinn focused on the point of contact and on his nervous system.

Then Malcolm decided to take Quinn to his place to work on it, and since Malcolm's parents were public Scientologists, this wasn't an issue. Yet another CSW later, and this, too, was allowed.

Malcolm's parents lived in a small condo on the fourth floor of a six-storey building in the northeast neighbourhood of Taradale, overlooking Stoney Trail, the Ring Road.

"Sorry it's so bare, my parents would rather put their money into the Church than a bunch of havingness stuff," he unnecessarily apologised.

The condo itself was painted a light beige throughout. The living room featured two old couches that looked like hand-me-downs. A large TV perched on an espresso-brown stand with glass doors. The other prominent feature in the living room was black bookshelves groaning under the weight of countless Scientology books.

The beige kitchen was perfectly clean, the fridge packed with food, which Quinn saw when Malcolm offered him a pop. Malcolm's beige room featured a double bed and a simple desk with his computer sitting prominently on top. The double bed had its right side pressed against the wall and was neatly made, with a soft mattress, clean blue sheets, and a blue striped comforter.

Neat, clean, a fridge full of food, a TV, and a computer—it was like everything Quinn had ever wanted had been put into one place.

"Have a seat," Malcolm told him as they went into his room, indicating the bed. Quinn sat stiffly on the edge.

"I'm going to try something else," Malcolm continued. "It's kind of like a locational assist; my friend from school who has anxiety told me about it. I thought it would help you when you're panicking."

"Ok, if you think it'll help."

Malcolm sat down in his desk chair and pulled it closer, so that he was right in front of Quinn. "Now, concentrate, and tell me about five things you see."

"You mean in here?"

"Yeah, any five things. Instead of focusing on one item, like in a locational assist, you focus on five."

"Umm…ok. I see you sitting, I see your computer, your desk, your blue curtains…um…the carpet?"

"That's good. Now, tell me five things you can hear."

"Really?"

"Yeah, you'll have to concentrate on the sounds. Like when we do a locational assist, you concentrate on the thing in front of you; now you're concentrating on the sounds. Close your eyes, if it helps."

"Oh-kay…"

Quinn closed his eyes, but at first, he had trouble hearing anything. It seemed the room was insulated, isolated from all sound, as if it were a world apart, existing on its own plane and on its own terms. Eventually, Quinn began to pick up small sounds he hadn't noticed before.

"I hear your reading lamp…it's…buzzing?"

"Good! Yeah, it does that, it's the filament in the bulb, I think. It's annoying as hell, and I can't get it to stop. I've had to slap it to make it stop. I hate that noise when I'm trying to read!" He laughed, a warm, rich, throaty sound. "What else?"

"You slap your light?"

"Yeah, I just get pissed off at it, and I slap the shade to make it stop. What else can you hear?"

"There's a…motor…I think?"

"That's the air conditioning for the building. That's really good, you've got two."

"You moved and your chair squeaked."

"How did you know I moved?"

"I heard your clothes against the chair, I heard you shift."

"That's four—the squeak and the fabric moving. Good! Just one more."

Quinn squeezed his eyes tighter, trying to hear anything else, but the only thing he could hear was his heartbeat in his ears.

"Nothing, I've got nothing. I can't hear anything else. Flunk." Quinn sighed.

"No, no flunk. It's not a flunk kind of exercise; you don't need to start over. Now, keep your eyes closed, and tell me five things you feel."

"Things I feel?"

"Yeah, it could be the mattress you're sitting on, the carpet under your feet, anything." His voice sounded closer, as if he had leaned forward in his chair towards Quinn. It was hushed and breathy, not quite a whisper.

"Hum...ok. I feel the mattress I'm sitting on."

"Right."

"I feel...itchy."

Without opening his eyes, Quinn reached up with his hand to scratch at the back of his neck where the collar of his second-hand green camo t-shirt brushed against his skin.

"What about your rash?"

"It's not itchy, although it hurts a bit. It's still sticky, though."

"Good. What else?"

Malcolm sounded even closer now, as if his face was centimetres away from Quinn's. His voice was just a whisper. Quinn wanted to open his eyes, but doing so would be an automatic flunk, and he was sure they'd have to start over again, despite what Malcolm had said.

"Hum... I don't know."

Quinn squeezed his eyes even more tightly closed, both to keep them from opening and to identify what he could physically feel. He was going to say something about feeling the comforter under his hands when he felt something press against his lips unexpectedly. It was soft and firm at the same time, like warm flesh, and it pressed harder against him.

Quinn's eyes shot open to find Malcolm's face filling his view, Malcolm's lips pressed against his own. Quinn jumped and backpedalled until his back was pressed against the wall, the width of the bed between them.

"W…what are you doing?" he gasped.

"Something I've wanted to do for ages," said Malcolm with a smile. He licked his lips.

Chapter Twenty-Four

"B...but...it's..." Quinn stammered.

"Perverted? That's what the Church says." Malcolm countered.

"And L. Ron!"

"Yeah, yeah, I've read it. I've heard it. Do you have any idea how many people outside the Church say the exact opposite?"

"But those are wogs!" Quinn wailed. "What do they know?" *Is he actually questioning The Source? LRH himself?* This was tantamount to high treason, and the severity of the punishment was unthinkable! Quinn's intestines were ice. He felt sick; his hands had suddenly gone so cold they ached. The air seemed to vanish from the room.

"How? How can you...Say that?"

Malcolm smirked. "Sometimes I think wogs know more than we do. Look, Quinn, I like you. I mean, I really like you, and I've been wanting to kiss you for ages. Everyone—and I mean everyone—I've talked to at school says it's not perverted, that there's nothing wrong with me liking you."

"Well...I don't care what they say! You need to get your ethics back in! It's wrong. You're sick, Malcolm." Quinn broke out in a cold sweat.

"No, I'm not sick. Tell me this... Did it feel good when I kissed you?"

Quinn opened his mouth to say *no*, but Malcolm held up a hand, stopping him.

"No, don't. Don't just feed me what the Church or L. Ron says. Tell me, did it feel good to you? You, Quinn. How did it feel to you? Was it real for you?"

Quinn wasn't sure how he felt. He'd been so startled he hadn't even considered whether it felt good or not; Malcolm's comment about LRH had driven every other thought from his mind.

"It felt good to me," Malcolm said. "It felt as good as I thought it would."

Quinn stared at him as if he were an alien. Malcolm got up from the chair and sat on the edge of the bed, closer. Quinn pulled his knees up until they were level with his shoulders, trying to make himself smaller.

"Well?" Malcolm prodded.

"Well…I…don't…hmm…"

"You're not sure?" Malcolm asked.

Quinn shook his head.

"Why don't we try again, maybe for longer, and see if you like it?"

Quinn started to protest, but Malcolm raised his hand again.

"If you decide you don't like it, I'll never do it or mention it again. But if you decide you like it, then…"

"Then what?"

"Then maybe LRH wasn't right about everything."

Quinn was horrified. "You can't say that! You can't question the Source material like that! Malcolm, you'd be declared if anyone heard you! Rejected by the Church and everyone in it! This is so wrong."

"I know I shouldn't. Are you going to write a KR on me, Quinn? Hmm? Do you know, one of my friends at school is Catholic, and do you know what she told me? She said someone can still be a good Catholic and disagree with the Pope. When has anyone ever said we can disagree with LRH?"

Quinn said nothing; they both knew the answer. Malcolm slid across the bed, and Quinn didn't move. He felt frozen, his blue eyes locked on Malcolm's dark brown ones.

"Maybe, just maybe, L. Ron was wrong about this," Malcolm went on. "You'll never know unless you try, Quinn. Let me kiss you again and see if you like it. If not, I'll stop, and it'll never happen again."

Quinn swallowed hard. His tongue felt thick, too big for his mouth. His heart pounded in his ears. All he could do was watch Malcolm move closer, while every part of him wanted to melt into the wall. He closed his eyes as Malcolm leaned in.

It felt like an eternity before Malcolm's lips touched his—warm and soft. Quinn's heart skipped at that first contact of flesh. Pressure, then a lightening, then pressure again as Malcolm pressed his mouth to his. Malcolm's lips began to move, opening and closing slightly as he kept kissing him slowly, deliberately.

The feel of lips against his own sent goosebumps racing over Quinn's skin. Heat crept up his face; he knew he was blushing. When Malcolm finally pulled away, Quinn opened his eyes a sliver and licked his lips. There was a sweet, tangy taste he couldn't name. He exhaled in a small pant; he hadn't realized he'd been holding his breath. Malcolm smiled.

"You can't tell me that wasn't nice," he whispered, leaning in again before Quinn could answer.

Quinn's mouth softened. Moving closer, he kissed Malcolm back. The goosebumps multiplied, a shock running through his whole body. Leaning towards Malcolm, he let each kiss grow deeper until Malcolm pulled away.

"See?" he whispered. "I knew you'd like it."

"It…feels…nice," Quinn said cautiously. "But…"

"But nothing." Malcolm kissed him again.

Moments later, they were lying on the bed, arms wrapped around each other, mouths welded together. Warmth spread through Quinn with every kiss; the tension bled out of his body as a need he'd never felt before overwhelmed him.

They clung to each other. With mouths open, they tasted each other's breath. Malcolm lifted his shirt, and his hand ran along Quinn's waist. Quinn's body answered with a familiar but unexpected response, starting to harden at Malcolm's touch.

Just then, the sound of the front door being unlocked and opened jolted them, followed by the cheery "hello!" of Malcolm's mother.

Malcolm swore under his breath as he broke away from Quinn and pulled back. Quinn sat up, staring at the closed door in horror.

Malcolm hurried over, opened it a crack, and called out, "I'm in my room with Quinn, Mom! We're working on touch assists."

That's kind of true, Quinn thought, but fear attacked him. *She'll know,* he decided. *No, she can't come in! She'll know!* Sweat beads grew on his forehead, and his hands were cold.

"Ok, I'm just dropping off some stuff and then going to the Org. Do the two of you want anything to eat?"

Oh, God, she's going to catch us! On the edge of hyperventilating, quick, shallow breaths filled his lungs, his hands ice. *We're dead! They'll send us to Ethics! They'll throw us in the hole! We'll be declared and tossed out of the church! Everyone we know will disconnect from us forever!*

"We're fine!" Malcolm answered his mother.

How the hell does he sound so calm? As if nothing is going on. Just as if he hadn't said what he said about LRH, just...normal. How can he lie so easily?

"Ok, there's frozen pizza in the fridge freezer, if you want it."

"Ok, thanks, Mom. We'll have one later." Malcolm closed the door and looked back at Quinn. He walked to the bed. "It's ok," he whispered to the panicked boy. "She most likely won't come in, and if she does, we're still working on touch assists, ok?"

"While l-laying down?" Quinn shot back in a frantic whisper. He swore to himself as the terror made him stutter. "She'll write a K-K-K...K-KR on us!"

"No, she won't! Just sit on the edge of the bed like you were."

"She's g-going to c-c-c-catch us!" Quinn whisper-moaned. Now beyond terrified, he slid over to sit on the edge of the bed, stomach roiling.

"No, she's not. Besides, it's worth the risk to kiss you." Malcolm leaned in for a kiss, but Quinn pulled away.

"You want to get c-caught?" he demanded in a hush. "Are you c-crazy?"

"No, but I can't help it, I like you so much. Besides,"—he leaned in again, putting his lips closer to Quinn's ear— "it's a thrill, isn't it? Knowing we could get caught?"

"You are crazy."

"Oh, come on! Don't you feel that...rush? Don't you feel excited? Don't you want to see how much we can get away with?"

"Not really, n-no, I don't want to end up in the h-h-hole. Thanks."

"You can't tell me you don't feel that excitement, the thrill of knowing she could walk in the door..." Malcolm took his shoulders and pushed him back onto the mattress. Standing over him, he planted his lips on his. Quinn tried to push him away, but Malcolm's tongue slid into his mouth. Quinn was horrified, shocked by the warm, wet, slithering thing. But as Malcolm's tongue explored his mouth, the same sweet, tangy taste as before relaxed him. His body responded with a rush of blood and adrenaline, making him rigid in seconds.

“I’m going now!” called Malcolm’s mother.

“Ok, Mom! Enjoy your course tonight!” Malcolm called back, pulling away slightly. His hands were still on Quinn’s shoulders, his gaze locked on Quinn’s. Quinn panted, staring back with wide, frightened eyes. They both heard the front door shut and lock as Malcolm’s mother left.

“I knew you felt the same,” Malcolm said, bending down to thrust his tongue into Quinn’s mouth again. Quinn went limp with relief. He willingly opened his mouth and wrapped his hands around Malcolm’s ribs, pulling him closer. Malcolm’s tongue explored Quinn’s back teeth as he moved closer, lying down on Quinn’s prone body. His hand slid beneath Quinn’s shirt, stroking his ribs and waist. Quinn’s body responded; his already hard cock grew even harder.

Malcolm pulled back and looked down at him, smiling. “I knew you’d like it. I knew you felt the same.”

“I’m n-not sure…”

“I am. You’re hard, I can feel it.”

Quinn glanced down and realized Malcolm’s thigh was pressing against his erection.

“That’s just ‘cause…”

“Don’t say it’s because you were scared. You like this.”

“M…maybe…” He couldn’t refuse to answer. It was too ingrained in him to admit everything; even though Malcolm wasn’t an auditor, the idea of lying never even occurred to him.

Malcolm smiled. “I knew you would.” He started to rub Quinn’s penis through his pants.

“No!” Feeling heat creep into his face, Quinn looked away. “Don’t.”

“How are you going to get rid of it, then? Hm?”

"I…I'll…take care…of it."

"You know as well as I do you'll get in trouble for it if they find out, so why not let me take care of it for you?" He leaned down on Quinn's body again, his face and lips brushing Quinn's cheek while his feet stayed on the floor.

Quinn was sure he whispered "no," but Malcolm either didn't hear him or ignored him. He rubbed harder through Quinn's pants, making Quinn moan. Quinn looked down in time to see Malcolm pull down his zipper. Malcolm was still smiling, eyes on Quinn's face, as he reached inside, wrapped his fingers around Quinn's penis, and began jerking him off.

Quinn gasped, the feeling far more intense than anything he'd ever experienced. He groaned and looked at Malcolm, who leaned closer to Quinn's right ear.

"I know Brittany did this to you," he whispered.

Quinn's eyes widened. *How?*

"She told me. She told me she has an intense affinity for you, wants to have you inside her, wants your babies inside her. I know she wants you, but I want you too. Brittany can have babies with anybody, but I need you. I don't give a fuck about the risk, I want you." His hand moved rapidly. Quinn writhed beneath his touch. Wave after wave of pleasure rolled through him, heightened by the adrenaline from his fear. He groaned heavily as he climaxed, the terror washed away in a rush of release.

Malcolm pulled his hand out of Quinn's underwear, covered in semen. He smiled, got up, and walked out of the bedroom.

Quinn stared at the doorway, breathless, suddenly worried this was some kind of trick, that Malcolm wouldn't come back. He exhaled in relief when Malcolm reappeared in the doorway with a roll of toilet paper in his hand.

"Here." He handed the roll to Quinn. "You should probably clean up before it stains."

Quinn hadn't even considered the stains. As he frantically wiped himself, fear rushed back. "What happens if they see the stain while doing the laundry?" he almost wailed. *We're in so much trouble, we're going to be in so much trouble, we're going to be…*

"Don't worry about it. How many times have you gotten your laundry back and it's not yours? If they notice, just say it's not yours."

Quinn looked up at Malcolm's smiling, confident face and felt himself relax again. He started to look away, only to be stopped by the sight of the bulge in Malcolm's pants. He looked back up, slightly shocked, to find Malcolm grinning.

"I think I need you to…take care of that for me," he said.

"How?" *What a stupid question.*

Malcolm laughed. "The same way I did for you, what else?" He undid his jeans and pushed them, and his underwear, down to his ankles.

Quinn stared, never having seen Malcolm's penis before. It was circumcised, thick, and curved slightly downward, springing from a dark, tangled nest of pubic hair. The tip was a darker shade than the rest of the flesh.

Malcolm bent to take his jeans and shorts completely off, then moved to lie down on the bed to Quinn's right. Quinn kept staring.

He tossed the used tissue onto the floor and reached out. Quinn hesitated before touching him.

"It doesn't bite," Malcolm teased, propping himself up on his elbows to watch.

Quinn swallowed hard and finally wrapped his fingers around the shaft. Malcolm exhaled heavily as Quinn moved his hand slowly up and down, eyes riveted to Malcolm's face as the sensation took hold. Malcolm closed his eyes and tilted his head back, giving in to the pleasure, biting his lip.

"Yeah," he whispered breathily, "faster, please. Faster."

Quinn obeyed, his hand moving more quickly as Malcolm groaned.

"Oh, yeah…yeah…Quinn…you don't know how much I've wanted this. Wanted you." He spoke through his teeth.

"Really?" Starting to tire, Quinn shifted his grip, fingers sliding down the length of the shaft so the head kept hitting the middle of his palm. As his hand kept moving, he felt the tip grow wet. *What the hell is that?*

"I've wanted you almost since we met," panted Malcolm.

Quinn watched colour flood Malcolm's face as he panted and grunted. Malcolm's eyes met his, and he smiled, a huge, happy grin.

I'm doing this. I'm…pleasing him… I think I am, anyway. "So…you're happy?" Quinn asked cautiously. He switched his grip back to the side, wrapping his fingers around the shaft again.

"Oh, God…yeah!" Malcolm moaned. "You always…make me happy, Quinn. You're all I think about…you're the reason I keep…going to the Org. It's the…only way I can see you."

"Me? You come to see me?"

"Because…I…want…you. I'm going to…" He couldn't finish. Quinn felt Malcolm's penis grow hot, almost fevered, before Malcolm climaxed and ejaculated over Quinn's hand. Malcolm fell back, panting, while Quinn stared at the white fluid. He'd seen his own semen, but had never really thought another man's would look the same. He didn't know why that surprised him.

Grabbing the toilet paper roll from the floor, he cleaned his hands. He glanced over and saw it had gotten all over Malcolm's stomach as well. Quinn pulled off another handful of tissue and began wiping Malcolm's stomach. Malcolm started to chuckle.

"I could have done that, you know."

"Oh, sorry."

"Doesn't matter. It feels nice, you doing it."

Malcolm sat up, reached for the back of Quinn's head, and pulled him in. Quinn grunted in confusion as Malcolm kissed him again, deeply, his tongue sliding into Quinn's mouth.

Quinn kissed him back, suddenly wanting to put his own tongue in Malcolm's mouth. He hesitated. Malcolm opened wider, inviting. Quinn found himself probing Malcolm's mouth, feeling his teeth, rubbing his tongue against Malcolm's. Malcolm responded in kind, their tongues caressing each other. Fear was a distant memory now, pushed aside by Malcolm's touch and Quinn's eager response.

By the time he finally pulled away, Quinn felt dazed. Malcolm gathered the used toilet paper and left the room. The toilet flushed a moment later, and Malcolm came back in. His penis was flaccid now, but Quinn still found himself staring as Malcolm climbed back into bed beside him.

Malcolm wrapped his arms around Quinn's shoulders and pulled him close, hugging him tightly. He kissed the top of Quinn's head. "I've wanted this for so long. I've daydreamed about it. I've dreamed about it at night. I've even masturbated more than once, imagining you touching me."

"Really?"

"Yep."

Quinn pulled back slightly so he could see Malcolm's face. "Was it…as good as you thought it would be?"

"Better."

Quinn smiled.

Malcolm pulled him closer. Quinn snuggled into his shoulder. Just being there with Malcolm, he felt safe, as if the Org and the outside world didn't exist.

"I didn't know it would feel like this," he whispered in Malcolm's ear. "I didn't think it would feel this good."

"I know. I don't understand why the Church is so against it. We're not hurting anyone, we're just…making each other happy. You are happy, aren't you?"

"Actually…yeah, I think I am. I didn't think I would be, but I feel happier than I have since…I don't know when," Quinn sighed.

"Same here. You make me happy. I'm always happy when I see you. I wish we could spend the night here."

"Hmm, that would be nice. No early morning wake up…"

"…No bed checks, no building demolition at three in the morning…"

"…No terrible food."

"Yeah. We could just be together. That won't happen, though, as long as we're in the Church." Malcolm frowned.

"Don't." Quinn suddenly felt sad. "Don't talk about it. I don't want to think about it."

"All right," Malcolm whispered in his ear. "I won't… But I want you to do something for me instead."

"What's that?"

"Open your mouth again."

Chapter Twenty-Five

The following weeks were filled with both terror and excitement. Malcolm took to ambushing Quinn as often as he could—quick stolen caresses, private moments in supply closets, passionate kisses that led to desperate rubbing that left them both breathless. Whenever footsteps approached, they snatched up brooms and swept as if nothing had happened at all.

Much to his dismay, Quinn found he liked it. The excitement. The constant threat of being caught. He would meet Malcolm's eyes across a room and feel a slow, knowing smile bloom across his face. Malcolm always smiled back, quickly looking away so no one would notice. But the kissing—*the kissing was amazing.* The more they kissed, the more Quinn wanted it, the wanting growing hotter and harder to deny.

Nights were restless. He lay awake thinking of Malcolm, his body screaming and aching, every nerve sharpened with hunger for Malcolm's touch. When sleep came, Malcolm followed him there: dreams of them standing together somewhere quiet and open, naked, pressed flush together, mouths exploring, cocks hard and needy. Beyond that, though, his imagination stalled—he didn't actually know what two men did together, how sex between them even worked.

Malcolm taught Quinn how to trick the e-metre, something Quinn hadn't even realized was possible.

"Patricia always uses the same machine," Malcolm said. "The can on the right—the one with the nick in the rim? Loosen your grip on that one. Hold it as lightly as you can without dropping it. And keep your hand near the bottom of the left can. I don't know why it works, but it does. Keeps the needle floating perfectly—like you're not reacting to anything. But you have to be precise. Bottom of the can, Quinn. If you don't do that part, nothing works."

"Got it."

"Quinn, you have to get this right. If they catch even a hint of what we're doing—"

"You don't need to tell me," Quinn blurted. "I know."

"Do you? You'll have to lie—it'll have to be a missed withhold."

"I *know, I know!*"

"You've told me you've never lied in session," Malcolm pressed. "Even though everyone else probably does. They're walking around with missed withholds piled high."

"Everyone doesn't lie," Quinn protested weakly. "But…I get it. I don't want to get caught."

"Then keep your cool during your auditing sessions, and we won't."

Auditing nights were agony. Quinn would lie awake beforehand, stomach twisting, acid burning his throat, exhaustion tangled tightly in his gut. Panic kept him restless even before sleep arrived.

His saving grace was the scarcity of auditing itself. No one was audited often—Patricia was the only auditor for all of Alberta, splitting her time between Calgary and Edmonton. Sessions were booked months apart. Staff schedules rarely allowed for long intensives anyway. You couldn't progress up the Bridge without them, but the delays bought Quinn weeks of fragile reprieve from his worst fear.

Warren, Sharon, and Tom had all gone Clear—and into OT levels. Everyone knew Clears could read minds. Surely one of them would look at Quinn—or Malcolm—and *see everything*. The thought made his stomach drop, nausea flooding him. Getting caught wasn't a matter of *if*—it was *when*.

Which was why it shocked him how long it all lasted without discovery.

The longer it continued, the more alive he felt. Alert. Happy.

How have they missed this? he wondered. *How haven't they read us yet?*

Or maybe—maybe they already have, and they're waiting to strike.

The thought made his skin prickle.

He didn't think anything could possibly feel better—until Malcolm joined staff.

The first night after, Quinn came into the dorm and found Malcolm sitting on the bed across the room, grinning like a conspirator. In one swift movement, Malcolm stood, shut the door, and pulled Quinn into a breathless kiss. Quinn wrapped his arms around him and clung as if he might never let go.

Soon, there were nights they lay together in silence, Malcolm carefully stroking Quinn through his underwear in case someone walked in. When nobody did, Malcolm grew bolder—skin on skin touches, bare hands exploring. They practiced climaxing soundlessly, biting down on gasps, stifling moans into the pillows so no one would hear.

Quinn lived in constant fear of random bed checks—but he couldn't resist Malcolm. Each touch only made the wanting stronger. He ached to please him, to give back even a fraction of what Malcolm gave him.

They both knew what would happen if they were caught.

Time in the Hole, absolutely. Forced labour. Physical punishment. Endless hours and days of Sec Checking. Public shaming in front of the entire Org. Golden Rods. Possible expulsion. Declaration as an SP.

That last punishment alone made Quinn feel hollow—cast out, friendless, severed from the only life he'd ever known.

The stress kept acid burning in his stomach, gas rising into painful bloating that ruined his sleep. Malcolm teased him relentlessly for it—called him "gaseous."

When they were alone, though—an hour here, two there—they could talk. And that was what surprised Quinn the most: how badly he needed to talk. How good it felt to be heard.

He told Malcolm about growing up in the Church, about joining the staff at fifteen to pay off coursework debts. About Joni trying to enlist him in the Sea Org, Elijah blocking it, and later defecting.

"He blew?" Malcolm asked. "Just like that? How did he even manage it?"

"I don't know," Quinn snorted. "They sure didn't tell me. One day he was here—the next he was an SP and Joni and I had to sign disconnection papers for the good of the Church."

The thought of leaving the Church chilled Quinn to the bone. Without it he'd have no friends, nowhere to live, almost no money— and no idea how to survive anywhere else. The fear tightened like a fist around his lungs. His rash flared under his arms, itching furiously until he scratched enough to make it ooze.

"I should end the cycle on him," Quinn admitted quietly. "But I can't. I keep wondering how he did it—how he's living. What it feels like out there alone." He swallowed. "It terrifies me."

"He's your dad," Malcolm said gently. "Of course you wonder. That's normal."

Normal? The Church would never agree.

"I'd leave," Malcolm went on, "if it didn't mean being kicked out by my parents."

"What?" Quinn whispered.

"If I could figure out how to get out—I would. This stuff isn't working for me." He turned on his side, eyes serious. "And it sure as hell isn't working for you."

Quinn stared at him.

"If I ever manage to leave," Malcolm said, voice tightening, "I want you to come with me."

"What?"

"Come with me. That's the only way we get to be together. And that's what I want more than anything." His jaw clenched. "I don't care about this place anymore. I want *you*. Let's leave together."

"Leave?" Quinn breathed. "The Church? My mom? Are you serious?"

"Yes. We could be free. Don't you want that?"

"Well…yeah, but—"

"There is no 'but'. They will never accept us. They'll never let us live like this." Malcolm's voice dropped. "We have to get out, Quinn."

The rash under Quinn's arms suddenly burned, itching fiercely, flaring in time with the panic rising in his chest.

One early morning, they were working together—along with most of the Org staff—gutting the burned-out mall that was being converted into new dorm rooms. The Church had purchased it cheaply from the city, and everyone was tearing the place apart so renovations could begin on everything *except* The Hole. That room was to remain untouched.

The Hole sat only metres away. Quinn saw its closed door from where he and Malcolm worked—a rectangle of scorched wood, once painted brown, now bubbled and peeled from fire damage, raw patches glaring through where paint had burned away.

They spoke in hushed whispers and darting glances; they were far from alone. The entire Org was present, everyone hauling debris, ripping out wiring, prying up tile.

"Aren't you scared of what'll happen to us?" Quinn whispered around a stifled belch as he heaved a chunk of drywall into the dumpster. His arms ached constantly now. He rubbed his right bicep, trying to soothe the pain.

"No," Malcolm whispered back. "I almost wish they'd catch us."

Quinn fought to keep his voice steady. "Why?"

Malcolm glanced sharply over his shoulder.

Tom was behind them, gathering the broken drywall.

Quinn followed Malcolm's look, and they both fell silent, working again as if nothing mattered.

Malcolm began casually chatting about how much damage the fire had caused.

"I once saw a fire-damaged house from the bus," Quinn offered as he hooked his hammer into the wall. "The siding had melted off— looked like the whole place was dripping."

"Didn't know siding could melt," Malcolm said between heavy swings of the sledgehammer.

"I guess anything melts if it gets hot enough," Quinn grunted, tugging stubborn drywall free. "Hey—hit here again?"

"Sure." Malcolm stepped closer. "Where?"

"Right here." Quinn shifted aside—and saw Tom had moved off again.

They were alone.

"What did you mean?" Quinn whispered urgently. "About wishing they'd catch us?"

Malcolm hushed him with a glance and swung the hammer.

Bang.

"That's why it stuck—there was a stud behind it," he said loudly, normal voice back in place.

A quick scan of the room.

Then, barely audible: "Because I hate it here. I wish they'd throw me out. My parents think going Clear will stop me from being gay." He raised his voice again immediately. "Hey, my parents are going up to Edmonton in a few days."

Sharon stood nearby, stripping wires from the wall, close enough to overhear.

"Yeah?" Quinn asked carefully.

"I'm going to ask if you can condo-sit with me," Malcolm said aloud. "We can keep working on your assists."

Quinn smiled. *Assists*—their coded word for kissing. "I'd like that." He kept his tone innocent, aware of Sharon's nearness. "They've been helping me a lot. How long will your parents be gone?"

"A week. Helping at the Edmonton fundraiser."

"Cool. I hope Warren and Sharon okay it." Quinn forced a gentle smile. "The assists really *are* helping."

Sharon was plainly listening.

Malcolm smiled faintly.

And it worked.

Sharon convinced Warren. The boys were allowed to spend evenings at the condo after Org work. Malcolm had to submit daily progress reports documenting Quinn's "case gains."

There would be gains, of course. Anything else wasn't acceptable.

The thought of being alone all night with Malcolm filled Quinn with wild nervous energy. He desperately wanted to be away from the Org—but the unknown terrified him. What would they do alone, without any chance of being caught? What happened when two men were truly free together?

Malcolm assured him, "Don't worry. I have ideas."

Quinn struggled to appear composed while Malcolm's calm poker face never faltered.

He envied it.

Later, he'd wonder if that inability to mask emotion made him responsible for what happened.

Quinn couldn't sit still. He rushed through work, knocked things over, and redid mistakes. He crashed straight into two bookcases at the shop, sending entire shelves tumbling to the floor.

"Get a grip," Malcolm hissed while helping restack books.

"I'm trying," Quinn whispered back. "I can't help it—I'm too excited."

"Calm down or they won't let you leave."

The nervous energy felt volcanic. He wanted to *run*. Run anywhere. Run to the bus. Kiss Malcolm the second they arrived. His body ached with an unfocused yearning only Malcolm could soothe.

Malcolm looked calm as ever—like this was nothing more than an errand.

On the bus to Taradale, he squeezed Quinn's hand discreetly, harder and harder the closer they came.

"I've figured out what men can do together," Malcolm whispered.

"You have?" Quinn scanned the bus anxiously. "I still feel watched."

"We're outside the Org now—no one here cares. It's just your nerves. And yeah…I know. We can give each other oral."

"Oral?"

"Blowjobs. But I figured—washing first."

"They don't usually clean?"

"Gross, right?"

"Yeah."

They agreed: washing first was perfect.

In the condo lobby, Malcolm pointed out security cameras. Quinn's breath stuck in his throat until the elevator doors closed.

Malcolm's hand shook as he unlocked the door, his calm expression finally betraying him.

The moment the door shut, everything ruptured.

Quinn shoved Malcolm into it, kissing him hard, hands tugging off shirts until both lay forgotten on the floor.

"I want to touch you," Malcolm whispered. "I wanna jerk you off—I wanna go down on you."

"Please," Quinn begged breathlessly. "Do anything—please—I want you."

They staggered toward the bedroom, fear finally stripped away in the pull of each other.

They never heard the door unlock.

Never heard footsteps.

Never heard the doorknob turn.

Ecstasy swallowed every sound—

Until the bedroom door slammed open.

"STOP!"

Perry stood in the doorway, drenched in sweat.

Tom shoved past him, grabbed both boys by the ears, yanked them upright and forced them naked into the hall.

Warren waited—arms folded, smirking.

Malcolm's mother sobbed beside him.

Joni stood stiffly nearby, eyes blazing.

Seeing his mother at all stunned Quinn—he hadn't seen her in ages.

Tom shoved them before Warren.

A *tsk* of disapproval.

Tom's grip crushed Quinn's neck.

"Did you think we didn't know?" Warren asked coolly.

He bent until his face hovered centimetres away. "Hm?"

Neither answered.

Cold sweat drenched Quinn. His rash burned. His knees shook. He stared at his bare feet—and nearly wet himself.

"Did you forget we see *everything* you think, say, or do?" Warren stepped closer, breath thick with onions and heavy cologne. Quinn gagged and looked down further.

"You thought you could indulge in your *disgusting perversions* without consequence?"

Tears streamed down Quinn's cheeks. He glanced at Malcolm— whose face was hard with fury.

"Answer him," Tom growled.

"N-no, sir," they stammered in unison.

Warren leaned close, eyes closed in something like pleasure. "I can't hear you."

"SIR—NO, SIR!"

He turned away. "We have long known of your vile impulses. Your one-on-one behaviour. Your degeneration will not rot this Church."

Malcolm's mother rushed forward. "Why would you relapse?" she sobbed. "Going Clear will fix this—"

"No!" Malcolm bellowed. "Clear won't fix what isn't broken! I'm gay—and there's nothing wrong with that!"

Her slap cracked like a gunshot. Another followed.

Malcolm glared at her.

Joni stepped toward Quinn. "How could you betray the Church like this?"

Tom's grip forced Quinn to meet her eyes.

"Mom—I—"

"DON'T CALL ME THAT. I WON'T HAVE A DISGUSTING PERVERT FOR A SON!"

"None of us wanted to see just how sick, how disgusting and filthy you both are," Warren went on, "but Tom and Perry were willing to take one for the Church and force themselves to witness your perverted behaviour. It was, sadly, required for us to catch you red-handed, as it were. This will mark the first step in your rehabilitation. Degenerates like you need to be brought to heel—once and for all— for your own good, for the Church, and for the entire world."

Quinn tried to hide behind his long curls. "I'm sorry," he whispered to no one. Tears ran freely down his cheeks, dripping from the tip of his nose. He had never felt so ashamed, so guilty—so unbearably sick inside.

"Quinn!"

Malcolm's voice cracked through the room like lightning.

Quinn's heart jolted as he locked eyes with him.

Tom's thick fingers were still crushing the back of Malcolm's neck, their knuckles gone pale with pressure.

Malcolm strained against the hold, forced to crank his eyes as far left as he could. "Don't say you're sorry!" he shouted. "You have nothing to apologize for! We haven't done anything wrong! Being together isn't wrong—we just want to be—"

Warren backhanded him.

The loosened grip sent Malcolm's head snapping violently sideways with a force far greater than his mother's blows.

Warren stepped forward. Drawing back his arm, curling his hand into a fist, he lunged with his full weight and punched Malcolm directly in the nose.

There was a sickening crunch.

Malcolm's head snapped backward, then wobbled forward again, blood instantly pouring down his face.

"Well," Warren said coolly as he straightened. Malcolm's head sagged forward onto his chest. "I think that settles that, don't you, Tom?"

"Definitely," Tom muttered, his hands never easing.

"Perry—escort Malcolm to his new home."

New home?

"No," Quinn breathed. Then louder, "No!"

He found Perry emerging behind Joni, moving closer to Malcolm.

"Please, don't—"

Warren turned sharply and stepped into Quinn's space. "Don't *what*?" he mocked. "Don't what, Quinn?" He leaned close until his nose nearly touched Quinn's face. Quinn turned his head away—but Warren followed.

"Don't take your lover?" Warren whispered cruelly. "Don't separate you so we might *help* him? Strip away those twisted, nasty urges? Hmm?"

He seized Quinn's face, fingers digging painfully into his cheeks, forcing eye contact.

"Or should we let you go back into that bedroom and—"

His voice dropped to a hush.

"—let you *fuck* each other?"

A pause.

"Would you rather be the one *getting* fucked, eh?"

Another pause.

"Would you rather catch than pitch, Quinn?"

"Stop—please!" Joni cried, covering her ears.

Warren released Quinn and straightened with a smirk twisting his beard.

Malcolm spat blood and shouted, "You make it sound dirty because you want it to be! But that's not what it is! We care about each other—we *love* each other! I care about Quinn—I—"

"How much *affinity* you have?" Warren cut in sharply, arms folding across his chest, chin tilted high with contempt.

Quinn's breath hitched.

Affinity.

The Church word for what wogs called *love.*

Malcolm hesitated only a second. "No—*love*. Love! That's what it is." His voice shook but stayed firm. "I love Quinn. He deserves to be loved. Being a man doesn't make that less true."

"Malcolm…" Quinn whispered.

Malcolm strained again to turn his eyes toward Quinn. "Quinn—I lo—"

Warren punched him again.

Blood erupted down Malcolm's chest as he collapsed, limp as Tom finally released him to the hall floor.

Malcolm's mother screamed.

Warren wheeled on her and struck her across the face with brutal force. She stumbled, clutching her cheek.

"Stop screaming!" he snapped. "Get a fucking grip!"

"Malcolm!" Quinn finally struggled, clawing uselessly at Tom's arm. Tom raised him slightly off the ground, squeezing harder until stars burst across Quinn's vision.

"Weak!" Warren suddenly screamed, stamping his feet like a child. "Weak! Weak! Weak! All of you are *weak!* None of you would last ten minutes in the Sea Org! You should be ashamed! What would LRH say if he saw how weak, pathetic, and perverted you all are?!"

He flew back to Malcolm's mother and began punching the back of her head and neck. The sound echoed—fist to flesh—wet and awful.

She dropped to her knees, arms shielding her skull.

"Don't you dare cover yourself!" Warren roared. "Arms down! NOW!"

Shaking violently, she lowered her arms.

Warren struck again.

And again.

And again.

With each blow he screamed, "WEAK!"

The impact noise turned stomach-sickening even beneath his shrieks.

Malcolm stirred, crying his mother's name—

Perry kicked him hard in the back of the head.

Malcolm fell still.

Quinn screamed Malcolm's name—but Tom's fingers crushed tighter into his neck until pain exploded up behind Quinn's eyes and his vision blurred with tears.

He could only watch Malcolm's unconscious body at his feet and cry.

In memory, the non-reactive part of Quinn's mind knew it couldn't have lasted more than seconds.

But it *felt* endless.

Time slowed brutally.

Warren—small, balding, red-faced—ranted like a possessed child, jumping, raging, consumed with hate.

Finally, he stood panting.

Malcolm's mother lay curled on the floor, hand covering her mouth as blood seeped between her fingers.

Warren snapped his fingers over his shoulder.

"Get them out of here."

Perry scooped Malcolm up in a fireman's carry, his limp body slung unceremoniously over his shoulder, and carried him away.

Malcolm's mother rose shakily and followed, sobbing.

"Malcolm," Quinn whispered—but his voice vanished into the empty hall.

He could do nothing as Malcolm was taken out of his life.

"Now," Tom purred softly behind him, voice crawling across Quinn's skin, "what do you think we should do with *you*, Quinn?"

"Yes," Warren added with a final smirk as he glanced back. "What ever shall we do with you?"

Chapter Twenty-Six

Malcolm vanished that night, presumably taken to another Org somewhere unknown to Quinn. Edmonton was the closest, but it could have been anywhere. He would never see him again; Malcolm simply disappeared, carried out of Quinn's life by Perry.

Their relationship hadn't felt wrong—if anything, it had felt exactly the opposite. Malcolm's lips felt no different than Brittany's had. Holding him had felt natural… exciting, yes… but also comfortable at the same time.

It couldn't have continued forever; the Church would never allow it. But Quinn had been so caught up in the rush, the secrecy, the closeness, that the certainty of being caught was pushed away every time the thought surfaced. He'd told himself they could hide indefinitely.

The guilt came only when Perry burst into the room.

Until that single second—until Perry had screamed at them to stop—there had been no shame at all. No guilt. Just two people caring for each other, wanting each other, their bodies and emotions answering back in unison.

The Hole.

Quinn shoved the memory away. He couldn't bear to stay with it.

Days blurred into weeks of Security Checks—nineteen, twenty hours at a time—meant to empty him of anything left unconfessed. He slept in fragments, two or three hours at most, before being marched from the Hole straight into the auditing room in the same wrinkled clothes from the day before. His mouth felt thick and sour. He couldn't remember the last time he'd been allowed to brush his teeth or shower.

He shuffled into the chair in front of Patricia like a sleepwalker.

By contrast, Patricia looked immaculate as always: brown hair smooth and perfectly combed, black T-shirt crisp, a trace of lipstick—like someone ready for a meeting rather than an interrogation. Quinn felt like he'd crawled straight out of a ditch.

He still dreamed of the Sec Checks: the endless questions looping again and again as Patricia watched the needle sway across the E-metre dial, the mind-numbing repetition of the framing of the questions. The words and the days blurred together after a while.

"You know the only way out is the way through, Quinn," she'd say smoothly. "You can get through this. You have to. Otherwise, you'll never get past it—and you want to get past it, don't you?"

"Yes, of course."

"Good. That's the right attitude! Now, let's begin. I am not auditing you. We are about to begin an HCO Confessional. We are not moralists. We can change people. We are not here to condemn them. While we cannot guarantee you that matters revealed in this list will be held forever secret, we can promise you faithfully that no part of it nor any answer you make here will be given to the police or the state. No Scientologist will ever bear witness against you in court by reason of answers to this Confessional. This Confessional is exclusively for Scientology purposes." Having given the required preamble, the Sec Check audit began.

"Are you upset about this security check?"

"No, not at all."

A lie.

"Thank you. I will now check the question. Are you upset about this security check?"

Quinn shifted his hands exactly the way Malcolm had taught him: loosening his grip on the right can until it was nearly slipping, keeping his left hand low on the other. He prayed for stillness.

"That seems clear at the moment."

No time for relief.

"Have you ever stolen anything?"

"No."

Another lie.

"Thank you, I will now check the question. Have you ever stolen anything? That seems clear at the moment." The ritual continued: "Have you ever been in prison?"

"No."

"Thank you, I will now check the question. Have you ever been in prison? That seems clear at the moment. Have you ever embezzled money?"

"No."

"Thank you, I will now check the question. Have you ever embezzled money? That seems clear at the moment. Have you ever been in jail?"

"No. Unless the Hole counts."

"You know it doesn't, Quinn. I'll repeat the auditing question: Have you ever been in jail?"

"No."

"Thank you, I will now check the question. Have you ever been in jail? That seems clear at the moment. Have you ever had anything to do with pornography?"

"No."

"Thank you, I will now check the question. Have you ever had anything to do with pornography? That seems clear at the moment. Have you watched pornography?"

"No."

"Thank you, I will now check the question. Have you watched pornography?"

The word *seems* landed hard when she repeated, "That seems clear…at the moment."

Quinn felt the warning settle in his gut.

"Have you ever been a drug addict?"

"No."

"Thank you. I will now check the question: Have you ever been a drug addict? That seems clear at the moment. Do you have a police record?"

"No."

"Thank you. I will now check the question, Do you have a police record? That seems clear at the moment. Have you ever raped anyone?"

"God, no!"

"Thank you. I will now check the question: Have you ever raped anyone? That seems clear at the moment. Have you ever committed adultery?"

"No."

How could I? I'm not married.

"Thank you. I will now check the question: Have you ever committed adultery? That seems clear at the moment." Then came the turn.

"Tell me about the times you heard a dirty joke and resented it."

"I don't think I ever have."

"There's something there."

The needle had moved—he just knew it.

"If you dislike dirty jokes, you resent them. I'll repeat the auditing question. Tell me about the times you heard a dirty joke and resented it."

"I can't think of any."

"There—that's it."

The needle again.

"I'll repeat the auditing question: Tell me about the times you heard a dirty joke and resented it."

"I don't resent them, I just don't find them funny."

"Still reacting. I'll repeat the auditing question, Tell me about the times you heard a dirty joke and resented it."

I have to answer, or she'll never stop asking. Right, the only way out is the way through. "…Mark told one that I didn't like. I don't remember how it goes, but the punch line was this little kid saying to his mother, "Mom, you'd better turn on your headlights, meaning her boobs, Dad's snake, his penis, is going into your bush, her vagina. I thought it was stupid, but everyone else laughed. I resented it because they made me feel like an idiot. After all, I didn't think it was funny."

She kept pressing.

He could feel sleep dragging him down.

Finally, desperate:

"…Mark once told a joke I didn't like…" He repeated the joke clumsily, ashamed even saying it out loud. "I resented it because everyone laughed, and I felt stupid."

"Thank you. Is that the only time?"

"Yes."

But the needle still danced.

Quinn spat out the first thing that popped into his mouth. Until he spoke, he hadn't even consciously remembered the joke; he had no idea where he'd heard it. "Two hookers were walking down the street. One hooker says to the other one, 'I smell semen.' And the second one says, 'Sorry, I burped.'"

Then another probing turn.

"Now, why did you resent it?"

"Because I thought it was stupid and gross."

"Thank you. I will now check the question. Tell me about a time when you heard a dirty joke and resented it?" Pause. "There's still something there. Did you resent the joke because that's what gay men do—because they suck each other's dicks?"

Quinn stared. "I never thought about—"

"Your needle is reacting."

She repeated it.

He stammered.

She cornered.

Finally: "I never thought of it that way."

"And male prostitutes—how do you know the joke wasn't about them?"

"I guess I don't."

Again the question.

He loosened his grip until his hands trembled.

"That seems clear… at the moment."

He heard the threat in the phrasing.

Then:

"Have you ever slept with a member of another race?"

"Kind of."

"I'll repeat the auditing question: Have you ever slept with a member of a race of another colour? Yes or no, Quinn."

She forced the wording.

"No. It didn't go that far."

"Thank you. I'll check the question now: Have you ever slept with a member of a race of another colour?"

Quinn held his breath, even though he knew what would happen.

But the needle jumped again.

Now she leaned in.

"What attracted you to Malcolm?"

The question struck him dumb.

"I… I don't know."

"Yes, you do, Quinn. You might not remember it, but the. The E-metre knows you do. It can read your deepest thoughts, even the unconscious ones. I'll repeat: What attracted you to Malcolm?"

"I just liked him."

"What about him did you like?"

Quinn stared at the faded blue of his jeans, blinking into heavy darkness. His head sagged. He bit his lip until pain brought him back.

"He made me laugh… smile. Being around him made me feel good. He told stories. He made me feel like I mattered—like I wasn't a fuck-up for once."

He hadn't meant to say it.

It was too much truth.

"Thank you. Yes, that was a strong reaction. Patricia's eyes sharpened. "So when he made you feel good… what was he doing to you?"

"Doing? No—"

"What sexual act was he performing?"

"It wasn't sex. This was before that."

"Still something there."

"I liked being around him. That's all."

"What specifically made you feel good?"

"He made me laugh."

"And who else makes you laugh?"

"No one."

Too fast.

The needle showed it.

"What about Brittany?"

"No."

"You laugh with her."

"Not like with Malcolm. I'm always on edge around her. I feel… brittle."

"Explain 'brittle.'"

"Fake… like I'm walking on eggshells."

"Thank you. Are you afraid of being found out?"

"Kind of. Yeah."

Then:

"Let's go back to your experience with Brittany…"

The instructions flowed automatically.

Close your eyes. Locate the memory. Begin.

"We were working at the farm…" Quinn began dully. "I was mucking out the barn. I was in a good mood. Brittany came in and told me to follow her…"

He recited the memory like a witness transcript, not a participant.

"She told me she liked me. I said I liked her too—just not that way. She grabbed my shirt and pulled me down to kiss me. I was shocked. I wanted to push her away… but I didn't. Her hands went around my waist… then lower… and she started squeezing my butt."

And still, in the room with Patricia, with the E-metre humming beside him, Malcolm's absence pulsed beneath every word.

"We were kissing for a while, I think, and then she put her tongue in my mouth. That really freaked me out. It was gross, but she kept pulling me closer. She didn't stop kissing me, and then she reached around and undid my pants. I wanted to pull away, but she said, 'I want to touch you, Quinn.' I felt her hand slide into my pants. I wanted to move, but I couldn't; she had reached into my underwear and started rubbing my dick. I didn't know what to do. It… started making me hard. No one had ever touched me before, so I got hard really fast. I was hard and she kept touching me. I know she was talking, but I can't remember what she said. I was focused on the feeling—on being touched, on being jerked off. I remember she said she liked me from the first day we met, and I came all over her hand. That's when Jeremy came around the corner and caught us."

"I understand. Now go back to the beginning and run through it again. Pick up any additional data you can contact."

Quinn began again, mechanically.

"Ok. I was in the barn mucking it out. It was summer, so the smell was really strong, but I like being with the animals, so I was in a good mood. Brittany came in and asked me to help with something behind the barn. When we got there, I was looking for what she needed, but she told me she liked me. I didn't know what she meant. I said I liked her too—I thought as friends. Then she stepped closer, picked at something near my collar, grabbed my shirt, and pulled me down to her. She kissed me. I was shocked. I wanted to push her away, but I didn't. I felt her hands on my waist, then lower, squeezing my butt."

"We were kissing, and then she put her tongue in my mouth. That freaked me out. It tasted strange, like lint, but she kept pulling me closer. She reached around with her right hand and undid my pants. She said, 'I want to touch you, Quinn.' Her hand slid into my pants. I wanted to move away, but I couldn't. She reached inside my underwear and started rubbing my dick. I didn't know what to do. I started getting hard. I got really hard and she kept touching me. I don't remember what she said after that. I was focused on the feeling—on being touched, on being jerked off. It felt like I felt my body for the first time, like everything suddenly woke up. I came on her hand. And then Jeremy came around the corner and caught us."

"I understand," Patricia said, smiling in what was meant to be reassurance. "Now go back to the beginning and repeat the incident. Pick up any additional data. Remember to relive it—don't just recount it. Think about what you see, what you hear, what you smell, what you feel."

Five things you see, five you hear, five you feel… Stop that.

"Ok," Quinn said and ran through it all again.

Several repetitions later:

"I understand," Patricia said again. "Now I have more questions. Go back to the beginning and scan for more data. When Brittany led you behind the barn, did you know what she wanted?"

"No."

"When she described her fantasies, did that turn you on?"

"I think maybe… but I was more focused on how it felt."

"And how did it feel, Quinn? To have a woman touching you?"

"Um… it felt good, I guess. No one had touched me before."

"You *guess*? Your needle says you felt something."

"I guess it felt good. I didn't want her to stop."

"And what did you want to do to her?"

"I don't understand."

"Did you imagine doing things to her while she touched you?"

"I… don't think so."

"You have perfect recall. I'll repeat the auditing question: Did you imagine doing things to her while she was touching you?"

"No."

"What else did she use?"

"Nothing. Just her hand."

"Did you orgasm?"

"Yes."

"Did you ejaculate?"

"Yes."

"On Brittany?"

"Yeah."

"Where on her body?"

"On her hand."

"Did you ejaculate on her face?"

"No."

"Did she touch your testicles?"

"I don't remember."

"You do remember. You have perfect recall. Did she touch your testicles?"

"I guess… yeah."

"Did you want to have sex with her?"

"I don't…"

"I'll repeat: Did you want to fuck her? Put your dick in her vagina?"

"I'm not sure."

"You wanted to, didn't you? That would be normal."

Normal desire… there's only one answer.

"I guess."

"When you were masturbating with Brittany, what did *you* use?"

"I didn't. She touched me."

"Why not?"

"We got caught."

"I understand. Now go back to the moment you were caught and review it. Pick up any more data."

He couldn't remember how many times he had run it before Patricia finally moved on.

"If you hadn't been caught, what would you have done?"

"I don't know."

"Yes, you do. I'll repeat: What would you have done?"

"I-I don't know how women masturbate."

"Would you have her show you?"

"I guess."

"And then you would get her off?"

"Yeah… since she did it to me."

"And if that meant using your mouth and tongue, would you?"

"Maybe. I don't know."

"Yes, you do."

"I guess I would."

"Did you want to have sex with her?"

"I guess. Yes."

"And would you have?"

"Yes."

"Do you think she'd let you?"

"Yes."

"Why?"

"Malcolm told me she said she wanted to."

"She told him she wanted to have sex with you?"

"Yes. She said she wanted me inside her… wanted me to get her pregnant."

"I've got that. We'll return to it."

"Have you ever practiced homosexuality?"

Here it is.

"Yes."

"When was the first time?"

"With Malcolm."

"I need a date."

"I can't remember. When we were doing touch assists at his place."

"Tell me about the first sexual conversation you had."

"It was after. Not before."

"Are you sure?"

"Yes."

"Thank you. Tell me about the sexual fantasies you had about Malcolm *before* anything happened."

"There weren't any."

"Your needle says otherwise."

"There weren't any. I just thought we were friends."

"So you didn't deliberately 2D flow him?"

"What was the first sexual act between you?"

"Kissing."

"Where?"

"In his room at his parents' condo."

"Who kissed whom?"

"He kissed me."

"And your reaction?"

"I freaked out and backed away."

“Why?”

“Because it’s supposed to be wrong.”

“And you knew The Source says homosexuality is an illness?”

“Yes.”

Then everything with Malcolm began to repeat as Brittany’s had—every kiss, every secret touch, every fantasy, dragged into the open and dissected until every memory felt violated.

“Tell me about that urge,” Patricia said. “Your needle is reacting strongly. Describe the desire.”

Questions circled endlessly until Quinn could barely tell where a memory ended and her phrasing began.

“Have you ever had intercourse with a family member?”

“No.”

“With an animal?”

“No.”

“Done anything your mother would be ashamed of?”

“She already knows everything.”

“Bombed anything?”

“No.”

“Murdered anyone?”

“No.”

“Been a Communist?”

“No.”

“A newspaper reporter?”

“No.”

“A baby farm?”

"No."

"Unkind thoughts about L. Ron Hubbard?"

"No."

"Afraid of the police?"

"No."

"Do you collect sexual objects?"

"No."

"Have you practiced sex with children?"

"No."

"Practiced masturbation?"

"Yes."

"What do you use?"

"My hands."

"What else?"

"Nothing."

"What sexual toys do you use?"

"I don't have any."

The question returned again and again.

"Why are you always getting caught in sexual situations?"

"I don't know."

"Are you addicted to sex?"

"No."

Then came the hypotheticals.

"If I allowed you to have sex with Brittany without punishment, would you?"

"I don't know."

"If she were tied up and you were told you could take her?"

"I don't know."

"If she were tied up and said no—would you still?"

"No."

"Even under orders?"

"No. I couldn't."

"She wants you, you said—so why not?"

"I don't— But you said *if she didn't want me…*"

His answers tangled.

And beneath every question, every answer, the same relentless ache pulsed through him:

Malcolm.

"All right, if she walked into this room right now, unzipped your pants, and started to suck your cock, would you stop her?"

"Yes."

"Why?"

"Because you're here."

"And if I wasn't?" Quinn could hear her eyes roll in her voice. "If it was just the two of you, would you still stop her?"

"Yeah. I think so."

"All right, so if she walked in right now, if I left the room and she stripped naked in front of you, would you fuck her?"

"I don't think so. No. I don't want her."

"What if I told you that you can have sex with Brittany as much as you like, but not with Malcolm?"

"I don't want Brittany."

"Does that mean you couldn't get an erection if she stood naked in front of you?"

"I don't know."

"Should we call her into this room and find out?"

"No!"

"How do you feel about being controlled?"

"I don't like it. I don't think anyone does."

"Have you ever practiced cannibalism?"

"No."

"Have you ever peddled dope?"

"No."

"Have you ever attempted suicide?"

"No."

Although the thought's pretty tempting sometimes. Like now.

"What sexual toys do you use?"

"I don't."

It went on for hours, until Quinn was falling asleep sitting up. He shifted his grip on the cans the way Malcolm had taught him, but Patricia still repeated the same questions again and again, each time phrased a little differently. Whenever his answer shifted even slightly, she seized on it, digging at why. She kept probing every deviation, exactly as she'd been trained.

By the time Quinn slunk out of the exam room, he could barely stand. More than once, Patricia had called Tom to help haul him back to the Hole.

Patricia told him his Sec Checks would "handle" his sexual orientation. Enough auditing would push his tone level higher, she said, until the homosexual urges disappeared, leaving only a distant shame. The longer it went on, the more exhausted Quinn became, the more desperately he clung to that promise—this would end, and all of it would fade into something far away.

One night, after twelve straight hours of auditing with no break, Quinn sat across from Patricia, barely awake, when something moved at the left corner of the E-metre. His vision was blurry from lack of sleep; he squinted, trying to focus.

He took a deep breath and shook his head. The moving thing was a light brown dot, slightly smaller than a pea. He watched it drag itself out of the corner seam of the metre and then pull out long, thin black legs that looked like thick hairs. The brown dot gathered those legs beneath itself, then stood up. Quinn recognized it as a type of spider known as a

A Daddy-Long-Legs.

He hated insects of any kind, and while a spider wasn't technically an insect, it was close enough to trigger that old rush of revulsion. Even half-asleep, his skin crawled as the spider adjusted its legs and walked along the left edge of the metre.

Another beige dot appeared where the first had been. It pulled itself free the same way, black legs unfurling. Quinn spotted a third one at the bottom right corner; this one had already climbed clear and was walking along the back edge of the metre, closest to him. He pressed his back into the chair, trying to get as far away as possible. If it touched him, he knew he'd scream, and screaming would be "out-ethics"—more trouble.

He saw two more dots on the top right, starting to walk down the side. When he looked back to the left, there were a dozen, maybe more, with dozens still pouring out of the bottom seam.

He turned his head and now the entire metre seemed covered—beige bodies, a blizzard of light brown polka dots in a writhing mass of black legs. He looked up at Patricia, stunned by the fact that she didn't react. She scribbled notes and watched the needle as hundreds of beige dots marched up her white t-shirt and coral cardigan, crawling steadily toward her face. She seemed completely unaware.

"Have you ever been arrested?" she asked, eyes still on the dial.

Quinn screamed, dropped the cans, and lurched to his feet, sending his chair crashing backwards. Patricia's voice came at him, sharp and demanding, but all he could do was point and scream at the spiders.

It took Patricia marching around the desk and slapping him hard across the face to shock him out of it.

He blinked, panting, and looked back at the desk. The E-metre sat there, a light grey box, both cans dangling by their cables where he'd thrown them.

No beige dots. No black legs. No crawling swarm.

Silently, cheeks burning, he picked up the chair, set it upright, and sat down again. The door behind him opened; someone—probably Tom—stuck their head in. Patricia glanced up, said "We're fine" in a clipped tone, and went straight back to the needle.

Quinn lowered his head and stared at his knees.

"Have you ever been arrested?" Patricia repeated.

"No."

The Sec Check went on.

Chapter Twenty-Seven

As he worked through everything—exhausting and mind-numbing as it could be—going over each incident and repeating events again and again, he started to feel better.

Clearing up each transgression, each mistake, made him feel lighter, more in control, even empowered. There were days when, despite the endless questions, he felt energised. Each time he recounted his "transgressions," he felt a little less embarrassed, a little less ashamed, and a little happier that he was finally getting through them and back in the driver's seat of his own life. It was beautiful and thrilling in a way he hadn't felt since he'd first started up the Bridge. He felt proud that he was finally "back on track" and in control of his destiny. He was getting those transgressions out of his universe and moving on.

But every day, he felt a bit better. Every day, he felt a bit lighter, a bit more peaceful than the day before. That was the reward, the "win." Since Elijah had already blown and been labelled an SP, suspicion around Quinn was even worse. He was the son of an apostate, a Suppressive Person naturally, that made everyone watch him even more closely.

There were days when all he did was rewrite the dictionary, a unique punishment Warren had come up with to make sure there were no misunderstood words ("MU's"). A simple misunderstood word, as Patricia reminded him relentlessly, was likely the root cause of his lapse, since MU's were often the root causes of overts of any kind. Over and over again, he rewrote the dictionary, clearing words with someone breathing down his neck to make sure he understood every single one.

Patricia would have him recite the dictionary while Quinn was on the metre. He'd hold one can while she watched for any twitch of the needle that meant a word he didn't really know. Malcolm's trick—

how to get the needle to float the way it was supposed to—came in very handy, and Quinn used it as much as he dared, just to get the ordeal over with. This part wasn't so bad, although he had to fight to keep from falling asleep over the page. He'd noticed, though, that the needle didn't always catch words he didn't know, even when he wasn't trying to trick the machine. Sometimes, stumbling over a word he *did* know, the E metre would throw a "false read."

Patricia had noticed as well and speculated that Quinn "half understood" those words, which, she said, explained the needle's odd behaviour.

He cheated. He had to. He didn't want to get bogged down in the dreaded word chains that every Scientologist hated. He'd look up a word and then be made to clear every single definition, each idiomatic expression and shade of meaning. If another misunderstood word cropped up anywhere in the chain, that one had to be cleared as well, and so on and so on. Quinn would lie and say he understood, parroting back and slightly rephrasing the definition to make it look like he'd got it. He despised word chains; pretty much everyone in the Church did.

Barbara preferred the "pop quiz" method. She'd open one of LRH's lectures at random—though *The Responsibilities of Leaders* essay was her favourite—and demand Quinn define whatever word she put her finger on. He frequently got it wrong, thanks to LRH's preference for odd, colloquial usages not listed in standard dictionaries. Then he'd have to endure her flunking him and screaming at him in Tone 40 about how stupid he was, followed by pages and pages of writing out the definition.

Perry liked pop quizzes as well, but he also made Quinn spell each word as if he were in a spelling bee. Perry loved to nit-pick, deciding that Quinn's definition wasn't good enough, which meant more dictionaries and more word chains. Perry liked word chains when he wasn't the one stuck in them.

Sharon preferred manual labour. She made Quinn clean the Founder's office on his knees with a hand-held vacuum and polish the desk with Q-tips. She watched him scrub the bathroom with a toothbrush and talked loudly to herself about how Quinn was such a letdown, how stupid and disgusting he was, what a pervert he was: "I can't believe I have to sit in the same room with such a disgusting pervert as this!" Quinn was expected to shout "Yes, sir!" every time she paused for breath. God help him if he missed one while trying to scrub the tiles at the same time. Sharon made sure everyone in the entire Org knew exactly what Quinn had done.

Quinn had never been the kind of person to hate anyone, but Sharon's attitude and consistently nasty tone grated on his nerves to the point that he frequently fantasized about punching her in the face until that smirk was gone and her ridiculous bouffant hairdo was ruined. She dampened his enthusiasm and made every tiny win feel harder than it needed to be.

He kept at it. He refused to give up; and no one in the Church would let him give up anyway. For his own good, they made sure he kept going. The only way out was through, so he kept ploughing on.

Warren never sat and watched Quinn; he sent Tom instead, who had his own version of the Cause Resurgence Rundown. It involved making Quinn march around the dorm building, reading aloud the most complicated, convoluted LRH writings Tom could find, in military style, hour after hour. While the real Cause Resurgence Rundown was supposed to make the Preclear realize they were in control of their own body and mind, Tom's version left Quinn shattered and made his anxiety clamp down even harder.

Whenever Quinn inevitably staggered, hesitated in his reading, mispronounced a word, or even twitched in a way Tom disliked, he got flunked—usually with a boxed ear and a stream of insults about how "weak" he was—and had to start again. Tom loved word chains; he was probably the only staff member who did, and he made sure Quinn got stuck in them frequently. Quinn would be running around the building with several dictionaries in his arms, looking up one word he couldn't even remember now. Once, he'd had six different dictionaries on the go for a single term.

Exhausted and half asleep, he spent hours writing and rewriting the Knowledge Report (KR) on Malcolm, accusing him of every crime they'd committed together, until Patricia was satisfied. She insisted that Quinn place all the blame on Malcolm, painting himself as the victim. Quinn knew that wasn't true; he was as guilty as Malcolm was, but he wrote what was expected because he had no choice.

He accused Malcolm of 2D flowing with him, of seducing him, of making all the advances. On paper, Quinn became an unwilling participant: Malcolm had instigated everything; Malcolm had made Quinn into his 2D even though Quinn "didn't want to be." Quinn hated writing that more than anything. He knew Malcolm would eventually be confronted with that KR, and it made it sound like Quinn hadn't cared about him at all.

The guilt ate at him. He'd thrown Malcolm under the proverbial bus, and he knew it. He'd had to write a KR once before when he was caught with Brittany, but this was different. This time he was betraying someone he'd wanted to be 2D with, someone he had more affinity for than anyone he'd ever met. He felt like a traitor.

And yet, his remaining feelings for Malcolm kept getting bowled over by the sheer joy and elation every time Patricia saw his needle not moving where before it had trembled like a branch in the wind. Every time he was able to talk about his withholds without a flicker of shame or panic, without that tight feeling in his chest, every time he felt unhooked from the past, Patricia lit up. She showered him with praise for each small win. She used words like "spectacular" and said things like:

"Oh my God, Quinn, you're on fire! You'll get through this Sec Check in no time! This is just a pebble on the road to Clear, you know that, right? Once these withholds are gone, nothing will stop you! This is nothing, just a small pothole! You're going to feel fantastic, you'll see!"

She told him he looked happier, that he was "glowing," that he'd gone to the brink of disaster and fought his way back. "Once this is done, nothing is going to hold you back! You'll see!"

Quinn was happy. He soaked up her praise, soaked up every moment he completed a task flawlessly. Every time he had to face that dictionary again, he remembered Patricia's enthusiasm and just knuckled down. He focused on the task in front of him and poured everything into it; the relief when it was over was overwhelming. He felt like he had wings when he could show Sharon the spotless bathroom and immaculate office, when he passed Barbara's pop quiz without a flunk, when he answered Perry's questions cleanly, without hesitation.

By the time Quinn was finished—by the time Patricia was finally satisfied with the report—he was on autopilot. He knew none of what he was writing was really true, but he had no choice. He wrote what Patricia wanted him to write. This was for the greater good of the Church, which was supposed to be the most important thing. Patricia told him this was not only for Malcolm's good, but his own as well. "It's the greatest good for the greatest number of dynamics," she'd told him.

The KR would get Malcolm back on track. The KR would help Malcolm get those perverted ideas out of his head and back onto the Bridge. Malcolm would get to Clear and go on to the OT levels. This was for Malcolm's own good. It was for Quinn's own good as well— so he could get back on the Bridge and start really moving up it again. After Patricia had drilled it into his head for the umpteenth time, with his eyelids impossibly heavy, he began to repeat it to himself: this was for his own good too. This would allow Quinn to save both his own soul and Malcolm's.

One day he'll thank me for this, he told himself. *He probably feels great too, working out his withholds and transgressions. I wish I could tell him how much better I feel now! And I'll be so proud of him when he does reach Clear! That'll be a great day, when he finally gets his certificate and...*

...forgets about me.

That thought slid in like ice water and stayed. The happiness and pride he felt imagining Malcolm's future accomplishments vanished as a bitter pain gripped his heart. It refused to let go, no matter how hard he tried to push it down beneath the joy of his "wins."

That was a one-off. A one-off overt, that's what Patricia said during the Sec Check, right? It was just a mistake, a lapse in judgment, probably brought on by an SP in a former life... we never had sex, not really, so it doesn't really matter, right? If we'd done it, if we'd really fucked, then it would've been different.

Quinn didn't know enough about love to know if that's what he'd felt for Malcolm, but he knew that losing him—being unable to speak to him or even know if he was all right—broke something inside. He'd cried every night for weeks, face buried in his pillow, trying to muffle the sound, to hide his tears, even though he inevitably had to confess them the next day. No matter how he tried to convince himself, no matter how many times he repeated that this was for Malcolm's own good, the words seemed hollow unlike Malcolm's almost-uttered four words.

Every day, under Patricia's guidance, he forced that "transgression" into submission until Malcolm's almost-spoken words felt as hollow as any other meaningless phrase.

All the colour vanished from Quinn's world when Malcolm disappeared, as if there had been an eclipse that never passed. The darkness felt endless, and the chill in his heart refused to loosen its grip. Everything was in greyscale—except when he was praised at the Church. When Patricia was pleased, when even Warren told him how proud he was of Quinn's efforts, of how hard he was working and how his perseverance would inevitably pay off, then there was colour again. Then the sun seemed to shine.

It was no surprise when Patricia confronted him with the KR written by Malcolm, in which Malcolm accused Quinn of the same things: being the instigator and forcing everything on him. Quinn wondered if Patricia had coached Malcolm the same way at the Edmonton Org, or if another auditor had been brought in just for him—assuming Malcolm was in Edmonton at all.

Then came the other, more surprising KRs from other Church members, reporting that Quinn had been 2D flowing not only with Malcolm, but also with Brittany and others, both men and women. Quinn hadn't even been consciously aware that he was flirting with anyone. He wanted to deny it, all of it, but instead, he did what was expected and simply bowed his head and accepted the blame.

Brittany's KR seemed especially bitter and angry, although Quinn didn't understand why.

Then there were the months of working through the lower conditions again, courses he'd already taken but now had to retake and complete before he could be considered back in relatively good standing. All of it he was supposed to pay for, on top of the huge fines he knew he'd never be able to pay off. He lost track of how much reading he was forced to repeat, how many essays he had to write on why homosexuality was banned by the Church. Homosexuality was an overt act, they said, that created more engrams and damaged the Church as a whole.

Twenty months.

It had taken Quinn twenty months get back in relatively good standing. Twenty months where he couldn't take new courses, couldn't work on going up the Bridge, twenty months where he was stuck, unable to go either forward or back, and under constant suspicion, which made everyone around him, living in terror of being expelled.

But the word clearing, the auditing, those had been the easy punishments. The memories of the rest, of everything else that had happened during those twenty months, loomed, but Quinn desperately pushed them away. *No. I don't want to remember. Stop it.* He'd just put his head down and powered through it, all of it.

Only after twenty months did Patricia give him the Proclamation to Forgive. "By the power vested in me, any overts and withholds you have fully and truthfully told to me are forgiven."

He'd then written out his "win", his success story, of how the Sec Check had helped him with a much-needed "ethics change". This was also a requirement; it didn't have to be a long document, but the longer and watch him even more detailed, the better. In conclusion, he'd written:

"I found myself in a situation that I never expected to be in. I found I was not only really out of ethics, but I was at risk of becoming an SP myself, something I'd rather die than become. I was at risk of losing my faith and throwing away my eternity for an unhealthy, meaningless 2D fling. I can't believe that I came so close to losing my eternity for nothing!

Thank you, LRH, for showing both me and humanity the right path. Thank you, COB, for all you do and for spreading LRH's words to the world. I can't explain how much I owe both of you."

Even now, his progress up the Bridge was still stalled. Despite his being "forgiven", it hadn't stopped the whispering, the outright accusations, the nasty looks. Quinn gritted his teeth and forcefully pushed the memories away again as his eyes began to prickle with tears as he tried vainly to focus on the parking lot, the breeze, and the apple.

And Quinn had accepted it, believing it to be worth it, since Malcolm would reach Clear, even if Quinn never did.

It was for Malcolm's own good and Quinn's.

Quinn was happy, feeling he was helping Malcolm, whom he still cared for more than anyone, to get back on the Bridge and take control of his life and eternity. He was willing to sacrifice his own spiritual progress if it meant Malcolm would be happier and more spiritually advanced.

Then it all fell apart, completely disintegrating in a moment. He was unexpectedly dragged into Sharon's office. She angrily threw a paper at him and started to command in a tone of 40. "Sign this. Now. Malcolm has been declared an SP. He's abandoned us, abandoned his eternity, abandoned his Church! He's perverted and out to destroy both this very Org but the entire Church itself! You will sign this, you will never speak to him again, you will disconnect, you will end the Cycle on him. Sign it."

Quinn signed it without hesitation, but inside his stomach was in knots. *Declared? Malcolm? That couldn't be right, could it? Is it because of what we did? Was he declared...because of me? I thought the KR would help him! I thought it would get him back on the Bridge! Why? Why would you do this? I don't understand what happened! What would make you give up your eternity? Your Church? Your friends? Me?*

He never found out what had happened; that was it. End of Cycle on Malcolm. The emptiness, the not knowing, was what ate at him most. All the questions that he wouldn't ever get answers for. *Why did you do this? How? How could you do it? Did I make you do this? How did you leave? Are you all right? Where are you now? How are you living? Eating? Is this my fault?*

Why would you, knowing that it means that I can't ever see you again? Talk to you again? Who got to you? Who turned you? Did some SP corrupt you? Why? Why didn't you tell me? Maybe I could have talked you out of it! Maybe I could have helped you!

Why did you leave me here alone? Why did you leave me?

He felt abandoned, with a crushed heart and shattered spirit; the colour had faded again from the world around him. Patricia kept telling him to get over it, to just move past that guilt and focus on clearing the planet. Nothing was more important than that, after all.

Chapter Twenty-Eight

"Only you. You're the only one I want. I don't give a fuck about the risk, I want you."

He'd never told Malcolm, or even Patricia, how much those words had affected him. The idea that someone wanted and needed him made Quinn more than just happy; the words themselves filled him up and made him feel whole. Malcolm had made Quinn happy; everything about him, from the way he spoke, the way he walked, to the way he touched him, had made Quinn happy.

I don't really think that I've been really happy since then. All my happiness went with Malcolm. Or did it? I feel happy when I'm with Larkin, I feel warm when I'm with Larkin. I smile. He smiles, like I make him happy, too. I don't want to lose... What? The feeling of happiness that's finally come back? The fact that I'm smiling again? The colour?

I don't want to lose Larkin the way I lost Malcolm. But that's stupid. The Church can't force Larkin to leave, can they?

Quinn took another bite of his apple, and the image of Malcolm being slapped across the face sprang to mind. He recalled how hard the blow had been, how Malcolm's face had violently snapped to the side as he was hit, how his eyes glared at his mother, full of anger and resentment. He tried to picture Warren doing that with Larkin, but every time he imagined it, the image shifted to Larkin simply using his skills to dump Warren on his butt, the same as he'd done at the lake to that stranger. The image kept making Quinn chuckle as he munched away and imagined the shocked and indignant look on Warren's smug face as Larkin effectively kicked his ass.

He frowned as a new thought struck him. *No, maybe they can't force Larkin to leave town, but they can make it impossible for me to see him. They can make it so that I'll never see him again, they could fair game him, Dead Agent him. Just like Malcolm, Larkin would vanish from my life forever.*

The thought of never seeing Larkin again hit Quinn hard enough that he doubled over as if he'd been punched in the stomach. *No! I won't be able to ever see him again. No! No! Larkin's...my... I have to stay close to him! I have to have him in my life! He's...*

It took a few moments for the feeling to pass, for the nausea and the pain to subside.

He straightened himself and squared his shoulders to regain control. Taking another bite of his apple, tears started creeping into his eyes at the thought of losing Larkin.

He's the only friend I have, really. He's the only person I know outside the Church. He's a wog, but he's the only thing that makes me happy. He's the only thing that makes the colours come back. But won't all this stuff go away when I get to Clear? That's what they say. Maybe once I get to Clear, I'll be happy again, maybe all the colours will come back then. Assuming I ever get to Clear.

Quinn's shoulders dropped and relaxed as he was starting to convince himself of this, trying to stay on this safe train of thought, when Elijah's words came back to him:

"I know you haven't attested to Clear yet, but after I left the church, I learned that all you have to do to have the Clear Cognition is to say, 'I've just realized that I've been mocking up my own Reactive Mind all this time, my whole life. But, I'm not doing that any longer.' That's really all you need to do to go Clear. None of them will tell you, so I know you're going to doubt what I'm saying, but it's true. I wouldn't ever, ever lie to you about that."

Quinn's confidence evaporated like steam. *That can't be right, can it? Your eyesight is supposed to get better, you never get sick, and you're supposed to be able to read minds. How can just saying those words, 'I've realized that I've been mocking up my own Reactive*

Mind, but I'm not doing that any longer,' be all there is to it? I mean, that's not going to keep you from getting sick, or fix your eyes or... Make me stop desiring a man that... a man that I'm...I have... strong affinity...feelings for.

Quinn took another couple of bites. *No, that's just stupid. There has to be more to it than that. There has to be. But if Warren can read minds, why didn't he catch Malcolm and me sooner? Larkin asked Warren why he was wearing glasses if he'd gone Clear. Why does he still need to wear them? Why haven't any of them realized that I'm having feelings for Larkin?*

Feelings for Larkin. What if I am having feelings for Larkin? What should I do? I'm having feelings for Larkin. What am I going to do when Patricia finds out? Or Sharon? What if she reads my mind and finds out? I mean, that's how they found out about Malcolm and me, right? That must be how they found out.

Quinn finished his apple and walked back to the green garbage dumpster. He tossed the core overhanded into it and heard a dull thud as it hit the side. He had to admit, he did feel better for having eaten, brighter and more alert. He slunk back in through the back door of Larkin's shop, only to hear the albino's even, but raised voice.

"*Ben là! Madame*, there's a very clear sign on the door saying that children are not allowed in this store, *ostie.*"

"I don't fucking care!" came a shout from a woman. The sharp edge in her tone made Quinn nervous; he reacted to the sheer force of her energy. He walked through the back and glanced over to see Sandra standing by the desk with a huge grin on her face. She was clearly listening and waiting to see what Larkin would do while remaining hidden behind the wall. Quinn pushed back the chain curtain with a rattle to peer into the shop.

Larkin stood with his arms folded across his chest, his face blank and expressionless, but his eyes narrowed in annoyance. A woman with mousy brown hair hanging around her earlobes was right in his face, less than an arm's length away. She was yelling and shaking her finger at him, almost touching his nose. She jerked a small boy around by the hand, yanking him this way and that, more focused on berating Larkin.

"What am I supposed to do, leave my kid outside while I'm in this damn shop?"

"Perhaps," said Larkin flatly. "Or perhaps you would consider leaving him at home when you're shopping in a place clearly not designed for children, *ostie.*"

"You listen here, you fuckin' freak! You need to work on your customer service! You're being very aggressive! I'm not leaving my kid outside or at home when I'm here to buy him a toy!"

Quinn cringed. *How can she call Larkin a freak? Is she blind? Aggressive? She's one to talk!*

"Madame, all our toys are antiques and quite valuable. I can promise you there is nothing here for your child, *ostie.*" Larkin snorted *criss* under his breath.

"What are you, stupid? You're just being too God-damned lazy to do your fuckin' job! There are toys right on that shelf!" She gestured wildly.

Quinn saw she was pointing at a few brightly coloured metal tops from the 1930s. They were only worth about thirty dollars or so, but Larkin clearly wasn't in the mood.

The woman released her grip on the child's hand. The boy immediately began to wander while she stayed locked on Larkin. Quinn quickly lost sight of him.

"Yes," Larkin retorted, "antique toys that are often quite valuable and highly collectible, as I said. Again, children are not allowed in this store. *Sacréfice!*"

"Do you know who I am?" the woman demanded, hands on her hips.

"*Non*, should I?"

"I'll have you know I'm good friends with the owner! I'm going to report you to him! This is terrible customer service! How dare you talk to a paying customer that way!"

"As you haven't yet bought anything, madame, you're not actually a paying customer, *ostie*."

Quinn snickered at that despite himself, but the woman heard him. She wheeled around to glare at him.

"What are you laughing at?"

His heart stopped, and his back and shoulders snapped to attention. "Nothing, ma'am. I…"

"Ugh! You must be faggots!" she snapped. "Only they could be this precious about some stupid toys! You two fags listen here! I am a paying customer, and if I want to bring my darling into a store, I'll bring him into the store! I know the owner, and I can't believe he'd hire two lousy queers like you!"

Quinn felt like all the air had been sucked out of the shop. *Fag… she called us fags… queers. She called me a fag. Is it that obvious? And did she actually just call her kid 'my darling'? Really?*

"*Ciboire! C'est assez!* You're done," said Larkin firmly. He'd moved closer to the woman; his eyes were narrow and very dark. "Get out."

He took hold of her elbow with the tips of his fingers and started guiding her toward the door. The woman jerked away theatrically.

"HOW DARE YOU! MANAGER! NOW!"

"No." Larkin's voice was flat and expressionless. He stepped away from the still-irate woman, who was now roaring something about suing.

Larkin moved to Quinn's side. He leaned in and whispered in his ear, "Lock the front door," as he dropped the key in Quinn's hand.

The warmth of Larkin's breath on his skin gave Quinn goosebumps. He hurried past him, almost running past the screaming woman to the front door, slid the key into the lock, and threw the deadbolt.

He flipped off the switch for the neon open sign and tucked the key into the front pocket of his jeans. Leaning back against the door, his spine pressed against the metal bars. Only then did he notice how damp his back was, the T-shirt sticking to his skin. He hadn't realized he'd begun to sweat so much.

"I DEMAND TO SPEAK TO YOUR MANAGER!" The woman stomped her foot like a child. She ignored her son, who'd begun poking her in the leg, asking her to look at something.

"Are you sure you wouldn't rather speak to the owner, since you know him so well, *ostie*?" Larkin had moved behind the desk, leaning on the counter, just watching her.

Quinn felt the urge to snicker again, but repressed it by biting his lower lip.

"Oh, I'll be sure to tell him about you two! Hope you've enjoyed having a job, because you'll be unemployed tomorrow! MAN-A-GER!"

Sandra, having heard how the entire situation was degenerating, pushed aside the chain curtain and glanced at Larkin and Quinn.

The woman spotted her immediately. "YOU!" She pointed at Sandra. "YOU! Are you the manager? You need to fire these two! They've been nothing but rude to me and my son and that freak over there..." Larkin was in the path of her pointed finger, "...assaulted me!"

"Mama!" The little boy was still poking her knee. "Look what I found! I have it?"

"Of course you can have it, sweetheart!" the woman suddenly cooed to the child, without even glancing at him. "And that man..."

she pointed to Sandra "…is going to give it to you! It's the least he can do after we've been treated!"

Quinn and Larkin both looked at Sandra, who raised her eyebrow with its silver piercing at the woman. Quinn lowered his head, trying to hide the grin spreading across his face as Sandra looked down at her chest, checking to make sure her breasts were still present and accounted for. He bit his lip harder, marvelling at how Larkin kept his face so blank in the face of this absurdity.

"Yeah, no," Sandra said. "First of all, lady, I'm not the manager; you need to speak with the owner. And secondly," Sandra emphasized the word as the woman tried to cut her off—"I think you need glasses, since I'm definitely not a man. And thirdly, that's an original 1972 Blythe doll your little crotch spawn is holding, worth six hundred seventy-five dollars, and no one here is just going to give it to you!"

Everyone turned to look at the little boy, who was playing with the dark-haired doll in a green and yellow paisley dress with a crocheted white collar, just as he pulled the head off, revealing the string running from the doll's head to the body.

"Mama, fix this?" The boy held up the broken doll. The mother just stared at the ruined toy.

Larkin took a deep breath and lifted his chin. "As she said, ma'am, that doll is an original 1972 Blythe doll. The dress is not original, but appears to have been hand-made and added later. Both the doll and the dress are in very good condition, and the detail on the dress is quite exquisite and shows fantastic workmanship. The string you pull to change the eye colour of the doll is also functioning, which is a rarity. Valued at six hundred seventy-five Canadian, although it could fetch more at open auction. Will you be paying by cash or credit card?"

"What? I'm not paying for this trash! I could buy this at Walmart for twenty bucks! Besides, no boy should be playing with girl dolls like that!"

She swung toward Quinn and snapped her fingers at him like he was a dog. "You! You! What's the name of the owner?"

Quinn, still shaken by her earlier comments, replied without thinking, "Larkin Childs."

"I thought you knew the owner?" Sandra smirked.

"Shut up!" barked the woman. "I want to speak to him now!! You! Give me his phone number!" She started snapping her fingers at Quinn again, who remained frozen.

"If you know the owner so well, shouldn't you already have his number?" Sandra inquired with seeming innocence. Quinn snorted around a repressed laugh.

"Would you prefer to speak to the owner in person, *madame?*" Larkin asked, deadpan.

"YES!! GO GET HIM NOW!"

Quinn winced as she roared, but he was impressed as well. *Her tone 40 is spot on. It might be one of the best I've ever heard.*

Larkin stepped back and turned to walk through the chain curtain, saying "*excusez-moi*" to Sandra as he moved past her and into the back. He was gone all of three seconds before walking back in.

"Well?" the woman demanded with a smirk.

"You asked to speak to the owner, madame. I am the owner, *ostie.*"

"Bullshit!"

Larkin walked over to her, pulled his wallet from his back pocket, and took out his driver's licence to hold up so she could clearly see his name and photo.

The woman stared at it for a moment, gaping as reality finally started to sink in.

Behind Larkin, still in the doorway, Sandra smirked.

"Now, again, *madame,* will you be paying by cash, credit, or debit?"

"This is bull! You're not the owner! And I'm not paying that for some stupid fuckin' doll!"

"Madame," Larkin's voice dropped, more measured now, as if he were holding himself in check. His eyes had gone darker and dangerous. "I am the owner, and you will not leave this shop without paying for the item your son damaged. Now…"

"But he's just a child!" The woman shifted from screaming to wailing, trying to elicit sympathy.

Larkin ignored the change in tone.

Sandra rolled her eyes, still smirking. Quinn's gaze flicked between them, following every move.

"Ben là! Yes, *madame,* he's a child who cannot be held legally responsible for his actions, which means you are legally responsible for his actions, *ostie.* You can either pay now or leave me your information, and I will take you to small claims court. Cash, debit, or credit?"

Instead of answering, the woman grabbed her son's hand and headed for the door, roughly dragging the now-crying child behind her. She shoved Quinn out of the way, hard enough to knock him off balance and into a display full of brass serviceware. There was a loud clatter as several pieces toppled to the floor. The woman yanked on the door, only to find it locked.

"Madame?" Larkin barely looked up from the computer screen behind the desk. "Any items damaged when you assaulted my staff will also need to be paid for, *ostie.*"

"What the fuck are you talking about? What assault? You can't keep me here!"

"You are correct. I can't and I won't—as soon as you pay. *Ça va, Quinn?*"

"*Pas mal,*" Quinn replied as he regained his footing.

"*Bon.* Perhaps we won't press charges then, *hein*? Is there anything on that display that's damaged?"

Quinn bent to look over the display. "Not that I can see, Lark."

"*Bon.* Now, madame, how will you be paying for the doll?"

"I'm not paying a damn thing! Unlock this door!" she hollered at Quinn.

"*Non*, madame, he won't."

"I'll call the police! This is false imprisonment!"

Larkin looked up with the slightest smirk on his lips; his eyes had shifted again, looking lighter. He moved from behind the counter to the front, leaned back, folded his arms across his chest, ankles crossed, and regarded the woman with cold eyes and an implacable gaze.

"Call them." His monotone still carried over the wailing child. He almost sounded bored. "Please do. I know the police well. They'll look at the security footage from the cameras *là, là, là, et là*. They record audio as well."

He straightened and walked up to her slowly. When he reached her, he leaned in so that his face was centimetres from hers, fixing his cold gaze on her eyes.

"Do you really think they'll side with you, *ostie*? I've had the police here before; they won't just take my word, they'll look at the videos, and they'll get your information for me. Then I'll take you to small claims court, where they'll watch the footage and make you pay anyway, as well as covering all my court costs and the assault on my staff, *ostie.*"

He leaned in even closer, almost nose to nose. "I have thousands of dollars' worth of stock in this store," he said quietly. "Do you really think I wouldn't have every inch of this place covered? Do you really think I haven't done this before? *Sacréfice!* I'm a small business owner, and you're just an entitled woman with an equally entitled brat. Do you really think the police will listen to you over me, *ostie*—especially when there's indisputable evidence that proves my version of events, including the wilful destruction of my property by your child? Do you really think I won't have you charged with assaulting Quinn if I have to go to the trouble of dealing with the police? And, of course, that's all on video as well. You can go to prison for assault, *vous souvenez, mademoiselle, ostie*? Prison—and away from your precious little darling for months, perhaps years, if the judge is in a poor mood."

The woman's eyes widened even more as Larkin straightened and walked back to the counter. When he spoke again, he didn't bother to look up: "Cash, debit, or credit?"

The woman hesitated, considering her options.

Quinn held his breath, waiting for her to explode.

"Credit," she finally mumbled.

Larkin slowly smiled, showing his teeth.

Chapter Twenty-Nine

"That was amazing!" cheered Quinn after the woman and child finally left with the broken, but paid-for, doll in hand. "Larkin, that was awesome! How'd you know she'd pay in the end?"

"He's good." Sandra laughed. "He's good!"

"*Merci*, both of you." Larkin was still smiling as he entered the sale into the computer. "I've been doing this for some time, *mon ami*. I knew she was going to be trouble as soon as she walked in, *criss*. I'd have lost more money than I would care to count if I didn't know how to deal with people like that. How do you feel, *cher*? Better? She didn't hurt you, did she?"

"Yeah, no, I'm fine. How long have you been selling antiques, anyway?"

"*Hum*, let's see… I started in Sarasota, that was...eight years ago, now."

"Did you own a shop there?"

"*Non*, someone I knew did, and I used to work for him. He taught me all about antiques."

"A friend of yours?"

"Not really." Larkin headed to the back, cigarettes and lighter in hand, calling over his shoulder, "Sandra, could you watch the shop, *mon amie*? I need a smoke after that." Quinn followed.

"Sure! No problem."

"What do you mean, 'not really'?" Quinn asked.

Larkin leaned against the side of the building and crossed his ankles. His face was briefly lit by fireglow as he flicked his lighter to life and lit his cigarette. He inhaled deeply, holding the smoke for a few seconds before exhaling. "A friend. *Oui,* but more than that as well."

More than that? Larkin—

"I'd really prefer not to discuss it, *mon cher ami.* Some memories are better left in the dust where they belong." Larkin put his left hand to his ear, fingers curled into a loose fist, and turned his head away slightly.

Quinn noticed every time he did it. It was an odd gesture; he didn't think Larkin was aware he was doing it. "Oh… Oh, sorry." Pause. "Can I ask you something?"

"But, of course."

"Does it...bother you?"

"Does what bother me, *mon ami?*"

"When she called you...us...fags?"

"That? *Mais non!* Why should it? People will say whatever they want, no matter what. Better to just ignore them."

"But, what she said—"

"It's not really an insult, *mon ami.*"

Quinn gaped. "It's not?"

"*Non.* Not to me. Why should it be? People are who they are, *mon ami.* It's only an insult if you think it is."

It's only an insult if you think it is. Quinn frowned at the ground, trying to understand what Larkin was saying.

They stayed that way for a few moments, Quinn's mind racing and Larkin exhaling clouds of smoke, one man with his eyes cast down and the other looking up at the sky. "*Ben là.*" Larkin sighed.

Quinn looked up to find Larkin staring at him. The way the sunlight struck him made his eyes almost glow. "Quinn, *mon ami*, I know that your church...has some very set ideas about such things, *ostie. Mais*, you should know that many disagree with them on that point in particular. I'm not trying to be critical. I know how you're taught to react to criticism. But you should be aware that not everyone shares your view."

Quinn felt his stomach flip over. He looked away to the side. "And you're one of those people who don't share that view?" he asked cautiously.

"Yes, I don't agree with their stance on that point."

Quinn frowned, but he still didn't look at Larkin. A puff of wind blew cigarette smoke across his field of vision. "Why?" *Why did I ask that?*

"*Pourquoi?*" Larkin repeated. "Because people are who they are. They are as *le bon Dieu* made them, no matter what."

"So, you don't think it's..." *Perverted? Disgusting? Revolting?* "...wrong?"

"No, I don't."

Agitated, Quinn started to walk away only to turn on his heel and stalk back. He did this several times while Larkin watched. "Why?" Quinn said suddenly as he stopped, his question in an accusatory tone. "Why don't you think it's wrong?"

"As I said, people are as they're made."

"That doesn't make it right!" Quinn started to pace again.

"Doesn't it? *Le bon Dieu* made me an albino; can I change that? No. Can I change my eye colour? No. My height? I'd love to be taller, but no, I am as tall as I'll ever be. Why should who we desire, who we love, be any different? I can't change that any more than I can change my complexion."

"But it *is* possible to change that! The Church says when you go Clear, that changes!" He stopped pacing to look at Larkin directly again, challenging him.

"*Vraiment?* Quinn, I was raised Catholic, did you know that?"

Quinn shook his head no.

"*Eh bien.* The Catholic church, too, has set ideas on that subject; they share much the same position as your church. I've known people who tried to turn themselves into something they weren't. There's a saying in English, 'pray the gay away'; it doesn't work, Quinn. Some people will pretend it does; they lie to themselves to please their families, the clergy, or society, but it really doesn't work. It just doesn't. Why do you think that is? Because *le bon Dieu* made them, He made them a certain way, and they can't change it, no matter how they try. Who am I to question how they were made? Who am I to question how Sandra was made, *hein*?"

"Sandra? What are you talking about?"

"She has a lovely wife named Beverly. Didn't you know? Adorable woman, I've met her more than once. Now, are they to be despised because they love each other, as *le bon Dieu* intended? Or how I was made, for that matter? There have been a great many people who think my appearance is gross and disgusting. Even that woman today called me a freak. Should I hate myself because they judge me by my complexion? Should I wear makeup and dye my hair to please them? Those are just masks, bandages. The truth is, I can cover it up, but I can't actually change. And why should I try to change to please others? For every one that thinks I'm gross, others think I'm angelic, elf-like, and beautiful. Why should Sandra and Bev hide who they are, hide their love, to please others?"

Quinn didn't know how to respond; he was unable to meet Larkin's eyes. *You're beautiful, to me, anyway.*

"The truth is, Quinn, people will judge you, no matter what, and it's a terrible thing to be forced to hate yourself, whether it's for being an albino, or gay"—Quinn winced at the word—"or for whatever reason. I don't think there is anything sadder than hating yourself."

There was a strange tone in Larkin's voice; he sounded sad as he took a step forward and put out his cigarette on the side of the dumpster. Quinn watched as he carefully pinched the burnt end between his thumb and forefinger before flicking it into the dumpster, following Quinn's apple core. "Besides," he said as he turned to look at Quinn, "I have enough darkness in me without adding someone else's reason to hate myself." With that, he turned and walked back into the store.

Hate myself...wait, what?

Quinn almost ran after him. "Larkin! What do you mean? Are you saying that you're..."

Larkin stopped and looked over his shoulder, then turned to face him. "I've been told I'm as rare as a unicorn," he said with just a hint of a smile. "I've always loved both men and women equally, although I don't think it's really so rare as that."

Quinn stared at him. The childhood crushes Larkin had mentioned suddenly meant nothing; this was confirmation.

"You? How can you be—" He couldn't finish the sentence.

"I believe the word that's commonly used is 'bisexual,'" Larkin replied, unconcerned. "*Mais*, I don't care for labels; they don't mean anything."

"But, but, I thought... I thought that because you're—"

"I'm what?"

"You're...so, well..." Larkin's head tilted to the left quizzically, eyes revealing nothing. "You're so...attractive, I thought you'd have all kinds of women after you!"

Larkin smiled at that, an open smile that showed his teeth. *Even his teeth are beautiful.*

"*Quoi ça?* There have been some women who've found me attractive, *oui.* I've even been called beautiful once or twice, but there have been many more who are disgusted or scared by me. Men, too."

The air started to leave the room. Quinn started to go external, something he'd never been able to do at will. He was watching himself from off to the right, floating above himself, and saw himself standing there in his threadbare jeans and blue T-shirt, as if he were looking at a stranger.

"The man...the one who owned the store that you mentioned..." His voice sounded like someone else's.

"In Sarasota. *Oui?*"

"You said…he was...more than a friend. Does that mean…"

"He was my partner, yes."

But that means...that means that if I...if I...he might... I could... We could... Quinn was suddenly in his own body again. His head spun, and the room seemed to close in around him. His vision tunneled in until he could only see a small amount of what was right in front of him. His head felt like a balloon. The floor shifted and tilted under his feet. Larkin had come closer and was speaking, but he seemed far away, and Quinn couldn't hear or understand what he was saying. Part of his mind wondered if he was going to faint.

He staggered as everything suddenly came rushing back and found Larkin had caught his arm and was steadying him. He would have fallen otherwise.

"Quinn! Are you alright?"

"Yeah…yeah. I think so. I don't know what happened." Still feeling lightheaded, he put his hand to his head and found that his hair was wet from sweat.

"You ok?" asked Sandra from the shop doorway. She'd heard the commotion and came to check.

"Yeah, I think so."

"I knew you weren't well. Come," Larkin took Quinn's wrist and pulled him towards the back door.

"I'm fine, Larkin! Honestly!" Quinn protested, but his eyes seemed riveted to Larkin's hand on his wrist as he pulled Quinn outside and headed towards his apartment door; he could feel the tips of his fingers pressed into his skin.

"*Non*, you're not. You're going upstairs to lie down."

"Really, Lark, I'm fine!"

"*Non!* No argument. You're going to lie down. Now."

Larkin's hand felt cold against his skin. Quinn stared at it. *If he shifted his grip, he'd be holding my hand.* He stopped arguing and just followed, Larkin only letting him go long enough to unlock his apartment door. He grabbed Quinn's wrist again and pulled him up the steep stairs and into the apartment and then began pulling him up the stairs to the bedrooms, which was when Quinn resisted, bracing his right heel against the bottom step.

"Ok! Ok! Larkin! I'll go and lie down!"

Larkin came back down the two steps and turned to face the young man. "Promise?"

"Yes! I promise!"

He let Quinn go, causing Quinn a pang of disappointment. "All right, if you promise. I want you to eat whatever you want out of the fridge and then go and lie down. I'll trust you if you promise."

"I promise. Ok? I promise."

"All right." He looked at Quinn for a moment, without moving or speaking, and then, surprisingly, he reached out and took hold of the back of Quinn's neck. He held the man still so that their eyes met. Quinn held his breath. Larkin's hand was cold against the back of his neck. "Quinn, you are my dearest friend, understand? I can't, won't, let anything happen to you. Not if I can help you. *Est-ce que tu comprends?*"

He looked at Larkin, looked into the amber eyes that were locked to him, and saw the intensity. "I understand, Lark," he said finally, quietly, voice just above a whisper. "Thank you."

Larkin let him go and stepped back; he still looked concerned, his eyes still frowning. "Eat," he repeated. "Eat whatever you want and then lie down, you clearly need it."

Quinn nodded again.

Larkin took another step back, but kept staring at Quinn, as if he were reluctant to leave. "Call or text me and let me know if you need anything, *cher*."

"I will, promise."

Larkin hesitated again, still watching.

"I'm fine, Lark, honest, I'll eat! I'll lie down!"

"*D'accord*," he said as he turned away and headed towards the door. "There are some hard-boiled eggs in the fridge, *cher*."

"Ok! Don't worry." Quinn waited until Larkin had left before sitting down on the steps. He didn't understand what had happened, why he'd suddenly felt so strange, and why he'd lost his balance. He put his face into his hands, vigorously rubbed his face to wake himself up, and shoved his hands up into his damp curly hair, trying to clear his head.

Larkin. Larkin likes men. He likes both men and women. He's not seeing anyone, or he didn't say he was, anyway. 'Cher' means dear. Does that mean I'm dear to him? "Quinn, you are my dearest friend, understand? I can't, won't let anything happen to you. Not if I can help you. Est-ce que tu comprends?" Yes, I understand, I'm your friend. But what if that's not what I want? What if I...want more?

Finding no ready answers, Quinn finally reached up to grasp the handrail, pulled himself to his feet, and slowly made his way to the fridge. There on the middle shelf was a small steel bowl full of hard-boiled eggs, along with a much bigger steel bowl overflowing with cut-up watermelon. He'd never had watermelon before, so he reached for the eggs first. He pulled out two eggs. He flipped up the lid of the small green food waste bin, cracked the eggshell on the counter, and began peeling one.

He stood at the counter, eating and going over everything in his head. *What do I want? Do I want to ignore this, all of this? If I want to move up the Bridge, I have to. I can't, can't act on this. But what if I can't ignore it? I couldn't help myself with Malcolm, so what if I can't ignore this? 1.1 one-one...overtly hostile. Out ethics. SP.*

Quinn could even remember the quote from the Source himself. *"The sexual pervert...such as homosexuality, lesbianism...is quite ill physically."* Out to destroy the Church. Pervert. Queer. Repulsive. Disgusting. Faggot. *"And for every one that thinks I'm gross, there are others who think I'm angelic, elf-like, and beautiful."*

While he ate, Quinn remembered the way the sunlight struck Larkin's eyes, making them glow, the light gold colour. Remembered his pale hands and long fingers, the delicate way he held his cigarette, fingers curved inwards. He considered every detail about Larkin, the way he walked with a natural grace despite his long limbs. Considered the man's feet, how they looked in sandals. He liked his feet, although he didn't really know why. He thought about the way the tattoos that covered his limbs moved, saturated colours and shading standing out sharply against the white skin. Then there were Larkin's pale pink lips, the way he licked his lips when he was concentrating, usually when staring at his computer screen. When he smiled, it often seemed almost fragile, making his face look softer, innocent, and open. It happened so rarely, but it was beautiful when it did.

He is beautiful. How could anyone think he isn't? Are their eyes painted on?

Quinn sighed as he went back to the fridge, both eggs now gone. He found the block of cheese that Larkin always seemed to have and pulled it out. He used a small paring knife to cut off two thick pieces before carefully rewrapping them and returning them to the fridge.

He looked again at the bowl piled high with pink watermelon. Eventually, he selected a smallish piece and went back to where he'd left the pieces of cheese on the counter. He took a bite of the sharp cheese, then took a small, careful bite of the watermelon. It was sweet and full of juice, which promptly ran down his chin and into his beard. *Water. Watermelon. Of course, duh.* He leaned on the counter in much the same way Larkin did, back against the edge and ankles crossed, occasionally wiping the water from his beard with his hand as he ate.

He thought about the way Larkin's left hand would go to his ear, fingers curled almost into a fist as he covered his mangled ear. Remembered the scar on his face, the way it went through his ear and followed the jawline to tick up at the end like a checkmark in reverse. *How did you get that scar, Lark?*

He eventually trudged upstairs, paused in front of the spare bedroom, and looked to the right. The door to Larkin's room was wide open. Quinn hesitated and then slowly went to the door to cautiously look inside. He didn't know what he had expected, but somehow the room didn't look like he'd thought it would. There was a white floor fan set close to the foot of the bed. The bed was unmade, the blue-and-white plaid sheets rumpled, with a thick, fluffy white blanket piled on one side. A bright red throw rug was at the foot. Bright white curtains with a stark black damask pattern hung on the overly large window, which was open to the wind.

The walls were the same nondescript beige as the rest of the apartment, and the hardwood floor gleamed. On the left side of the room was a large cherry wood dresser with a huge oval mirror and carved ornamental swirls that framed the glass. There was a large pile of books on the cherry wood nightstand to the right of the bed, which had a small light sitting on top of them. On the other side was another chest of drawers, made of a dark wood that Quinn couldn't identify, a black chest sitting on top. Carefully, Quinn took a step inside, as if the floor was laden with traps.

I shouldn't be here. But he took another careful step, his eyes on the black chest. It reminded him of a pirate chest. About the size of a bread box, it was dull black with what looked like leather bands along the edges, and another that went straight up the middle. The middle band featured a brass padlock. Creeping like a burglar, he moved further inside the room, going to the side of the bed to contemplate the chest. The padlock looked old, and the key wasn't anywhere to be seen, so there was no possibility of opening it. Not that he would. Quinn guessed that Larkin wouldn't take snooping well. He rapped the lid lightly a couple of times with a knuckle, to be greeted with a thin, hollow sound. *Yeah, plywood, that's the right word. Larkin taught me that.* Quinn smiled to himself. *"My secrets keep themselves." What did he mean by that? Is whatever is in this chest one of his secrets?*

Quinn sat down on the edge of the bed, which sank slightly beneath his weight, when a familiar smell suddenly caught his attention.

Peppermint, with a trace of old dust. He turned and looked around but saw nothing that could cause the smell. He took a moment to look at Larkin's closet; the door was open, and he could see countless pairs of jeans neatly folded and hung up, as well as a few dress shirts mostly in dark colours. He looked back down at the bed and, after hesitating again, reached out to pick up Larkin's pillow and hold it close to his face. Quinn inhaled deeply and was rewarded by the familiar smell. He held the pillow away from his face and looked at it, the blue and white checkered pillowcase soft beneath his fingers.

Peppermint again. That means...the peppermint smell is Larkin's scent. The dust must be from the stuff he works with. Larkin. He smells of peppermint. How weird is that? I love peppermint.

He held the pillow to his face again and inhaled more deeply. Immediately, he felt himself relax; he felt the tension leave him, tension he'd become so used to that he wasn't even aware of until it drained away, leaving him feeling limp and a bit dopey. *I must be really tired. I need to get up and go lie down in the other room.* But he couldn't; he wanted to get up, but his body refused to listen to him. Instead, he found himself almost falling over into the bed.

I'll get up in a few minutes. Larkin won't know I was here. I'll get up in a minute. He kicked off his shoes and heard them clunk against the floor as they fell away, and he tucked the pillow under his head. He lay on his left side, with his arm under the pillow to support his head and his knees bent. Just a couple of minutes. He reached over and pulled the white blanket over himself, finding it to be surprisingly soft and comfortable. The smell of peppermint surrounded him, and he smiled to himself.

As he felt himself relax further, his mind wandered back to that horrible night that he and Malcolm were caught. He tried to push the memories away, but his internal darkness fought back and asserted itself against Quinn's will.

Chapter Thirty

"Yes." Warren looked over his shoulder with a smile like a razor blade. "What will we do with you?"

The only mercy he was shown was that Warren allowed him to get dressed, all while Quinn wept uncontrollably.

They all piled into the elevator, Tom's death grip on Quinn's arm so tight it felt like the bone might crack. Quinn kept his head down, tears still flowing, unable to look at anyone. No one spoke, but he thought he heard Joni sniffle. She might have been crying, but she managed to hold herself together enough that Warren ignored her. Warren didn't speak until they got out of the elevator.

"Make sure he doesn't lose consciousness, Tom," he instructed as he headed towards the van without so much as a glance at Quinn. "He needs to go through this to see the error of his ways, to see how ill he really is. It's the only way to get him back."

"Yes, sir!"

The punishment began as soon as they got out of the black former police van that the Church owned. Warren got in the front to drive, while Joni climbed into the passenger seat. They'd parked in the back of the building near the green dumpsters. Quinn could smell the garbage and saw bits of trash near his feet as he stared down at his shoes.

Tom grabbed him by the front of his shirt and the waist of his jeans and tossed him into the van like a rag doll; Quinn's slight frame was no challenge for the bigger man. The bang when he hit the bare metal floor was deafening. The wind was knocked out of him at once, and the congestion from crying only made it worse. He gasped like a fish on land.

He tried to roll away as Tom climbed into the back and slammed the doors shut. There, in the dark, Quinn felt Tom's thick fingers in his hair as he hauled him further into the van and away from the doors. Quinn cried out at the sharp pain and tried to grab Tom's wrists, only to be met with a series of punches to his face before Tom let him drop to the floor, forehead striking the metal. He'd heard the expression *seeing stars* before, but never thought it was real until all he could see were bright lights and colours behind his eyes and all he could feel was blinding, electric pain. His brain felt like it was vibrating from the deepest point outward until it hit his skull. His vision and thoughts blurred. He tasted blood and spat it onto the van floor.

He felt the van begin to move, the rocking motion only adding to his misery. Pain radiated through his body like waves on a pond, leaving him both dull and raw.

"How could you let us down like this?" Tom demanded as he pulled Quinn to his feet by his shirt, then drove his knee into Quinn's stomach. Quinn dropped in a heap, coughing and retching. He tried to curl into a fetal position, but it didn't help.

"You're on staff!" Tom bellowed as he began punching the back of Quinn's head. "UGH! You're supposed to set an example! Fuckin' faggot! How could you do this?"

Quinn whimpered, unable to reply. He didn't hear the sound of Tom taking off his belt or see him fold it in half, buckle in his left hand.

"This is your own fault!" Tom screamed as he brought the belt down on Quinn's back.

Quinn felt the buckle; he heard it rattle as it hit his flesh, heard the sickening whack as it struck, felt the deep pain spreading through his spine and ribs. He tried to roll away again, only to feel more blows across his back. His eyes squeezed shut. Tom was throwing his weight behind each blow, punctuating every word.

"This is because of your actions!" ***Whack!***

Quinn rolled towards him, but the blows shifted to his ribs and stomach.

"Your choices caused this!" *Whack—whack!*

He rolled back onto his stomach, but there was no escape. Instinct made him cover his head. Tom brought the belt buckle down on his knuckles in an explosion of pain. Quinn was certain his hand had been broken, but he bit his tongue trying not to scream, biting down so hard he tasted blood again.

"See what you're making us do?" *Whack—whack—whack!*

Gritting his teeth, Quinn tried not to scream but ended up coughing up more blood.

"See what you're making *me* do?" *Whack—whack—whack—whack—whack!*

"Please," Quinn managed to whimper, but Tom acted as if he hadn't heard.

"This—" *Whack!*

"Is—" *Whack!*

"For—" *Whack!*

"Your—" *Whack—whack!*

"Own—" *Whack—whack—whack!*

"Good!" *Whack—whack—whack—whack!*

Quinn couldn't hold it any longer. He began to cough and sputter, finally retching up whatever he'd eaten earlier along with more blood.

"You're scum. Ugh!" Tom watched him vomit, voice full of disgust. "You turned your back on the entire world, do you realize that? The entire world is counting on us to Clear it, to make it a better place, and you want to throw that all away for what? To...ugh, fuck a man? You're disgusting. Fuckin' nasty, gross faggot."

Quinn tried to get to his knees, but his arms were wrapped around his stomach, so he braced himself with his forehead and drew his knees up to his chest. He could taste the dirt on the van floor, taste and smell metal and blood, the sour reek of his own vomit surrounding him, making him feel sick all over again. His mouth was full of nothing but blood and bile.

"People like you have to be brought to heel," Tom continued, parroting Warren's phrasing. "You need to take responsibility for what you've done. You pervert and disgrace the good name of our Church for sensuality and deny the truth of L. Ron's vision, of his words. LRH would beat you into the ground if he were here." His voice sounded rehearsed, as if reciting a script.

"Please," Quinn whispered, his face still pressed to the floor. "Please."

"PLEASE," Tom mocked, mimicking Quinn's tone. "Please. Please, what? Please let me go so I can mock the Source even more? So I can spit in the face of the Chairman of the Board again? So you can spread lies and misinformation about the Church? So you can push your filthy gay agenda onto our members? Eh? Please what, queer?"

There was a loud thunking sound as Tom moved around Quinn's prone body, his heavy footsteps unmuffled by his running shoes. His heels struck the van floor with force.

"P… Please, I wo...won't…"

"Won't what?"

"I...w-w-wouldn't… I w-won't…"

"You're repeating yourself, scumbag."

"I'm…"

"Say you're scum," snapped Tom as he kicked Quinn in the stomach. Quinn let out a deep groan, followed by another hacking, retching cough. Tom pulled his leg back as far as possible, and Quinn felt another intense impact in the same spot. The kick landed high and in the centre of his body. An intense cramp seized his lower ribs on top of the pain of the blow. He couldn't breathe.

"Say it!" Tom screamed and kicked him again in the same place.

There was nothing but the pain, nothing but the tightening cramp. Quinn felt himself exhale whatever tiny bit of air he had left. Then there was nothing. Just blackness.

The next thing he knew, he was being dragged by the back of his shirt. The floor beneath him was smooth and cold. He thought he could hear Joni crying, pleading, but she seemed far away. Warren was yelling again, but that, too, felt distant.

Mom, he tried to call. *Please...Mom... Mommy...help...please.* He didn't know if she could hear him. So overtaken by the abuse, reality had abandoned him. He didn't know if his plea had actually left his lips, but he hoped it had. He managed to crack his eyes open just enough to see grey tiles sliding past beneath him. He closed them again. He knew where he was going. He heard a door being unlocked, felt Tom drag him inside and toss him unceremoniously onto a lumpy mattress. There was a loud thud as yet another spring broke.

"None of us want to do this, Quinn," he heard Warren say from behind Tom.

Quinn turned his head and managed to open one eye to see Warren move past the larger man and stand over him. "We have no choice. You are ill, Quinn, seriously, physically ill. So that some good can come from you, even though you are a worthless, filthy faggot, we need to make an example of you. We must make it clear that even a disgusting piece of shit like you can be cured of your illness, so you won't stop us from Clearing the planet. We'll get you back on track, and your example will become a shining beacon of what can be done if you have the right attitude. This is all for your own good, remember that."

"P…Please," Quinn mumbled.

Warren bent stiffly at the waist, arms folded behind him, looming over Quinn. "Hmm? I can't hear you."

"Please…don't…" Even the tiniest breath sent pain through his ribs. He couldn't speak above a mumble.

"Don't what?"

"D…don't…hurt…Malcolm. Please."

"Malcolm? How touching, you're worried about your unnatural boyfriend?" Warren sneered. "I'd be more worried about yourself, Quinn. Son of a low-life apostate and now this. Tsk, tsk, tsk. The congregation won't accept you back so easily; it will take a great deal of effort on your part to get yourself back into our good graces, to heal yourself. You already have two strikes against you. You should ponder your life choices and actions, Quinn, and decide what it was that influenced your overts, what led you to this place. It's time to pay the piper, as they say. Remember, this is for your own good."

Quinn stared at Warren's feet, watched the brown loafers turn on a heel and walk out. He heard the door slam and then the locks being fastened.

The Hole in the Calgary Org. A tiny, windowless room that had most likely been a storage closet once, with just a twin mattress, a sink, and a bucket for a toilet. The single light bulb hanging from a bare wire began to sway from the force of the door slamming, causing shadows to stretch and dance wildly around him. Quinn couldn't look; their crazy movements made him want to vomit again.

He closed his eyes, buried his face in the filthy, flat, caseless pillow, and started to cry all over again. He wasn't sure what he was crying for—Malcolm, himself, the embarrassment, the shame, the fear—or all of it.

He wept for a long time. When he finally started to calm down, he realized that at some point during the beating he'd wet himself. Disgusted, he began taking off his jeans. Every movement rubbed his injuries raw again, sending flares of new pain through him.

He pulled himself into a sitting position and, moving slowly and carefully, undid his jeans and started to peel them off. He didn't have the strength to stand, so he leaned back and managed to lift his hips just enough to drag them down. He pulled them off along with his shoes and socks. The smell of urine was overpowering, so he threw the jeans across the room. They hit the wall a couple of meters from the foot of the mattress with a dull, wet thwack, but that was as far away as he could get them. His boxers followed.

Cold, aching from head to toe, disgusted and miserable, Quinn found the edge of the itchy, dirty blanket and pulled it over himself as he shivered on the mattress. He looked at his hand, the one he was convinced Tom had broken. The back of it was one massive, deep purple bruise. It had swollen to the size of a tangerine, and moving his fingers sent a shot of blinding pain through him. Both eyes were starting to swell shut, and he could still taste vomit and blood. Anything beyond a shallow breath caused crippling pain. Quinn wondered if his ribs were broken.

He pulled his knees up as much as he could, curling into a fetal position to try to relieve the pain. It took time to find a position where every bone and muscle didn't scream quite so loudly.

My fault. This is all my fault. I brought all this on myself, pulled this in. How could I have been so stupid? How could I let this happen? Joni will never forgive me. I'm so stupid, I'm such a failure. I failed. I failed everyone. I let everyone down. I failed Joni. I failed Warren. I failed the rest of the members, my friends. I failed the Church itself. I failed LRH. I failed the planet. I failed at my job. I've failed at my job lots and lots of times, but this is the worst. They'll never forgive this. A total failure.

I even failed Malcolm! I couldn't protect him, I couldn't stand up for him, or keep him from being punished. If I were really in love with him, I should've told them it was all me. I took the blame and saved him that way. Malcolm. Malcolm, I'm so sorry! I'm so, so sorry!

They're going to expel me and declare me! I just know it! Oh, God, what will I do? I don't know anyone, I don't have anything, anywhere to go. I'll be on the streets! Elijah. Elijah just blew. Maybe, if I could find him. Maybe…

But what's the point? He'll probably reject me as well. Besides, he's an apostate, like Warren said. God knows what kind of degrading shit he's into. Probably drugged up by doctors, trying to destroy the Church. That's who I've turned into? An enemy? An actual Suppressive Person? I'm such a loser!

I should just kill myself and do everyone a favour. No one actually needs me, needs me to be here…

His thoughts went around and around like this until he finally managed to drift off to sleep, despite the pain, despite the cold and the shame. Despite everything, he managed to sleep, if only fitfully.

Chapter Thirty-One

Quinn startled out of his dream, breathing heavily. He looked around the room, trying to get his bearings. Instead of the filthy walls, dirty mattress, and dingy blanket he expected, he saw a fluffy white blanket, clean beige walls, and a nightstand with a pile of books written in French.

He looked around, trying to understand what he was seeing. *Where the hell am I? Oh wait. Oh my God! I went to sleep!* He threw the blanket off and looked down in horror at where he had dropped his shoes. There they were, neatly placed side by side, toes against the dresser, waiting for him. He could still see them clearly in the rapidly fading evening light. *Oh shit.*

He picked up his shoes by their backs, as if they were a pair of snakes. Then he realized that the door had been shut and that the fan, which hadn't been on before, was now running, the air cool against his damp face. Panting, mind racing, he stood.

He saw me. He came in and saw me. Saw me in his bed. Asleep. What is he going to think? What will he say? He'll be mad, I know it. He'll kick me out. What am I going to do?

He stood there, head hanging in dread, trying to slow his breathing before finally going to the door. He slipped through and carefully shut it behind him. Padding to the top of the stairs, shoes in hand, he looked down.

Larkin was sitting on his cream couch adorned with ugly orange flowers, a dark green mug perched on the arm, his knees bent, bare feet resting on the sofa, a large art book in his hands. His head was almost lost under giant black noise-cancelling headphones. Despite the hardware, he looked up, apparently having some intangible clue that Quinn was there. "Ah! You're up, *mon ami!*" he called, taking off the headphones and pressing a button on his tablet to stop the music. "Did you sleep well? How do you feel? Better?"

"Larkin, I'm so sorry." Walking carefully down the stairs, he waited for Larkin to yell, certain it was coming.

"For what?"

"For…well…"

"Falling asleep in my bed?" The tone of his voice held a hint of a smile.

"Yeah, that. I didn't mean it, I don't know how it happened. I wasn't trying to, you know, snoop around your room or anything." *Only, that's exactly what I was doing.*

"*De rien, cher.* It's fine. I told you, my secrets keep themselves. I don't mind."

By now, Quinn was at the bottom of the stairs and saw Larkin's face. He actually looked amused; his expression was a cross between a smile and a smirk. Even his eyes seemed to be smiling. Quinn couldn't believe it. No yelling, no anger, just wry amusement.

"But I—I shouldn't have gone into your room!"

"If I were that interested in keeping you out of my room, *cher*, I'd have shut the door, don't you think?"

"But there was no one here when you got up this morning!"

"True, but I could easily have gone upstairs and shut the door when I brought you up here, *non*? It's fine. You looked unhappy in your sleep, though. Did you have a nightmare?"

"Kind of, yeah."

"Well, there's food in the oven. *Pardon,* I didn't wait for you to get up, I ordered for you. I wasn't sure what you'd want, so I hope you like it." Larkin looked back at his book, leaving a confused Quinn standing there. After a few seconds, he looked up again. "*Kessé?*"

"You're really not mad?"

"Mad? *Hein?* Why should I be? I admit I was surprised when I didn't find you in the spare room, and even more surprised to find you in my bed. But you looked so comfortable, and you were so worn out, I had no intention of waking you. Besides, I always heard it was a poor thing to wake someone from a dream, even a nightmare. What were you dreaming about?"

"Oh...uh…someone I used to know, that's all. You're really not upset?"

Larkin set his book aside and looked up at Quinn, eyes smiling and an actual slight smile on his lips. "No, *cher*, I'm not angry, or upset, or mad, pissed, or whatever synonym you care to use."

Quinn smiled back.

"Now, go eat, *mon ami.* Everything is in the oven on low to keep warm. Just help yourself."

He could breathe again. He hadn't even realized he'd been holding his breath, but the relief was so tangible he had to lean on the handrail for a moment to steady himself before setting his shoes down on the bottom step and heading to the kitchen, a smile brightening his face. He opened the oven and found several round tin containers with cardboard lids inside, as well as a plate with half a dozen brown, cigar-shaped things that looked like they were made from pastry.

"Hey, Lark, what are these little things on the plate?"

"Spring rolls, *mon ami.* Be careful, the plate will be hot. I didn't want to leave them in the container, as they would get soggy. Dip them in that yellow liquid in the little containers on the counter; it's delicious."

"Yellow liquid?" Quinn turned and saw several small, round, clear plastic containers sitting on the counter. "What is it?"

"Fish sauce. Doesn't sound wonderful, but it is, really."

"Ok." Quinn took the oven mitts off the hooks above the stove and began pulling the containers and the plate out of the oven. He picked up one of the spring rolls and dipped it into the yellow liquid as Larkin had suggested. He bit into it, the thin, crisp pastry breaking easily, and found it full of bean sprouts and other vegetables. The liquid gave it a subtle flavour he couldn't describe. "Mmmm, Larkin, these are good!"

"I hoped you'd like it."

Quinn opened the aluminum containers while munching more spring rolls and found each one full of cooked noodles and vegetables, things he couldn't even name. One dish had been partly emptied and contained shrimp and other seafood along with thick noodles. There was another plate of fried rice with more seafood, also partly emptied. Larkin must have eaten part of those two. Another container held two roasted chicken leg quarters on a bed of plain white rice.

"You got chicken, Lark? Even though you won't eat it?"

"I may not eat it, but I knew you would. You need protein, *mon ami.*"

"Thanks!" He took out a large dinner plate and began helping himself, still munching on the spring rolls. The smell was fantastic; he just stood inhaling it, reveling in it. He piled the plate high. Carefully, he carried everything into the living room and sat down at the end of Larkin's mustard couch with the ugly orange, yellow, and white daisies on it. It meant he could be closer to Larkin, even though he was on the other couch.

Larkin glanced up as he sat down, noting the heavily laden plate. "You could have seconds, *tsé,*" he said with a chuckle.

"Sorry."

"*De rien,* Quinn. I'd rather you eat it than it be left over. I ordered it for you, really. Turn the TV on, if you want."

"Won't that bother you?" Quinn mumbled around a mouthful of noodles.

"No, not at all. I learned to read around noise years ago." Larkin reached over, picked up the remote, and handed it to Quinn. "Here."

Quinn balanced his plate on his knees as he leaned to take it. "What do you want to watch?"

"Whatever you'd like."

He stopped eating while he flipped through the channels, looking for something to watch. He never had time to watch TV at the Org, so everything seemed new and interesting. Eventually, he stumbled on a live show featuring police at their jobs and settled in, starting to wolf down his food, beginning with the roasted chicken. Within moments, Quinn was lost, both in the show and in the food.

Everything Larkin cooked or ordered always seemed incredible, with flavours and textures Quinn didn't have the vocabulary to describe. The vegetables were bright and crisp, paired with noodles, and were so good he couldn't seem to eat them fast enough—which was probably why some finally went down the wrong way and he started to cough. He set the plate down on the coffee table to keep from spilling it.

"You ate too fast; you should take your time." Larkin set his book aside and headed to the kitchen. Quinn was still coughing and sputtering when he came back with a large glass of water. "*Là.*"

Quinn managed a hoarse "thanks" as he took the glass.

"The food isn't going anywhere, Quinn. You don't have to eat that fast."

"Sorry. Habit."

Larkin sat back down, looked at Quinn, and smiled. His teeth weren't showing, but it looked genuine.

Quinn watched him for a moment before looking down at the plate in front of him, though he didn't pick it up. "Larkin?"

"Hm?"

"Did you mean everything you said before?" *Why in hell am I bringing this up again? What am I doing?*

"About what?"

"About…."

"Being bi?"

Quinn winced. "Yeah, that."

"Of course. Why?"

"It's just…"

"Kessé?"

"If I told you something, you wouldn't…tell anyone else, would you?"

With narrowed eyes, Larkin stared at him for a long moment. "Wait," he said, getting to his feet again, "wait here." He headed for the stairs to the bedrooms, bare feet padding on the tiles.

What am I doing? I can't tell him about Malcolm and me, can I? What would he say? What if Warren found out? But if Larkin promises… Can I trust him not to reveal anything to anyone?

Quinn looked over his shoulder as Larkin climbed the stairs, then turned back to his plate and continued eating. The spring rolls now gone, he poured the remaining fish sauce over his entire plate. He was shovelling stir-fried broccoli and carrots into his mouth when he heard Larkin coming back down the stairs.

Larkin sat down on the couch and held up his hand in front of Quinn with what looked like a necklace dangling from his fingers. It was composed of dark beads and a silver chain, with larger, single white iridescent beads interspersed here and there. The bottom of the necklace featured an oval silver medallion, from which descended another white bead, followed by three more dark beads and one more white iridescent bead, ending in a cross.

Quinn looked at it as he finished chewing his enormous mouthful and swallowed.

"Do you know what this is, *mon cher ami?*"

"No."

"It's a rosary. I told you I was raised Catholic—well, this belonged to my maternal grandmother."

"What's a rosary?"

"A rosary is a pattern of prayer, a way of praying. The beads are how you keep track. It belonged to my grandmother. The Silent Revolution meant nothing to her; she was a staunch Catholic until the day she passed—fish every Friday, I've been told. A rosary is an essential part of the Catholic tradition, Quinn. It's something we take very seriously."

"Really?"

"*Oui.* Each bead represents a type of prayer. We start here, at the crucifix, we say the *Our Father* and the *Apostles' Creed* while holding the first bead, here." Larkin indicated the large white bead. "Then these three dark beads are each for one *Hail Mary,* this bit of silver chain? That's another prayer called the *Glory Be,* then there's another *Our Father,* and then you go off to the right and say another *Hail Mary* for each of these smaller beads. There are ten, so it's known as a decade. Then we say another *Our Father* when we reach the white bead here, and so on."

"That's a lot of praying. You have to do the whole thing? How long do you have to do it for?"

"*Oui,* the prayers themselves aren't very long, but it does take time, although there isn't a set amount. Many people find comfort in the pattern, the repetition. Why am I showing you this? Because I want you to understand how seriously I take this, Quinn." Larkin held out his hand. "Give me your hand, *cher.*"

Quinn swallowed hard, even though he hadn't taken another mouthful. He leaned forward and set the plate on the table, hesitated, then reached out to take Larkin's hand. He held his breath. Larkin's hand felt warm and soft; his fingers seemed to caress Quinn's hand, like waves slipping over sand on a beach. Larkin reached over and wrapped the rosary around both their hands. Quinn stared at the dark beads against their skin, his pale and Larkin's ghostly skin together entwined.

"Quinn." He looked up to meet the intense whisky eyes boring into him. "I'm making this promise on the rosary so that you'll know how serious I am. To break a promise like this would be a terrible sin. Do you understand?"

He couldn't speak; his mouth was dry, but he nodded.

"Quinn, I promise, I swear on my grandmother's rosary, on her grave, on all that is good, before the Divine and all the angels, if they exist, that I will never tell anyone anything you say to me in confidence. Nothing you say will pass my lips to anyone else. Ever."

His lips.

"*Est-ce que tu comprends?*"

Still unable to speak, Quinn nodded again.

"*Et voilà.* Now you can tell me anything you like, *cher.*" Larkin unwrapped the rosary from their hands, let Quinn's hand go, and sat back.

Quinn looked at his hand, still feeling the warmth. He was both elated at the touch and disappointed that their contact was over.

"Do you make a lot of promises on that rosary?" It was the first thing that popped out of Quinn's mouth, and he immediately regretted how stupid it sounded.

"No, this is the first I've ever made. *Ma grand-mère* must be rolling in her grave that I have it." He could hear the beads clicking together as Larkin gathered them in his palms.

"Why?"

"She wanted to be buried with it, but *mon oncle* René took it from her dead hands, where they lay across her chest, and replaced it with another, newer rosary that had been blessed. It's a family heirloom." Larkin held the rosary up again, letting it dangle from his fingers. This time he leaned forward and held it higher so the lamplight shone through the beads.

Quinn was startled. "They're blue! They're so dark, I thought they were black!" Larkin's eyes smiled. "Are they sapphires?"

"Sapphires? Ha!" Larkin scoffed. "This would be worth more than my life if they were! No, *cher,* I believe they're Swarovski crystals. Still precious, but not so much as sapphires!"

Worth more than my life. "Tell me more about your grandmother, Lark. Please?"

"I will later, if you like. She died not long after I was born. I have stories about her that I was told, but I don't remember her. But you were going to tell me something first, *non?*"

Quinn's stomach flipped; he stared at the plate in front of him, suddenly not feeling hungry.

"Does whatever it is have to do with your nightmare, *mon ami?*"

Quinn nodded.

"*Eh bien,* like I said, whatever you tell me will go no further."

I want to tell you that I'm attracted to you, that I want to be more than your friend, that I want to touch you again. I want to know what it's like to kiss you.... What the hell am I actually going to say? "There...was...this guy that I knew in the Church—"

"Yes? That's who you were dreaming about?"

Quinn nodded, trying to think quickly about what to say. *Wait, I could leave out who Malcolm was with. Would that work?* "He...was caught...with a man by Warren, Tom, and Perry."

"You mean, in an intimate moment?"

Quinn nodded.

"What happened?"

"It…was awful. What I heard was that they just took him away. No one knows where."

"Je ne comprends pas ce que tu dis," said Larkin. "What do you mean, 'no one knows where'? Surely Warren knows."

"He does. He'd have to, but no one else in the Org is allowed to know."

"Doesn't your friend have parents? Family?"

"His parents are public."

"Ah! In the church but not on staff. I understand. But they took him away from his home and family for that?"

"Yeah. And—"

"And?"

"They…beat him up and put him in the Hole."

"The Hole?"

"All of the Orgs have one, Warren says. We'd never had one before, but Warren made sure there was one once he took over."

Larkin didn't say anything; he just sat looking at Quinn, waiting.

"I heard they beat him pretty bad, Lark. It's not just that the Church has a problem with it. It's…dangerous to get caught."

"And so you had a nightmare about it, because our conversation brought it to mind."

"I guess."

"Ah. *Mon cher ami,* no wonder you seemed so surprised by my views. Were you close to this man?"

"Kind of, yeah. He was my friend."

"Then it's hardly surprising that you dreamed of him, *eh?*"

"I guess."

Larkin was silent for a few minutes, seemingly staring at nothing. He sighed. "I don't know what to tell you, *mon cher ami.* I really don't."

Quinn stared at him. "You don't?"

"*Non,* I don't. I disagree with that rule, and certainly no one should ever be beaten and...kidnapped..." He paused. "I can't think of a better word for it *en anglais.* But those are the rules of your church." Larkin sighed again. "Quinn, I have always been cautious about what I say and don't say regarding the church around you. I mentioned before that I dealt with them years ago, and I know how you're taught to react to even the suggestion of criticism. So I try not to speak of it at all, but when I do, I choose my words with great care—except when I'm overtired and cranky. Given that, I'm at a loss for words. I disagree with it, I don't think it's right, but...I can't be critical, or else I risk losing you as my friend." Larkin turned to look at Quinn. "...And I'd do anything to prevent that, to prevent losing you. If I must bite my lip and my tongue, I'll do it, if it means you remain in my life, *mon cher.*"

Quinn stared at his half-full plate and said nothing. *I choose my words. I'd do anything to prevent that, to avoid losing you.*

"What do I do, Larkin?" he asked after some time. *Damn it, I slipped.*

"What do you do? It depends on what you want, *cher.*"

"They're...still trying to get me to convert you, you know."

"I'm not surprised. They're putting pressure on you, *je pense,* to show some progress?"

Quinn nodded.

"*Eh bien,* I have thought about this." Larkin got to his feet and walked over to his computer desk. He knelt and rummaged around on the bottom bookshelf. "*Et voilà!*" he cried out after a few minutes and headed back towards Quinn with a book in his hand. "*Ce livre,* this will be how you make progress, *eh?*" he said as he held it up for Quinn to see.

It was a copy of <u>The Way to Happiness</u>. Quinn recognized the cover immediately as an edition from maybe ten or fifteen years ago. "Have you read it, Lark?"

"Many years ago, but that's not the point. Quinn, can you get me this exact edition? This exact book from your Org?"

"I think so, I think we have old editions stored somewhere. Why?"

"You must get me this exact copy, *comprends?*"

"I understand, but why?"

"Because, *mon cher ami,* you're going to tell them I want to read it. And then, as proof that I have, you're going to take this copy back to them after a suitable amount of time has passed."

Larkin opened it with smiling eyes, and Quinn saw handwriting and highlighted sections. Larkin flipped through the pages, and Quinn saw more and more notes and bright orange highlights.

"Did you make all those notes?"

"*Non,* someone I used to know did. But, Quinn, for this to work, I need this exact edition. They don't know my handwriting, so you're going to tell them I wrote all of this."

"What if I can't find one? Then what?"

"Then I'll rewrite the notes. Actually…" Larkin frowned as he looked down at the book. "That might be a better idea."

"What?"

"I'll just rewrite these notes, *en français.* They'll really believe it was me, since I generally don't write notes to myself in English." He paused. "Yes, I think I like this better. Bring me whatever copy you have and I'll do that, *là.*"

"You'd go to all that trouble for me?"

"*Bien sûr!* Writing out notes like this is a trivial thing. I'm happy to do it, if it helps you."

"They want money to put towards the Ideal Org."

"I'm sure they do. *Mais,* that won't help you in the long run, *cher.* In fact, it will make it worse. If they get money once, they'll keep putting pressure on you to get more. I won't give you money."

Quinn had to admit that this was true. The requests for donations never seemed to end. If they weren't looking for donations for the planned Ideal Org, they needed them to cover the lawsuits the Church was facing, brought by people who were out to destroy it. He hung his head and said nothing.

"Quinn…"

He looked up to find that Larkin had sat down on the other couch near him again, the book on his knees and his light whisky eyes locked to Quinn's blue ones. "I meant it when I said I would do anything to keep you in my life. Anything but give you money, that is. I wouldn't do anything to make things more difficult for you."

The intensity of Larkin's gaze, the way he seemed to stare into Quinn's eyes without blinking, finally made Quinn look away.

"Thanks, Larkin."

"*De rien, cher.* Now, eat as much as you like, and eat all of it. It's getting late, so I'll drive you back if you want." He got up again to take the book back and drop it onto the desk by his computer.

Wait… Did you say "if I want"?

"*Oui.* If you want to stay the night, you're more than welcome to."

"—And if I wanted to stay longer than a night?"

Larkin's eyes were smiling as he came back to stand in front of Quinn, looking down at him. His lips slowly joined his eyes in a smile.

"What's that saying—*mi casa es su casa?*"

"What does that mean?"

"It means 'my house is your house.' It means you're welcome here any time, for as long as you want. Think of my home as your home, too."

"Really?"

Quinn couldn't understand how he felt. Tears were creeping into his eyes, but his heart leapt at the same moment, and the sudden rush of pure joy caught him off guard. He couldn't look at Larkin; he could only whisper a "thank you."

"My door will never be closed to you, Quinn. Please don't ever forget that. Be it right now or ten years from now, my door is always open."

Quinn looked up and found Larkin's eyes still smiling at him.

"No matter what, know that you always have somewhere to go. I'll even leave a light on for you, like the song says."

Chapter Thirty-Two

"Leave it to Warren to pick the hottest day of the year to campaign!" grumbled Blaise to no one while putting out the *Free Personality Test* and *Free Stress Test* A-frame signs near the edges of the stand.

"It's always hot during Stampede," snorted Jeremy, who was setting out the plastic folding chairs that would be used to interview wogs for their tests. "Quit yer bitchin'."

"Warren always seems to manage to pick the hottest days of the year," Blaise replied. "I think he uses those Clear powers and does it on purpose."

Quinn, who was arranging the display of *The Way to Happiness* books and trying to smooth the green plastic tablecloth, didn't believe that for a second; even Clears couldn't control the weather.

"Will you two knock it off?" Rochelle snapped as she fiddled with the green-and-gold pennant banner that would hang on the front of the green tent. "We're supposed to be extra cheerful, remember?"

"Yeah," chimed in Brittany, who was setting up the E-metres. "How are we supposed to book personality test appointments and sell books if you two look like you're melting?"

"Maybe Warren should've thought of that before he decided to send us to the Stampede on a day when it's a billion degrees out!" Blaise shot back.

Boy, there's a KR in the making, Quinn decided. *Actually, I haven't done one in a while, so it's probably a good idea to do one about Blaise.*

Quinn immediately felt guilty; he hated writing Knowledge Reports and felt terrible about getting anyone into trouble—especially since he was often in trouble himself—but he didn't really have a choice. All Scientologists were expected to write KRs on other members, and he would be considered an accessory to Blaise's insubordination if he didn't.

It wasn't like Blaise was saying anything they weren't all thinking, but saying it out loud like that, speaking disparagingly about the executive director, was a guaranteed KR. *Even if I don't write one, Brittany, Rochelle, Jeremy, and Dickson certainly will. And then Patricia and Barbara will want to know why I didn't do one, too.* That alone would put Quinn in trouble, adding to his already low statistical position. *Better to do a KR as well and cover my ass. Blaise is going to be sent to ethics anyway; the others will make sure of that, so my report isn't going to change anything.*

Warren had managed to get one of the best locations on the Stampede grounds for the Church's stand, outside the BMO Centre building, right near the main entrance gate. This meant literally thousands of people would walk right by them all day, every day, for the entire ten days of Stampede. The Church had arranged stands at every Stampede for as long as Quinn could remember, but never before had they had such a prime spot.

Their tent was the only green one in a sea of bright white, planned to stand out as much as possible. Instead, it gave everyone and everything under it a strange, sickly cast that was off-putting. It also absorbed the heat from the sun, so it was actually hotter under the tent than outside it, making the whole thing even more miserable.

Quinn would be forced to talk to more people in a single day than he could count simply because of the stand's position. He leaned on the table and took a deep breath, trying to steady himself. The thin, dark green plastic tablecloth wrinkled under his weight as he tried to settle his stomach.

The rash under his arms had flared up a week ago and now throbbed and itched intensely. Quinn had to resist the urge to scratch, knowing it would only make it worse. It had begun to weep two nights ago, and applying cornstarch had only resulted in a sticky, caked-on mess instead of absorbing the fluid like he'd hoped. He'd managed to wash the cornstarch off, but now his deodorant (a gift from Larkin) made the rash burn and ache even more.

The Stampede grounds hadn't even opened, and there were already more people around than Quinn could comfortably deal with. *People are setting up booths, and others are starting to cook in the food tents.* Sudden bursts of loud music and voices shouting "Check, check, check," into microphones at deafening volumes as the sound systems on the stages were tested. Servers setting up tables and chairs in the makeshift patios for the bars and beer gardens. Everywhere there was loud talking, laughing, and shouting.

Quinn had to keep repressing the urge to run. Run away from the noise, the crowd, the commotion. He could feel sweat running down his back that had nothing to do with the heat.

The Org members were all dressed in their best urban cowboy Stampede gear. The men were in heavy blue jeans, with Jeremy, Blaise, and Dickson wearing long-sleeved plaid shirts. Dickson wore a white hat, Jeremy a black one, and Blaise had one made of straw. Dickson had even added a bolo tie, a silver-toned cattle skull clasp at his throat and braided black leather cords with silver metal tips hanging down the front of his shirt.

Rochelle and Brittany looked like typical Stampede buckle bunnies, with very short denim skirts and worn cowboy boots bought from a second-hand store. They wore short-sleeved plaid shirts they'd only buttoned partway and then tied in a knot just under their breasts, topped with cheap cowboy hats to complete the look. Brittany had her blonde hair tied in pigtails, while Rochelle left her short brown hair loose. Their revealing clothing was much cooler than anything worn by the men.

Quinn didn't really have anything that looked like Stampede gear and was the only one without a hat, so Jeremy had loaned him a simple denim button-up shirt with long sleeves. He'd rolled the sleeves up and unbuttoned the front partway down, but between the shirt, his running shoes, and heavy jeans, he was already sweating profusely in the early July heat, and it wasn't even 11 a.m. yet.

I hate being posted to Div 6. Why the hell can't I be posted to something else? I hate Div 6. God, I hate Div 6. Why the hell do I have to do this?

"Right!" yelled a familiar voice.

Quinn forced himself to straighten and look at the woman approaching them. Sharon was decked out in blue jeans that looked a size too small, paired with a black belt and a large silver buckle. She wore a short-sleeved T-shirt in her favourite leopard print and a bright white cowboy hat perched atop her bouffant, bleached-blonde hair. A clipboard sat in her right hand. Even from a short distance, her bright blue eyeshadow, clumpy black mascara, and too-bright pink lipstick stood out against her pale skin. The foundation was clearly visible in the creases of her face, making her appear older.

Another buckle bunny.

"Everyone, this is a significant day!" Sharon went on. "This is the first day of Stampede, and our first day to get a lot of fresh meat in through our doors! I expect everyone to exude as much theta as possible. Please put on your best *Theetie-Weetie* personalities and get 'em to sign up for a personality test! If you absolutely cannot do that, at the very least, get a flyer or book into their hands. You need to put on your best faces and your best smiles! Quinn! I'm talking to you! Stop lookin' like a wet week and fuckin' smile!"

"Yes, sir," replied Quinn promptly, while Rochelle outright laughed and Brittany smirked.

"Today is significant for you, Quinn. The more books you sell or appointments you book, the more you'll be up to date. God knows you need it."

"Yes, sir."

"As for the rest of you," the older woman continued, "don't get smug. There isn't a single one of you who doesn't need to get your stats up; there isn't one of you who doesn't need to work on this as hard as possible! And let's not forget the commissions you'll all earn! Ten percent on all processing sold and fifteen percent on all training done for your selectees, on the ones you bring in. You need to chat up as many people as possible! Sell those books! Get those appointments! We need this! The Church needs this! This is do or die, people! If we fuck this up, they'll cancel the Calgary Ideal Org plans and put it in Edmonton instead! We can't allow that to happen, can we? We can't lose to Edmonton!"

"Sir! No, sir!" said everyone in unison.

"Right! It looks like the gates will be opening in five minutes! Everyone, get ready!"

"Yes, sir!" everyone responded again.

Quinn went behind the tables to check the coolers. Sharon had insisted they needed coolers with lots of bottles of water. Warren had initially refused, but Sharon convinced him that hot, sweaty ambassadors possibly suffering from heat stroke wasn't a good image for the Church, so he'd finally relented.

Quinn stuck his hand in and rooted around in the cooler to see how many bottles of water had been put in to chill. He found that there were only a few sitting on the top of the ice, while underneath, there was nothing. He started pulling bottles out of the case that sat under the table and began burying them in the ice, so that the already cold bottles on the top would be used first. *What am I going to do? What can I do? I have to do my best, that's all. He sighed.*

He had texted Larkin that morning: "Hey Larkin. Just wanted to remind you that I'm not going to be coming in today because we're working the Stampede."

"Pas de problème, cher," came the response. "The weather is supposed to be beautiful today. Not a cloud."

"Yeah," Quinn had texted back, his hands already shaking. "I was hoping for rain, then there wouldn't be so many people. I don't know how I'm going to do this. I'm scared! There's going to be SO MANY PEOPLE!" He didn't give a damn about the commissions, since anything he earned would immediately go to paying off his fines; he'd never see a dime himself.

"Do your best, *mon ami*. Remember to breathe slowly and deeply, it'll calm you. Try not to push yourself too hard if you can help it. If you need to talk I'm here for you. Text or call me when you can," had been Larkin's reply.

If you were here, I could probably muddle through it. If I could stay close to you, I know I'd be all right. I could get through. Larkin, I wish you were here. Just having you here would make everything better. I'd feel more keyed out, stronger, if you were here. I really wish you were here, Lark. He heard Sharon yelling over the general din that the gates were open. Quinn stood up to face the throng.

He hung back, trying to figure out how to approach someone without tackling them, the way Jeremy, Blaise and Dickson seemed able to do.

Rochelle and Brittany had tightened up the knots in their shirts, undid another button near the top to reveal even more cleavage, and were focusing on flirting with the men who were walking by. Sharon, too, was flirting and batting her eyelashes at the older men, but wasn't having nearly as much luck getting them to talk to her as the younger women. There was a part of Quinn that couldn't help but be pleased by Sharon's failure, since she was so much further up the Bridge than he was, and yet she was failing as well.

After about ten minutes, she turned away, frustrated, only to catch Quinn hanging back. "Quinn! Get out there!" she snapped at him as she walked back to roughly grab his arm. "You're never going to get over this, not wanting to talk to people unless you actually do it. So, go do it!" She forcefully shoved him towards the front of the stall, hard enough to make him stumble, while he mumbled a "yes, sir".

He had no idea what to say or what to do, so he looked helplessly at the massive crowd around him while biting his lower lip. Men, women, families, most wearing urban cowboy chic, hundreds of people milling past, talking, and laughing. There was loud music from the midway, crying children and the smell of beer and things frying in the air. It was loud, crowded, bustling with people going every which way. Quinn desperately wanted to hide under a table and stay there.

Larkin. I wish you were here to tell me what to do. Wait! What would Larkin do? He'd probably just step up to someone, say "excusez-moi" and start talking. Can I do that? Maybe, if I pretend to be Larkin, if I act like him...

Quinn looked up and saw a young woman who appeared to be alone approaching from his right. Blaise and the others were on his left, so no one had spoken to her yet. She was wearing a pretty yellow sundress with spaghetti straps and multi-coloured flowers and had a wide-brimmed straw hat to shade her face. Her wavy hair looked perfectly black, deep, and rich. She had an open, round face and her lips seemed inclined to turn upwards into a smile. She was walking slowly, looking at the booths and smiling here and there.

If I were Larkin, if I were in the shop.... He'd make small talk first. Nice day, haven't seen you before, whatever. I don't know if I can do that, but...

"Excuse me," said Quinn quietly as he stepped towards the woman. She looked up at him with pale, ice-blue eyes. Quinn realized for the first time just how pretty she actually was. "H-hi," he stammered.

"Hi," she smiled.

"Hum - It's a beautiful day for the first day of Stampede, isn't it?" Quinn tried to smile in a way that didn't make him look creepy, although he wasn't sure how successful he was. The woman didn't look at him strangely or run away, however, which he considered a win.

"Yes, it is," she smiled again, a big, honest smile with perfect teeth. Her black hair rested fetchingly on her shoulders.

"I w-w-w-w-was w-w-w-won-wondering if you would be i-i-interested in a free p-personality t-t-test?"

"Personality test?"

"Y-yes." His mind raced, trying to remember what he was supposed to say. "It's a scientific test created by O-Oxford University." Quinn suddenly went blank on the actual name of the thing, so he skipped it and went on. "It will show you areas of your p-personality that might be c-c-c-c-causing you problems or holding you back. B-by addressing problem areas, you can reach your full potential as a person. It's totally free, and there's no obligation at all. Would you like to spend just a few minutes taking one?" He exhaled heavily, feeling like he'd somehow been holding his breath or that he'd run a race. He felt his face smile, simply because he'd managed to get through, he'd managed to talk to a stranger.

The pretty woman shrugged her shoulders. "Sure, why not?"

Quinn had a hard time repressing a huge grin as he asked Jeremy to set the lady up with a test sheet. Once the sheet was filled out, Sharon would enter everything into the tablet and discuss the results with the lady. It was Sharon's job to convince the woman that she needed Scientology courses to improve her weak or problem areas, usually by talking the person into an E-metre reading. The others could also do this if Sharon was busy, but Quinn hadn't gotten nearly to that point yet. They were responsible for the 'hard sell' as Field Staff Members (FSMs) that Quinn couldn't do. He was still too low on the Bridge to be trusted to do that.

But talking to someone and getting them to simply agree to take the test was huge for Quinn. He was ecstatic. *Oh, my God! I did it! I tried to act like Larkin and it actually worked!*

"Good job, man," Dickson said in Quinn's right ear as he slapped him on the shoulder. "Good job."

He had an overwhelming urge to call Larkin, to tell him of his accomplishment, his win. To tell him how he had helped Quinn without even being there, but he couldn't. *Later.* He beamed. *Now, to do it again.... To talk to someone again. If I imagine I'm Larkin, I can do this. I can do this.*

It didn't take long for the intense heat to sap both Quinn's strength and enthusiasm. The blazing summer sun, along with the heat reflected back up from the asphalt, and the body heat from the sheer number of people, became stifling. At one point, Quinn simply stood there, turning his face to the sweet summer wind, so common to the point of almost being ceaseless in the Alberta foothills, but it offered little relief.

Within a couple of hours, Quinn was drenched in sweat. The novelty of having talked to one person had long since worn off, as Quinn hadn't been able to replicate the result again. A few who had hit the beer gardens early simply told him to fuck off, while others were more polite. He noticed that the others were having similar issues, but they were definitely having more luck than he was, so he couldn't shake the guilt. *I keep letting everyone down. I'm still going to be down stat. I'm always going to be down stat, no matter what I do, aren't I?*

There was a knot in his stomach that felt like a rock, he felt sick. His head was pounding, and his eyes were hurting from the sun's glare, giving him an intense headache. His limbs felt like lead, and he desperately wanted to lie down somewhere cool and sleep. He kept drinking water, trying to settle his stomach, but it didn't help. He walked back to the cooler and began scooping up the still-cold water from the melted ice and splashed it on his face and neck, trying to cool himself down.

It's never enough, is it? I'm never enough. No matter what I do, it's not good enough. I'm not good enough. I can't talk to people. I can't get back online. I'm always down stat. I'm always freaking out over stupid things. Everyone's always pissed off at me. I'm so stupid, *so useless. Worthless. Except....*He gave up trying to splash himself, deciding to crouch down and dunk his entire head into the cooler. He thought he heard the muffled voice of Rochelle yelling at him, but between his own thoughts, the water and the ambient noise all around, he had no idea what she was saying.

Except when I'm with Larkin. I don't feel stupid with him. If I don't understand or know something, he just explains it. He doesn't seem to mind. I think he kind of enjoys it. I love being with him, I love just hanging out with him. I feel better when I'm with him. I feel like I can do things when I'm with him. I'm keyed out when I'm with him. He evens me out, calms me down. He makes me happy. He makes the colour come back. Larkin. I wish I was in the shop, or in your truck, or anywhere that you are. I just wish I was with you, just near you. That would be enough. I guess I really am in love with you, aren't I?

He sighed to himself as he pulled his head out of the cooler to hear Rochelle loudly complaining about how "unhygienic" it was, how he'd contaminated all their water bottles.

"How stupid can you be?" she huffed. "Now what are the rest of us going to drink?"

"Calm down," Blaise snorted. "The bottles are sealed, remember? There's nothing wrong with them."

"I don't want to drink something that Quinn rubbed his nasty hair all over!"

"It's not like he took the bottle top off and then stuck it in his ear!" Blaise shot back with a laugh. "You get thirsty enough, you'll drink it."

"Yuck."

"Here, Quinn, let me have a go," Blaise said. "It looks refreshing and I really could use it."

"Not you too!" wailed Rochelle. "Sharon, tell them! Tell them to knock it off!"

"It's really cold," Quinn quietly pointed out to Blaise as he smoothed his curly wet hair back off his face.

"Perfect," muttered Blaise as he, like Quinn, crouched down and stuck his entire head in the cooler.

"You're missing the point of why we're here," said Sharon as she came out of the tent with one of the people who had agreed to take the personality test. "Thank you so much, Joe," she said to the muscular, brown-haired man who followed her. "I'm so happy you've decided to come to one of our lectures! I promise you won't regret it. You'll look back and think it was the best twenty dollars you've ever spent!"

Quinn tuned out the man's response, instead watching Blaise as he finally popped up again, splashing water all around him as he stood up straight.

"Geez, that'll take your breath away! Feels good though! Good idea, Quinn."

Quinn smiled. "I come up with a good idea every once in a while," he said, trying to be funny.

"You mean, every once in a blue moon!" laughed Brittany from the other side of the table, dropping her Theetie-Weetie facade for a moment.

Everyone started to chuckle and Quinn felt his face getting hot, but not from the heat. Reluctantly, he went back out to the front of the table. He looked off to the right again just in time to see an older lady approaching.

She was small, although she was bent over slightly at the waist and so appeared even shorter. She had short, very white hair that had been tightly curled into small ringlets and silver-rimmed glasses. Royal blue dress pants accentuated her wide hips and a simple white t-shirt with a print of a blue vase of daisies completed the outfit. She wore black orthotic shoes and walked with an aluminum cane with a grey curved handle. She walked slowly and stiffly, rolling to her right with each step as if she were unable to bend her knees.

"Excuse me." He stepped towards the woman. "It's a beautiful day, isn't it? Are you...hum... enjoying the S-S-Stampede? I was w-w-wondering if you would be interested in a free p-personality test?"

The old woman looked up at Quinn, who, at six feet three inches, loomed over the woman like a giant. "I'm sorry." The woman smiled, her voice slightly raspy and high-pitched.

"P-pardon?" Quinn had to lean down, putting his ear close to her. "I'm s-sorry, it's so noisy. What did you say?"

"I'm sorry," the woman said again.

"Sorry?" Quinn frowned. "For what, ma'am?"

"I'm sorry you have to do this, that you have to be here on this beautiful day when you should be off enjoying yourself. You should be off somewhere with your friends, or your girlfriend, the people you love and having fun. Life's much too short, young man, believe me, to spend years of your life doing a job you hate." She laughed quietly at that and walked away without another word.

Life's too short...to spend years of your life doing a job you hate. Life's too short. ...On this beautiful day... you should be off enjoying yourself. You should be off somewhere with your friends, the people you love.

The words echoed in his mind, racing around his head. Quinn stood there, processing. He ruminated over her words, words that should have created a cognitive dissonance in his mind, but there wasn't one. There was no conflict, no doubt, just one single, clear thought that wouldn't leave. One single sentence that stood out, making all the sense in the world, so that his mind yelled to him:

I don't want to be here.

Chapter Thirty-Three

Why am I here? Why am I doing this? I'm no good at it anyway. I'm useless here. I don't want everyone to be angry with me anymore. I don't want to be here. I want to be with Larkin, where I'm happy. I don't want to be here anymore. Not one day more. Not one minute. I want to be with Larkin.

It was as if a veil had been lifted; he could see himself from a distance. He could see himself standing there, just staring off into space; he could see how tired he looked. Sweat soaked through his clothes, through his wet hair, water dripping down his shirt. He knew it was true: he was tired of all of it—Div 6 especially—and he didn't want to be there at any cost. There was no trace of cognitive dissonance in his mind, no question, just certainty.

He needed to do what seemed right to him.

He needed to do what was right *for* him.

He was done.

There wasn't a conscious decision; he began to move, his body acting on his desire before his reactive mind understood what was happening. He looked carefully at everyone around him. Jeremy and Rochelle were both in the open tent, giving personality tests. Blaise was in the tent, entering personality test information into the tablet, while a middle-aged woman waited to hear her results.

"In my experience," Quinn heard Blaise telling the woman, "the only really accurate information you're going to find or receive about Scientology is by being in a Scientology church and doing Scientology auditing."

"So, I shouldn't Google Scientology then?" she asked.

"No, definitely not," was Blaise's predictable answer. "We only deal in truths, which are only found when you observe them for yourself, instead of reading someone else's thoughts."

Quinn didn't bother to listen to the rest.

Brittany was busy flirting with not one but two young, muscle-bound urban cowboys, one of whom blatantly licked his lips while watching her. Brittany laughed and mirrored the gesture, which caused the two men to look at each other and laugh with big, shit-eating grins. Quinn wouldn't put it past Brittany to have sex with both of them if it got them enrolled. He'd heard rumours about other women in the Org doing just that, but he'd never put much stock in the stories until now.

Dickson was talking to a woman whose two friends were trying to get her to leave, so he was really focused on trying to convince all three to stay. "I don't know that word, Xenu," Quinn heard Dickson saying to one of the girls. "You shouldn't focus on the negativity; you should concentrate on what will help your life right now. That stuff on the internet is designed to mess with your head."

He turned to Sharon last, who was distracted by the older man she was talking to. He was tall, attractive, with a caramel complexion and a bushy silver moustache. This was the first person to stop and speak to Sharon in quite a while, so she was giving him her full attention. She smiled, laughed, and frequently touched his arm. "Our religion is the fastest-growing religion on the planet. It's huge."

"Sharon," Quinn interrupted, "I'm going to go to the bathroom." He pointed to the BMO Centre nearby. "I'll be back in a bit."

"Wait!" she barked, forgetting herself and reverting to a Sea Org order-type tone. "Take..." She looked to see which of the others would be free to accompany him, but they were all busy talking to the homo-saps, the wogs. The man next to her said nothing.

"No one's free," Quinn pointed out.

"You'll have to wait until someone's free, then," Sharon concluded, turning back to her mark.

"I can't, I really have to go. I drank too much water. Send someone when they're free, I'll probably still be standing in line, anyway."

"No," Sharon replied. "You'll have to wait, there are too many people for you to handle, Quinn, you know that. Sorry about that, these young people have no self-control sometimes," she said to the older man while smiling. She had to act nice; she couldn't let her Sea Org self out while the man was standing beside her.

"No worries," the man replied with an easy, warm grin.

"Sir, I'm sorry, sir, I really can't."

Sharon looked at him for a long moment, which caused Quinn to look down and away to avoid meeting her eyes; it was his usual response to such a look.

"That request goes against regulations, you know that," she huffed, her annoyance starting to show.

"Yes, sir, I know. I'm terribly sorry, sir." Quinn didn't look up; he just kept staring at his running shoes.

"Fine. But come straight back, and I'll send someone to accompany you as soon as possible." Quinn's use of the word *sir* had no doubt placated her, and she couldn't react the way she usually would in front of the wog she was talking to. She turned to the man. "Now, Jeevan, what were we discussing?"

"Thank you, sir," Quinn replied as he headed towards the BMO Centre building. He tried not to hurry, to walk normally, even a little slow, which was simple, as people kept walking in front of him and cutting him off. He had to wait in line to get into the building. Even with the large double doors, people had to wait to get inside; the line crept forward a few steps at a time.

As soon as Quinn managed to get in through the main doors near Hall A, he was struck by the air conditioning, which hit him like an invisible ice wall. The deafening noise of the crowd bounced from the walls, and the smell of hot dogs filled the air. He headed right, the fingers of his left hand in his mouth as he bit off the nails one at a time, slowly, trying to get through the throngs of people. Looking down, all he could see were legs and boots and summer sandals. Every spot on the chunky, backless wooden benches that lined the hallways was occupied, and there were even people sitting on the floor with their backs propped against the milk-chocolate-coloured brick walls.

People, everywhere. People going every which way, some darting through any tiny opening in the crowd, others snaking their way down one side of the hallway. There was shouting and laughing.

All the commotion should have been overwhelming, should have freaked Quinn out, but he was focused—focused on simply getting through this crowd, focused on finding an exit, concentrating on not being seen or stopped. It was enough, in that moment, to distract him from the fear creeping into his stomach and spine.

He could smell hot dogs and saw people walking by with food in their hands. Others walked by with ice cream cones or small plastic buckets of mini donuts, covered in cinnamon and sugar. The freshly fried donuts reminded Quinn that he was extremely hungry. His stomach began to assert itself by growling, even while it lurched sickly. His mouth was watering enough that he was forced to swallow repeatedly, swallowing bits of fingernail as he did so.

He saw three security guards in neat black uniforms standing near the wall on his left, talking to a man who was holding a plastic cup of beer he'd smuggled out of one of the beer tents. The black uniforms stood out sharply against all the denim and plaid, making the tall, broad-shouldered security guards look even more imposing. Briefly, Quinn considered asking for their help, but he remembered the power of attorney and decided against it.

Years ago, when Quinn joined the staff, one of the many documents he was required to sign was a power of attorney. While he couldn't remember every detail, he knew that the POA allowed the Church to assert itself as Quinn's guardian. It meant that even if he went to the police, Sharon could walk in with the POA and walk out with Quinn, no matter what Quinn might say. The POA gave the Church authorities carte blanche to make any medical or legal decisions for the member, meaning they could force him to go with them, and the police wouldn't be able to lift a finger.

So, no point in asking the police for help.

He quickly walked past the vast, open, and brightly lit exhibit halls, the din of the crowd deafening. He headed past the washrooms and towards the Corral exit, deciding that it would be far enough away from the booth that he wouldn't be seen. Once again, he had to impatiently wait in line to exit the building, ending up stuck behind a middle-aged woman pushing her friend in a wheelchair. His right thumb was in his mouth now, as he bit and pulled the nail free. The pointer finger followed in short order.

It was only once outside that Quinn dared to reach into his back pocket and pull out his flip phone; no doubt Sharon had forgotten he had it, for which he was infinitely grateful. He moved away from the entrance, still moving to the right and deeper into the grounds, his hands shaking. Cold sweat was starting to drip down the sides of his face, and his palms were wet. He felt his rash throbbing and itching to the point that it was maddening, but he didn't touch it.

Larkin's cell phone number popped up immediately. He pushed the button to call it without thinking and held his breath while it rang three times, pointer finger now in his mouth, teeth trying to find a bit of nail to pull on.

"Allo, Quinn," came Larkin's familiar voice. "*Ça va, mon ami?* How's the Stampede going?" He sounded cheerful, happy to hear from Quinn twice in one day.

“I’m done,” Quinn replied around his finger before he could think about it.

“*Quoi ça?* The campaign’s over already?”

“No, I mean, I’m done with everything. I can’t. I just can’t anymore.”

There was silence between the two.

“Quinn,” he sounded cautious now, “what do you mean, exactly?”

“Larkin, you said if I ever needed a place to stay, even for a while, that I could stay with you. Did you mean it?” After the words escaped his lips, the terrifying thought closed in on him. *What if he says no?*

“But of course!” came the immediate response.

Quinn felt himself breathing again. “Lark, I... I... I can’t do this anymore. I need to get out. Get away. I don’t want to be here anymore. I want to stay with you.” He felt his throat tightening, felt the fear starting to strangle him.

I want to tell you I’m in love with you, but I can’t. I’m too scared you’ll reject me. I can’t even think of not being with you, near you. I can’t even consider doing this alone.

“Where are you right now?” Larkin’s deep, soothing voice snapped him out of his thoughts.

“Outside the Corral doors at the BMO Centre. Lark, what do I do? Can you pick me up?” He could feel the panic rising now as he looked around, desperately scanning for familiar faces. *Am I really going to do this? What do I do if I see someone I know?* He had no idea as he began to work on the right middle finger, now pulling the nail with his teeth.

“Any other time, *oui*, no question, but with all the Stampede traffic, it’ll take forever to get there and longer to find you.”

"What do I do? Larkin, help me, please!" He pulled at the nail, tearing it off in a large strip that took some of the flesh with it. He didn't even wince, despite the sharp pain, and gave the blood now oozing up from the wound only a passing glance.

"All right, *écoute*, go back into the BMO Centre and walk towards the casino."

"The casino?"

"*Oui*, there will be cabs there, lots of them. Catch a cab and take it here, *là*."

"But I don't have any money."

"*Pas de problème*, I'll pay for it."

"Are you sure?"

"Of course I'm sure! Unless you think you're better off taking the train. Go, start walking and stay on the phone with me, *cher*."

"No, if I walk to the Victoria Park station, they'll see me. Lark, what do I do if they see me? Oh God, what do I do?" He began weaving his way through the crowd, heading back into the building. His head had started to throb again, and he pressed the heel of his hand to his forehead in a futile effort to dull the pain.

"Take a deep breath, they won't see you, and if they do, we'll cross that bridge if we get there. I'm with you, even if I'm not there beside you."

"Ok." Pause. "Lark, I'm scared!"

"I'd be surprised if you weren't, *mon cher ami*. This is a huge thing, but you're not alone, remember that."

"Ok."

"Where are you?"

"I'm in the building, like you said... which way do I go?"

"If I remember correctly, the exit you want is called the Palomino exit. It's on the far side of the main entrance. Go back to the main doors and then go down the hallway to the left."

"They'll see me if I do that! Sharon was going to send someone in with me!"

"Not in all those people, they won't. Just put your head down and go, *cher*. And if you do happen to see someone you know, don't look at them."

Quinn was breathing heavily as he worked his way through the crowd. "Why?"

"People sense when someone is looking at them; they're more likely to spot you."

Quinn was still picking his way through when he looked up and saw a familiar figure in a white hat. Quinn's heart stopped, but he quickly looked away and down like Larkin had instructed and whispered: "Dickson." *Damn, it's like we planned it.*

"Quinn? What's happened? Do you see someone?"

Quinn didn't answer and did the only thing he could think to do: put his head down and turn left at the nearest entrance into the Market Hall area, the massive open space where artists and craftspeople had set up tables and stalls to show their wares. It was slightly less packed than the hallway, but Quinn was hopeful Dickson wouldn't think to look for him there.

"Quinn! What's happening?"

"I think I'm ok. I don't think he saw me. I think it's ok, Lark." His voice was shaking, despite his reassurances. He suddenly, desperately, wanted to pee.

"Where are you now?"

"Market Hall."

"Perfect! There are other exits further down. Keep going left."

"Ok."

More and more people, but at least Quinn was just one more amongst hundreds, just a body lost in the crowd. More smells of food frying, along with the flowery scent of essential oils spread by diffusers, made him feel light-headed.

"Quinn?"

"Yeah?"

"I'm proud of you for doing this, for taking this step, this risk. I know it's not easy. I know you must be terrified, but I'm proud of you. And Elijah would be, too."

Quinn froze, stopping in the middle of the aisle, and was promptly bumped into by several people, a couple of whom gave him dirty looks.

"You're... proud... of me? Really?"

"Of course. You're being courageous."

"Really?... Thank you, Larkin."

"Are you close to the Palomino exit?"

"N-no, on my way." Quinn started walking again, suddenly feeling warm inside. *He's proud of me. Larkin's proud of me. Elijah would be proud of me.* He started to smile despite the fear still creeping deeper into him.

"Are you alright?" Larkin asked after a moment.

"Yeah, I'm ok. I feel like I'm going to puke, but I'm ok."

"That's your nerves, *cher*. Not a surprise."

"When's the last time you came to the Stampede?" Quinn wanted to take his mind off what he was actually doing, even as he kept weaving through the crowd. He got bumped by someone—a burly man with massive muscles, nearly a metre taller than Quinn—who almost knocked him into a table.

"I'm sorry!" the man said, turning to him.

"N-no problem. It's fine."

"Quinn?"

"I'm ok, I just got bumped. Larkin, talk to me. Please." The sound of his deep voice made Quinn feel stronger, like everything would be fine. He switched the phone to his right hand so he could start biting the nails on his left again, but there was nothing left.

"It's been years since I've been to Stampede," Larkin replied, clearly following Quinn's lead. "I've been thinking about having a small table or booth there myself."

"Yeah?"

"*Oui,* in addition to the store being open. I might have to take on some extra temporary help for that, though."

"Temps aren't going to know about antiques like you do."

"True. I've thought of that. Where are you now, *cher*?"

"I think I'm getting close to the door."

"Good. Is it packed?"

"God, yeah. There are tons of people."

"There usually are. Stampede is always packed if the weather's nice. I know you dislike crowds, but that crowd works in your favour today."

Quinn managed to get through the door and found himself in an area facing a wall of windows, with a door to the outside off to his left. Through the glass and over the heads of the milling crowd, he saw the blinking yellow lights of Cowboys Casino. "I'm just through the door, Lark. I see the casino."

"*Très bon!* Now go outside, and you should see several cabs in front of the casino. Go to the front of the line and take the first cab."

"Why can't I take any one?"

"It's cab etiquette. The ones in the back of the line won't take you—they'll tell you to go to the front."

"Ok."

Once Quinn exited through the double doors, the intense summer heat hit him like a punch. He almost ran past the line to the first cab, a crisp white Toyota Camry with the words "Calgary Cab" emblazoned in white against a black banner. He bent down to look at the older man inside, who promptly rolled down the window.

"Hi," Quinn said, phone still to his ear, "can you take me to 432, 16 Avenue Northeast?"

"Sure. Hop in." He turned to enter the address into the GPS clipped to the dashboard just to the right of the steering wheel.

Quinn opened the back door and climbed in, greeted once again by cool air conditioning. He set the phone down as he buckled his seatbelt, then picked it up again as he heard Larkin say his name.

"I'm here, Lark," he explained. "I'm in the cab. I'm in."

"*C'est fantastique,* Quinn! Now all you have to do is wait. You'll be here in no time." He sounded thrilled; Quinn didn't think he'd ever heard him so pleased.

Quinn looked over his shoulder back at the building and the crowd as the cab slowly pulled beside the parking-lot gate. Then he looked forward just long enough to see the gate arm rise before glancing back again. Sweat trickled down the back of his neck and along his ribs, his shirt sticking to his skin despite the air conditioning.

"Larkin… did I really just do this?" The feeling of needing to relieve himself suddenly asserted itself. Instead, Quinn tore off another massive chunk of nail from his left middle finger, focusing on the metallic taste of blood and the pain.

"*Oui, mon cher ami,* you did. I'm so proud of you!"

Quinn didn't respond. His hands and blood felt frozen, while his skin remained clammy from sweat. His head and eyes ached, and the rash had begun to burn again.

"How do you feel, Quinn?"

"I… don't know."

"It may be that the reality hasn't hit you yet, *cher.* I know you must be terrified, but you are not alone, *hein?* Remember that."

"You always wanted me to leave, didn't you?"

"I wanted you to be happy, *mon ami.* If you were truly happy there, I would have accepted it. But you weren't. Anyone could see that you weren't."

This surprised Quinn. "What do you mean, anyone could see I wasn't happy?" *I just saw how unhappy you were. I saw my own misery reflected in your face, in your eyes.* Wasn't that what Elijah had said? Now Larkin was saying much the same thing.

Quinn looked out the window, watching the cab inch away from the crowd as it turned off Roundup Way and headed into traffic.

"Quinn, you always looked tired, ill, and terribly hungry. Grey is not the right complexion for someone so young. The anxiety, the panic attacks, the way you tried to crawl into the floor when that *trou de cul* Warren appeared… the way you were afraid to go back after our trip to Banff, because you were afraid you'd be in trouble."

"I was. I was in trouble." Quinn couldn't help but smile; he didn't know what *trou de cul* meant, but he could guess it wasn't flattering.

"Exactly my point. No one should live their life in fear, Quinn. Trust me—it's a shadow-life, a terrible existence."

Quinn said nothing, trying to absorb what Larkin was telling him. He began biting the remnants of the nail on his right ring finger.

"They made you afraid to live," Larkin continued, "to live a life that was your own. To explore the world and your own heart. You were prevented from doing whatever you wanted to do. That's no way to live—believe me."

Quinn kept turning to look out the back window. He couldn't shake the fear of being followed. He felt winded, as if he'd been holding his breath too long. He blinked sweat from his eyes and wiped his forehead with his right hand when it didn't help.

Life's much too short, young man, believe me, to spend years of your life doing a job you hate.

"You almost sound like you've done that yourself."

"In a way, I have. My life was not my own for some time."

"What do you mean?"

"*C'est pas important,* Quinn. Where are you?"

"I think we're on Edmonton Trail. Larkin… is this real? I mean, I just walked away. I just walked off and blew. I didn't think it would be so easy." He hunched his shoulders as sweat raced down his spine from the base of his neck.

"In any other situation, it wouldn't have been, *cher*. Lucky the Stampede provided you with perfect cover, *non?*"

A sudden realization struck Quinn. "They're going to know exactly where I am, aren't they?"

"I would think so."

"They're… going to come for me, aren't they?" Panic crushed in on him as the urge to pee vanished under fear.

"Probably. They won't get far, *mon ami*."

Quinn felt a fresh stab of terror. "Larkin… what if—"

"*Oui?*"

"What if they come after you?"

A snort of amusement came through the phone. "Let them. It wouldn't be the first time I've crossed paths with them. *Ne t'inquiète pas,* Quinn."

"But—"

"Don't worry about it," Larkin repeated. "Don't let your anxiety get the better of you and make you lose your nerve. I can handle them. *Ne t'inquiète pas.*"

"What if they fair game you, Lark? Or declare you an SP?" Fair game, the directive from the founder that allowed for enemies of the Church to be "utterly destroyed". Whether that meant financially, their reputation, or even physically, it was a declaration of all-out war.

"I'm surprised they haven't already, *mon ami*."

"Lark—"

"No, no second-guessing. Don't worry about me. I've handled bigger bullies than them. Quinn, don't go back and be miserable because of what they might do to me. You've made this choice—and I am so very proud of you for it—but now it's time to see it through."

But Quinn couldn't help himself. He started hyperventilating; his clothes were so drenched with sweat it looked as though he'd stepped out of the shower. The tips of his fingers were bleeding where he'd torn the nails down to the quick. The pounding in his head wasn't just back—it was worse. He couldn't keep his eyes open; the glare of sun off passing cars, asphalt, and windows stabbed at his skull. He dropped his head, Larkin's voice drifting distantly as he lost the thread of what was being said.

He wanted to cry—to sit and weep with both relief and fear—but his headache was too intense to bring tears. Each ragged breath whistled into a wheeze as fear clenched tighter around his chest, squeezing out every scrap of air. Somewhere, dimly, he heard the driver asking if he was okay, but Quinn couldn't answer.

Larkin. I need to be with you. It'll be ok then. I'll be fine then. Oh, Lark... what have I done? I think I'm too sick to be excited. Maybe that'll come later?

The cab ride felt endless—every light red, every intersection clogged, pedestrians darting across traffic. At one point the driver slammed the brakes, pitching Quinn forward. The driver rolled down his window and yelled at a drunk man who had staggered out between cars into the cab's path. Quinn watched blankly as the man flipped the driver off and wandered away, leaving the driver swearing.

There were car horns, the occasional roar of motorcycles, people yelling and laughing, and a cacophony of music pouring from every bar they drove past. Quinn jumped at a sudden piercing whistle from somewhere beside the car at a stoplight. He lowered his head and finally closed his eyes. The driver asked once more if he was alright.

Quinn looked up as the cab finally pulled into the parking lot— and saw Larkin waiting by the front door, his bright red t-shirt a beacon in the sunlight, colorful tattoos gleaming on his legs, cell phone held to his right ear, and a broad smile lighting his face. The cab had barely stopped before Larkin moved toward the back passenger door.

"Larkin!" Quinn cried as soon as he got the door open.

"I'm here, *mon ami*. I'm here."

"Oh my God, what have I done?" Tears spilled down his face. His head throbbed, his eyes burned with sharp, piercing pain. He nearly collapsed into Larkin, who caught and steadied him.

"What you had to do, *cher*. Come—hop out while I pay the driver, *hein?*"

The driver rolled down the passenger window and Larkin leaned in. "*Merci, monsieur,* for bringing my friend home; he's not well in this heat. How much is it?"

Quinn didn't hear the amount; he began pacing in tight circles, fists buried in his hair, gaze swinging from his shoes to the glaring blue sky above.

"Oh my God, Larkin, what have I done?" he wailed. "What have I done? I've lost all my friends! I've lost my home! Everything I was working for! My eternity! *My mother!* Oh my God, Larkin—I'll never see my mother again!"

"Shh, Quinn." The cab pulled away as Larkin stepped in close. He laid a steady hand on Quinn's shoulder, the weight anchoring him. "*Respire, Quinn.* Slow down and breathe. You're going to hurt yourself."

Quinn turned into him and broke down, sobbing into Larkin's shoulder as Larkin wrapped both arms around him and rubbed his back. They stayed that way for several moments—Quinn crying uncontrollably, Larkin holding him, allowing the storm to pass.

"What am I going to do?" Quinn finally wailed. "I've got nothing!"

"You have me," Larkin said firmly, easing him back just enough to meet his eyes. "And you have a safe place to stay, a warm bed to sleep in, and food to eat. Many people don't even have that."

"But—"

"*Non.* Come inside where it's cool, *cher.*" Larkin slipped his arm around Quinn's shoulders and guided him toward the door. "Let's get your temperature down. I think you might have heat stroke." He pressed the inside of his wrist gently to Quinn's forehead.

"Heat stroke?"

"Your skin is cold but you're sweating heavily. Come in so you can cool off."

"My head and eyes are killing me. I think I'm going to be sick."

"You may be having a migraine."

Quinn didn't remember going inside or using the bathroom, but he must have, because the next thing he knew, he was sitting on Larkin's ugly mustard couch, folded over with his face buried in his hands, forearms braced on his knees.

Larkin sat beside him, holding a cool, damp cloth to the back of his neck. Quinn felt the cloth adjusted, then Larkin's hand rubbing slow, steady circles across his hunched back. He was crying again, shoulders shaking. From time to time, Larkin murmured softly, "It's ok. It'll be ok," but mostly he let Quinn unravel in silence.

Suddenly Quinn stiffened. "I'm gonna be sick."

"Go."

He bolted for the half bath near the outside stairs, flipped up the lid, didn't bother with the light, and dropped to the toilet. He stood there in the dimness, hands gripping the bowl's edge as his stomach lurched. He retched again and again, bringing up nothing but water. When the spasms finally eased, he slid down onto his knees.

He heard Larkin's voice somewhere nearby, then felt hands grasp his biceps and haul him upright, but he couldn't process what was being said. *What have I done? Did I really blow? Did I really walk away? What am I going to do?*

"Did Elijah feel this bad when he left?"

"I wasn't there, *cher,* but I think he did."

Quinn hadn't realized he'd spoken aloud until Larkin answered. "I feel like shit."

"You're sick, overtired, overheated, and *ton anxiété est au maximum.* Come—let's get you upstairs, undressed, and cooled down. You'll feel better after some sleep."

He let Larkin lead him upstairs to the guest room, his long fingers curled weakly around Larkin's wrist.

"I guess this is my room now, huh?" he muttered.

"Oui, mon ami, for as long as you want it."

Quinn nearly collapsed onto the bed. He couldn't open his eyes; each attempt sent knives of pain through his head and behind his eyes. His stomach quivered, threatening another round of vomiting. He sat frozen at the mattress edge, afraid to move. Larkin was talking, but Quinn couldn't make out the words. He cracked one eye open just enough to see Larkin setting a tabletop fan on the desk and aiming it at the bed.

"Quinn, *cher*, you need to get these heavy clothes off."

"I can't move."

"I'll help." Larkin began unbuttoning Quinn's shirt, his pale fingers efficient and gentle. His hands settled on Quinn's shoulders as he eased the heavy denim off. Under different circumstances, Quinn would have flushed with pleasure; now he was simply too sick to react.

"Cher, if I help you stand, can you undo your pants?"

Quinn wasn't sure if he nodded, but Larkin lifted him anyway. The room began to spin and Quinn squeezed his eyes shut. He found the zipper by feel, tugged it down, and managed to lower his jeans a little before he sank—more fell—back onto the bed.

"Sorry," he whispered. "I think I'll throw up if I move too much."

"It's all right. Don't worry."

Through one half-open eye, Quinn watched Larkin bend down. He felt the jeans being pulled free from beneath him, slid down his legs, and his shoes were tugged off without the laces being touched. He stared at the crown of Larkin's head—the straight, white hair parted near the ear, the faint ghost of scalp visible beneath it.

Larkin set the shoes aside, stripped off the socks, and removed the jeans completely. *He's taking my clothes off. I'm almost naked in front of him, and I'm too sick to even enjoy it.*

"Here, *cher*, lie down."

Larkin lifted Quinn's ankles and swung them up onto the bed. Slowly—so slowly—Quinn eased himself back until his head rested on the pillow. Larkin went to the window, threw it open, then drew the dark brown curtains with their vine-and-leaf pattern, cutting the glare of daylight except for brief pulses when the breeze billowed the fabric. As soon as the fan reached his legs, cool air washed over them—wonderful relief—though his torso and face still burned.

"Larkin?"

"Yes?"

"Could you move the fan? It's only hitting my legs."

"Ah—of course. Better on your face and body; it'll cool you faster."

The breeze shifted. His hair stirred. Quinn sighed—the relief was immediate. His limbs loosened, the tension draining away as exhaustion pulled him under.

"Thanks, Lark."

"*Pas de problème, Quinn.* Rest. Everything always seems better after some sleep. A nap cures many ills."

"Larkin?"

"What is it?"

"I'm… really grateful."

He felt Larkin's hand against his brow, fingers threading gently through his curls. "It's all right, Quinn. I'm glad you came to me."

"Of course I came to you," Quinn murmured thickly. "Who else would I go to? There's no one else I trust… no one else I can count on but you. You mean everything to me." He tried to shift, but the weight of sleep pinned him down.

"And you mean the world to me, Quinn," Larkin answered, just before darkness claimed him.

Chapter Thirty-Four

There was yelling—he could hear it. Voices raised in anger, but only the tone reached him, muffled as if through a pillow.

Then there were other voices, one he recognized as Larkin's, along with a woman's voice. No shouting this time—only concern.

He felt hands on him, someone easing him upright and coaxing a pill between his lips. The bitterness of the medication bloomed on his tongue, chased by the clean taste of cold water. Fabric brushed his skin, but it felt irritating, so he kept pulling at it, no matter how lightly it lay against him.

Gentle hands sifted through his hair, stroking his head. He thought it might be Joni or Elijah; the idea soothed him. He felt like a child being cared for by his parents—safe, small, protected. He tried to call for them, but his jaw wouldn't move, his mouth wouldn't open. A faint doubt flickered—*that isn't right*—but who else would it be?

Someone lifted him again, tipped something to his lips, and the cold taste of water returned. He swallowed reflexively. The chill slid down his throat into his stomach, spreading outward in a way that felt astonishingly good. He drank in long gulps until the glass was taken away, and he drifted back into deep sleep.

He was in a room, though he didn't know where. It looked like Warren's office, with the dark carpet and shelves—but the wall that should have been crowded with Scientology awards was bare. The room was empty. He wondered suddenly if he had missed something. *Did everyone go to the farm and leave me behind?*

He rose from the couch and stepped toward the door with his right foot—only to find his left refusing to move. Looking down, he saw the blood-colored carpet bubbling up around his feet.

He tried to pull away and instead felt himself sinking deeper, the red fibers sliding over his shoe. He stepped back and froze in horror as his right foot stuck fast as well. Off balance, he wobbled, arms windmilling to keep from falling.

Then he heard it: a sound he couldn't quite place—shuffling, but sharper, scratchier.

He scanned the room, saw nothing, looked back down at the carpet now swallowing him to the ankles, and heard it again. He lifted his gaze to the far wall—and it was no longer smooth. It was riddled with holes like a honeycomb, scattered in uneven patterns. The randomness unsettled him, and he stared, searching for meaning or order as he fought to keep his balance, forgetting about his trapped feet.

It was louder now: clicking, skittering.

The "holes" moved—dashing across the wall in wild trajectories that made the hairs on his neck stand on end. And then he saw it: legs. Eight of them. Spiders.

They weren't holes at all.

Great, dark, tarantula-like spiders poured down the wall and spilled across the floor.

Quinn strained to wrench himself free, but the carpet held him fast. He watched in paralyzed horror as the spiders skated effortlessly toward him, gliding atop the carpet as if it were ice-crusted snow. Another skittering rose above him—he tilted his head back and saw thousands more spiders crawling across the plain white ceiling.

Quinn screamed and bolted upright, flinging the sheet away. Panting, drenched in sweat, he stared around the dark room, trying to orient himself. As his breathing slowed and reality snapped back into place, he knew where he was.

Three soft knocks sounded at the door. "Quinn? Are you alright?"

"Yeah, come in." He scrubbed his face hard with both hands until his skin tingled.

The door opened and a bar of light cut across the room as Larkin stepped in. "You're awake," he said cheerfully.

"Yeah."

"How do you feel, *mon ami? Ça va?*"

"*Pas mal,*" Quinn answered.

"Your French is improving." Larkin's eyes warmed with gentle amusement.

"How long was I out?"

"Three days."

"What? No!"

"*Oui, c'est vrai.*"

"I didn't—I mean, how is that even possible?"

"You needed it. My aunt used to say if someone falls into a deep sleep, their body clearly needs the rest. Otherwise, sleep stays light."

Quinn suddenly became aware of intense pressure in his bladder. "I gotta pee."

"Go." Larkin shifted aside to let him pass.

So focused on reaching the bathroom, Quinn forgot he was wearing only briefs. He flipped on the light; the brightness stabbed behind his eyes. Squinting, he was relieved to see the seat already up. He moaned quietly as relief flooded through him.

"Better?" Larkin called from down the hall.

"Oh God, yeah. Sorry—I didn't realize I was that loud."

"We've all made that sound at one time or another, *cher,*" Larkin replied, clearly amused.

I did it. I really did it. I'm here. I'm here with Larkin. What do I do now?

"Are you up to eating, Quinn?"

His body answered with a loud growl. "Yeah," he chuckled. "I guess I am."

"*Bon!* How about comfort food? Macaroni and cheese—the real kind, not from a box."

"Oh, that sounds amazing!" He washed his hands.

"*Parfait.* I've left clothes on the desk for you—come down when you're ready, *mon cher ami.*"

Larkin's footsteps thudded down the stairs, and Quinn resisted peeking out to confirm it was really him—he sounded happier than Quinn had ever heard him.

"Your father used to love my mac and cheese," Larkin called up.

Quinn rested his hands on the sink and studied his reflection. His curls were a wreck—flattened in some places, spiking in others—but the deep circles under his eyes were gone, despite pillow creases etched into his face. He felt clearer, steadier. The last time he'd felt this rested was the stay at Larkin's before their Banff trip, after Elijah's funeral.

"Elijah," he whispered to the mirror. "You left. You did this. Were you this scared? This sick? Or were you relieved—excited to be free? Where did you go? Who did you turn to? You didn't know Larkin. Were you alone?"

The thought of doing any of this alone made his stomach clench. He couldn't imagine walking away without knowing someone was waiting—without having somewhere to land.

"I'd be on the streets," he murmured, "if it wasn't for Larkin. Is that what you did? Sleep outside? How did you manage the first days? Did you plan it? Save money? Or did you just go, the way I did? *How* did you do it?"

His eyes burned. "I wish I'd asked you when I still could. And now I'll never know."

The finality hit him again—the unbridgeable gulf between what he knew and what he longed to understand. Elijah's absence felt like a severed limb, an empty space that would never close. He bowed his head.

"Elijah. I'm sorry. I'm so, so sorry. If you can hear me…forgive me."

On the desk lay the neatly folded clothes Larkin had promised—far more than Quinn expected: stacks of T-shirts, several pairs of shorts, two black jeans, three blue jeans, a light gray sweatshirt, a heavy purple hoodie, plus unopened packs of briefs and socks.

The sheer choice overwhelmed him. It took much longer than it should have just to decide what to wear.

"Larkin, this is amazing!" he finally said around a mouthful of food. He sat barefoot at the kitchen counter, now dressed in black shorts with gray trim and a white T-shirt bearing a blue-and-white flag and the words *La Belle Province* scripted beneath.

"*Merci.* I'm glad you like it." Larkin watched him eat while calmly finishing his own plate.

"Oh my God, this might be the best thing I've ever eaten in my life!" Quinn tried to slow down, to savor it, but hunger drove him to shovel forkful after forkful. Creamy, orange-cheese sauce stretched in glossy strands from plate to fork.

"It can't be that good," Larkin laughed, eyes shining. "But it's only as good as the cheese. Better when you mix more than one kind. I made plenty—help yourself, *mon ami.*"

Quinn rose before finishing his plate and went for seconds anyway.

"Thanks for the clothes, Lark. I don't know when I can give them back."

"Pas de problème. Keep them."

"Are you sure? You gave me so much stuff. This shirt might even be too small," he tugged at the hem.

Larkin smiled, genuine warmth in his eyes. "I'm sure. They hang on me like sacks anyway. It fits you better."

"Really?"

"Oui."

"This is the Quebec flag, right?"

"Oui. The Fleurdelisé—*the lily-flowered."*

"Lily-flowered?"

"Oui. The *fleur-de-lys* are the lilies, for the Virgin Marie, and the white cross comes from old French royal banners."

"La Belle Province... 'the beautiful province,'" Quinn translated softly.

"Your French improves daily, *mon ami."* He was grinning openly now.

"Thanks—you're a good teacher."

"And you are a good student."

Heat rushed into Quinn's cheeks. He turned back to the stove, loading his plate to hide the blush.

"I had some weird dreams," he said, still facing away.

"Did you?"

"Yeah—people yelling, and I was in Warren's office, and my feet sank into the carpet, and there were spiders everywhere." He shuddered. "That's what woke me."

"You dislike *les araignées,* Quinn?"

"I hate bugs." He sat beside Larkin again, chewing more deliberately now. "God, this is so good."

"*Merci.* You said you heard voices?"

"Yeah. Someone yelling."

"Could you hear what was said?"

"No. Just yelling."

"Hm."

Quinn studied Larkin's face. The unreadable calm had returned, but something beneath it wasn't quite right, and unease coiled in Quinn's chest as they ate in silence.

"What's wrong?" Quinn asked at last, forcing Larkin to meet his eyes.

"*Rien.*"

"Larkin."

"*Rien.*"

"That's not true, I can tell by your eyes. What is it?"

Larkin's eyes frowned at him. "You can tell by my eyes?"

"Yeah. What's wrong?"

Larkin looked back down at his nearly empty plate and sighed. "It's as you said—they knew where you were. That was the yelling you heard."

"You mean…"

"*Oui.* Tom was here, with two women—Sharon and Barbara, I believe. They were demanding to see you, to speak with you, *ostie.*"

Quinn felt his blood go cold, even though his stomach—too full— didn't flip the way it usually did. "What…else did they say?"

Larkin snorted. "Some nonsense about having power of attorney over you, *crisse*. I told them a POA only applies if you're unfit to make your own decisions, and you're far from that, *ostie*. The Calgary *sûreté* agreed without hesitation. They said your people would have to go to court and have you formally declared unfit if they wanted to act on that POA." He huffed a laugh. "Then Sharon was foolish enough to *show* the officer the document. I thought he'd laugh until he cracked a rib, *ostie!*"

"Why?"

"It was for a billion years! It even claimed it applied to 'all future lifetimes,' or some such ridiculous wording. *Crisse de tabarnak!*"

"Warren said the Sea Org contract works the same way," Quinn murmured. "A billion years."

Larkin's mouth tilted into a sharp smirk. "I'd love to see them try to make *that* stand up in court, *sacréfice!* A contract—even one signed by both sides—has to be reasonable. You can't enforce something absurd, like lending someone twenty dollars and demanding thirty million back in interest when they don't even have a job. Judges throw nonsense like that right out."

Quinn stared. "Really?"

"Of course. It's unenforceable, *ostie.*"

"They always said it was ironclad—untouchable by any court. They said it protected us from SPs and the government."

Larkin snorted softly. "Well, *cher,* of course they'd say that, wouldn't they?"

"I guess." Quinn looked back at his plate.

"They depend on you *not* questioning things," Larkin said. "On your trust. Fear works well when people don't question the story they're told."

"Larkin…are you sure you're okay?" Quinn asked, unable to hide the tremor in his voice. "They can't hurt you, can they?"

"Yes, I'm sure. Tom began with bluster—said they know *all* about me, my past and such drivel, *ostie.* If he truly knew half of what he claimed, he'd think twice about provoking me. *Tabarnak.*"

"What do you mean?"

"*Ce n'est pas important.* Just know I can defend myself against bullies."

"Yeah, but these aren't kids on a playground."

"*Non,* but the principles don't change. Don't worry about me, *cher.* I can handle them."

"But—"

Larkin turned fully, fixing Quinn with his clear whiskey gaze. "And I can take care of *you* as well," he said firmly. "*Ne t'inquiète pas, Quinn.* As long as I draw breath, no one will force you to do anything against your will."

"Larkin…" Quinn whispered. The words felt like they emptied the air from his lungs.

"*Non, non—ne t'inquiète pas.* Understand?"

"Yeah. I do. It's just…"

"Yes?"

Quinn lifted his eyes and met Larkin's stare, tried to hold steady the way Larkin always did with him. "Thank you—for everything. I don't know what I'd do without you."

"*De rien, Quinn.* You're welcome. I'll help however I can. I promise." On the final words, Larkin reached out and rested a hand on Quinn's left shoulder, the pale fingertips pressing gently above his elbow. "*Ok?*"

"'Kay. I'm…really grateful."

"There's no need, but *merci*. Now eat. You'll need strength for your new life—your new adventures."

Quinn turned back to his plate. A small smile spread across his face, but the knot of fear still sat heavy in his stomach, unwilling to loosen its grip.

Chapter Thirty-Five

"A billion years, that doesn't make sense. Why would they say that?" Quinn blurted. The thought had been weighing on him ever since Larkin told him about the Blow Team's visit.

"Kessé? What was that, *cher?"*

"Why would they say I signed a contract for a billion years? That's only done for Sea Org members. Besides, I don't remember signing anything like that."

"Je ne sais pas." Larkin shrugged, eyes still on the online auction he was watching. They were in the back room of the store since there were no customers—Larkin at the desk, Quinn on the ugly floral couch. "That's just what they said."

"Did you see it? The contract?"

"Non. Besides, it was a POA, not a contract, and when they said it I just laughed at them. It wouldn't matter if they had it or not; such a thing wouldn't ever hold up in court. *En plus,* I doubt you read every word of everything they've asked you to sign, *là."*

Quinn didn't reply, but frowned as he remembered signing the notice saying he wouldn't go to Elijah's funeral—he'd done it without reading a word. "They have to have lots of contracts, paper trails," he said instead. "The government, the RCMP, the FBI in the States— they make it so hard for them to do anything, so they have to have everything documented. LRH insisted on it. It's the only way the Church can keep doing all the good it does. It has to be able to defend itself."

"En tout cas?"

"What does that mean?"

"It means that if that's what you say, that's what it is."

"You don't believe me." The tension in Quinn's body spiked; his back straightened and his shoulders squared as if for a fight.

"It's not that. I'm just surprised you're defending them, considering you've left, that's all."

"Just because I couldn't hack it doesn't mean I don't believe in LRH. It doesn't mean they aren't working for the good of humanity."

"*Eh bien.*"

"It's true! LRH's technology is amazing, and it makes people's lives so much better; it makes them free."

"*Si tu le dis, Quinn.*"

"It does! LRH's work has helped millions of people worldwide. I was just too weak to take it, I guess—to really get the most out of it. That's all."

"If you say so," Larkin repeated in English.

"But it's true! Scientology didn't fail, neither did the tech. *I* did."

"All right."

"They probably feel bad that I won't get to be a part of all the good things they do," Quinn added after a moment.

"Of course."

"Why do you sound like you don't believe me?"

"I didn't say that, *cher.*"

"No, but you sound like it."

"*Chu désolé,* it wasn't intentional."

Larkin abruptly let out a string of French profanity Quinn couldn't follow, though the repeated *"merde"* and *"tabarnak"* left little doubt about the gist.

"What happened?"

"*Ostie de câlice de tabarnak,* I got sniped! Someone outbid me in the last three seconds! *Ciboire! Bâtard!*"

"That's too bad, Lark."

"*Christophe Colomb,* I have a collector ready to buy that stupid Fitz and Floyd teapot, so I put in a bid for probably twice what it's worth, just to make sure I got it. And this *maudit toton* outbid me anyway! Idiot!"

"That sucks."

Larkin continued to mutter under his breath as he logged out of the auction site. He got up and headed to the hot plate to put the kettle on for yet another mug of tea.

"Hey, Lark?"

"*Oui?*"

"Can I use your computer? I want to look something up."

"Of course. You can use the one here if you'd like. Just don't download a virus or anything, *là.*"

"Yeah, yeah, I won't. Don't worry," Quinn replied with an eye roll. "I'm going to look up all the good stuff that the Church does, so you can see for yourself why I feel bad about leaving."

"Quinn—" Larkin stopped and shifted his tone. "If you like. But you don't need to convince me, *mon cher ami.*"

"We were helping during the flood in 2013. I'll start there. I'm sure it was in the news."

"Would you like some tea?" Larkin asked.

"I don't understand this," Quinn kept muttering to himself. The shop interior was in shadow; Larkin had closed it and gone upstairs to order pizza, but Quinn had stayed in the back room on the computer. "Why can't I find anything?" His frowning face was lit by the bluish glow of the screen, the only light in the room.

He'd thought it would be easy. Scientology did so much good in the world; he'd assumed there would be countless websites devoted to its good works alone, and even more singing its praises.

But there was nothing. No mention of Scientology helping during disasters like the flood in Calgary. No mention of the work overseas, in the poorest and most dangerous regions of South America, Africa, Honduras, or Iran. Nothing at all about Narconon's work with drug addicts in the cities, about their success getting people off fentanyl or crack. He couldn't even find a single mention of the homes and schools that were supposedly being built in Africa, or the wells for fresh water in drought-struck areas. Of the medicine they provided to people in the third world, there wasn't even a hint.

Nothing. Zero. *Rien,* as Larkin would say.

"This is crazy! There has to be something! Unless the mainstream media is repressing it, that's possible, I guess." That thought was strangely cheering; it would explain so much of what Quinn was, or wasn't, seeing.

The sound of the shop's back door opening startled him.

"Quinn? The pizza's here. *Enwèye,* come and eat."

"Sure, in a minute. Hey, Lark?"

"*Oui?*"

"How hard is it for the media to repress information?"

"These days, it's almost impossible. Everyone has access to a phone, the internet, and social media. Is your search not going well?"

"But they could if they really wanted to, right?"

"Once something is posted, it's almost impossible to remove it completely. Even things like accident photos. It doesn't take long for people to share them, and then some websites specialize in such things. They pick it up, and there it stays."

"That's disgusting! And people go and look at that stuff?"

"Sadly, yes. Come, *mon ami,* leave it for now and eat. I got you that bacon and mushroom pizza you like."

"What did you get?"

"Smoked oysters."

"I never knew you could put smoked oysters on a pizza. I don't understand why I can't find anything. Wait! I'll Google all the awards given to LRH! He won war medals, even though everyone knows that the official records were 'sheep-dipped', that they were altered to hide the secret intelligence work he was doing. But LRH won what, twenty-seven medals? Or was it twenty-nine? I can't remember. There's got to be records of at least some of those! Everybody knows that's how he started to develop Scientology. He was wounded, crippled, and blind, and he used *Dianetics* to heal himself while in the hospital. I'll look for that."

"*Eh bien,* just don't let it get cold, eh?"

Quinn's search went from bad to worse. The Church websites listed that L. Ron Hubbard had received a total of twenty-nine medals, including a Purple Heart and medals for marksmanship. LRH had been awarded medals from France, the Netherlands, the UK, and the Philippines. Surely they couldn't "sheep dip" those files as well.

But again, there was nothing—no lists of Hubbard's wondrous deeds on other sites. He was accused of "stolen valour," of claiming medals that weren't his or were outright fakes. No medals of honour from anywhere. The US Navy called his service "at times substandard." Worse, LRH hadn't been in the hospital for war wounds, but for something unrelated. One website read:

"According to the Church's chief spokesman, if it was true that Hubbard had not been injured, 'the injuries that he handled by the use of Dianetics procedures were never handled, because they were injuries that never existed; **therefore, Dianetics is based on a lie; therefore, Scientology is based on a lie.**'"

No, this isn't right. I remember them saying there was another set of records, one that the US Navy repressed; these must be the official ones that were altered, that's all.

Elijah's voice suddenly came back to him: "Quinn, Ron Miscavige left."

"That's a lie," Quinn responded under his breath, as if Elijah's voice had spoken aloud to him.

"Yes, he blew as well. If the father of the church leader leaves—"

No.

"He was OT 8, the highest Operating Thetan level there is, and says now he doesn't believe in any of it."

That's… that can't be right, can it? He stared at the computer screen, knowing there was really only one way to find out. Reluctant fingers slowly typed *Ron Miscavige* into the Google search bar; he held his breath.

The search brought up YouTube first. Apparently, Ron had conducted numerous interviews, had his own channel, and had even written a book. The titles were things like *"Scientology took my family from me!"* He'd even written a book entitled <u>Ron Miscavige: Life After Scientology.</u>

The shop phone rang—no doubt Larkin calling to remind Quinn to eat. Quinn ignored it and instead picked a video at random, pressing play.

Chapter Thirty-Six

The night was deep, and Peter's Drive-Inn was long closed. On the roof, the only light came from the pale orange streetlamps below, so the glowing ember of Larkin's cigarette and his ghostly hair stood out sharply in the darkness. He took a final drag before snuffing it out in the ashtray. Lighting another, the flame flared like a spotlight on his pale face as he cupped it in his long fingers.

"Larkin?"

He looked up. "Quinn! Your pizza is cold, *mon ami.*"

"Is it true?"

"Is what true?" Larkin asked cautiously.

"Is… Scientology, the Church, is it all a lie? All of it?" His tone was low, each word sounding like it hurt to say.

Larkin exhaled, the smoke puffing pale and wispy in front of his face. "*Oui,* it is. I am truly, truly sorry, *mon cher ami.*"

"Is that why Elijah left? He found out it was all… fake?"

"I don't believe so. From what I understand, he left first and then started to do his research afterwards, just like you did."

"I don't understand. I mean, how could LRH lie to everyone? All his writings, all the speeches, all the books? How could he lie like that?"

"Quinn, come sit down, eh?" Larkin gestured to the empty bistro chair. "It might have started as, well… a con. But I believe Hubbard came to believe it himself later. From what I've read, he was not well mentally near the end of his life."

A con, Quinn repeated silently. He remained standing several feet away from Larkin, ignoring the chair, unmoving as a stone. "Is that what it is? Is that what I've been believing my whole life? I believed in a con?"

"You and a great many others. Cons are effective because they play on people's good nature—in this case, the desire to belong and the need to believe in something bigger than oneself. You said yourself the church was making the world better, and you wanted to be a part of that. Who wouldn't? To help the world and to help people are the best of intentions. And, sadly, as they say, 'the road to hell is paved with good intentions.'"

"You knew, and Elijah knew. Why didn't you tell me?"

"Would you have listened? Or believed us?"

"You could have made me! Elijah could have!"

"Remember when we met in Chinook?" Larkin asked around, another puff of smoke. "Elijah did try to explain, as gently as he could, but you weren't interested, *non?*"

Dianetics is based on a lie; therefore, Scientology is based on a lie.

"But millions of people are joining every day! That's what they said!"

"*Oui,* I'm sure they did say that. If they said the truth—that there are only a few thousand active Scientologists in the world—would you still have wanted to stay? Or would you have wondered why so few people were involved?"

"But David Miscavige took over as Chairman of the Board when LRH dropped his body! He has to know!" Quinn started to pace around the roof in tight circles, hands flailing like he was drowning. "He has to know that... that... it's all... bullshit! I saw the birthday party they had for LRH! They listed award after award that he got posthumously! They said the attendance was through the roof! There were awards from the US Congress and the state of Washington. The original Church is a national historic site! There were hundreds of awards, and you're saying the COB just made it all up!"

Another puff of smoke curled in the night air. "So it would appear."

"But why? How? How could he do that?"

"Probably for the same reason Hubbard created it in the first place—to make money."

"But people believe in him! He's the Chairman! He can't be wrong! They believe in LRH! They believe in the tech, and you're saying that the e-metre can't detect thoughts? That it's just a… a… knock-off lie detector? That it's all nothing!"

While Quinn floundered, Larkin remained statue-still.

"All that time, all the work I did! The sleepless nights! I even cut my leg open doing those fuckin' renovations! And it was all for NOTHING?" His voice rose into a scream, then broke into a wail. "I gave my life to the church! So did Elijah! And Joni! She's still there! She's still buying all this bullshit! Everything I am is because of Scientology! I had a life, I had security, I had a home, a family! Without the church, what am I? Who am I? I don't even know!"

"You're free, that's what you are."

Quinn stared at Larkin, who finally rose from his chair. Cigarette forgotten in the ashtray, he walked over and took Quinn by the biceps. His amber eyes bored into Quinn's with fierce intensity.

"You're free," he repeated. "You can start again, *là*. You can find out who you are now, without anyone's influence. You can be whoever and whatever you want to be, Quinn. Yes, you've lost much, but there is so much out there for you to find. I've been in your place— having to start over again, having to reinvent myself. It's not easy, and it won't happen overnight, but it will happen. Elijah did it too, remember? He struggled with it, right up until he died—he struggled but was winning against it, against their brainwashing. You can too. You're as strong as he was, *mon ami.* You can do this. You can move forward."

"How? How can I move forward knowing everyone I care about is still in that… hell?"

"Everyone?"

"Everyone but you, I mean. You really are my only friend, Larkin."

"Sometimes one is all you need, *cher.*"

"I… feel so stupid."

"You're not stupid."

"Yes, I am! I must be! How the hell else could I believe all that crap? And that fuckin' Xenu bullshit! Aliens dropped into a volcano and then bombed by spaceships that looked like 1950s fighter planes! And now their souls are stuck to us! I mean, it doesn't even make a good story! It doesn't make any sense! I'd heard the word, I'd heard wogs—people—mention it, but I thought they were making it up! I never believed that we were supposed to actually believe all of that shit!"

"Tell me, Quinn, did you ever get that far? To the Xenu story? No, I know you didn't. There's a reason it's one of the last things they tell you. From what I've learned, that story has driven many away. As for being stupid, I know for a fact you are far from that. You trusted these people; they raised you, and you had no reason to doubt what they told you. It was normal for you."

"Stupid. I can't believe I was so stupid."

"How many other people have they lured in, eh? How many other intelligent, well-meaning people have they corrupted? You're not stupid, and neither are they."

Slumping into Larkin's grip, the energy left him like water running down a drain, leaving him weak and exhausted. "What do I do now?"

"First, you eat your pizza. Then you try to sleep. In the morning, and for days and days afterwards, you'll think. In the meantime, you put one foot in front of the other, and sooner or later, you'll find your path. And I'll be there as much or as little as you like. We'll find your new life together, *bien?*"

"So, you're not going to throw me out?"

"*Mon Dieu!* Why would I do that? My home is yours for as long as you want it, Quinn. I've already said that."

He didn't realize he had started to cry until he blubbered out a "thank you," only to find himself wrapped up in a hug. Sobbing on Larkin's shoulder, he almost missed Larkin whispering in his ear, "*De rein, cher.*"

Chapter Thirty-Seven

Blue golf shirt with collar…check.

Khaki shorts…check.

Sandals? Downstairs, but check. Is this too dressy? I don't really know how to dress for a date, and I don't want it to look super obvious that it is a date.

But it was. It was an actual date with Larkin, and Quinn could barely contain himself.

Wallet? Shit, where the hell…oh, there it is. Can't pay for dinner without my wallet! I've never paid for dinner in a restaurant before. I never had the money, barely had enough to scrape together for a cheap pizza once in a blue moon. But I can now, with all the money Larkin's been paying me. Besides, I want to do something nice to show him how grateful I am for everything he's done for me. Yeah, that's it, this is a thank-you dinner. Not a date at all…

Looking at himself in the mirror, he grinned, barely recognizing the person looking back. Larkin had decided he needed a change and had taken him to a fancy downtown barbershop. Styled like something out of the Old West, with striped poles and wooden floors, it was the kind of place Quinn would never have had the nerve to walk into alone. But the women working there greeted Larkin by name.

"Please, *mesdames,* make my friend here look less like a sheepdog, *ostie.*"

Quinn let them have free rein.

Once they were done, his tangled curly hair was cut to a medium, business-like style that accentuated his face. The long, scruffy beard had been trimmed down until it looked more like Quinn hadn't shaved in a few days. He could actually see his blue eyes, which somehow looked darker under his chocolate curls, and was rewarded by an astounded look from Larkin, who seemed flustered.

"Very nice, *mon ami.* Who knew there was a man under all that hair, *là?*"

He'd never considered himself vain, but the drastic change delighted Quinn, made him really feel like he was starting a new chapter in his life. The fact that Larkin kept staring at him when he thought Quinn wasn't looking was a definite plus. And now they were going out: Quinn in his new-to-him clothes, and Larkin looking decidedly dressy in a pale yellow short-sleeved button-up and denim shorts. Quinn was too nervous to talk much during the cab ride down to the Stephen Avenue Walk.

The Stephen Avenue Walk was four blocks of Eighth Avenue closed to vehicles, allowing tourist-laden foot traffic to reach some of the city's best restaurants and pubs. The large steel sails by Bankers Hall were an iconic sight and cut the powerful wind gusts that plagued other city corridors.

"So, where do you wanna go, Lark?" Quinn hopped out of the cab and waited for Larkin to light a cigarette.

"*Ça n'a pas d'importance,* Quinn. Wherever you like will be fine."

"But I don't really know any of them. Geez, you really do smoke a lot, don't you?"

Amused, Larkin snorted. "*Oui,* I was a chain smoker for years, but I've cut down. Well, there's The Unicorn; it's a nice pub, but it can be a bit noisy, especially when the Stampeders are playing. James Joyce is really nice, the food is Irish and delicious, but that's a bit expensive."

"Let's go to James Joyce then, I'm paying, after all!"

"Yes, yes, I know, you're insisting on paying the cheque."

"That's right," Quinn said proudly, "I'm paying for the sex… **cheque!**"

His hands flew to his mouth as he stopped and stared at Larkin in complete horror, eyes wide as plates. Larkin's eyebrows shot up; he smirked slightly.

The next thing Quinn knew, he was running down the street towards Bankers Hall, away from Larkin and away from what he'd said, sudden terror, propelling his feet without his consent. *What the actual fuck did I say? Oh my God, what did I say?* He bumped into people as he ran, feet pounding on the cobblestones. *Oh my God, what did I say? What the fuck did I do?*

He ran past the street that led to the base of the Calgary Tower, where a life-sized workhorse sculpture made of scrap metal stood proudly. Slowing down, he leaned on the sculpture to catch his breath. *Oh God, I fucked up. I so fucked up. Why the hell did I say that? What am I gonna do…*

He was so wrapped up in his turmoil and racing thoughts that he didn't see Larkin until the other man raced up and grabbed his arm. Quinn started to sputter, trying to think of an explanation even as Larkin pulled him around so they were face to face. Quinn was terrified by the hard look in Larkin's whisky eye, but he didn't resist as Larkin pressed his back firmly against the rusted metal horse. His eyes widened as Larkin moved closer, lips right by Quinn's ear.

"You'll never have to pay for sex with me, *cher,*" he whispered with a Cheshire cat smile. "It'll always be free, but that doesn't mean that you'll get it on the first date, *là.*"

Before Quinn could process what had been said, Larkin moved in and pressed his lips to Quinn's. The words scattered from Quinn's mind like mice. The taste of his mouth was obscured by tobacco, but the feeling of his lips was clear. He blinked when Larkin moved back, staring at him as if he'd never seen him before. Larkin's face frowned and darkened, confused.

"Quinn," he breathed, "if I've made a mistake, if I've misunderstood…"

"Are you kidding?"

Quinn stepped up to Larkin, cupped his face, and pulled him into another kiss. He was in a daze as Larkin took his hand and guided him along the street until they reached a bench near the base of the sails. People didn't exist; there was no one on the crowded street, no one coming out of Bankers Hall, no one at any of the bar patios. It was just the two of them. Larkin's lips, his hands on Quinn's waist, then holding his hands; the smell of peppermint, tobacco, and old dust was everything.

The shadows had gotten long by the time they came up for air.

"I've wanted to do that for so long," Quinn panted.

"Me too."

"Lark, I wasn't sure if you liked me. I really like you so much and I didn't know how to talk to you about it…"

A genuine smile spread across Larkin's features. "Anyone else would probably have kissed you much sooner, *cher*. But you terrify me."

"Me? Why?"

"My past relationships haven't gone well and ended worse. I had given up on it, *ostie*. But you, with your eyes, I can't get you out of my head."

When Quinn looked confused, Larkin went on, "The world seems new to you, like you've never seen it before. When I saw how your face lit up when you were feeding the deer in Canmore, that was it. That smile, your face beaming. I couldn't fight your charm."

"Really? You put up a great front."

Larkin laughed. "Years of practice; I learned to have a great poker face."

They looked at each other for a moment, both smiling, their hands entwined.

"Quinn, what do you say we go home, eh? I don't feel like being in a crowded pub. I'd rather go home with you and order a pizza."

"Ok, but on two conditions."

"What conditions?"

"One, that you let me pay for the pizza. I've never had the money to do it before, and I really want to."

Larkin rolled his eyes. "*Oui, oui,* and the second?"

"We get to kiss more."

"Oh, *cher,* I was counting on that."

They stood, still holding hands, as Quinn glanced around. He noticed that no one was paying any attention to them at all. No one looked at them strangely or negatively; people were milling around, going about their own lives without paying any attention to the two men. The complete lack of negativity delighted and emboldened him as they walked beneath the Plus 15 bridge, which connected Bankers Hall to the mall across the road.

"Hey, Lark?"

"Hm?"

"Who the hell says *'cheque'*?"

Larkin sputtered. "It's an American idiom I picked up, *tabarnak.* I know that here in Canada, we say, 'I'll pay the bill.' But if I hadn't misspoken—"

"I wouldn't have messed up."

"And we wouldn't be here. Thank *le bon Dieu* for Freudian slips, eh?"

"Freudian slips? What's that?"

They were so engrossed in each other's company that neither of them noticed the man by Bankers Hall watching and taking photos of them. He took several more as they walked away. Neither of them knew that the man was sending the pictures with a text:

I'm guessing this is what you were looking for, Warren.

The reply came back quickly:

Yes, thank you, Murray, the pictures are exciting. Please continue to keep an eye on our prodigal son. And please continue your research into his companion. I want to know everything. We need to find his ruin.

Murray Frere quickly typed back: Will do.

Acknowledgment

I'd like to thank the following people for their assistance in making this book possible:

My fantastic and crazy husband, Garry, and our fur children, without whose constant love and support, I'd simply fall apart.

Thank you, Shawn, for letting me annoy you with questions.

My amazing editor, Connie S., for her much-needed kick in the butt, which helped me finish it.

My fantastic partners at Lincoln Writes, Noah and Mujtaba, who helped me navigate unfamiliar waters and occasionally talked me off the proverbial ledge.

My aunts, Valerie and Peggy, and my friends Sandra, Beverly, Peter and Betty, Sandi, Judy, and Lila, for their invaluable emotional support and belief in me.

I'd also like to thank Anne Rice for showing me what was possible. A special thank-you to everyone involved in _The Duchess of Duke Street_ TV series for creating my childhood hero, whose lessons I never completely forgot—although I did have to relearn them for myself.

"We're born to be real, not perfect." — Min Yoon-gi

Author's Note

While the preceding novel is a work of fiction, in that the characters and their experiences are fictional, there are many elements of this work that are, in fact, quite real. Most of the locations described are real places that can be visited to this day. Calgary is a beautiful and fun city. Alberta is an incredibly beautiful province, boasting some of the greatest areas of natural beauty in the world. I would highly encourage you, dear reader, to visit.

The experiences of Quinn and the other members of the Scientology organization, as portrayed in this novel, while fictional, are heavily based on first-person accounts of former members. I firmly believe I have remained true to the source material and have represented this organization as accurately as possible from the perspective of a "never-in."

For anyone seeking assistance, the Michael J. Rinder Aftermath Foundation is a fantastic resource and can be found on Facebook, Instagram, and through their website:

http://theaftermathfoundation.org/

North America: 1- 888-FREE-002

UK: 0800 090 3372

contact@theaftermathfoundation.org

The Michael J. Rinder Aftermath Foundation

414, 4833 Front Street B

Castle Rock, CO., USA 80104

There are also a large number of anti-COS groups on Facebook, YouTube, and Reddit, full of emotional support and advice. I encourage anyone interested to check them out and investigate further. To those who got out and were willing to put your lives, hearts, and souls on the line to shine a light on this organization, I would personally like to thank each and every one of you for your strength of spirit and willingness to stand and fight. Without your bravery—your willingness to come forward, reveal your experiences, and take a stand—this book would not exist. For your resilience, strength, courage, and all the personal sacrifices you've made, I thank you. All of you. Your courage feeds my own and never fails to inspire.

"You have to figure it out. Stand up and walk. Keep moving forward. You've got two good legs, so get up and use them. You're strong enough to make your own path."

- Edward Elric, *Fullmetal Alchemist: Brotherhood*